THE HOSTAGE OF ROME

THE HISTORIES OF SPHAX SERIES

BOOK THREE

ROBERT M. KIDD

The Histories
of Sphax series
~ book three ~

Dedicated to
Alice Dixon

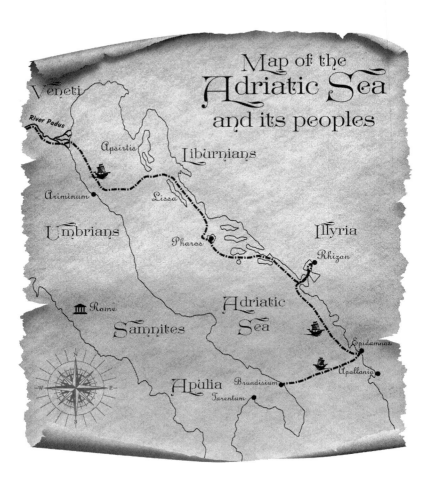

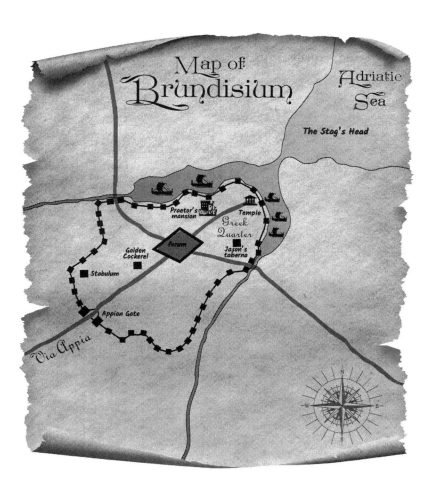

Map of
Brundisium

Adriatic
Sea

The Stag's Head

Praetor's
mansion

Temple

Greek
Quarter

Golden
Cockerel

Forum

Jason's
taberna

Stabulum

Appian Gate

Via Appia

LIST OF PRINCIPAL CHARACTERS

Characters marked with an asterisk are real historical figures. The rest might well have been.

Agbal Numidian. One of the youngest members of Sphax's eshrin, with keen eyesight

Alkibiades & Alexandra of Epidamnos
Cleon's grandparents and Corinna's suspicious in-laws. Alkibiades, rich beyond measure, is leader of the council of elders in Epidamnos

Cleon Corinna's two-year-old son, held hostage of Rome in Brundisium

Carmo Boy from Gaul and lead oarsman, rescued from slavery by Sphax's party

Corinna Daughter of Queen Teuta of Illyria* and mother of Cleon, a hostage of Rome held in Brundisium

Damon Greek publicanus (tax collector) in Brundisium

Demetrius of Pharos*
Illyrian/Greek nobleman. Flees to Philip of Macedon after defeat on Pharos by the Roman consular army of Aemilius Paullus in 219 BC

Drust   Noble Cavari warrior and trusted lieutenant of Idwal

Elpis   Greek boy rescued from slavery by Sphax's party

Glavus   Elderly Illyrian sea captain with a wealth of knowledge of the harbours and coasts of the Adria

Hannibal Barca*

Born 247 BC, Carthage. Renowned Carthaginian general who invades Italia in 218 BC

Hannon   Numidian veteran in Sphax's eshrin

Idwal   Son of Lord Cenno, chief of the Cavari Gauls. Idwal is the leader of the Cavari contingent in Hannibal's army and Sphax's closest friend

Jugurtha   Numidian veteran and chief scout in Sphax's eshrin

Menda   Untrustworthy former advisor to Demetrius of Pharos*

Nikolaos   Loyal ex-servant of Corinna who lives with his aged mother in Brundisium

Queen Teuta*

Wife of King Agron,* who gains the throne after his death in 231 BC. Defeated by Rome in the First Illyrian War (229 BC) she sues for peace and is banished to Rhizon in the north of Illyria. History remembers her as the Pirate Queen

Scardus   Captain of Queen Teuta's* guard at Rhizon

Sempronius Falto

Vicious centurion, commander of the Roman garrison of Epidamnos

Sphax   Born in Numidia, January, 235 BC. Son of Prince Navaras of Numidia* and Similce Barca,* sister of Hannibal Barca*

Titus Voltina

Quaestor and secretary to praetor Marcus Rufus. Secretly holding Corinna's son Cleon a prisoner in Brundisium

Zwalia   Corinna's faithful Nubian servant

PART ONE

THE HUNTERS AND THE HUNTED

ONE

Sphax watched anxiously as Jugurtha, Hannon and Agbal threaded their javelins. He knew perfectly well his Numidians had done this a thousand times before, could do it in their sleep, yet all their lives now hung by those slender leather threads. Since dawn, equites from Placentia had been hunting them down; now he was sure they were closing in for the kill. But they were not their immediate problem.

All eight of them were crouching, wet and miserable in a swampy grove of alder, staring at the dozen Roman legionaries guarding the two river craft moored alongside the wooden jetty that stretched into the great river. Sphax could hear the sound of distant hoof-beats. He knew it must be the equites. It was now or never.

'Now,' he said, sprinting forward to cover the eighty paces of open ground before they could close with the enemy. After thirty they were spotted. The cry went up and there was a desperate scramble for spears and shields. But it was too late. The legionaries' undoing was that they were scattered around in small knots, some around a campfire, others pacing the jetty or the riverbank.

Four fell to Numidian javelins before Corinna and Zwalia flung their lethal daggers. The two scarlet-cloaked hastati resolutely standing their ground by the jetty met the full force of Idwal's shield boss before Drust finished them off with a scything sweep of his blade. Two trapped on the wharf saved their skins by leaping into the river, whilst those on the riverbank turned and fled.

It was over almost before it had begun. But those insistent hoof-beats were drawing closer. Tossing their supplies and gear into the belly of the boat, the rest boarded, leaving Sphax and Idwal to untie the mooring ropes. In desperation Idwal had to slice through the last of these. Time had run out. Behind them they could hear the clatter of horses' hooves on the wooden planking of the jetty.

'Jump!' screamed Corinna, and the two of them leapt, landing painfully on the rowing benches. Corinna and Zwalia had oars in their hands, pushing with all their might against the wooden pillars of the jetty. At last the craft caught the current and began to drift downstream. They were safe ... for now.

It was Corinna who'd selected the vessel they'd seized, a wide-bellied oared boat, low in the water and no more than twelve paces in length. Now she gripped the two steering oars in the stern and began yelling orders.

'Find oars. Jugurtha and Agbal one side, Sphax and Hannon the other. Zwalia, the mast and yard. Get Idwal and Drust to help you set the sail.' Dutifully they began wielding four of the oars that had been stowed away, Agbal immediately striking Jugurtha a mighty blow that almost sent the veteran sprawling overboard. In the next instant Hannon somehow managed to lose his oar over the side. At last all four held an oar and settled on the benches facing downriver.

'Face me, you slackheads!' shouted Corinna. 'Turn around on the benches and face me! Don't lose any more oars, we only have eight aboard.' For the sake of his men, who had no Greek, Sphax did his best to translate the stream of invective flowing from Corinna's lips, but even he was struggling with some of her more colourful oaths. In any other circumstance, anyone witnessing such a comedy would have been rolling around in fits of laughter. But their present predicament was not a laughing matter.

'Slide the oars into the thole pins and lock them,' Corinna was instructing. Sphax was defeated by this. What was a thole pin? Did Numidians have such things? 'Hera spare me from such empty vessels! You dumbwits couldn't find a woman's fanny if she spread her legs and pointed to it! On the gunnels, you limp-pricked Scythians. On the gunnels!' What in the name of Ba 'al Hamūn was a *gunnel*, pondered Sphax? And 'limp-pricked' was an unfamiliar term to Numidians.

In the end, Corinna had to step down from the stern platform and lock each oar into place herself, much to the embarrassment of the four novice rowers. For good measure, she barged Agbal aside on the rowing bench and demonstrated herself how to use the oar. At last a measure of comprehension dawned on the faces of her shamefaced crew.

'On my command you will all pull together, as if as one. Do you understand?' After Sphax had translated they all meekly nodded. 'Pull,' she shouted. And again, 'Pull! Pull!'

It took some thirty or so strokes before Sphax and his men began to sense the rhythm of it, and learned how to twist the oar-blades cleanly out of the water on the backstroke. Sphax found himself grinning across at Agbal, surprised how satisfying and pleasurable this gentle exercise was proving to be. He could even feel the thrust of each stroke on the planks beneath his feet. After forty strokes Corinna ceased to call out, 'pull,' and fixed him with that wicked smile of hers.

'What a pleasure it is to command Numidians,' she crowed. 'As my crew, I feel it necessary to introduce you to some of the mysteries of sailing and boat-craft,' her eyes firmly fixed not on them but on the next bend of the Padus. 'The oars I hold in each hand are the steering oars that guide our vessel left or right. But to achieve what we mariners call steerage, our boat must be propelled faster than the current or tide that holds us in sway. Otherwise, we would be enthralled to the mercy of the river's whims and currents, and just as easily drift on to a sandbank or find ourselves grounded on an island.' Corinna's eyes narrowed. 'As we are being shadowed by a turma of Roman equites, grounding on the southern bank would be most unfortunate.' Sphax scanned the southern bank and saw them for himself.

'We seem to be pulling away from them,' he observed. 'Roman stallions don't have the stamina for the long haul. Give me an eshrin of jennets and we could follow this craft all day long. They'll give up soon enough.'

'I wouldn't count on it,' she said, frowning. 'They recognised you and that beaverskin cloak of yours on the wharf back there. What Roman would not want to kill Sphax the Numidian? I'm afraid there's a price on that princely head of yours, my darling. You are being hunted, and they won't give up easily.'

'One thing is certain.'

'What's that?' she asked, still frowning.

'The Gauls in these parts call this river the Bodencus, which means bottomless, so those equites won't be crossing it in a hurry. So if you do run us aground, make sure it's on the northern bank.'

Corinna snorted. 'I have no intention of running us aground on either bank, but I have every intention of outrunning them. Zwalia has raised the mast and yard, and is about to set the sail. The fore and aft stays are in place and Idwal and Drust are about to tie the sheets. With this stiff westerly behind us it should double our speed.'

'Are you enjoying this gentle exercise?' Sphax addressed his Numidians.

'No!' came the resounding cry from the bench behind him. 'If Ba 'al Hamūn had meant us to row over water he would have given us oars, not legs to straddle a mare.' It was Hannon, chief bellyacher in his eshrin. Suddenly the wind caught the sail, and Sphax felt the craft lift and surge forward with renewed vigour.

He couldn't tear his eyes away from Corinna. She was standing on the stern platform, a steering oar in each hand, her lovely hazel eyes darting ceaselessly between the square sail and the river banks, the hood of her crimson riding cloak tossed back revealing raven curls abandoned to the wind. She looked radiant. Sphax recalled that on Roman merchant ships the graceful figurine of a swan's neck protruded where she now stood, elemental yet animal.

'I can see this is your true element, my love,' he said, gazing up at her. She flashed him a brilliant smile.

'I am the rider of the wind and salt spray, I am the sea nymph Thetis, mother of Achilles, and every breath of wind draws me closer to my son.'

* * *

Two weeks ago, with the passing of the shortest day, the next had dawned bright, the mid-winter sun arcing across a cloudless blue sky. Since the great battle beside the Trebia that had shattered the armies of Rome, no one had stirred from tent or pavilion except to attend to the needs of horses or livestock. Snowstorms and icy blizzards had raged incessantly, whipping the flurries into drifts that could bury a horse. The winter of winters had saved her final savagery for the dying light of the year, exacting a terrible toll on the men and beasts huddled together in hope of warmth. Hiempsal's elephants had suffered grievously from the cold and lack of fodder, and every day elephants froze and perished. Now few were left.

When that first day dawned clear, Hannibal was eager to assess the extent of his victory and gain news of the withdrawal of the enemy. Maharbal, his chief of cavalry, was tasked with sending out scouts. Sphax was given ten eshrins and ordered to cross the Trebia and find out if the old Roman camp had been repaired after Hiempsal and his mahouts fired it, then he was to scout the area between Placentia and the great river. After making his final report to Hannibal he trudged wearily back to his own pavilion in the growing twilight. It had been a long day and he was dog tired.

Between mouthfuls of food and wine he began to tell Corinna about the events of the day and what the other captains had reported seeing. At some point he was surprised to see she was nodding and listening intently, her face more animated than he'd seen for days. He fell silent and smiled at her.

'It's good that I've aroused your interest at last. I have been worried about you, my love. I know you suffer ... I see it every day.' For days Corinna had wandered listlessly around their pavilion or sat with vacant gaze by the brazier, worried and fretting about her son Cleon, a hostage of Rome, hundreds of miles to the south of them in Brundisium. Dasius, the wretched creature who'd seized and taken away her child was now dead, but before Corinna had killed him, she'd discovered the name of the steward who now held her two year old son captive. The world a better place without Dasius, though Sphax had refrained from asking how she'd wheedled the name of the steward out of the brute.

'Go on with your description,' she said, tenderly reaching out for his hands. He told her how they'd chased off a single turma of cavalry, but met their match when they'd come up against legionary infantry who'd fled on to a jetty by the Padus that served to supply Placentia. That's when the questions began, thick and fast.

How many boats had been moored at the jetty? What was their size? Did they possess oars or sails? How many defended the jetty? Was there cover at the river's bank? After incessant questioning, his eyelids began to droop and tiredness seeped through his body.

'I must rest now, my head is spinning,' he said wearily.

'Forgive me, I have been selfish, you must be exhausted. Sleep now, I will join you in a while.'

He hadn't protested. Kissing her lightly on the cheek he'd walked over to their sleeping couch and sank into its softness, covering himself in furs. Sometime later, Sphax had no way of knowing whether it was an hour or four, he awoke and reached out to where Corinna's warm naked body should have been.

Turning over, he saw that she was still seated beside the brazier, lost in thought, a cup cradled in her hands and a single lamp burning on the table. Despite the brazier, the pavilion felt as cold as the tomb. Draping a great bearskin around his shoulders he padded over and sat beside her, teeth chattering.

'What's wrong, Corinna?'

For some time she didn't answer, staring into her empty wine cup. Finally she turned and gazed into his eyes, a comfortless smile on her lips. 'Your uncle's camp marshals came round this afternoon. Many are to leave this camp and move into winter quarters in towns and villages of the Insubres, north of the Padus.' Sphax nodded. 'It sent me into a black despair. Three or four months spent in idle inactivity. Months I cannot spend with my child. Months of his life I will miss and never regain. I cannot bear it, Sphax … I cannot bear it any more!'

He had no words of comfort to ease her pain, all he could do was draw her to him. For a while they clung to each other before Corinna broke the silence. 'Everything you told me this evening gave me hope. Perhaps it's only a fool's hope, but nevertheless, you kindled a spark that lit a flame. I have a scheme to rescue my son.'

Sphax removed his arms from her shoulders and stared into those fathomless hazel eyes that could melt stone. 'Tell me your scheme?' He listened dutifully, without interruptions or questions. When she'd finished he said simply, 'We will need help. Tomorrow we'll talk it through with Idwal before we approach my uncle. Now, can we retire to our sleeping couch?' adding with a weary grin, 'I'm cold.'

'Certainly, my darling,' sliding her warm hands inside his bearskin, 'but forget about sleep.'

The following morning, after Idwal had listened in silence to Corinna's scheme, he declared in admiration, 'You are full of surprises, Corinna, I had no idea you could sail a vessel and navigate the seas.'

Corinna laughed, her spirits perfectly restored. 'All Illyrians can sail, they are born with salt in their nostrils, just as Numidians are raised on the backs of horses. Do you know how Rome refers to my mother, Idwal?'

'I dread to think,' shaking his head, 'but I'm sure it won't be flattering.'

'They call Teuta the pirate queen, and as her daughter, I shall revel in the illustrious title of pirate princess! I'm not fond of my mother, but I do take a certain pride in her reputation.'

'My concerns are not with your mother, or her reputation. Neither are they with your scheme to capture a vessel from Placentia's jetties, sail it down the Padus and across the Adriatic to Rhizon. And I'm certain your mother will offer you every assistance to recover her grandson. My concerns are much closer to home.'

'Namely?' queried Corinna, taken aback.

'Hannibal,' he said emphatically. 'Since Adherbal's death, our general of cavalry has come to rely on Sphax's leadership. And though I don't flatter myself that I'm in any way indispensable, nevertheless, Hannibal has come to rely on me, if only for my influence on the other Gaulish chieftains. Neither Maharbal nor Sphax's uncle would release us on what they would see as a wild goose chase.'

Sphax watched Corinna's frame visibly shrink into the couch she was sitting on. 'Then we must think of necessities, both strategic and tactical, that will make Cleon's recovery essential to the prosecution of my uncle's war with Rome.'

'Exactly,' Idwal grinned, encouragingly, 'and they are legion, pardon the expression.'

'Key to this, Corinna, is alliances,' Sphax explained. 'I know my uncle. What will persuade him are sound strategic reasons for sanctioning your scheme. Within days our cavalry patrols will range far and wide, cutting off all the land routes to the south and east. Rome's hold on Liguria can only be maintained if her garrisons are supplied along the Padus river.

'We need to acquire allies capable of prosecuting the war by sea and river. Illyria and Macedon are the only powers capable of this. If your mother could muster a fleet of Illyrian lemboï, Rome's trade on the

Padus could be decimated in a week. Our next target should be Ariminum, the source of her seaborne trade in the northern Adriatic. With the Padus closed and Ariminum blockaded, Roman power in the north of Italia would be at an end.'

'I too know something of your uncle's mind, Sphax,' Idwal began ominously, 'and I know with certainty he will not be persuaded by whimsical statements about high strategy. Only cold reason and hard fact will sway him.

'Firstly, how will we convince your mother, Corinna, to ally with Carthage and risk everything on another war with Rome? Illyria's last war ended in humiliating defeat and her own banishment. Airily you claim that a fleet of lemboï will decimate shipping on the Padus, Sphax. How many is a fleet? Does your mother possess such a number, Corinna? And secondly, how can Macedon be drawn into this? An alliance with Macedon would be a great prize, one that Hannibal would move mountains to achieve.'

Corinna had been listening intently to the arguments and counter arguments. Now she raised a hand to silence them both. 'The key to this is Demetrius of Pharos.'

'What?' cried Idwal. 'That treacherous snake switched sides, betrayed your mother and took control of the young king Pinnes. He's Illyria's chief calamity and a puppet of Rome. Your mother must loathe him!'

'He's no one's puppet,' Corinna replied calmly. 'You're not abreast of events, Idwal. Two years ago, after Demetrius foolishly sponsored piracy once more,

Rome sent an expedition that crushed him on Pharos. He's since fled to Philip of Macedon.'

'It would appear that I'm not,' Idwal conceded, startled by this latest news, 'but your mother must be overjoyed—'

'—Rome left him little choice!' Corinna interjected, eyebrows arched. 'You should know that my mother is not blameless in her relations with Demetrius. The fates were set in motion when my mother disdainfully rejected his marriage proposal.'

Sphax exchanged significant looks with Idwal. 'Is there something you're not telling us about your mother's relationship with Demetrius?'

'Maybe,' she answered, without giving anything away. 'Anyway, the true serpent and architect of my mother's downfall was Demetrius' advisor, Menda. The less said about him the better! Demetrius is not only a trusted advisor of Philip, he has a small Illyrian army with him, fighting for Macedon.'

Idwal was shaking his head, 'I still don't see how you can persuade your mother to forgive a man who switched sides and betrayed her to Rome. How can you reconcile the two of them?'

'You don't know my mother, Idwal. She has ships but no men. Demetrius has an army, albeit a small one, and the ear of Philip of Macedon. Don't you see? Everything fits into place perfectly. If Illyria *and* Macedon were allied to Hannibal, all would benefit from their mutual support.'

'Don't look at me like that, Corinna,' Idwal smiled wryly, 'you will only get the chance to convince your mother, if you first convince Hannibal.'

'Aren't you both forgetting about the young king, Pinnes?' asked Sphax.

'Through the lineage of my mother, my son Cleon's claim to the throne of Illyria is just as strong as Pinnes' claim. If we can rescue my son, my mother will proclaim Cleon Illyria's next king, not Pinnes.'

Sphax and Idwal stared speechlessly at one another as this last revelation sank in. Rome would wail and wring its hands in horror if a grandchild of Queen Teuta's was named king. But Rome was their sworn enemy, and they were about to persuade the queen to join them. Rome's treaties or opinions counted for nothing.

'Leaving these momentous questions aside for a moment,' Idwal said at last, 'how will we rescue Cleon? An Illyrian vessel would never be permitted to enter Brundisium's harbours. How will we reach the city?'

'From Rhizon we must sail to Epidamnos,' Corinna explained. 'My late husband's father is head of the council of elders and the wealthiest merchant in the city. He owns a fleet of ships. Cleon is his flesh and blood, his grandchild. Surely he'll want to help me recover my son! I'm still a hostage of Rome. So I'll have to enter Brundisium in secret and rescue my son by stealth, not by force of arms. So the fewer that go with me the better.'

It was almost dark when Idwal had risen from his seat to leave, but by then the three of them felt ready to face Hannibal's inevitable interrogation. Before he reached the vestibule, Corinna ran towards him and gripped his shoulders.

'Believe me, Idwal, I'm truly grateful. But why are you risking your own life on my son's account?'

'Because I'm fond of you and Sphax,' Idwal answered, turning to grin at her. 'But like you, Corinna, I can't bear the thought of being cooped up in an Insubres roundhouse for three months when adventure beckons!'

'You requested an audience, but I see you've brought a delegation, nephew,' Hannibal had begun ominously.

Sphax had come to dread a summons to his uncle's grand pavilion. It usually meant he was in deep trouble and would be slowly spit-roasted over an inquisition of gruelling questioning. On these occasions, Hannibal had often been flanked by his Greek tutor, Silenos, and the venerable historian, Sosylos, on couches either side of him. But that evening had been an audience, not a summons, and their places had been taken by Maharbal and Hannibal's younger brother, Mago. Sphax was encouraged by the fact that the three of them were offered seats, even refreshment.

'Corinna and Idwal are only here, Sir,' Sphax began, 'so we can give you a fuller and more complete account of our proposal.'

'Which is?'

He'd taken a deep breath and launched into the speech he'd spent all afternoon preparing. After the first sentence he noticed his uncle had closed his eyes, a familiar habit of his which Sphax had always assumed was to rest the eye plagued with its milky cast that required daily medicine from his Greek physician. Sphax had never minded this much. Better that than Hannibal's penetrating and disconcerting gaze. When his address was over and his uncle opened them again, that disconcerting gaze had fallen not on him, but on Corinna.

'Tell me, my dear, what could your mother possibly gain from an alliance with Carthage?'

'Much, Sir,' Corinna's rich low voice had answered assuredly. 'But if I were permitted to turn your question on its head: what has she to lose from such an alliance? She's been left to wither on the vine in a small kingdom in the north of Illyria, surrounded by her enemies and torn from her family.'

'Surely the same vultures would descend the instant Queen Teuta sealed an alliance with us. From my understanding, Scerdilaidas holds your stepbrother Pinnes captive at Scodra, and he's a client of Rome. He would be obliged to curb your mother's ambitions. As for your mother's betrayer and chief calamity, Demetrius, such an alliance would give him the perfect excuse to crush her and by so doing, win back favour with Rome.' Sphax had not been surprised by his uncle's grasp of affairs beyond the Adriatic, but other than himself and Idwal, everyone in the pavilion was utterly astonished by what Corinna had said next.

'Not if there was a reconciliation between my mother and Demetrius, and both of them allied themselves with Philip of Macedon.' For a few moments there had been a stunned silence as everyone stared at her.

'Surely Hades would have to release its dead before this could happen, madam?' Hannibal had said at last.

'That would not be necessary, Sir,' she'd replied coolly. 'My mother and Demetrius were lovers of long standing until she drove him away. This bitterness and Demetrius' overweening ambition caused him to betray her to Rome. Both deeply regret the rift, and I believe a reconciliation is—'

'Are you saying that Demetrius' defection to Rome was the result of a lovers' tiff?'

'Indeed I am, Sir, for that's what it amounts to. Demetrius knew full well that Illyria could not hope to win a war with Rome, as did my mother, but he'd more to gain from changing sides. I have known him since childhood. Despite his spitefulness towards my mother to gain control of Pinnes, I know him to be a noble and honourable man.'

'You truly believe there could be a reconciliation between them?' Hannibal had asked, still unconvinced.

'He's lost everything, Sir, his lands in Pharos, power over Pinnes. Rome is now his enemy, forcing him to seek the protection from his only friend, Philip of

Macedon. It's common knowledge that Demetrius and his army have fought bravely in Macedon's many wars. The three fates have dealt my mother and Demetrius equal blows, but in levelling them, I believe Clotho has woven a web that also unites them in a shared purpose.'

Hannibal had been utterly bemused by these revelations, spreading his arms in a gesture of bewilderment before bringing the palms of his hands together and raising fingertips to his lips. An unsettling silence had descended on the pavilion where his uncle's eyes never left Corinna's unflinching gaze. 'If we imagine,' he continued, 'for the sake of logical reasoning, that a reconciliation could be arranged between your mother and Demetrius, what could this unholy alliance offer Philip of Macedon?'

'What Philip and Macedon have long since desired, Sir, access to the Adriatic sea.'

'But surely that would mean giving up Illyrian lands to Macedon?'

Sphax had watched nervously as a brazen smile formed on Corinna's lips. 'Not if we offer them a Greek city that has already been stolen from our land, Sir.'

For the first time since he'd known him, Sphax witnessed his uncle burst into spontaneous laughter. 'You are indeed your mother's daughter,' he'd said, slowly shaking his head and turning to the general seated on the couch to his left. 'My dear Maharbal, remind me never to go to war with this lady, she would be a match for any of us.'

'Indeed, Hannibal, never in a woman have I encountered such an unscrupulous intellect. But tell me, Sphax, how many men do you need for this enterprise?

'Three from my eshrin, Idwal and his lieutenant, Drust, Corinna and her servant, Sir.'

'And who will navigate this vessel you steal from under the noses of Rome's legions?'

'Corinna, Sir.'

It had been Maharbal's turn to burst out laughing. 'It seems there's no end to the list of your accomplishments, madam.'

Hannibal turned to Idwal. 'Do you have a sound plan to recover Corinna's son?'

'We do, Sir, and have studied every contingency.'

'Then all is settled,' Hannibal had said, clapping his hands. When servants appeared he spoke with a flourish, 'Bring more wine, we have much to celebrate,' and turning to Corinna, 'Tomorrow I will have Silenos draw up a document that Carthage will only recognise Cleon as the future king of Illyria, and as my three representatives, I give you licence to treat with Queen Teuta and Philip of Macedon at your discretion. May Melqart bring us allies and swiftly launch them across the Adria.'

TWO

They'd glimpsed the vessel struggling upstream at midday. It was making heavy weather of a contrary breeze, and the river's currents. Earlier that morning they'd watched as the equites following them failed to keep pace. With every passing hour they'd fallen further astern. By mid-morning Sphax felt certain they'd given up the chase and returned to Placentia, which meant they could safely beach on the southern bank and take a closer look at the approaching craft. A bigger vessel would be more suitable for facing the perils of the Adria.

'There's a sandbank ahead,' shouted Corinna, 'we need to rein in our speed. Untie the sheets and let the sail flap, Idwal. Numidians, on my command stop rowing and brace your oars under the water to slow our progress.' Throwing all her weight against a steering oar Corinna yelled, 'Now!'

Sphax braced himself as the boat juddered to a halt amidst the sickening sound of grinding sand, a sound which set his teeth on edge. Leaping overboard,

Corinna and Zwalia soon had the vessel moored by a painter and a stern rope to willows on the bank.

'What now?' Corinna asked, looking uncertainly at him.

Sphax couldn't resist chuckling. Since they'd set sail, Corinna had commanded like a Greek naval strategos at the battle of Salamis, but the instant her feet touched dry land she was deferring to him. 'We take a look at this vessel and decide how to capture her.'

'What are we waiting for?' asked Drust.

'Wait!' protested Corinna. 'I know I said she looked bigger than ours, but that doesn't necessarily make her more seaworthy than the vessel we already have. Because of the serpentine bends in this river, I've only caught glimpses of her. I suggest we leave men behind to guard this vessel.'

'Agreed,' said Sphax, acknowledging Idwal's nod. 'Numidians, stay on board and guard our vessel until we return.'

On this stretch of the Padus, its banks were lined with a narrow strip of sand six paces deep before they met a tangle of birch and willow. They couldn't risk being spotted walking on the sand, so having no choice, began forcing their way through the almost impenetrable barrier of trunks and branches, leafless in this season. Eventually the trees thinned and gave way to grassy water meadows, making progress easier at last. Their first glimpse of the vessel came as a complete surprise.

What caught their attention was not the craft, but a pair of horses hauling her upriver, with a young boy plodding beside them. In the face of a contrary wind, the oarsmen were doing little more than overcoming the river's current, which was hardly surprising, as the oarsmen were little more than young boys. Headway was being maintained by the harnessed horses pulling a long painter tied to the vessel's prow. As a slave in Rome, Sphax had witnessed such sights every day. Her marketplaces were supplied by goods hauled up the Tiber by teams of horses. It was a commonplace sight.

'What now?' whispered Idwal, as intermittent glimpses of the vessel and her struggling oarsmen came into view through the scrubby corridor of trees that hid them from the river.

'I don't know,' Corinna answered, without taking her eyes off the craft. 'But I'm certain of one thing: we must capture her. She's twice the length of our vessel, has benches for twelve oarsmen and a high freeboard far more suitable for the open waters of the Adria.'

As whispered suggestions on how to capture the vessel were bandied around by the rest of them, Sphax continued to watch the horses closely. A grain of an idea had occurred to him. He'd noticed the horses were not being worked hard, and they were big sturdy creatures, capable of much more than they were giving. The boy, who must have been no more than twelve, was simply walking beside them, not having to coax or exhort them to the easy effort they were making. Sphax judged the rope to be no more than twenty paces long, and the vessel was being rowed as close to the bank as the oars would allow. All they needed now was to wait for a wide sandbar, and move fast.

Sphax could see from the nodding heads and broad grins they thought his idea might work. Walking quickly now so as to draw ahead of the horses, the five of them headed back up river, looking out for a wide stretch of sand. They found such a place after a few hundred paces: a sandbar thirty paces across before it met the tangle of trees higher up the bank.

Unstrapping the buckles of his dragon sword from around his chest, he handed it to Corinna and passed on his clutch of javelins to Zwalia. 'I don't want to be encumbered by anything when I try this. Besides, you may need them.'

Corinna smiled. 'They're only boys, Sphax, probably slaves, and the man on the steering oars looks ancient. I don't think they'll give us any trouble.'

'I wonder what the vessel's carrying upriver?' mused Sphax.

Corinna laughed, 'Food and wine fit for a Consul's table, I hope.' Narrowing her eyes she added, 'I see it. We'd better get into position.'

Making for the widest stretch of the sandbar he weaved his way through a tangle of ivy-clad alders that gave excellent cover, crouched down, and waited. Gazing to his right he could see the others were ready, crouching down in the undergrowth, awaiting his signal. Sphax could see the horses now, less than a hundred paces downstream. The harness that bound the two together seemed to be a simple arrangement of leather neck collars yoked by a wooden bar to which the painter had been attached. It should be simple, he thought.

'Now,' he shouted, sprinting as fast as he could over the sand. The boy noticed him soon enough, but simply stared at him, paralysed to the spot. After two more strides Sphax leapt on to the back of the nearest horse, a big chestnut stallion, which instantly snorted and reared up its hind legs, throwing his harnessed partner into near panic. Sphax knew he had only a few heartbeats to calm them down before he lost all control and they bolted.

Letting out a stream of sing-song words to soothe the creature, he began gently stroking the stallion's neck whilst riding the bucking and kicking of its front legs. Eventually Sphax had him under control, but by then his own heart was racing.

Finally he was able to gently nudge him up the sandbar and away from the river. With his right hand he reached over to the other stallion, fed his fingers through his browband, and gently tugged so the two of them would work together. Immediately he felt the tension on the rope and the yoke strain. Now it called for a supreme effort.

Digging his knees into the chestnut's shoulders Sphax felt him respond instantly and break into a trot.

Ten strides later the stallions could pull no more and ground to a panting halt. Closing his eyes, Sphax sank his forehead into the stallion's mane and breathed a mighty sigh of relief. Until now he had not dared to look over his shoulder. Now he did.

Somehow, they'd managed to haul the entire vessel and her crew clean out of the water and onto the sand. The boy who'd walked beside the horses was still staring at him. And Idwal and Corinna were strutting on board as if they'd just captured her. Which they had.

Dismounting, Sphax grinned at the boy still gaping at him and reached for his hand. Idwal was at last grinning. 'Well done, Sphax, it worked perfectly.' Hauling a terrified old man by his loosened hood, he continued, 'May I present Lucius, merchant and captain of Ariminum, with a cargo bound for Placentia.'

If Idwal was grinning, Corinna was smirking. He knew that look. 'You almost lost it, my little dove, didn't you? Those stallions were about to bolt.'

'I must confess it was a close call,' Sphax admitted, grudgingly. 'But have we not promised Idwal never to use those *endearments*, Corinna?'

'I'm sure he'll allow me the occasional indulgence,' she replied with a mischievous grin, 'otherwise life would become far too dull.'

Drust was busily binding the hands of a shifty-looking youth who'd received a bloodied lip. Sphax took one look at him and knew straight away he was the enforcer—the one that would beat the slave boys and keep them in check. 'Meet Cyrus, Sphax. Thug, bully and general dogsbody.'

Sphax stared at the boys huddled together on the rowing benches. They seemed to be drawn from several races, but the majority were fair-haired Gauls, the oldest no more than fifteen. 'What in the name of the gods are we going to do with this lot?'

'Welcome to my new crew,' replied Corinna; 'they might be boys, but they row better than Numidians.'

Sphax flushed, staring at her. 'Not as slaves!' he snapped. Having been one himself, he knew something of the misery of slavery. 'If they row for us it will be as Numidians rowed, as free men—'

'But they're not men, Sphax, they're boys—'

'Exactly! That's why our responsibility for their welfare is even greater. We must ask each in turn whether they wish to serve us for wages, or try to make it back to their homelands and families. From this moment onwards they are free, and as free citizens they have rights that *will* be upheld.'

'That's ridiculous!' In exasperation she appealed to Idwal, 'What do you think?' She was appealing to the wrong man.

After borrowing Aristotle's treatise on slavery from Hannibal's venerable historian, Sosylos, Sphax and Idwal had debated the philosopher's flimsy arguments for months. 'I agree with Sphax,' Idwal said coldly. 'They're now free, and at liberty to choose their own destiny.'

'Very well,' snapped Corinna, 'but let's get on with it. We have to transfer everything to this vessel and we're wasting the wind.'

Sphax tried to step over the freeboard onto the vessel, but the boy wouldn't let go of his hand. 'What's your name?' he said in Latin. The lad just stared up at him, blankly. He tried Greek, but got no further. There was something familiar about his clear blue eyes, fair hair and complexion. The boy began repeating a word incomprehensible to Sphax. In desperation he let go of Sphax's hand, pointed at Idwal then patted his own chest. He was Cavari.

'Idwal,' he yelled, 'come and talk to this boy. I'm sure he's Cavari!'

Lifting the lad on to the vessel, Idwal sat him on a rowing bench and begun an earnest conversation in Gallic. Immediately, four other boys stood up and joined them, along with Drust.

'Dog's twat, Sphax!' cried Idwal at last. 'You did us a mighty favour when you killed that bastard Vertros and sent him into the arms of Morrigú. He was selling his own people into slavery. All five are Cavari!'

Vertros, a vicious warlord of the Cavari, had insulted Sphax beyond measure. Challenging the man to single combat, Sphax had slain him in a fair contest. They'd always known he'd enslaved neighboring tribes such as the Allobroges, but that he'd stoop so low as enslave his own people had come as a terrible shock to Idwal and Drust.

Sphax glared at Corinna. 'How would you feel if we'd found your son Cleon a slave on this vessel?' Corinna paled, but said nothing. 'There is only one word that describes slavery: misery!' Stepping on to the vessel he added, 'Now let's talk to these boys and ask them if they will serve us willingly, or be released.'

For most of them, including boys from Corinth and Rhodus, their homes were so far flung that return would have been impossible. The Cavari boys were keen to serve Idwal, and when Sphax found the stick Cyrus had used to beat them and cast it angrily into the river, it sent them all a clear message. Four boys were from the Cenomani tribe whose territory lay downstream. Naturally, they wanted to return home, but all the rest raised an arm and willingly agreed to serve.

'It seems you have your crew, Corinna,' said Sphax at last.

'What do we do about those two?' she asked, nodding at the Ariminum captain and Cyrus, bound together on the stern platform.

'I tied those knots,' replied Drust. 'Believe me, those two aren't going anywhere.'

'Neither are the horses,' added Sphax, 'so let's go back, sail our other craft down river, then transfer our supplies to this vessel.'

'That would be quickest,' agreed Corinna. 'But once we've done that we should scuttle the other vessel so it can't be used for trade by Rome.'

'At last we *all* agree about something,' Idwal said, smiling at Corinna.

* * *

'I never asked,' said Sphax as they began retracing their steps upriver, 'what goods is our latest craft carrying to Placentia?'

'You will be delighted, my love,' Corinna answered, grinning, her mood considerably improved. 'There's grain, salted meats, fine wine … even honey. Nothing but the best for the tables of Placentia.'

'I wish Rome had a taste for mead,' Drust said whimsically, to no one in particular. 'I do miss it.'

'Me too,' agreed Idwal, wistfully. 'What would I give for a bowl of milk sweetened with that honey?'

'Milk!' cried Corinna, quite disgusted.

'Shut up all of you,' groaned Sphax, 'I'm hungry enough as it is!'

Half a mile later he first heard it, but dismissed it as branches creaking in the wind. When he heard it for a second time he was sure. Striding ahead, he turned around and put a finger to his lips and beckoned everyone to be still. Sphax heard voices. Distant and faint, but definitely voices, and they were coming from upstream.

Now Drust could hear them. 'It doesn't sound like your Numidians,' he whispered.

'I think they're speaking Latin,' Sphax said with rising panic, fearing for the safety of his men. As the five of them began running as noiselessly as they could manage, the voices grew closer with every stride. He could now distinguish some words and phrases. Together the five of them plunged into the dense undergrowth of the trees and crept forward to where they gave way to sand.

Much to his relief, the sight that met him could almost be construed as comical. His Numidians must have cut the stern rope and cast off from the sandbar. They were now standing on the platform at the back of the vessel, clutching their javelins. As the vessel was still attached to the painter at its bow, the craft was bobbling in the river's current, some way from the bank. Meanwhile, on the sandbar, three dismounted Roman equites were hurling insults at their would-be captives, whilst two more lay dead on the sand, skewered by javelins. It was a perfect stand-off.

If the Romans cut the painter the craft would drift downstream and the Numidians would escape. If they approached the vessel and tried to board it they would meet with certain death. So the battle was being fought with insults, and the jeering Numidians were giving as good as they got.

Strutting up and down the sand out of javelin range a decurion in a fancy helmet and a fine mailcoat was yelling, 'Tell me where Sphax the Numidian is, you pieces of rat shit!' Except for two words, his Numidians would understand none of this.

Sphax glanced at the faces crouching beside him, mimed the drawing of a sword then tied his slender iron saunion with his throwing thong. Idwal and Drust had left their shields behind, but no Roman eques was the equal of Cavari swordsmen, and Corinna still had his dragon sword at her waist.

'Where *is* he, you shitheads?' bellowed the decurion.

'He's right behind you,' Sphax shouted, striding towards him with levelled saunion. 'Quid ergo vis eum tecum?'

Of this there could be no doubt. 'His severed head,' snarled the man, swiveling around and charging towards him with sword raised. Sphax's saunion snuffed out his life before he'd taken another stride. No mailcoat yet made could withstand a saunion. The remaining equites fought bravely, but they were no match for the blades of Idwal and Drust. He could hear his Numidians cheering as they jumped from the bow and splashed onto the sand.

'What kept you?' demanded Hannon. 'We're all as sick as dogs after bobbing about on that river all afternoon.'

'It's a long story,' sighed Sphax, grinning at the three of them affectionately. 'You look perfectly well to me.'

'I'm starving, captain,' pleaded Agbal.

'You're always starving, Agbal. But there's good news. The latest vessel we captured has plenty of food, and your days as oarsmen will soon be at an end.'

Jugurtha was eyeing the mailcoats, helmets and warm crimson cloaks the equites had been wearing. 'It would be a shame to leave this stuff behind, Sir. Those mailcoats alone are worth their weight in gold!'

Corinna had been listening to their exchange. 'He's right, Sphax, at some stage we might need a disguise. They might prove useful.'

Sphax nodded. 'You two collect what you can from the dead whilst Agbal releases their stallions tied to the trees over there.'

'I warned you they would not give up,' nagged Corinna, frowning at him.

'My guess is that the turma did give up, but this decurion was persistent and managed to persuade four of them to continue the chase.'

'You now have a reputation, my love, and that worries me. I could see the hatred in his eyes as he leapt at you.'

Sphax shrugged. 'It didn't do him much good, did it?'

* * *

Within the hour they'd rowed downriver to where the larger vessel was beached. Everything was as they'd left it except for Cyrus' face. The more courageous of the slave boys—or the ones that had suffered most from his stick—had exacted their revenge. Sphax could hardly blame them, but he should have foreseen this. Cyrus was moaning and in a bad way. He asked Zwalia to bathe his face and do what she could for him.

They now had a vessel that could ride the waves of the Adriatic Sea and a crew of twenty that would be reduced by four when they reached Cenomani territory. But that was more than enough, and what's more, young as they were, at least the boys knew what they were doing. After everyone had eaten their fill, he and Drust led the ex-captain, Lucius, and his slave master Cyrus from the vessel and helped them onto the stallions. Sphax didn't even bother to remove the harnesses and yoke, it would slow them down.

Standing on the more spacious steering platform, Sphax could see that Corinna was once more back in her true element. Because the boys rowed more efficiently than Numidians, she'd suggested that only eight oars were required, which meant that twelve of them could rest and be rotated so as not to tire them unduly. Zwalia was left to supervise six of them manning the sail, but they needed little supervision. Even though the boat was almost twice the size of the vessel they'd seized at Placentia, she was quite cramped and difficult to move around in. Wooden chests and clay jars filled virtually all available space in the belly of the craft, and clumsy landlubbers found the rowing benches awkward to negotiate on a swaying vessel. When any of them had to traverse the length of the boat it was usually accompanied by much cursing. Sphax and his men eventually found quarters beneath the steering platform, whilst Idwal and Drust joined Zwalia in the bow.

'It's cold up here,' Corinna said to him, 'stand with me, my darling, and keep me warm. Perhaps we can share your cloak.' Standing beside her he draped some of his cloak over her left shoulder and slid his hand around her waist. 'Much better,' she said. 'Now I'm content.'

For a while he was happy to gaze out at the southern bank and watch the trees and landscape slide by. It would soon be dusk, but as the breeze had stiffened, Corinna was eager to make progress while they had the light. As they rounded another great bend in the river that set them on a northerly course, he suddenly saw lights and fires twinkling out of the distant gloom.

'It must be Cremona,' he said anxiously, 'can we sail past it before night is upon us?'

'I don't know, it's difficult to judge how far away it is. Dusk would be the perfect time to sail past it unnoticed, but I wouldn't want to be on this river in the dark, it's too dangerous. Is there a moon tonight?'

'Agbal,' he shouted, whilst answering Corinna's question with a shake of his head. 'Get up here and take a look at this.' Agbal had the sharpest pair of eyes in his eshrin. Sphax swapped places with him. 'How far?'

'It's getting dark out there. I'm not a cat, Sir.'

'Then guess!' Sphax demanded.

'Four … maybe five miles,' he replied, uncertain.

Sphax stared at Corinna. 'Can we cover that distance before nightfall?'

'I'm not sure. But it will be close.'

'What if we get all twelve boys rowing together and ask them to speed up the … what do you call it—'

'Stroke!' cried Corinna. 'That's it, Sphax. It will certainly improve our chances.'

Sphax turned and sought out Idwal in the gathering gloom. 'Idwal,' he yelled over the rowing benches, 'I need you to explain to the boys there's an emergency. Turn around and see for yourself.' Pausing for a moment, he continued. 'Ahead of us is the Roman garrison town of Cremona. We have the perfect conditions to sail past it undetected, but if we fail and land on some sandbank in the dark, we'll be in grave danger at first light. I need all twelve of the boys to row for their lives. If we're captured they will all be taken back into slavery. Remind them of that.'

As Idwal's plea in Gallic began, the rowing benches leapt into action as boys resumed their places and began their work in earnest. Zwalia had also resumed her position amongst the boys manning the sail.

Sphax was once again huddled against Corinna on the steering platform, giving warmth and whatever encouragement she needed at this fateful moment. 'Carmo has already increased the stroke. He's a good lad, that one.'

'Which one is Carmo?'

'He's the lead stroke, the boy on the first rowing bench on the left. All the rest follow his lead. That Greek lad, Elpis, is opposite, he's also a strong oarsman for his age.'

Sphax was amazed. 'So, you've got to know some of these boys?'

'When we were arranging the rowing teams,' she answered, slightly abashed. 'I took to heart what you said to me. Cleon could well end up at the mercy of vicious slavers like that Cyrus.'

'He won't!' Sphax said fervently. Staring ahead at the flickering lamplight of Cremona, he willed it nearer, knowing they were now in a desperate race against the darkness. It was a strange coincidence that the young boy from Corinth had the same name as his own teacher, Elpis, also from Corinth. For some reason a fragment of a poem, from some half-remembered lesson came into his head.

Out loud he recited, 'Be present, Goddess, to thy suppliant's prayer, desired by all, whom all alike revere, blessed, benevolent, with friendly aid dispel the fears of Twilight's dreadful shade.'

'That's beautiful, Sphax, is it from a poem?'

'I was thinking of the goddess Nyx, our current enemy, feared even by Zeus, and the lines came into my head. And yes, it's a hymn by Orpheus.' Ominously, he could see the lights growing brighter with every stroke of the oars, which meant the goddess was winning. He watched as Idwal and Drust climbed on to the prow. Had Zwalia asked them to act as lookouts?

'I know what I must do,' said Corinna. 'If I hug the northern bank on this north-easterly course until a mile or so from the city, I can then swing due east, heading for the southern bank.' Sphax said nothing, realising that Corinna was just thinking aloud. 'Due east would give us all the wind and take us far away from prying eyes. See! The river loops back on itself, so we would cut a corner. I must beware of cross-currents that drive us north. May Hera make my right hand strong and dispel the fears of Twilight's dreadful shade.'

They were close now. Sphax could even distinguish between torchlight and lamplight as the city illuminated herself from the coming night.

'Look out!' Idwal and Drust screamed, pointing ahead of them. Corinna saw it and threw all her weight against the right-hand oar. All Sphax saw was a jetty looming out of the gloom, like that built into the river at Placentia, but this was much longer and alarmingly solid looking.

'Help me, Sphax!' Corinna gasped, 'I can't hold it!' Swivelling around and crouching slightly, he gripped the oar with both hands below her quivering fingers. Sphax felt the vessel's planks groaning and straining, but she was coming about, swinging to the south.

Everyone seemed to be shouting at once. Carmo was shouting a succession of orders to the boys on the benches whilst Zwalia was yelling and wrestling with a tangle of flapping ropes. For a heartbeat all was chaos, but nevertheless the vessel continued to swing. The last thing he saw of the jetty was the last two enormous wooden piles looming above him. By a miracle they'd cleared it by a whisker.

'You can let go now,' gasped Corinna with a heartfelt sigh. It was only then he saw that Carmo had got all the boys on his side to ship their oars out of the water, otherwise, every single oar would have snapped into splinters on those massive wooden piles sunk deep into the river. The boy's quick thinking had saved them all.

At last Sphax could feel the full force of the wind as the sail swelled and drove them onwards. Carmo was shouting again, ordering the boys to lower their oars and begin rowing. But darkness had already overtaken them. Without moon or stars, the only light left in the world was coming from the receding glow of Cremona.

'We're now in the hands of the gods. Whilst I could still see it, I took a sighting from the far bank and will continue on that bearing, but this is fraught with danger. I have much instruction for you to pass on to Idwal and Zwalia, so listen carefully.' After she'd finished he took off his cloak, draped it around her shoulders and feeling his way, gingerly stepped down into the belly of the boat and made his way to the last rowing bench.

'Idwal,' Sphax shouted, 'these are Corinna's instructions. Our oarsmen are to ease their stroke to that which keeps us a little faster than the river's current. Carmo will understand why this is necessary.'

Pausing, he waited for Idwal's translation. Ahead of him he heard Carmo say a few words before Idwal spoke again. 'Carmo says they'll make sure Corinna has steerage, whatever that is.'

'Don't worry, Idwal, I know what it means. You must tell the boys to be ready to raise oars the instant they feel the vessel grounding. They must brace themselves for this.'

Once Idwal had finished speaking, Sphax added, 'Zwalia is to take down the sail and you should brace yourselves for the grounding.'

With that he stumbled back to his men and explained what was going to happen, relieved in the circumstances he couldn't see their expressions. Corinna's exposed position on the platform worried him. 'I'm joining you on the platform, Corinna, you need to—'

'No!' she yelled. 'Stay where you are.' Ignoring her, he felt for the hand rails, gripped them tightly and heaved himself on to the platform. Without warning, it was then that the vessel struck.

All Sphax remembered was Corinna's body slamming into him, his hands giving way and the two of them being propelled backwards. Then all his senses merged into the darkness.

THREE

His first sensation when returning to the world was the exquisite touch of fingers combing their way through the curls of his shoulder-length hair. Sphax decided he could happily bear his throbbing head for all eternity if those fingers continued their sensuous progress. But then will and necessity intervened, forcing his eyes open. In mellow lamplight he saw Corinna kneeling above him, anxious and concerned, cradling his head in the palms of her hands. 'Thank the gods! You're awake.'

'How long have I slept?' he asked, groggily.

'Not long, my love. When the vessel struck I was propelled forward, but you were there to save me and stop my flight. You fell backwards and I landed on top of you.' She suddenly grinned, 'An unusual position to find myself in. Remind me to cut your unruly hair before I present you to my mother. How's your back?'

He flexed his shoulders and sat up. 'I'll live. Is anybody else hurt?'

'Not a scratch. Hera answered my prayers and beached us on a steep sandbank.'

'On which bank?'

'That's the problem,' she frowned, 'the northern bank.' Sphax glanced sharply at the oil lamp. Corinna caught his movement. 'Don't worry, the vessel can only be seen from close by, and Idwal has posted sentries on the riverbank. None of the boys seemed to know what was in the chests and amphorae, so we needed light to examine them. But they did know where Lucilus hid this.'

She opened the lid of a cedar chest, raising the lamp so he could view its contents. Reaching out her left hand she plowed her fingers through a small mountain of silver coin. 'We have a war chest, my prince.'

It proved to be a bitterly cold and uncomfortable night for everyone on board, but they all managed some sleep, and after midnight, Sphax felt well enough to take up his responsibilities on watch.

But as dawn's first fingers of light glistened on the surface of the water downstream, they realised they had a new problem: the vessel was well and truly stuck on the sandbank and wouldn't budge. At one point they almost gave up and considered abandoning her and capturing a new vessel in Cremona. One final attempt with all the adults heaving and the boys rowing away from the bank at last succeeded. But the sun was already high in a wintry grey sky when at last they set off down river.

The westerly wind had almost deserted them that morning, blowing so fitfully that for long periods their sail hung limp and impotent. Corinna insisted the rowing teams be rotated well within the hour so as not to tire their young oarsmen, but Sphax was encouraged to see how eagerly they stuck to their task. He also noted that beyond Cremona the nature of the river itself had changed: gone were the vexing serpentine bends prohibiting views downriver, now its broad waters held a steady easterly course, drawing them on to the sea that lay beyond.

Once more Sphax took up station beside Corinna on the steering platform, not so much to keep her warm as to relieve the monotony of her lonely vigil at the steering oars. By mid-afternoon the wind had dropped to a whisper, so Zwalia and her young assistants took down the mast and sail that was now acting as a drag on their momentum. Even so, as the uneventful hours passed by, Sphax thought they'd made excellent progress.

Negotiating a sudden bend that swept them in a north easterly direction, an opportunity arose that called for a swift decision. Ahead of them Sphax could see that the Padus diverged into two separate channels before uniting its waters half a mile beyond. Between them lay the perfect sanctuary—an island with a northerly sandy beach and ample driftwood for fires. There was at least another hour of light left in the day, but for once, Sphax and Corinna agreed that a further six miles was not worth a fleabite. So they beached, flushing flocks of cranes that took to the air, honking in protest.

* * *

It was bitterly cold again that night. When darkness fell, Sphax asked his men to scan both banks for signs of settlements or habitation, but they reported seeing nothing. For once they were alone in the wilderness, on an island in the middle of the deepest river in Liguria; with no need of sentries or watches. Tonight they would sleep easy. After settling the boys around two campfires, the eight of them edged as close to their own campfire as possible. Jugurtha, the most elderly amongst them had taken upon himself the task of feeding the fires with fresh driftwood. His old bones felt the cold more than most.

It felt good to stretch legs and eat hot lentil stew and chopped pork. It felt even better after he learned why his men were whooping and dancing around in the middle of their vessel. What they'd discovered was a labelled jar of the sweet raisin wine Passum, a favourite of all Carthaginians, grown on scores of vineyards near Carthage. It was as if they'd discovered their mothers' milk, an authentic taste of home.

When his men were not looking, Sphax carefully examined the clay tablet attached to the neck of the jar. He hadn't the heart to tell them the Latin clearly stated the grapes were harvested in the year of Consul

Gaius Flaminius, which meant that for the last five years, Rome had been making its own version of Passum. It was Flaminius who'd signed his parents' death warrants. The wine began to stick in his craw and he refused another glass.

But something else had been weighing on his mind that evening. Sphax took a deep breath, knowing Corinna would not like what he was about to say. 'Corinna, my darling, I want you to share your duties on the steering platform with Zwalia. Not only have you to contend with the twists and tribulations of the Padus, ahead of us lie the perils of the Adriatic. You will need to rest and retain your strength for the trials to come.' He was avoiding her eyes, but out of the corner of his he could see she was glaring at him.

'You are depriving me of something I love,' she cried, her eyes flashing with outrage, 'what I was born to do!—'

'Listen to the man, Corinna!' Zwalia interrupted, sharply. 'I watched you carefully as you stepped down from the platform this evening. Your shoulders and arms were shaking from the effort you've made this day.' More soothingly she added, 'Your strength will return, my dear, but not overnight. Sphax is usually right about such things. For the moment you need to share this task with me.'

'She's right, Corinna. This is not a reflection on your strength or skill,' Idwal echoed, with his innate conciliatory tact, 'but a measure to preserve them.

Ultimately, all our lives are in your hands, so we must take every precaution to preserve your strength.'

That clinched it. Without another word of protest, Corinna nodded acquiescence.

* * *

For the next two days Corinna and Zwalia shared the work on the steering oars. The journey proved uneventful, and without breaking into food stored on the vessel they were able to feast themselves royally from the abundance of wildfowl on the river.

By mid-morning on the third day, Brennos, one of the four boys from the Cenomani, began pointing excitedly at the northern bank. Sphax guessed by now they must be deep into the tribe's territory, and the lad was pointing out landmarks he recognised. Idwal gathered the four of them beneath the prow.

Sphax was standing beside Corinna on the steering platform as Idwal began to make his way to the stern. 'They say that in a mile or so we should see fishing boats tied up at a wharf,' he shouted up to Corinna. 'Brennos says his village is half a mile inland.'

Corinna nodded, already hauling on her left-hand oar to set a course for the northern bank. Rounding a gentle curve in the river they could see it ahead, not a highly engineered Roman jetty, but a crude wharf formed from rough-hewn logs sunk into the river's edge bound together by strips of hide. Sphax counted three small rowing boats bobbing in the current alongside. Corinna now had such an understanding with Carmo and his opposite number Elpis that a few gestures sufficed to bring them to a gentle halt beside the wharf.

Idwal was burdened by that familiar frown of his. 'Bearing in mind we have no idea what reception we'll receive from the Cenomani, I suggest Drust and I hand over the boys, alone.'

'No, Idwal. We restored their children's freedom from Rome, and my uncle has scattered Rome's legions. I mean to remind them of it.'

'This is madness, Sphax, they're allies of Rome!'

'Then it's about time I reminded them of this misalliance.'

Idwal stared at Corinna, imploringly. 'Don't waste your breath, Idwal,' she shrugged, 'just try to bring him back alive.'

'That might prove difficult,' Idwal sighed, resigning himself to the situation as he and Drust began shepherding the four boys onto the wharf.

Seeing his Numidians sharing out javelins, Sphax rounded on them. 'I'm prepared to risk my skin, but not yours. You three stay.' At which all three started laughing, reaching for their hide shields. Now it was his turn to bow to the inevitable.

Once clear of the wharf and a belt of willow, the village came into sight immediately. But it wasn't a village, it was a large settlement, wreathed in a fog of wood-smoke clinging to a myriad of thatched roundhouses and grander halls. Sphax realised they would have more to contend with here than a few grey-haired elders. They would be as welcome as a pack of ravenous wolves in a hard winter. With the four Cenomani boys leading the way, they made their way along a dung-strewn track that seemed to be leading to the centre of the settlement. As doorways opened and the inhabitants poured out of their houses to gawp at the strangers, an ominous silence descended on the place.

Sphax noticed the Cenomani were not fair like Gauls, with shaved faces and generous mustachios the colour of Idwal's. Most were clad in Gaulish leggings resplendent in autumnal russet hues, whilst the women favoured waist-length shawls in similar colours. But he met faces with unfamiliar features, as if from a different race, faces with prominent cheekbones, raven hair and sallow complexions. Idwal was fond of telling him that all Gauls were cousins, but to Sphax's eyes, these people looked like very *distant* cousins.

Ahead of them he could now see a complex of larger buildings; one of them he guessed was a feasting hall, similar to Idwal's father's in Nages. Sphax didn't have fond memories of such places. Guards, hefting great shields and wielding spears stood stony-faced outside the entrance passageway. Idwal said something to one of them and he disappeared inside. They were made to wait. Deliberately, he suspected.

Finally, two figures emerged from the darkness of the passageway and strode boldly out to meet them.

Sphax guessed the elder of them to be a Cenomani chieftain, and the younger, a boy of no more than fourteen, to be his son. The resemblance between the two was striking.

Both were unarmed except for long blades strapped to silver chains around their waists and both were wearing sumptuous versions of the russet-coloured cloaks and leggings he'd already observed. What marked them apart was the gold torques of authority, emblazoned around their necks.

Sphax couldn't understand why he felt dismayed that both father and son shared the same sallow complexions and wore their shoulder-length raven hair plaited. Nevertheless, he did. Nervously he began twitching the iron saunion he carried, and out of the corner of his eye he saw his men discreetly threading their throwing thongs.

Idwal was a head taller than the chieftain, a fact exaggerated by his bronze helmet laced with silver and gold. His thigh-length mail coat and cape was of the finest quality, and his blade, along with his own personal courage, was legend. In Sphax's eyes, Idwal was the embodiment of everything that was noble about the Keltoi, what his Greek teacher called 'the tall ones.' But Sphax feared that he was facing not a distant cousin, but a different race, with its own set of rules, and more significantly, its own allegiances.

On the appearance of the chieftain and his son, the four Cenomani boys sank to their knees and solemnly bowed their heads, giving Idwal his cue to speak. Sphax listened in ignorant silence as Idwal explained their mission to free the boys from Roman slavery. At times the conversation grew heated, especially when he noted that his name, and that of his uncle were mentioned.

By now a mob of chattering townsfolk had gathered around them, but these were a simple people, farmers and fishermen, and Sphax was relieved to see none carried weapons. When both parties eventually fell silent, Idwal turned to him.

'Carmanos, chieftain of the Cenomani, welcomes the release of slaves to his kingdom. But it is only through common courtesy and Gaulish custom he's allowed me to speak. As for you and your Numidians, you are not welcome, and seen as enemies of the Cenomani. If we are to get out of this place alive, Sphax, please temper your remarks.'

Before he could open his mouth to say anything, Carmanos hissed in bad Latin, 'When Rome's legions return, the Cenomani will fall on the invader and drive you like dogs from our lands. Numidians and Libyans are foreigners to the Cenomani, and will be hunted down and slain.'

Sphax allowed himself the time it took to thread his saunion to compose a reply. 'My uncle has destroyed the legions of Scipio and Longus,' he said evenly. 'Rome will never return to these lands. You are without allies, Carmanos.'

'You're a black-faced devil, Numidian! You speak lies unworthy of a serpent—'

'Then I will spell it out for you, Carmanos, chieftain of the Cenomani. All lands on the southern bank of the Padus now belong to Carthage. Our allies, the Insubres and Boii have claimed the Padus for themselves, so all fishing will cease, as will all your commerce with Rome. Do you understand?—'

'—Morrigú awaits you!' snarled the chief, reaching for his sword. His fingers had barely closed on its hilt when he froze in horror as three javelins were raised and poised for flight. Seizing the moment, Sphax leapt forward, grabbed the chief's startled son by the arm and dragged him back to where his Numidians were standing their ground. He soon had the boy in an iron grip with the barb of his saunion at the boy's throat. Carmanos let out an animal cry of pain and gaped helplessly at his son.

'Your son is now my hostage, Carmanos. If he's to live, you will dismiss your guards and tell your townsfolk to return to their homes. Only when we are safely aboard our vessel will he be released. His life is in your hands ... what say you?'

'I beg you, Numidian ... spare him!' the chief bleated, gazing in horror at the expression of terror screwed on his son's face. 'You're free to leave, I swear it ... I swear by Morrigú!' A demented Carmanos now began waving his arms and screaming at his guards and the crowds to disperse.

Forming a protective ring around Sphax, who was still gripping the boy's arm like a vice, they managed to retrace their steps through the town. Behind them they could still hear the chieftain yelling at his townsfolk to return to their homes. Only when they'd reached the open water meadows beyond the settlement did they offer a collective sigh of relief.

'On the whole,' said Drust cheerily, 'I thought that went rather well.' At which point Sphax and Idwal were so convulsed with laughter that he loosened his grip on Carmanos' son, who managed to wriggle free and sprint back to the settlement. No doubt into the joyous arms of his father.

Sphax and Idwal were still chuckling to themselves as they clambered aboard the vessel and asked Corinna to cast off. Behind his smile, however, Sphax knew full well he'd used up another of his lives.

FOUR

'What can you see?' shouted Corinna from below. Sphax settled himself in the leafless crown of the ancient oak he'd climbed and looked to the east. It was another grey windless day, barely warmed by a wintry sun, but in the east, the horizon seemed limitless, and wherever he looked it sparkled with motion. 'I'm coming down,' he said at last.

That morning, two days after their encounter with the Cenomani, they'd entered a wild land, a land fit only for animals and birds, a land that people shunned. Sphax had never encountered such a place before, nor could he ever have imagined such places existed in this world. Not by choice had they entered this horizonless water-world of lakes and lagoons, threaded by myriads of reed-choked channels flanked by water meadows rich in willow, ash and gnarled old oaks. With alarm they saw bears feasting in fishing ponds, beavers nuzzling great logs through reedbeds and lynx, normally shy and reclusive, hunting amongst the patchwork of meadow and woodland that lay beside the waterways and lagoons. The air was thick with the calling of birds, many unfamiliar to him, and high above their heads eagles circled, their great white tails glinting in the wintry sunlight.

Who in the name of the gods would enter such a place by choice? No, somehow they'd lost the main channel that led to the sea and entered this watery wilderness by mischance. Earlier, they'd noticed the great river was dividing into a dizzying number of separate channels, each one as inviting as the next. Corinna had always selected the broadest and most promising, yet the river had deceived them, and now they were marooned, short of the Adria.

Swinging down from the last branch to join the seven of them gathered around the gnarled trunk, he found himself grinning for the first time that day. 'There is some good news,' he offered. 'The Adria is less than half a mile away to the east, so we are very close, but too far to carry the boat.'

Corinna's shoulders slumped. 'Close is not close enough. We need to retrace our steps and try another channel, but there are scores of them. I fear we'll be trapped in this Hades for days.'

'Don't despair, Corinna,' Idwal assured her, 'as Sphax has said, we're close. I'm sure we'll find a way out of this watery maze.'

At that moment a great bellowing sound erupted, and all eight of them froze. What new horror is this? thought Sphax, turning round to where the sound had come from. The horror was a great black ox, the size of a small forest elephant, with vicious, forward-pointing horns that could have skewered a bear, let alone a man. It looked mean, irritable, and was bellowing at them from less than sixty paces away.

'Dog's twat!' cried Agbal. 'In the name of Ba 'al Hamūn, *what* is that?'

Drust placed a hand on Agbal's shoulder. 'That, young man, is an aurochs.' Sphax translated for the benefit of the Numidians. 'Where I come from, young men hunt these wild cattle in the forests and valleys of the Pyrenees. Their horns are much sought after as drinking horns. But I suggest you leave it well alone; they are notoriously unpredictable and extremely dangerous.'

'So it's just a wild cow!' Agbal scoffed. 'Then I'm having it,' he continued, selecting a javelin and searching for his throwing thong. 'I haven't tasted beef in months.' His mouth already watering.

'Then your belly will be the death of you, Agbal,' Idwal observed soberly, 'I doubt if that javelin of yours would pierce the beast's hide.'

Agbal looked affronted, and appealed to his fellow Numidians for support. Jugurtha and Hannon looked sceptical. 'What's wrong with duck?' they chorused. Duck had become their staple.

'I'm sick of it,' Agbal replied, 'it gives me the shits.'

That seemed to convince his countrymen, who began threading javelins. Idwal appealed to Sphax. 'Aren't you going to put a stop to this?'

Sphax shrugged. 'Three javelins should bring it down; besides, why should I ruin their sport?' Turning to Drust, he asked, 'How do your people hunt them?'

'They dig a pit, cover it with branches, then get as close to the beasts as possible. That's when their courage is tested. Facing their quarry, they taunt and goad the creatures into chasing them—that's where the excitement comes in—aurochs are surprisingly light on their feet! Once the creature's stuck in the pit they dispatch it with great spears used to hunt boar.' Carmo approached, curious to know what was afoot. 'Just the boy I was looking for,' grinned Drust. 'Would you fetch our spears, we may have need of them?'

'If you don't mind,' said Corinna tartly, 'Zwalia and I will leave you boys to the pleasures of the hunt. This is obviously more important than getting us out of here.'

Sphax couldn't take his eyes off the beast still bellowing at them, pawing the ground menacingly. Quickly he threaded his saunion then fingered the ivory image of Artemis. He had a nagging feeling he might need divine intervention, and who better than the goddess of the hunt?

By now his Numidians were heatedly discussing the best way to bring down their prey: Jugurtha and Dubal favoured aiming at the head, whereas Agbal insisted that only a javelin to the neck would slay the beast. As Idwal reluctantly selected his spear from Carmo, only Drust seemed eager for the sport to begin. Sphax was terrified! He would rather face a turma of Roman equites than the creature that was steadily regarding them with evil intent.

Tactics agreed, his Numidians stalked forward cautiously. Ominously, the beast ceased its bellowing and pawing, casting its sinister gaze on its would-be hunters. As the Numidians crept nearer, he could see them tightening throwing thongs and stealthily raising javelins. Surely they were in range by now, thought Sphax, watching nervously? How close were they going to risk?

Without the slightest warning the beast suddenly charged. An aurochs isn't just light on its feet, it's as fast as a bull elephant in must! But *mating* wasn't on this creature's mind. A chorus of startled cries marked the point when the hunters became the hunted as they turned on their heels and fled for their lives. It was only the fact that the three of them shot off in slightly different directions that confused the beast long enough to spare one of them evisceration. Sphax was astonished how fast the elderly Jugurtha could sprint when he put his mind to it!

Now all was madness. The Numidians were leaping backwards and forwards with the aurochs undecided as to whom to skewer first. The beast seemed to have it in for poor Agbal. Perhaps it had sniffed out its chief nemesis. After much skipping and dancing on Agbal's part, the creature managed to corner the luckless Numidian against a huge oak. Luckily, the girth of the ancient tree allowed Agbal, pursued by a not-sonimble aurochs, to circumambulate its trunk before hoisting himself onto a branch and clambering higher, putting himself out of range of those lethal horns. The creature bellowed foul-play and pawed the ground in frustration.

All of which allowed Jugurtha and Hannon time to stalk the beast and finally launch their javelins. Both proved ineffectual, bouncing off the aurochs' impenetrable hide as easily as from a Campanian bronze cuirass. Idwal had been right all along. The only effect it had on the beast was to increase the volume of its bellowing.

Sphax had to do something: the aurochs showed no sign of ending its sport with them, and one of his men was stuck up a tree. He decided on a diversion. 'Spawn of Geryon,' he yelled, heart pounding as he strode towards the beast. 'Heracles has come to round you up.' The beast responded by turning around and facing him, but at least it ceased its bellowing. Perhaps it would do what cattle normally do, thought Sphax, wander off in search of fresh pasture. The two faced each other, forty paces apart. The beast began sniffing the air as if taking the measure of this new scent. Then it charged.

Heracles could not have sprinted faster than Sphax did that day. His effort was truly Olympian as he overtook both Idwal and Drust, splashing into the lagoon where their vessel was berthed and slithering aboard, closely followed by Idwal, Drust and two red-faced Numidians, gasping for breath.

Unfortunately, they'd overlooked one small detail: this watery world was the beast's domain. It was equally at home in the water as out of it. Its progress was more in the nature of a wallow than a charge, but its intentions were no less alarming.

'Row, boys!' screamed Sphax. But it was hopeless. Corinna, Zwalia and the entire crew were helpless with laughter. 'Where's Agbal?' he cried. As if on cue, the Numidian suddenly shot out of the waist-deep water caked in a black slime darker than the creature's hide. To evade the aurochs he'd held his breath and plunged under the water. It was difficult to say which of them was more surprised at his re-emergence. For the first time the beast looked alarmed and backed away, giving a terrified Agbal the opportunity to splash his way over to the boat and clamber aboard.

For the rest of the afternoon Sphax and his fellow hunters tried to maintain a dignified silence, but every time Corinna or Zwalia caught sight of Agbal they burst out laughing and there was much discussion about the merits of duck and beef. One thing their encounter with the aurochs had taught them was that this watery wilderness was a dangerous place. When dusk descended they chose their camping ground carefully, lit fires early, and took turns to keep watch throughout the night.

* * *

Late morning next day found them in yet another reed-choked channel, having to paddle rather than row to make any progress at all. Corinna was trying to retrace their route westwards to where the main channel of the river had begun to divide, but nothing looked familiar to them that morning. This was their second day in the wilderness, and it was obvious they were completely lost.

Once more Sphax was standing beside Corinna on the steering platform whilst poor Agbal, up before dawn to scrub his cape and tunic, had been told to stand on the prow and look out for obstacles blocking the channel. Twice that morning they'd had to retreat due to a fallen tree and a beaver dam.

'The Bora is running this morning. It's a pity we cannot avail ourselves of its help,' grumbled Corinna.

'I suspect this Bora is the icy wind that's presently chilling our backs,' Sphax observed.

'Quite so, my darling. It blows in the winter from Illyria to the west; useful for trade with Italia. That is if merchants were to risk sailing in the storm months.'

'January being a storm month.'

'Yes,' she frowned. 'We risk much by sailing in the dead of winter, but what choice did we have?'

'When do the storm months cease?'

'Rome would have you believe that sailing is only safe after the Ides of May, but they are as children when it comes to knowledge of the seas. Illyrians will happily sail after Martius has blown itself out.'

With a shout, Agbal suddenly started waving his arms at them and pointing to the north. They both saw it at the same time. At least four hundred paces north of them a vessel was heading westwards in what must have been a separate channel. Between them lay dense stands of willow, so their view was intermittent, but two things were obvious: it was enormous, and travelling at twice the speed they were able to manage. Astonished at the sight of it, 'In the name of the gods, what is that?' Sphax asked.

Corinna was smiling and looked more relieved than he'd seen her for days. 'That's a Roman trading vessel called a cybaea. As you see, her mainsail and raked artemon foresail aren't spilling a breath of the Bora this morning, and her twenty oarsmen make her the perfect craft to navigate the Padus. This vessel has sailed directly from Ariminum, I'm certain of it. Like us, if Placentia and Cremona are not to starve, Rome has been forced to brave January storms. But we have found the main channel to the sea, my darling!'

Catching a brief glimpse of the elegant swan's neck on the vessel's stern he was reminded of his own ill-fated journey on such a ship. 'The last time I boarded a vessel with a swan's neck on the stern I spent three days spewing my innards for the benefit of the rats in the hold, and in the face of the terrible tempest we faced, it was a miracle that Fionn and I ever reached Massilia. I must confess to being a poor sailor,' he added, shamefacedly, 'and the sea terrifies me.'

'You are right to fear the sea, it is the first lesson all mariners must learn,' she assured him. 'As for your guts, all you need is something to occupy your thoughts. I have the perfect remedy.' Sphax looked unconvinced. 'Once we are settled on the Adria, you will begin your first lesson in steerage. Believe me, you won't have time to think about your guts.'

Sphax could feel the strength of the Bora blowing his unruly curls hither and thither, but their reed-choked channel was so overgrown with branches of willow that hoisting the sail would have been impossible, so the boys had to paddle as best they could.

Hour after hour, progress westwards was painfully slow, thwarted by every obstacle the wilderness could throw at them. Several times they had to retrace their steps because of blocked channels, fallen trees or beaver dams. It was as if the wilderness intended to hold them prisoner for trespassing on its sanctuary.

It was late in the afternoon when Sphax, sharing his cape with a shivering Zwalia, saw the channel suddenly widen. To their joy they could both see open water ahead of them and a broad channel that would lead them east into the Adriatic. The gods had released them from Arcadia and the wiles of Pan, but Sphax would now have to take his chances with Poseidon.

As their channel widened, it ran beside water meadows with scattered copses of willow, ash and birch that made perfect camping grounds for their last night on the great Padus. At least Agbal was happy. After they beached, Jugurtha and Hannon had disappeared into the woodland and returned with a stag they'd managed to skewer with their javelins. Red meat was back on the menu.

* * *

'Haul on your left oar, you dumb-witted Numidian,' yelled Corinna for the twentieth time that morning. 'You're doing it again ... drifting inshore! How many times do I need to tell you, arsewit, your course is that headland marked by those feeble eyes of yours and the vessel's bowsprit? They should be aligned as straight as one of your precious saunions.' Sphax grinned obedience and did as he was told. But he did regret providing Corinna with the ammunition of another choice curse-word that until now had been reserved for him by his javelin teacher, Dubal.

For two days since entering the Adria they'd rowed steadily southwards, following the coastline of the lands of the Boii. Sphax had received his first lesson on the steering oars yesterday, and much to his amazement he'd found it fascinating. It helped that there hadn't been a breath of wind, and the sea was like a polished mirror that morning. In the afternoon, Zwalia had taken on Drust as her apprentice at the steering oars—Sphax guessed Corinna had more than a hand in this—for now there was a strong element of competition between them.

Corinna reckoned the Roman harbour of Ariminum was only a day and a half south of them, so that morning all eyes were on the lookout for shipping. If they had the misfortune to encounter a Roman trireme, their fate would be sealed, for they hadn't a hope of outrunning such a warship.

'Remember,' Corinna reminded him, 'the waves are continually trying to push you ashore, so you must correct your course frequently with the left oar.' Deep in concentration, Sphax barely nodded. The headland came and went, as did the next bearing and the one after that. By midday he felt drained by the relentless concentration required to keep the vessel on course and weary from handling heavy oars. When Corinna suggested he take a rest, he breathed a sigh of relief and willingly handed them over to her. For a while Sphax watched her in silence, admiring how few adjustments she had to make once the course was set. It all came so naturally to her, he realised.

When Zwalia and her eager apprentice took over in the early afternoon, it was evident they were making excellent progress, even though Corinna had asked Carmo to set a leisurely stroke for the boys to follow. By mid-afternoon, Agbal's keen eyes could see Ariminum to the south west. After a brief discussion between Corinna and Zwalia, it was agreed they give the place a wide berth, even though Agbal saw no shipping coming in or out of the port. It was as they were heading out to sea that everything suddenly changed. And what changed was the wind.

What started as a gentle breath of wind from the west quickly became a steady breeze, then a stiff wind. To Sphax's alarm, the surrounding sea quickly transformed itself from a mirror to a turbulent confusion of white-topped waves. For the first time on the Adria, the vessel began to bob and weave in time with his innards.

After a rapid-fire conversation in Illyrian between Corinna and her handmaiden, Corinna hurried forward, straddling the rowing benches, yelling, 'Raise the sail, Idwal. Raise the sail! Tomos, Alanus, go and help.' Idwal leapt into action. He had no interest in steerage, his aim was to be the lord of the wind. Once the sail was erected and spilling not a breath of wind, the craft surged forward over the foam-tipped waves. They were no longer heading just out to sea, they were about to cross it. Now there was no turning back.

Sphax was mightily relieved that when the vessel reached her top speed she ceased to bob and weave. Occasionally she would sink into a trough between waves, but his stomach could cope with that. He likened it to a horse at a trot or a canter: a trot bounced the rider every which way, whereas a canter simplified the motion either backwards or forwards. That day he managed to eat and drink without the embarrassment of throwing up over the side. Corinna decided the oars were making little difference to their progress, so the boys were told to ship them and rest.

Once Corinna was satisfied that Idwal and the four boys could manage the square sail efficiently, she and Zwalia shared the steerage in watches throughout that late afternoon and into the long night ahead. Idwal and his Numidians cleared an area below the platform, gathering all the spare furs and cloaks so the women could sleep and rest between watches.

As dusk approached and the wind began to stiffen, his apprehension grew. They were now bound on a course to take them across a great sea, with a crew of boys, on a vessel with a freeboard not much greater than a humble fishing boat. Night descended suddenly. All at once they were enveloped in an all-encompassing darkness, relieved only by a pale crescent moon and the stars in their courses. Now they were little more than a speck of dust on a vast empty sea. Never before had he felt so abandoned and helpless in the face of nature.

Sleep escaped him that night. Sometime after midnight he felt his way to the steering platform and shared his beaver skin cloak with Corinna. 'Are we on course?' he asked, tentatively.

'That depends, my love, on what you define as a course. Zwalia and I intend to reach landfall in Illyria. Better still, somewhere in Illyria we recognise.'

'But in this darkness, how do you know where Illyria is? Are you being guided by the moon?'

Corinna chuckled. 'No! Certainly not. Then we truly would go round in circles—though I'm grateful for Selene's pale light this evening.' Although he could only make out the silhouette of her hooded cloak in the moonlight, Sphax recognised from her tone she was smiling. 'Look up at the sky to your right and tell me what you see?'

'Nothing! It's dark—'

'—Look more closely, arsewit!'

'I wish you wouldn't call me that! It's Dubal's favourite endearment, and it's reserved for me.'

'Then look more closely and I'll moderate my barbs.'

Slightly mollified, he did as he was told. 'I see stars, Corinna, but there are hundreds of them. What use can they be to anyone unless they're an astronomer, or a farmer who wants to know when to plant his barley?'

'But I *am* an astronomer, my darling. Those stars are keeping our vessel on course.'

Now Sphax was interested. 'How?'

'Look to your right and search the sky for three bright stars in a row.'

At first he struggled to detect any patterns in such a bewildering confusion. Then all he saw was pattern. It was only when he ignored the dimmer stars that he saw them. 'I think I've found them,' he said at last.

'You're looking at what the Greeks call Orion's belt; we Illyrians have a different name for it. The three stars are perfectly aligned from east to west. Your hero Ulysses found his way home by observing their course, and I will find my way home by the same observations. Below it, do you see a bright star between two lesser stars?'

'I see them,' he replied, astounded.

'That's what the Greeks call Orion's sword. Illyrians find this rather fanciful, but it's useful for navigators, because the brightest star points due south.'

Like a bolt of lightning, suddenly Sphax remembered something from his childhood, a distant memory, a memory of warm evenings in their courtyard, when his parents feasted merchants returning from a caravan that had crossed the great desert. They returned with far more than profit in gold and ivory. They returned with stories of fantastical beasts and kings so laden with garments adorned with gold they had to be carried around on litters. They also told of how they navigated the endless sands of the desert: by the stars!

It was all beginning to make perfect sense. Besides Orion, there was mention of another star he remembered, equally as important, and he was keen to hear what Corinna had to say about it. 'But what of the stars in the north, Corinna. What of the north?'

'I'm pleased to see you're so interested, my darling.' Again, he sensed she was smiling. 'If Orion's sword gave you the direction of due south, then look to the northerly sky, and tell me what you see?'

Looking over her shoulder he stared up at another confusing myriad of stars. 'What am I looking for?'

'Brightness of course, but you're really looking for patterns, always patterns. What can you see?'

'I can see one bright star, below which a thread of stars leads to a box-like square of stars.'

'By Hera, my love, you have a real gift for observation,' kissing his cheek as reward. 'What you've described perfectly is what we Illyrians call the Great Wagon, and the thread of stars are its oxen. Greeks call the bright star Kynosoura—the dog's tail—but it's known by many names. Carthage is descended from Queen Dido and ancient Tyre, so your mother's people would know it as Phoenice—'

'— That's it!' he cried. 'The star of the north. Phoenice!' Excitedly he told her of the caravans of horses that set out across the great desert laden with salt harvested from the lagoons on the coast. How they were armed only with a knowledge of the desert's hidden wells and underground watercourses, risking the burning heat and storms of sand to reach the lands of the south in the heart of Africa, lands fabulously wealthy in gold, ivory and precious jewels. Lands where salt was worth its weight in gold. And to reach these fabled lands they followed Orion's sword south whilst Phoenice brought them home.

When he fell silent, Corinna observed, 'I think I would rather face an empty ocean than that desert of yours, it sounds a dreadful place.'

'I remember it as being quite beautiful ... and mysterious. But as a child I was only allowed to explore its fringes. Mostly I remember the fantastical tales the merchants told of the lands beyond.'

As a child he'd often puzzled about Orion's miraculous sword. Numidians had little time for swords; their weapon of choice was the javelin. The only sword he'd ever seen was his father's, a magnificent blade with a hilt decorated in silver with a solid-gold pommel. It had been a gift from his father-in-law, Hamilcar. Somehow, in his childish imagination, his father's sword became Orion's, mysteriously sailing through the skies above the great desert, guiding the travellers to their destination. Now he knew better, he even understood how they'd returned safely, thanks to Phoenice, and for the first time he'd grasped the true meaning of the old Numidian proverb; *don't look to your feet to cross the desert.*

'Tell me some of these stories,' she asked eagerly. 'I know nothing of Africa.'

He'd long run out of stories when hours later, Zwalia relieved them on the steering platform. Draping his cloak over the maid's shoulders, Sphax helped Corinna down from the platform, and buried under a pile of furs, they fell instantly asleep in each other's arms.

* * *

They were woken by Idwal. Rubbing the sleep from his eyes Sphax saw that dawn had broken on another grey January morning.

'Drust has taken over my duties on the sail,' Idwal said, yawning deeply and stretching his arms as if measuring his tiredness. 'Zwalia looks weary too,' he added, gazing up at her rooted to the steering platform, 'perhaps she needs to be relieved. I'm going forward to get some sleep.' As he began clambering back over the rowing benches he turned and grinned at Corinna. 'By the gods, we covered some miles yesterday!'

Corinna was already on her feet. 'So we did, sail-master, and I can already sense the wind has stiffened. If the sea nymphs favour us, we will sight land before the day is out. Sleep well, my friend, you've earned it.' Turning to Sphax she said, 'I'm going to take over from Zwalia.'

'Oh no you're not, my love! You are going to have breakfast. When you've eaten and drunk your fill, you may ask permission from me to take over the steering oars. If Drust can sail, I can steer. Besides, as you've already pointed out, if through my inexperience we lose half a mile, the stiffer breeze this morning will surely make up for it.'

To Sphax's amazement she didn't protest. Agbal was the only Numidian awake at that hour. 'You will see to the Lady Corinna's every need this morning, Agbal, and wait upon her. Is that clear?'

Agbal stiffened. 'Perfectly, captain, I am her obedient servant.'

Zwalia needed no such persuasion, but had to be helped down from the platform by Agbal, who carried her to the bed of furs Sphax and Corinna had just vacated.

The Adria felt different that morning: disturbed, in tumult, out of sorts with itself. And the wind had indeed picked up, its icy blasts chilling his back and shoulders, obliging him to tighten the hood of his cape. As a pale sun had barely risen above the horizon, at least steering a course east had been made easy: all he had to do was keep the bowsprit pointing at it.

Much sooner than he'd hoped, Corinna was demanding to take over the oars, but she had breakfasted, and looked refreshed. Reluctantly Sphax agreed. He himself hadn't eaten since dawn and was now ravenous. At midday he took over for an hour so Corinna could eat and rest. Idwal's team were once more manning the sail. As the afternoon passed uneventfully, they all began to look forward to sighting land, beaching the vessel and lighting fires. Fire meant warm food, something they'd been dreaming about for two days.

It was Carmo who saw it first, leaping to his feet and pointing to the west, yelling something at Corinna in Gallic. By now Idwal was also on his feet. 'He's shouting *storm*, Corinna. Look to the west. Look behind you!'

Rushing on to the steering platform, Sphax stared along with Corinna at the western sky. Behind them a lowering wall of leaden cloud was fast approaching. Even as they watched, the light seemed to diminish from the world. Moments later the first squall hit, splattering the hull with hailstones as the mainsail billowed, lurching them forward almost out of control.

'We can outrun it. We *must* outrun it!' he heard Corinna mutter under her breath before she yelled, 'Carmo! Elpis! Man every oar! Row for your lives!'

FIVE

It all happened with such shattering suddenness. Now all around their fragile wooden walls, the sea foamed and seethed as white-capped waves began to boil and shower them with spray. Lashing hail turned to driving rain and soon they were shivering and soaked to the skin. What until now had been a steady breeze had become a tempest, its squalls and gusts assailing them from all points west, making steering impossible at times, and control of the sheets a challenge. Zwalia had joined Idwal and Drust to work the great square sail, but sitting in the belly of the vessel they were constantly being thrown and tossed around, causing the sail to flap and billow. Sphax stood behind Corinna, his arms wrapped tightly around her waist to shield her from the worst of the icy blasts. Grimly, he'd made up his mind that whatever happened, he would not leave her and would cling on to her for as long as he had breath in his body.

Above all, Sphax found the bolts of lightning searing down from the darkened heavens the most terrifying sight he'd ever witnessed. Astrape, shield bearer of Zeus, seemed to be aiming her bolts at their helpless craft. As each blinding flash struck the sea, the waters sizzled and boiled, dowsing their deadly fire.

For an hour they tried to outrun the storm, riding the lurching vessel as a horseman clings to a bolting stallion. And in that desperate hour, they were saved by sixteen ex-slaves, not much older than children, who rowed on in perfect synchrony, indifferent to the tempest raging all around them. But Sphax knew it was a race they couldn't hope to win. Their lives now depended on reaching land.

Sphax saw it first, yelling to Corinna above the howling wind, 'Land! I see land, Corinna. We're saved!' Looming suddenly out of the gloom ahead of them was an island whose low shoreline seemed to stretch for miles.

'I think it's Apsirtis,' she cried, 'and its shores are notoriously rocky, so we are not saved yet, my love!' In the dead of winter, Sphax was amazed by the sight of verdant pines, rising from the shoreline, half a mile ahead.

Corinna was frantically signaling Zwalia to take down the sail whilst yelling and gesturing at the boys to ship oars. At last Zwalia turned, saw the looming shoreline, understood what she must do and realised there was not enough time to do it. Sphax watched as she used her knife to sever the hemp sheets, but at that moment the craft dipped into a deep trough and the freed sheet caused the sail to swing as the entire vessel yawed sickeningly sideways.

In that instant Sphax dragged Corinna from the steering platform onto the piles of furs as a wave hit them amidships and broke over the gunnels. To his horror the next wave lifted the craft and hurled her towards the shore as if she was little more than a cork stopper. Amidst the sickening sound of splintering wood and grinding keel they came to a juddering halt in knee deep water.

Sphax still had his arms firmly around Corinna. Managing to raise her to her feet, he half-carried her from the craft, hauling her up the shore and into pinewoods. Corinna was too shocked and stunned to be of much help, so he left her propped up against the trunk of a tree and dashed back to the stricken vessel.

All was chaos inside. When the wave lifted and catapulted them towards the shore it had partially tilted the hull, smashing and overturning much of its cargo. On the rowing benches some of the boys lay spread-eagled and senseless amongst a tangle of splintered oars, whilst the ones who were unhurt were beginning to scramble over the gunnels and lurch on to the shore. Sphax picked up one of the boys and carried him ashore before returning for two more who were out cold. With utter relief he saw his three Numidians clambering over the sides, bruised and shaken, yet miraculously unharmed.

'Thank Ba 'al Hamūn you're all safe,' he cried above the howling wind.

Drust joined him. 'Help me, Sphax,' he yelled, 'Idwal's trapped and he's not moving.' Racing to the prow they both leaped aboard. Idwal lay wedged against a clutter of upturned barrels and jars, half-covered by what was left of the sail, flapping and tearing at the last sheet still holding it in place. Sphax knew they had to get him out quickly. Powerful waves were still crashing into the vessel's hull, causing her planks to creek and judder. Any moment a wave could smash her into a thousand pieces.

Working together, they frantically began dragging away the barrels and jars that were trapping him. Soon they were able to reach down, grab an arm and raise him to his feet. Judging from the blood trickling down his cheek, Idwal had received a blow to his temple from one of the barrels. 'Don't worry, Drust,' he shouted, 'he'll live. One of the barrels must have hit his forehead.' With a tremendous effort they managed to manhandle him over the side and carry him to the safety of the trees. Then a sudden panic gripped Sphax.

'Where's Zwalia, Drust?' he yelled. 'When did you last see her?' Drust stared at him, wide-eyed, shaking his head. Once more Sphax dashed back to the half-upturned vessel, and despite successive waves spewing over her sides, searched the craft thoroughly for anyone still alive. Striding over the prow he then followed the rocky shoreline north. At last he saw her. Reaching for his ivory image he prayed she was still alive, but it didn't look good.

He gave thanks. Zwalia was still alive, but badly hurt. She must have been thrown from the vessel when it was hit by that second wave and flung around like a cloth doll by successive waves. Her cape was nowhere to be seen and her stola was in shreds. Her face, arms and hands were covered in blood and she was bleeding profusely. Thank the gods she was slight and Sphax could easily pick her up and carry her over his shoulder.

Corinna had recovered enough to gather everyone together in a sheltered clearing in the pinewoods. When she saw him carrying Zwalia she let out a cry of alarm. 'Is she hurt, Sphax?'

'I'm afraid so,' he said gently. 'You need to attend to her immediately. She's lost a lot of blood.' Lowering himself on to one knee he eased Zwalia to the ground as best he could.

Corinna gasped when she caught sight of her handmaiden's face. 'Oh, Zwalia! My poor Zwalia.' There was nothing more he could do, so Sphax left Corinna frantically tearing strips from the tunic she wore beneath her stola, and strode over to where the boys were huddled together on the ground, hugging their knees to keep themselves warm. His Numidians were doing what they could for them.

'I don't suppose any of you have a fire striker, flint and kindling wool on your person?' He knew what the inevitable answer would be the instant he'd posed the question.

To his astonishment, Jugurtha was grinning at him in delight and already fumbling with a cord around his neck from which he produced a leather pouch. 'I know you never believe me when I tell you such things, but I swear by Ba 'al Hamūn that your father, Navaras, gave me this advice during the Truceless War: a man should never be separated from his fire starter.' The veteran Numidian had indeed fought with his father in that war, but besides being the finest scout in the Carthaginian army, Jugurtha was also a renowned storyteller, and Numidian storytellers seldom drew a line between fact and fiction.

'Then I'm delighted you followed my father's advice, Jugurtha. Would you mind lighting a fire for these shivering boys? Dry firewood will be a problem. Perhaps Hannon can help.' Why they hadn't already lit one defied explanation.

'Two boys have not been accounted for,' said Agbal, gravely.

'What! Dog's twat, Agbal, why didn't you tell me earlier?' If Zwalia could be thrown from the vessel, so could these missing boys. Soon, what little light remained in the day would be lost. 'Follow me, Agbal, we need to look for them.'

Arriving back at their stricken vessel he sent Agbal north, whilst he searched the shoreline to the south. The howling gale had lost none of its strength, driving each wave on to the rocky shore with a deafening crash, but for now at least, rain was not lashing his face. Far out to sea the lightning was still spearing down from the heavens.

Sphax guessed he'd searched the shoreline for more than a mile when he decided to give up and turn back. Agbal was already waiting for him by the vessel, and a solemn shake of his head told him all he needed to know.

'Those poor boys,' he said grimly, 'what a terrible way to die, cast into that seething Hades.' It was almost dark now. With a last look out to sea Sphax turned to Agbal. 'We will search again at first light. I pray Jugurtha's managed to light that fire.'

It was a long and miserable night, one he hoped he would quickly forget. Nobody slept, or if they did it was in snatches that brought little rest. At last Idwal and Zwalia woke up, Zwalia in considerable pain, swathed in dressings, Idwal to an almighty headache. But at least Corinna was no longer worried about her maid. Except for the deep gash to the back of her head which had knocked her out cold, her cuts and scratches were not deep and would heal in time. Two of the boys had broken bones in their arms, which Jugurtha skilfully set and bound with splints he cut and fashioned himself.

But there was no let up from the howling wind, which raced through the feathery branches above their heads and brought squalls of rain that repeatedly soaked them. At least they had a spluttering fire, but even that was more of a comfort than a provider of real warmth. The boys, normally talkative and full of banter, had fallen silent, already mourning the loss of their friends. Sphax felt guilty that he didn't even know their names, nor could recall their faces. Somehow he knew their search tomorrow would be fruitless.

For hours Corinna had sat beside her handmaid, close to the fire, but when Zwalia at last fell into a restful sleep, she covered her with her own crimson cloak and came to sit in front of him, nestling her head on his chest.

Enfolding her in his arms he whispered, 'What were the names of those two boys? I'm ashamed to say I don't know their names. It seems I'm keener to stand up for my principles than behave as you have, befriending them and getting to know them.'

'You have nothing to feel ashamed of. Your principles and your sense of honour are why your men would follow you into Hades. It's not why I love you, but it's what I most admire about you. Idwal has similar qualities, but he doesn't make me laugh! Jugurtha has told me such stories about you and your father ...'

'In the name of the gods, don't believe a word that Numidian tells you, he's a storyteller.'

'They were called Gáeth and Ciniod,' she said gently. 'Both Gauls. I seem to remember Idwal telling me they were from the Tricastini tribe. If you hadn't grabbed me when you did, we would have shared the same fate.'

Dawn didn't bring light into the world so much as renew its greyness. Somewhere far to the east, the sun had risen and begun its journey, but it didn't make an appearance above the island of Apsirtis that morning. As for the tempest, it raged on. When the greyness became pale enough to see by Sphax gathered everyone together to begin a thorough search of the shoreline for the missing boys. Idwal felt well enough to join them that morning, so the two boys incapacitated by splints were asked to stay behind, feed the fire, and look after Zwalia.

When they reached their beached vessel, everyone was surprised to see she was still in one piece. Whilst Sphax was dividing them into two search parties he noticed Corinna was carefully looking over the craft for signs of serious damage. When she'd finished her examination she joined his party, which was to search the shore to the north, and as agreed, if after two hours they had found nothing, return to the vessel. Spreading out across the shoreline, they painstakingly searched for several miles before giving up and turning back.

Once they arrived back at the vessel, Corinna resumed her examination. 'This craft has not given up on us. I think we can save her, Sphax.'

All he could see was the remains of an enormous horse trough, filled to the gunnels with seawater. Barrels and clay jars were floating freely inside her belly, barrels and jars so heavily laden they could crush a man's hand or leg in an instant, and every fresh wave driven ashore by the tempest threatened to tear her apart. Last night they'd continually returned to the craft to gather up anything that had spilled over her sides. In this way they'd retrieved everything from oars, to Sphax's dragon sword and the jar of honey that Corinna had smeared over Zwalia's deepest cuts. Entering the vessel amidst those jostling barrels seemed nothing short of madness to him. 'It's too risky, Corinna. Jugurtha will be fashioning splints for the rest of the day if we try it!'

'Not if we work carefully,' Corinna argued. 'There's enough time between each wave to rope a barrel and pull it to the side, wait for the next trough and manhandle it ashore. Once we've freed all the loose barrels and jars we can climb aboard and begin to bail her. As we bail she'll lighten and the waves will push her further ashore and out of danger.'

At that moment Idwal's party arrived, the Cavari shaking his head. 'Nothing, I'm afraid,' said Idwal. 'But we did find this,' adding in Gallic, 'do any of you boys recognise it?' He was holding up a threadbare grey cloak, with a leather drawstring around the hood.' Most of the boys nodded. 'It's Gáeth's, Sir, I would know it anywhere,' Carmo answered for them all.

'Then I'm truly sorry,' continued Idwal, solemnly. 'For I fear Gáeth and Ciniod are lost. Now is the time to grieve, and grief begins by sharing your memories of them with each other, so their lives can live on in your remembrance of them. This is how we face the trials of life. As best we can, tonight we will feast and remember their brief lives amongst us.'

Although Sphax hadn't understood a word of the Gallic, judging from the bemused expression on the boys' faces, Idwal had been preaching to them. 'What did you say to them?'

'I told them that tonight we feast, share their grief and remember the friends they've lost.'

'Ah! The rituals of a true stoic,' Sphax observed. 'But I think it's an excellent idea, and it might dispel some of the gloom that's descended on us all. Providing a feast might be a problem, though. You better listen to Corinna's suggestion. I think it's risky, but you might disagree.'

After Idwal had heard Corinna out he stared at the vessel and watched as three or four waves pounded her, spewing foaming white water over the gunnels and up the shingle beach. 'We could at least try it,' he told Corinna. Frowning at Sphax he added, 'if we are to get off this island, we need that vessel.'

Sphax shrugged, accepting Idwal's casting vote. 'Let's go back and find the rope we retrieved last night.'

Sphax soon found the coiled rope he'd placed beside the undamaged oars last night. The six of them headed back to the vessel, leaving Corinna to clean and dress Zwalia's wounds and a party of boys to search for fresh water, which wouldn't be difficult after the deluge the island had received over the last days.

An extraordinary sight met them when they returned to the shoreline. It was as if the gods had suddenly drawn aside a curtain. Above them winter's storm clouds were still lowering, but far out to sea the sparkling blue sky of a perfect spring day was heading their way. They didn't need to risk life and limb in those waves—all they had to do was wait for the calm those blue skies promised, tie down those barrels and start bailing. Already the waves had ceased spilling over the gunnels, and he could feel the ferocity of the wind dying as each wave reached the shore.

Sphax was relieved. He hadn't relished the prospect of tying off those jars and lifting them from the vessel in the teeth of a howling gale and battering waves. 'Are we all agreed,' he said at last, 'we wait for the storm to pass over before we attempt this?'

Idwal had been staring out to sea. 'My guess is that we'll have less than an hour before the storm clears, so it makes sense to wait.'

Sphax translated these thoughts and conversations to his Numidians. They too seemed relieved, settling down amongst the pines for winter to pass and spring to arrive. But mostly he knew they were thinking about their bellies, especially Agbal. All the food was stored on their vessel, and last night they'd managed to recover so little of it.

Idwal had been right, within the hour spring arrived. For the first time that winter Sphax felt real warmth in the sunlight as the gale dropped to a whimper and the raging sea became a gentle surf caressing the shoreline. But in the warming air a terrible stench was coming from the vessel. She reeked of it. The rancid smell of garum fish sauce. A jar on board must have smashed and spilt its pungent contents. Slaves were never treated to this Roman delicacy, so Sphax had been spared having to eat such excrement. Nothing that morning would have persuaded him to bail from *inside* that vessel.

By the time Corinna returned to check on their progress two hours later, they'd removed all the cargo that could be saved, and thrown overboard smashed shards of amphorae and splintered barrels. All that was left was a sickening, ankle-deep slop in the belly of the vessel's hold. 'What's that terrible smell?' she asked, wrinkling her nose.

'Garum fish sauce,' Sphax announced, 'laced with rotting sardines and rancid oil.'

'It smells worse than a camp shithouse! Can't you tip the vessel over and rid us of this stink?' pleaded Corinna.

With help of some of the boys, the men managed this, swilling down the bottom of the boat with seawater until the smell became bearable. At least they now had the means to give the boys a feast to remember that night.

When everyone had eaten their fill and the fires had been stoked, Idwal and Drust took charge of the proceedings and made fine speeches in honour of Gáeth and Ciniod. At least Sphax guessed they were fine, judging from the boys' expressions and thigh-slapping when they were over. For this was a night for Gauls, conducted in Gallic, their common language.

At first tongue-tied and shy, as the evening wore on the boys began to reminisce and tell stories about their lost friends. The modest amounts of wine Idwal had been plying them with helped to loosen tongues. Before long, the boys were eager to get to their feet and tell the next story. Idwal's stoic instincts had been right all along. Gentle remembrance and kindly laughter were the best remedy for grief, not stiff mourning.

Corinna begged Idwal to translate some of the boys' stories. In this way they discovered that Ciniod had possessed a beautiful singing voice and had taught them a number of his songs. Late into the night the boys began to sing Ciniod's songs. Music was lost on Sphax's ears, but listening to Ciniod's plaintive melodies and the boys' sweet voices touched him deeply that night.

> Sore suffering to me, and O suffering sore
> his death that used to lie with me!
> Sore suffering to me is Caeo, and O Caeo is
> a suffering sore
> that the wave should have swept o'er his
> white body ...

* * *

They woke to a perfect, spring-like day, with the risen sun shining from a peerless blue sky and not a cloud in sight. Even the air itself was still and breathless. Unfortunately, after last night's late-night feasting and wine, many of the boys' heads were far from clear and shining. Corinna wanted to make an early start, but Sphax and Idwal insisted they leave the boys to enjoy a leisurely breakfast to clear their heads.

In any case, lifting the craft to where the shallow tide would re-float her and stowing away all the items they'd recovered took up most of the morning. Corinna supervised the placement of every single jar, barrel and chest, to ensure the weight was evenly distributed throughout the vessel. This done, she insisted they use the last of their hemp rope to secure the heaviest jars and barrels together, so in the event of a sudden grounding, they wouldn't create havoc.

When the invalids with broken bones and the much recovered Zwalia were safely aboard, Sphax asked Corinna the obvious question: 'Where now, my love?'

'The island and harbour of Pharos.'

Frowning, he asked, 'Will the daughter of Queen Teuta be welcomed in the homeland of Demetrius?'

Corinna raised an eyebrow, smiling playfully. 'I may, or may not choose to reveal myself. But you needn't worry, Demetrius' supporters fled, along with their master, to Macedonia. Those that were not so fortunate the Romans sold into slavery. I'm hoping that Demetrius' chief advisor stayed behind and managed to avoid this fate.'

'Who's he?'

'A reptile called Menda. If anyone can lie low and stay out of trouble it's Menda. He's adept at bending with the wind. If I were Demetrius, the person I would rely on to stay behind and look after my interests would be him. If he's still on the island he's our best hope of contacting Demetrius.' As Corinna glanced over the vessel her smile disappeared. 'We urgently need repairs. There are only eight serviceable oars left. When we lost the other four in the storm they damaged the thole pins, not to mention the iron cleats that were ripped out, mast stays lost and a sail left in tatters! Our list of repairs is long, but Pharos has excellent shipwrights.'

'How long is the journey?'

'Two days,' she answered gazing out to sea, 'if Poseidon will grant us a tide.'

* * *

It took three. But Sphax didn't mind. For him it was a journey through Arcadia, through a land so breathtakingly beautiful that wherever he looked his eyes feasted on the perfect harmony between land, sea and sky, where glittering blue waters lapped the golden sands of natural harbours and sheltered bays, where gentle hills rose from the depths of the Adria to ridges the colour of white marble, all clothed in lush forests. This was a land of a thousand islands. Corinna named the largest of them, but there were so many. Later, he could only recall Pirosima, Lissa and Olynta from the scores she mentioned. What delighted him was their rich colours, so green and verdant with varieties of pine and cedar that seemed to have found a way of cheating winter's desolation. Corinna pointed out the darker trees, giants of the forest, long-prized for their colour and sweet fragrance and said to cover the mountainsides of Lebanon, the ancient homeland of the peoples of Carthage.

For three days there was not a breath of wind and the sun shone from a clear blue sky as their oars cut through waters as still and limpid as a mountain lake. Sphax partnered Agbal with duties at the oars, grateful for the exercise, as were Idwal and Drust. But winter returned each evening as they huddled around fires lit on some sandy beach and drew their cloaks tighter to stave off the chill.

By the afternoon of the third day Zwalia felt well enough to take a turn on the steering oars, and it was she that announced the sighting of Pharos and set a course for its natural harbour in the heart of the city.

SIX

Pharos was in truth, hardly a city. But it did have its charms, and several fine public buildings. Clusters of stone houses with red-tiled roofs crept up the steep hillside above the harbour, finishing beneath the ramparts of the citadel Roman legions had stormed and then dismantled after Demetrius fled. That was two years ago, and though the senate had deemed Pharos a protectorate and a friend of Rome, there was little evidence of this friendship in the conversations Sphax had with its citizens, in fact quite the reverse. Rome and its people seemed to be universally unpopular. Given that a Roman legion had been billeted on the town for months at Pharos' expense, this came as no surprise.

What did come as a shock was that Illyrians were seen as worse, lower than thieves and scoundrels. The truth of the matter was that Pharosians were a proud Greek people who hadn't always lived in harmony with their native Illyrians, let alone with what they saw as those *pirates* on the mainland.

As soon as they'd hauled the vessel out of the water on to the sandy beach, they were surrounded by a crowd of merchants, petty officials and the inquisitive. After listening to a score of conflicting recommendations, Idwal and Drust set out to find rooms for them all whilst he and Corinna began the ritual haggling. When they returned less than an hour later having found splendid rooms in a grand hospitium close to the market, taxes had been paid, their cargo sold to the highest bidders, and awkward questions about where they'd come from, dodged. Once back at the hospitium, they gathered in Sphax and Corinna's spacious room to discuss their next move.

'Tell them what you know about Menda, Corinna,' Sphax prodded. 'Beside repairs to our vessel, that's why we're really here on this island, isn't it?'

'Yes,' she frankly admitted. 'Menda is a poisonous toad, who began life as a lowly steward and rose through intrigue to become Demetrius' chief advisor. After king Agron's death when my mother was free to remarry, Demetrius proposed to her. Since I can remember they had been lovers. Foolishly thinking she could make a more illustrious match, she refused him and drove him away. That's when Menda plotted revenge and opened secret negotiations with Rome. My mother's calamitous war with Rome provided Menda with the perfect opportunity to put his vile scheme into operation.

'Night and day he poisoned the ear of Demetrius, whispering that Teuta had betrayed his lifelong love and devotion. If he switched sides, Rome would reward and advance him, and if he took control of king Agron's young son, Pinnes, he would become the most powerful man in Illyria.

'Demetrius is charming and courageous, but hardly the cleverest scholar in the schoolroom. He believed Menda's lies. And I suppose Rome did reward him in a way—by leaving him alone for eight years!

'But when Demetrius broke the treaty and began raiding Greek cities that were supposed to be friends of Rome, his former allies lost patience and ousted him from Pharos. I suspect his ill-advised raiding had little to do with Menda. It's not his style, he much prefers treachery.'

'Can you be certain of all this, Corinna?' Idwal questioned. 'It does put a different complexion on Demetrius' actions during your mother's war with Rome, though it hardly excuses his switching sides.'

'I was not idle in Rome and Brundisium. I was desperate to know the truth, to find out why someone I'd looked upon almost as a father, had betrayed me and my mother. During my years in Brundisium I interviewed scores of people who corroborated exactly what I've just told you.'

'But how will this help us to persuade him to contact Demetrius, Corinna?' Idwal persisted. 'Surely Menda has much to hide, and a reconciliation between your mother and Demetrius would only bring his sordid role in all this to light. Surely it's in his own interests to avoid this at all costs!'

'You're right of course, so we must look for some hold over him. If I made it clear my mother would be fully informed of his treachery if he didn't comply, that she might be tempted to take matters into her own hands— Rhizon being but a day's sail from Pharos—I think he may be persuaded to do our bidding.'

'Can you be certain he's even on the island, Corinna?' asked Sphax.

'Rumour has it that he fled to the Veneti after Demetrius' defeat. But I'm certain he's returned to crawl under some stone, like the reptile he is. He knows this place.'

'Where do you suggest we start looking, Corinna?' asked the ever-practical Drust.

'Tomorrow, I suggest you men trawl the bars and tabernas and start asking questions. Zwalia and I will supervise the repairs on our vessel, and we need to buy new clothes for the boys. We can't let them walk around in those rags.'

After Sphax had translated this for his men, Hannon grinned. 'What an excellent way to start the day,' he said approvingly.

***

Next day those same menfolk soon realised that the name Menda either brought on a fit of amnesia, or an ignorant stupor. Either way, citizens were not forthcoming about his whereabouts. But at least they'd found a taberna where Corinna wouldn't be accosted as a common whore. The respectable Helios catered for the merchant classes, specialised in hot food, and possessed two braziers to keep out the winter chill. Even so, Corinna had pinned back her hair like a respectable married woman and covered her head with a shawl.

Around noon, as Zwalia and some of the boys bought hot food to take back to their rooms, the rest of them settled at tables and benches in a corner of the spacious bar, licking their lips at the prospect of a hot meal that would not be eaten amidst the stink of fetid garum.

They'd almost finished when six men barged their way through the crowded room to the counter. Sphax knew immediately they meant trouble. A bartender was already pointing at their tables.

Corinna had also spotted them and was fidgeting. Sphax guessed she was fumbling beneath her palla for the handle of her knife. Only Idwal and Drust had blades strapped to their waists. He and his Numidians were unarmed. Lightly kicking Idwal's shin, Sphax flicked his eyebrows to signal that trouble was heading their way.

An elderly bald-headed Greek, wearing a chiton tunic under a grubby cloak, approached their table and glared at Sphax. 'I understand you're making enquiries about the whereabouts of Menda. Is that correct?'

'Do you know where he is?' answered Corinna, innocently enough.

'That depends ...' the Greek hesitated, without removing his eyes from Sphax.

'On what?' asked Corinna.

With his eyes still locked on Sphax the Greek demanded, 'Who are you, and what's your business with Menda?' It was as if Corinna was invisible.

'Ask her,' protested Sphax, gesturing towards his spokeswoman.

Corinna struggled on, determined to be seen as well as heard. 'We are simple merchants with a cargo for Epidamnos. As to our business,' she added, 'that is our own.'

'Then we'll make it our business!' someone hissed as three of the younger men pushed forward, lowering over them.

Until now, Idwal and Drust had gauged the temper of the exchanges through the expression on Corinna's face, but as this had remained an inscrutable smile, they were none the wiser. Now they both swung their legs over the bench to gaze up at what they were confronting.

Casting his eyes over the Numidians, the young man standing above Idwal growled, 'And who are they? Egyptians?'

'Yes ...' Corinna began, but was cut short.

'I wasn't asking you, bitch!'

Further questioning from him would prove difficult, for in that instant Idwal's knee struck him viciously in the crotch, after which he was only capable of incoherent animal noises. A language soon to be shared by the youth standing next to him as Drust's knee delivered a similar blow. In a heartbeat, Idwal had drawn his blade and had it pointed at the throat of a blond-haired youth in the front rank.

'*Stop!*' shrieked the elderly Greek who'd first spoken. 'He is my son! He means you no harm.' With two of their party writhing amongst the lavender on the floor and a third about to have his throat cut, the *delegation* backed away as a tense silence descended on the bar.

The old man tried again. 'Please, release my son and I'll tell you where you can find Menda,' he pleaded. 'We can't stop you joining his ruffians.'

'See to your young men!' commanded Sphax, rising to his feet. 'They are in pain and in need of willow leaf.' Now outraged, he continued, 'What has happened to common civility and politeness on this island? Are you not Greeks? You are behaving like barbarians and bring shame on our gods!'

Idwal withdrew his blade from the golden-haired Greek boy, sheathing it as the bar came alive with whispered conversations.

Gesturing for the young men groaning on the floor to be gently removed, the elderly Greek glared at Sphax defiantly. 'If I have offended the gods then I will make offerings. But Menda's ruffians are the barbarians, and they're bleeding Pharos dry. His tyranny must be stopped.'

Corinna exchanged a knowing look with Sphax. They were all too familiar with Menda's history of double dealing and treachery. Corinna's inscrutable smile returned. 'If we were to remove Menda from Pharos, could we count on your help?'

'Remove him!' answered the Greek, taken aback by Corinna's offer. 'Or replace him?' he continued, now unsure. 'I will take you to meet our leader, Diodorus. Only he can decide.'

At last the elderly Greek politely introduced himself as Pallas. The seven of them followed him out of the bar and through the town. Corinna had given up trying to question him after receiving nothing more in return than monosyllabic grunts, so the journey was largely passed in silence, during which Sphax sensed Corinna's growing irritation. When they passed through the town's northerly gate it was Idwal who finally asked where they were meeting Diodorus.

'At this hour my master takes his daily exercise at the gymnasium,' replied Pallas, 'that's where we'll find him, gentlemen.'

Corinna threw her hands in the air in exasperation, all the while glaring at Pallas. 'That rules me out! I will not be allowed to enter.' Shunning her stare, Pallas turned on his heels and hurried on.

Sphax was now in an agony of indecision. Secretly he was desperate to see inside a gymnasium. His Greek teacher Elpis had told him so much about these unique institutions where men gathered to discuss philosophy and exercise in the Olympian disciplines. Where the cultivation of the mind *and* the body were seen as equally important for a healthy balance between matter and spirit. But stepping foot in the place seemed to Sphax almost like crossing a forbidden threshold, that between infidelity and idle curiosity. In the grand scheme of things, he knew what was more important.

'I will share Corinna's exclusion from this meeting, but I urge the rest of you to meet Diodorus and hear him out. We'll await you in our rooms at the hospitium.' But Sphax was curious. On their stroll back to town he asked, 'Why are you so vexed by the attitudes of Greek men, Corinna? You've told me yourself your true education only began when you married your Greek husband. Are Greek women treated so badly?'

Corinna stopped dead in her tracks and glared at him. 'How many women have you seen on the streets of Pharos today? How many were seated at the inn?'

Sphax considered. 'Well ... none,' he had to admit.

'That's because their husbands, or should I say their jailors, have them under lock and key!'

'But I was taught to read and write in Greek by Airla, the wife of my tutor, Elpis.'

'Then you were fortunate, my darling, for falling into the bosom of an enlightened couple.'

'But your late husband educated you—'

'—Only because he was torn between the desire for a hetaira and for a dutiful wife!'

Sphax frowned. 'I thought hetairai were common whores.'

Corinna laughed, 'There's nothing common about hetairai! Have you not read Sappho? They're the best educated women in Greece, and hardly loose with their favours ... unlike the hetairai in the gymnasia.'

Sphax was quite shocked. 'You mean to say that your late husband—'

'You've led such a sheltered life, my darling!' she said between fits of laughter.

* * *

Two hours later they were all seated on their stools and klines in Sphax and Corinna's room. Both he and his Numidians had been quite taken with these folding chairs with a comfortable seat made from strips of colourful linen. Corinna had called them diphroi, and told him it was fashionable in Epidamnos for slaves to carry them around for their mistresses. Greek ladies, apparently, objected to standing for too long.

Idwal had already recounted in detail their meeting with Diodorus. It was much as Corinna had conjectured on their stroll back to the hospitium. A power struggle was in progress between Greeks and Menda's ruffians.

With its rich farmlands that grew everything from wheat to lavender and a busy harbour on the lucrative amber road, Pharos was a wealthy island, a prize worth fighting for. That's why Corinna had been sure that Menda would have returned after the Roman occupation. Patience would have rewarded him with great wealth. All he would need was a small army to cow the Greek citizens, then all the taxes, tithes and rents from the island would have fallen into his lap like rain from the heavens.

Diodorus had told Idwal that Menda invented a new tax every month, and that his tyranny had become boundless and had to be stopped. 'In two days' time,' he'd told Idwal, 'his lieutenants will march into town to collect taxes. We will tell them what is rightfully due and they will demand double that sum.' Drust had pointed out that Pharos had high walls and strong gates that could be barred and defended.

'What would be the point?' Diodorus had answered, 'we would be besieged, and as most of our food comes from our farmlands to the south, we would soon starve. Trade by sea would never be enough to meet our needs.' Shortly after this, Idwal and Drust had left, promising to meet him again at his residence in the city this evening. All they needed now was a plan.

'How many men does Menda have?' asked Sphax.

'About forty,' Drust replied with a wry grin, 'but according to Diodorus, they're armed to the teeth and some are Veneti mercenaries.' When Sphax translated this for his Numidians, they were outraged.

'What! cried Agbal. 'There must be thousands of Greeks in this town.'

'Surely Pharos can take on forty?' echoed Jugurtha.

Corinna was laughing, 'Especially as they train so diligently at the gymnasium!'

'This isn't getting us anywhere,' pointed out Idwal, soberly. 'For whatever reasons, the citizens of Pharos are not prepared to take on Menda's bullies, so it's up to us to solve their little problem for them. We want Menda, and Pharos wants rid of him. Our aims converge, do they not?'

'Does Menda accompany his men on these tax gathering expeditions to the city?' asked Sphax, thoughtfully.

'No he doesn't,' answered Idwal, smiling at his friend's astute question.

'Then are you thinking what I'm thinking, Idwal?'

'Yes, I believe I am. It gives us a golden opportunity to round up Menda without his men to defend him.' Idwal allowed time for Sphax to translate this exchange for his Numidians before adding, 'Will our vessel be repaired in two days' time, Zwalia?'

'She'll be ready tomorrow,' she replied confidently.

'We need to provision her and take on fresh water,' added Corinna, 'but Zwalia and I will do that tomorrow.'

Lost in thought, Idwal's familiar frowning expression returned. 'Which leaves us with the thorny problem of what to do about Menda's little army.'

'They may flounder for a while without Menda,' conjectured Corinna, 'but sooner or later they'll realise they don't need him to carry on fleecing these cowardly Greeks! In a week or so they'll simply take over Menda's lucrative operation.'

'That's not our problem,' griped Drust, 'it's up to the citizens of Pharos to defend themselves. Why should we fight their battles?'

'That's settled then,' Sphax summed up, 'we offer to remove Menda from the island. That's all.' Everyone nodded. 'So, how do we capture the slimy bastard?'

* * *

In their preparations the next day, the only problem they encountered was finding eight horses and a spare for Menda. Donkeys and mules were common on the island, but horses were as rare as dragon's teeth. Menda had taken over Demetrius' country villa, five miles south of the town, close to a village his mercenaries had taken over, so they could have gone on foot. But if they did run into any of Menda's men left behind, none of them relished the prospect of fighting from the back of a mule! A soldier on foot that could challenge mounted Numidians was yet to be born. So finding horses had been essential.

If Idwal, Drust and the Numidians' task of finding horses proved difficult, Sphax's trials that day were only just beginning. After Elpis and some of the boys had carried supplies back to their vessel, Corinna and Zwalia marched him back into town to a barber that had been recommended. Worse was to come.

Against his will he was shoved into a merchant's shop selling furs and ordered to buy a new cloak. Sphax loved his beaver-skin cloak. Idwal had given it to him as a gift. It had kept him alive on their journey through the Alps, the battle on the Ticinus and the dreadful winter beside the Trebia.

But Corinna was adamant, 'It's so infested it's quite capable of crawling back to Gaul by itself. I can't present you to my mother with *that* over your shoulders! I love the fact that I've never seen you with a mirror, but my mother isn't like that … she never strays far from one, and would have sold me into slavery to get her hands on the elixir of youth. She will judge you on your bearing and appearance, not your intellect and integrity—she doesn't give a fig for such things.

'Am I going to like your mother?' he asked warily, frowning.

'I doubt it. But I must prepare you, we'll need her help, remember.'

Trying on a handsome bearskin cloak that fell in graceful folds to his ankles, he caught Zwalia grinning at him. 'She'll like you well enough, dressed in that,' she laughed. Corinna agreed, so he purchased it, along with a practical woollen cloak for travelling. Thinking this had put an end to his trials his mood lightened. He couldn't have been more wrong.

Back on the street the two women completely ignored him. 'We have no choice but to dress him in the Greek mode, which means a chiton and himation, and he must get rid of those ridiculous braccae. He looks like a Gaulish waif in them!'

'Your mother always approved of Greek fashion,' agreed Zwalia.

'Come, my darling,' commanded Corinna, grabbing hold of his arm. 'Let us make a peacock of you.'

One weary hour and an interminable number of shops later, he was the owner of two chiton tunics and a white himation with embroidered neck and hem, a garment more fearsomely complicated than a toga, and one he would never be able to master.

As he was agreeing the amount of silver with the shopkeeper, Zwalia sidled up to him and whispered, 'My mistress requires new clothes. See to it!' Before he could reply she'd sidled to the back of the shop, pretending to examine chlamys cloaks. Back on the street, Sphax received a further reminder in the form of an elbow in the ribs when Corinna paused momentarily before a merchant specialising in silks from the island of Kos.

'Let me return the compliment, Corinna,' he said brightly, determined to do this with good grace. 'Surely you need something new for our audience with your mother, if only to prove to her that I'm attentive to your needs … and Zwalia too, of course,' he added as an afterthought.

Corinna laughed, smiling at Zwalia before fixing him with that wicked smile of hers. 'You are always attentive to my needs, my darling. But you are right, this palla has seen better days, and Zwalia's stola is threadbare.' Sphax gestured for them to enter, and braced himself for a long wait.

A stool was found for him by a small brazier away from the draughts in the open shopfront. Again, he was quietly ignored as the two of them began an earnest conversation with the shopkeeper and his wife. As Sphax listened to the fascinating story of how silk was produced he'd begun to count the tiles on the shop floor.

At last he heard someone say, 'I have the very thing,' at which Corinna, Zwalia and the shopkeeper's wife retreated into a room at the back of the shop. Sometime later, to be precise, six-hundred and thirty tiles later, Corinna drifted back into the shop and stood before him. Sphax's jaw dropped. It was as if the gods had granted him a vision of loveliness.

Zwalia had removed the pins from Corinna's hair, so that her raven curls fell on to the shoulders of a revealing, diaphanous garment that shimmered and flowed freely in elegant folds to her sandaled feet. The silk seemed to hug her shapely form, emphasising the curve of breast and hip. She twirled around like a little girl at her first banquet as the shopkeeper and his wife brought oil lamps to illuminate this darker part of the shop where Sphax was astride his stool.

Dyed in rich reds, oranges and ochres, and embroidered with fantastical vertical patterns resembling stars, palms and fronds, the garment seemed to have a life of its own whenever Corinna moved an arm or a leg. It was as if he was seeing her anew, yet somehow it renewed that first breathtaking sight of her when she'd fallen from her horse and he'd cradled her in his arms.

'Well?' she said finally, inviting an opinion.

Sphax grinned up at her, knowing he must break the spell or forever fall under it. 'Are you not cold, my darling?'

Momentarily her eyes flashed disappointment, before she burst out laughing. There could be no mistaking the look of rapture on Sphax's face. 'You are right of course. A fine silk peplos such as this should be worn in summer. In winter I'll have to wear it beneath a woollen himation, embroidered with similar silken motifs. They are expensive, but you are so attentive to my whims I know you will not begrudge me more silver.'

Silver to pay for all this extravagance was beginning to worry Sphax. Extra clothing for Corinna, and a pretty double-chiton for Zwalia, virtually wiped him out. 'Don't worry,' Corinna had whispered, 'tomorrow we'll all be rich beyond our wildest dreams.'

* * *

Tomorrow dawned bright, promising yet another day of clear blue skies without a breath of wind. After carefully going through the instructions for Carmo and his crew they'd mounted up an hour after first light and ridden through Pharos' southern gate.

Not that any of them were pleased with their mounts. Jugurtha had generously described them as workhorse nags, and four of the owners they'd rented them from were amazed when Jugurtha had removed the saddles, bits and reins. It was shameful for Sphax and his Numidians to be seen riding with these instruments of torture, when all the beasts required for instruction was a touch to the flank or neck. But at least the creatures had got them to the top of a hill they'd chosen, two miles south of the town, overlooking the track from the south. And there they waited.

The sun was high when Agbal's keen eyes spotted them. A ragtag column of men on foot, armed with a variety of spears, pikes and swords. None were helmeted and few carried shields, let alone wore armour. Two of the men had mules in tow, presumably to carry back the plunder looted from town. As they drew closer, Sphax counted thirty-eight of them.

Which left few behind to spring a nasty surprise at Menda's villa. That is, if Diodorus' estimate of forty was to be believed. Sphax had cast doubt on this, to which Idwal and Drust had added their concerns after their second interview with the Greek. Idwal suspected double dealing, so they'd planned for all contingencies. Or so they hoped.

Once the column drew abreast of them they nudged their mounts to the south, being careful to remain hidden in the lee of the hill. For a mile or so they kept to the east of the track before finally veering westwards to rejoin the track and head south. Even in the barren depths of winter it was evident this was rich farmland. They passed neat orchards of bare fruit trees, olive groves and fields already laid out for wheat, awaiting the spring plough and the first sowing. And all within sight of the sea, for the glittering blue of the Adria was never more than a mile or so to the west of them.

At last Demetrius' villa came in sight. With its grand porticoed entrance and red-tiled roofs, it was obvious the past master of Pharos had spared no expense on his country residence. Last night they'd agreed their best tactic would be to rush the place, surprising any guards by galloping directly into the inner courtyard. From there they'd reckoned on overpowering anyone foolish enough to stand against them.

Sphax had already handed his dragon sword to Corinna, who now drew it and waved it aloft with a prayer to Hera. Idwal and Drust did the same with their Gallic blades, whilst Sphax and his Numidians reached for their throwing thongs and selected a javelin. When Sphax signaled 'forward', the sluggish progress of their mounts took the edge off the exhilaration he was feeling. It was not so much a full-blooded charge as a plodding canter. How Sphax yearned for his swift jennet!

But at least they all arrived in the courtyard at roughly the same time, to the astonishment of the elderly man dressed in a long white chiton, clutching a swaddled baby to his breast. Seated on a chair below him was a blond-haired beauty, not much older than the boys in their crew. Out of the corner of his eye as they'd ridden into the courtyard, Sphax had noticed several figures bolting for exits and doorways: servants or slaves he'd guessed. None of them was carrying arms, at least.

Whilst the rest of them formed a loose cordon around the two figures, Corinna dismounted and boldly strode towards the elderly Greek, standing transfixed beside the seated young woman. As Corinna approached, the woman let out a sudden cry of alarm and dropped both the spindle and distaff she was holding. Corinna ignored her, stopped within a couple of paces of the rooted Greek, and demanded, 'Do you not know me, Menda?'

Recognition slowly dawned on the man's penetratingly dark eyes. 'Why of course, my dear!' he said at last, his voice deep and rich. 'The last time I saw you was at your wedding feast in Epidamnos. You were a comely bride, Corinna, but I see you have blossomed into a remarkable beauty.' There was a pause as he handed the baby to the seated woman gaping up at him. 'May I present my son, Aeneas, and my wife, Elantia, of the Veneti.' With an ingratiatingly smile, he continued, 'How may I serve the daughter of Queen Teuta?'

Sphax looked on anxiously. What new mischief was brewing? Menda was too composed, *too* in control of events. Where had those servants fled to? Menda seemed to be playing for time. Before Corinna could answer he yelled, 'Jugurtha, Agbal, Hannon, keep watch outside the villa.'

As his men nudged their horses towards the courtyard entrance, Menda stared at Sphax. 'In the name of the gods, I never thought to hear Numidian spoken in this house.'

Corinna sensed Sphax's suspicions, and ordered Zwalia to join his Numidians. 'You may serve me, Menda, by quickly gathering what possessions you need for a journey and handing over the silver you've stolen from the Pharosians over the last two years.'

'And where will this journey take us, my lady?' he asked, still unflustered.

'To Rhizon, where you have business with my mother.' Sphax dismounted and stood beside Corinna.

Menda's fawning smile returned. 'My business with your mother ceased years ago when she rejected my master, Demetrius.'

In that instant, Zwalia burst through the courtyard entrance, shouting, 'Men are coming on foot. They're armed. We don't have much time!' In the next moment Corinna snatched the baby from his mother's arms, yelling at Sphax to take the girl. Grabbing a wrist, he yanked Elantia from her chair and began dragging her away from Menda.

'My people will *kill you!*' she screamed. At last Menda reacted and lunged towards Corinna, but Corinna was too quick for him. Clutching the swaddled baby in her left arm she swiveled her blade so that it pointed at his throat. Menda froze.

'What's it to be, Menda? You either come willingly, or you'll never see your wife and son again.'

A look of pure hatred fell like a shadow over Menda's face. 'Very well,' he spat the words.

'The silver first,' Corinna hissed, 'and a cart to transport you all.'

Sphax had his hands full with Elantia, who was trying to kick and bite him, but he'd a firm grip on her wrists and she was only a slip of a girl. 'You and Drust join my Numidians, Idwal, and slow down the rescue party. If they're Veneti, kill them all, the bastards are allied to Rome. Corinna and Zwalia can handle Menda.'

After binding the girl's hands behind her back, she began spewing forth a torrent of curses in some

Gallic tongue as he hoisted her over the back of the spare horse and grabbed the reins. Corinna, still with the baby cradled in her left arm and the sword in her right, followed Menda as he made his way to the far end of the courtyard where another gateway seemed to lead to the back of the villa. Zwalia reached for the reins of Corinna's horse, drew her dagger, and nudged her mount to walk behind Menda.

'There's a wagon and horses in the stables,' Menda growled, pointing, his voice flat and defeated.

'Take the baby, Zwalia, and bring the wagon to this entrance,' Corinna instructed, without taking her eyes off Menda. The baby began wailing as Zwalia bundled him into her arms and trotted off. 'Now there's the small matter of silver, Menda. Lead the way,' she demanded, deftly severing the threads of Menda's chiton around his scrawny neck to remind him she had a blade she was prepared to use.

As Menda led the way down a corridor with Corinna's sword at his back, Sphax walked the horses out of the gate where he had a clear view to the south. He was desperate to see if Idwal, Drust and his Numidians needed help. He needn't have worried. Menda's little relief force was in a sorry state, backing away in retreat, with several of them already strewn on the ground, either dead or trying to crawl away, badly wounded.

Elantia had given up cursing and was now wailing louder than her child. Sphax reached into the sack around his horse's rump and removed more hemp rope to tie her ankles together. What was keeping Zwalia, he fretted? Then he saw that the wagon was a solid, four-wheeled farm vehicle, used for carrying grain, and Zwalia must have saddled and harnessed two horses to it with lightning speed, even finding time to find hay on which to deposit the swaddled child.

'Well done, Zwalia! Now it's time to re-unite mother and child.' And with that he unceremoniously lifted Elantia from the horse, carried her to the wagon and lowered her on to the hay beside her child. Miraculously, the wailing ceased immediately.

Idwal trotted back from the skirmish at the same time as Menda staggered into view under the weight of a great wooden chest with bronze clasps. 'They're retreating to a village down the road to lick their wounds,' Idwal stated coolly, 'they won't be back.'

'So much for the renowned Veneti,' grinned Sphax, taking the chest from Menda, who looked as if he couldn't carry the burden a step further. Sphax thought the chest satisfyingly heavy!

'There are three more where that came from,' said Corinna, gleefully, 'and I have the key. So I'll need your help, Idwal … and perhaps Drust's.'

Sphax reached for more rope, ordered Menda to climb into the wagon and kneel with his hands behind his back. Menda knew by now that protestation was futile; he'd been defeated, so in sullen silence he meekly obeyed.

Which only left one nasty surprise for them that morning.

The Numidians returned with the news that Menda's little army was returning from town in a mighty hurry, and they were no more than half a mile down the track. Sphax left them and sprinted down the corridor he'd seen Corinna emerge from. At last he found them. 'We must hurry!' he shouted. 'Menda's men have returned from town and are spoiling for a fight.'

'That's not possible ... unless—'

'—We've been betrayed by Diodorus.' Idwal finished Corinna's sentence.

'Never mind about that now,' Sphax pleaded, relieving Corinna of the chest, 'let's get a move on!' The four of them began running down the corridor as best they could, considering the burdens they were carrying. At last they arrived panting by the gate and heaved the chests into the wagon.

It was almost too late. His Numidians were already having to fight off the fittest of Menda's ragged army, who'd sprinted forward. But as three javelins spun towards their targets, Menda's men would come to regret their haste.

And then it was all over. With Zwalia at the reins, the wagon was thundering westwards at a pace no man on foot could keep up with, surrounded by six horsemen and a horsewoman. More than a match for any of Menda's rabble.

They had always suspected that Diodorus and the Greek faction on Pharos might betray them in some way, but figuring out the form this might take and what they could gain from it had defeated them. That the gates of Pharos had been barred to Menda's ragged army was certain. Sphax liked to think the Greeks had at last found their courage.

As they approached the designated cove and began looking out for their vessel, Sphax was pleased that at least they'd removed one hostage to fortune. At first light, as the eight of them had ridden through Pharos' southern gate, their vessel had slipped quietly out of its harbour with Carmo at the helm. Corinna had given him clear instructions how to find a sheltered cove less than a mile west of Demetrius' villa. To his joy and relief, he now saw fourteen youthful faces, beaming and cheering in their direction.

PART TWO

THE
PIRATE
QUEEN

SEVEN

'Rome is finished, Menda,' snapped Sphax. 'Her cavalry was routed on the Ticinus, and she lost two Roman legions and all four of her alae legions on the Trebia. It was a slaughter. Which means that Placentia and Cremona are already lost to them. In the spring it will be the turn of Arretium and Perusia, and finally Rome itself. Hannibal's army is superior in every respect. Nothing can stand in the way of our conquest.'

'You've gambled on the wrong runner, Menda,' observed Idwal, coolly.

Menda looked shocked as he gloomily stared into the campfire, his dark eyes glinting in the firelight as the fingers of his right hand nervously combed through his long, silver-grey curls. Sphax guessed that in his youth he must have been something of a peacock, trading on his good looks. But after an uncomfortable day tied up in the belly of their vessel, he looked old beyond his years, and he was fifty if he was a day.

They'd beached the boat and pitched camp for the night near the mouth of the bay of Kotor. Corinna told him it would be a calm and easy row to Rhizon tomorrow, so Sphax and Idwal had suggested they use the opportunity to talk to Menda about the strategic situation and the new power that had descended on Italia.

Discovering Menda had a baby son and young wife solved a major problem. How to coerce him to undertake the mission to Demetrius and Philip of Macedon? Holding his wife and son hostage in Rhizon meant they would have his complete cooperation. Corinna also thought it ensured success: that Menda wouldn't dare return without Demetrius and a letter from Philip.

But Menda had still to be convinced that Demetrius would be welcomed by Teuta. And somehow, they had to supply juicy titbits to tempt Philip to throw in his lot with Hannibal.

Whilst the three of them tackled Menda. Drust led off Elantia and her child to a distant campfire, where all they heard that night was laughter and animated conversation.

Earlier, Menda had told them he was aware the Boii and Insubres had risen. But he'd assumed Rome would put down the Gauls as they'd always done: brutally. When Idwal described the battles in Liguria over that winter of winters, Menda had listened in astonished disbelief. He told them he'd heard nothing more than rumours that Rome had received a setback. When Sphax told him of the numbers in Hannibal's army, and those recruited to their cause, Menda had been staggered.

At last Menda gazed over to where Corinna sat, leaning against Sphax. 'I know that you and your mother will never forgive me and my master, but believe me, Rome also betrayed us. I have no love of Rome.'

Corinna held his gaze. 'I myself will *never* forgive you, Menda. I know it was you and not Demetrius who opened secret negotiations with Rome. But my mother is unaware of this. She blames Demetrius, not you. Even so, I think I can persuade my mother to be reconciled with Demetrius and receive him once more. But I have need of your silken tongue to persuade him to return to Rhizon.'

'Why, Corinna?' exclaimed Menda, perplexed. 'What purpose would a reconciliation serve? If my master returned to Rhizon, Rome would send its triremes and legions. History would undoubtedly repeat itself!'

'What legions?' demanded Idwal. 'Haven't you been listening? When Hannibal's army marches south this spring, Rome will be involved in a life or death struggle for its very survival. As for sparing legions—Rome will need every legion she can muster to counter Hannibal's threat. And it will not be enough! Believe me, Menda, Illyria will be the last thing on Rome's mind. And the idea of her being able to *spare* legions is preposterous.'

'It's a compelling argument,' echoed Sphax. 'Rome already faces Hannibal's brother Hasdrubal in Iberia, a seaborne threat to Sicily from Carthage, and its greatest peril of all, our march on Rome. She does not have the resources to fight a war on so many fronts.'

Menda glared at Corinna. 'Do you believe Hannibal will destroy Rome?'

'Yes, I do,' she answered fervently. 'And with powerful allies, such as Macedon and Illyria, the outcome is certain.'

'Then Demetrius is the bait to hook a bigger fish,' observed Menda, astutely. 'I see your eyes are already fixed on Philip.'

Corinna smiled appreciatively at the man's wit. 'I have not introduced you formally to your jailors, Menda. I shall do so now. The man keeping my back pleasurably warm is Sphax, a Prince of Numidia, who happens to be a nephew of Hannibal. To your right is Idwal, Lord of the Cavari, one of the most powerful tribes in Gaul now solemnly pledged to Hannibal. Both have been given free rein to open negotiations with my mother, Demetrius, and Philip of Macedon. If you are ever to see your wife and son alive, you will do our bidding. Is that clear?'

Menda nodded grudging acceptance.

'Then you can be useful to us, Menda, and usefulness will be rewarded. Now is your opportunity to make amends by recognising the new power in the land, and forging alliances with it.'

'I have no influence over Philip of Macedon,' Menda replied, curtly.

'But you have influence over your master—too much it seems to me—and Demetrius is a trusted advisor to Philip. Bringing news of Rome's defeats on the Ticinus and Trebia will whet his appetite and open the door to persuade Philip to send envoys to Hannibal to negotiate a treaty. We have much to offer, and Philip much to gain—'

'—Hardly!' sneered Menda, scornfully. 'What has Philip to gain by making himself an enemy of Rome?'

'An alliance with Hannibal will ensure Rome's destruction,' Corinna countered, coolly. 'And without Rome's backing for one Greek League or another, Macedon will have a free hand to make war on whom she pleases. If Rome is not eliminated, she will always tip the scales in favour of the League that is against Macedon; for Rome fears Macedon, and intends to keep her weak by thwarting her every ambition. Philip understands this perfectly, and will need little persuasion.'

'Then you don't need me,' Menda shrugged. 'Any one of you could persuade Philip.'

'You've forgotten the small matter of Demetrius' return to Rhizon. Only your silken tongue will be able to persuade him he'll be welcomed. He certainly would not believe any of us! And once you've convinced him of its merits, Demetrius is the best person to put the case for an alliance with Hannibal to Philip. Demetrius is the key to all our hopes, so you must win him over to our cause.'

'I'm not so sure ...' murmured Menda, sweeping grey curls from his forehead. 'Why should he risk the wrath of the woman he betrayed?'

'Because she also betrayed and rejected *him*, if you recall,' Corinna countered persuasively. 'The scales of guilt are equally balanced, so it's time to put aside the bitterness and close the door on the past. My mother has ships but few men; Demetrius commands a small army of battle-hardened veterans, but is doomed to exile in Macedon. If Illyria is to honour its alliance with Hannibal, it will need those men, as well as a general to lead them. That's why Demetrius must be persuaded to come home and take up his rightful place beside my mother. Once he understands that you have come from my mother's court in Rhizon, and have her blessing, he will trust what you have to say.'

Sphax could see that Corinna was in something of a quandary, choosing her words carefully. A large part of persuading her mother depended on telling her the truth about Menda's sinister role in Demetrius' betrayal. But she could hardly tell *him* that!

Menda was lost in thought for a moment before he bestowed another leering smile on Corinna. 'You forget, my dear, that Scerdilaidas holds the real power in Illyria, for he controls its future king, the boy Pinnes.'

'You were most careless,' Corinna teased, 'when you lost your grip on the boy and allowed Scerdilaidas to take control of him.' A fact that wiped the smile from Menda's face. Sphax watched as Corinna turned the tables and returned Menda's smile with one laced with contempt. Somehow he knew she would save the best till last.

'Rome decided that Pinnes would be Illyria's future king,' she began, innocently enough. 'Understandably,

Hannibal disagrees with Rome's choice. He's chosen a different line to ascend to Illyria's throne. One he can trust as a natural ally.'

'And who might that be?' Menda asked, incredulous.

'My son Cleon, grandson of Queen Teuta.'

Menda's eyes narrowed to darkened slits. 'You have a son!'

* * *

'This is Elysium, Corinna, I would willingly give up the desert to feast my eyes on such breathtaking beauty.' Sphax was standing in his usual position on the steering platform, with an arm around Corinna as she guided the steering oars.

'It became my home after my mother was exiled here after the war with Rome, but I soon came to love the place. Although the mountains are forbidding, it's really quite a populous province of our Ardiaei people, with a myriad of settlements and harbours dotted here and there. The waters are so sheltered that in any season it's safe to journey by boat. This is where I truly mastered the art of the steering oars, and this is where the best shipwrights in Illyria ply their trade.'

That morning they'd awoken to another perfect day, with a cloudless azurite sky mirrored in the glittering waters of the Adria. The air itself seemed sharp and crystalline clear, with not a breath of wind. Here the bay of Kotor cut deep into a mountainous country whose steep-sided valleys were clothed in pine and cedar. They had celebrated the solstice less than a month ago, but here, even in the depths of winter, Sphax saw a green and verdant land that seemed to defy the seasons. After an hour or so of leisurely rowing they'd entered a triangular stretch of water that appeared to form a narrow channel at its apex.

Several boats were crisscrossing the bay's sheltered waters. 'What are these strange craft?' he asked Corinna, intrigued by their sleek hulls that finished in elegant curves at prow and stern.

'You will see a great variety of these vessels from now on. They are lemboï, a gift to Illyrians from the sea nymph, Alcima, who also founded our city of Rhizon. Alcima, like my mother and Rome, offended Poseidon and was banished into exile. Lemboï are the swiftest and most manoeuvrable craft that ever sailed the seas. Though they carry no sail, the largest have a crew of fifty oarsmen, are armed with bronze rams and have space for fifty warriors. They are the scourge of the Adria, feared by Roman and Greek alike, but the craft you see around you are probably carrying nothing more threatening than cabbages.'

As they approached the narrowing passage, Corinna described the inner waterway beyond the channel as shaped like a butterfly. Its wings formed the extent of the bay's waters, whilst the slender body of the insect represented the narrow passage they were heading for. In all, she guessed it was about seven miles from wingtip to wingtip, with Rhizon seated on the butterfly's upper left wing.

Rhizon was much smaller than Pharos and lacked a wall and gates. Red-tiled stone houses were dotted along the shore and lined a stream that fed the bay's waters, but none looked grand or imposing. Beside these sat disordered clusters of mean-looking wooden shacks, thatched in simple reed. To Sphax's eyes the town was unremarkable. What *was* remarkable was the hive of activity on the shoreline and its spectacular position, for Rhizon sat at the foot of towering mountains that rose in great cliffs of white rock that shimmered and danced in the winter sunlight.

Corinna pointed to the citadel, set high above the town. It had been constructed from the same white stone as the mountain on which it sat, giving the illusion that it had been carved into the mountainside, rather than built upon it.

All along the shoreline numerous quays and rickety jetties were thronged with vessels loading and unloading everything from iron ore and amphorae of wine to travellers, whilst around them smaller fishing craft jostled to unload their catch. As they neared the shore the air came alive with screaming seagulls and the cries of merchants, bartering with captains or servants and housewives complaining at the price of lobster or bream. Illyrians, it appeared, were a clamorous folk.

Sphax saw that Corinna was staring fixedly at where the river entered the bay. This area seemed to be given over to shipbuilding, and he could see several huge vessels under construction with swarms of shipwrights hammering and shaping with adze and chisel. Three seemed almost complete, and were being fitted out with masts, spars and rigging. Corinna was frowning.

'What's wrong?' he asked, puzzled by her expression. This industrious scene looked innocent enough to him.

'My mother is breaking the treaty with Rome.'

Sphax laughed. 'Does it matter?' adding, 'we'll be asking her to tear it up this evening.'

Corinna was still frowning. 'I'll explain later … but she's definitely up to something!' Tearing her eyes away she began instructing Carmo to ease the boys' stroke. They were about to make landfall in Illyria.

After hauling her a little way up the shingle beach and making her fast, they left Zwalia and the boys on board with the Numidians guarding Menda. As the four of them trudged up the beach, Idwal observed drily, 'There was a time when I thought I'd never live to see Rhizon. So what's next, my fair captain?'

'We find another captain, of my mother's guard, a man by the name of Scardus. I've known him since I was a little girl. What little skill I have with knife and blade is down to him. I'm hoping he'll take in our *guests* and keep a watchful eye on them. Presenting Menda, his wife and child to my mother would be like handing her a serpent on a silver plate. At all costs we must keep his presence in the town a secret until we can send him on his mission to Demetrius. I would trust Scardus with my life, and he won't ask too many awkward questions.' Grinning at their bemused expressions, she added, 'Follow me, he has a villa near here.'

They were shown into a spacious courtyard by a slave who promptly left to search for his master. Moments later a giant of a man appeared before them, beaming from ear to ear and dressed in a smart white chiton. Lifting Corinna effortlessly by the waist, he swung her around in circles until both of them collapsed in helpless laughter before beginning an animated, quick-fire conversation in Illyrian, a language so removed from Greek, Latin or Keltoi that none of them were any the wiser. At the mention of their names they'd courteously bowed before the gentle giant, and being offered wine, repeated the gesture. At the mention of the name Menda, however, the captain's attention sharpened, but otherwise, what had been agreed between the two of them remained a mystery until they withdrew and gathered on the street outside his villa.

'Scardus is happy to accommodate Menda's family, Sphax, if your Numidians are willing to be responsible for them. He's suggested rooms for our crew can be found over there,' she said, pointing to a ramshackle stone building across the street.

'It's not the grand hospitium we found on Pharos, but they take in merchants and sailors, and will be grateful for the trade in this slack season. As for our newfound wealth, including Lucius' merchant hoard we found hidden in the vessel, it would be safest under the roof of Scardus, with your Numidians guarding it.'

'So when do we present ourselves before your mother?' asked Sphax.

'After we've installed the boys in their lodgings and carried our worldly goods to Scardus' villa. We must dress in our finest, wait for the hour of dinner and surprise her, unannounced. Tonight I want to wrong-foot her and keep her on the defensive. May Hera grant us good fortune.'

'And Artemis,' whispered Sphax, fingering his ivory figurine and wondering how he would feel about meeting the Queen who had cost his mother and father their lives.

* * *

'By all the gods ... my daughter! Corinna! What an unexpected surprise,' exclaimed Teuta, as if she'd been summoned to an unforeseen funeral. After rising from the table and staring at the half-remembered face, it was not the fourteen-year-old girl she'd handed to a husband six years ago she'd recognised, but the face reflected every morning in her mirror. For Corinna was the spitting image of her mother. But whereas Corinna's beauty was blooming, Queen Teuta's was fading.

Even so, dressed in the fashion of her people she presented an extraordinary sight, and her upright bearing more than compensated for a face etched with a few more lines or hair tinged with strands of silver-grey.

On her head she wore a circular leather helmet studded with rich metals and jewels, with a fringe of pure gold ornaments that dangled across her forehead. A shawl, woven with exquisite golden thread depicting exotic birds was draped around her shoulders, beneath which she wore a diaphanous silk peplos of the deepest Phoenician red. Teuta, it seemed, did not believe in hiding her wealth away, but instead, flaunted it in the form of ornament for all to admire. She was drenched in gold and amber. From earrings and bracelets, to an elaborate necklace and girdle made up of threaded amber beads, Teuta sparkled and shone like honey and gold.

Earlier, with a stroke of good fortune, two of the citadel guards had recognised Corinna, so they'd been escorted to the audience hall, where her mother was holding a banquet in honour of a Liburnian embassy who'd arrived that afternoon. Corinna explained that the Liburni were Illyrian neighbours to the north of the Ardiaei. And so, as the doors of the hall were flung open by the guards, they were able to make their dramatic entrance, unannounced and uninvited. Just as Corinna intended.

Recovering her composure, Teuta clapped her hands, summoning servants. 'Bring chairs and prepare places for our newfound guests. Place them across from me, I have many questions for my daughter.' Then remembering her guests, she smiled graciously at the astonished faces of the score or so men either side of her. 'Dear Malavicus and Volsus, would you and the rest of your delegation indulge an old lady. I haven't seen my daughter for over six years, and feared she was lost to me. Her sudden appearance has both shocked and delighted me, and I'm all atremble.' All around her there was a murmur of willing agreement before she stared again at her daughter. 'Will you introduce your companions, child?'

'May I present Idwal,' Corinna began, 'Lord of the Cavari Gauls, and his lieutenant, Drust, also of the Cavari.' In turn each bowed low to the queen. 'And this is Sphax, nephew of Hannibal, and a Prince of Numidia.' Sphax did not condescend to bow, but nodded.

At the mention of Numidia a shadow passed over the queen's face. 'It's over ten years since Illyria had dealings with Numidians, and as I recall, it ended badly and blackened Illyria's name in the eyes of the world.'

'Mother! Hold your tongue!' cried Corinna, horrified at what she might say next. 'Illyria's good name pales into insignificance when compared with the fate suffered by Sphax.'

Before Sphax could intervene, Corinna steeled herself and seized the moment. She knew her mother was perfectly innocent of the fate that had befallen Sphax and his parents; nevertheless, Teuta had to acknowledge the pain and suffering her reckless war with Rome had caused, including her own exile as a hostage and cruel separation from her son.

Corinna seemed to grow in stature as she ripped open an old wound and poured in fresh venom. 'Sphax is indeed the son of Navaras and Similce, mother, whose embassy to Illyria you failed to protect. As a boy of seven he was forced to witness the brutal murder of his parents by legionaries, then he was sold into slavery and spent the next ten years of his life as a slave in Rome. Only last year did he escape this bondage and join his uncle. Because of Sphax, I myself am no longer a hostage of Rome, but my own son still remains a captive of our enemy.'

'You have a son…' whispered Teuta, visibly paling under this onslaught as she sank wearily into her chair and lowered her eyes to an untouched plate.

'Sphax, as well as three of his men, Idwal and Drust,' Corinna explained in a gentler tone, 'are risking their lives to help me free my son Cleon, who is held captive in Brundisium.' All around the table there was now a hushed silence as the Liburnians strained to catch every word of this extraordinary exchange between mother and daughter.

By now servants had laid plates and brought chairs. 'Come, Corinna,' Teuta gestured, 'join me at table. I must hear your story and news of my grandson.'

For a good half hour, Corinna talked and her mother listened, occasionally questioning or shaking her head in disbelief, but as their conversation was in Illyrian, none of them understood a word of her account. Instead, as the wine and the sea bream were excellent, Sphax was quite content to eat in silence. But this was not to last.

A Liburnian, who introduced himself as Aetor, asked him in hushed tones if he'd come from the camp of Hannibal. Sphax had nodded, and shortly after found himself surrounded by Liburnians eager for news. Beginning with the cavalry action on the Ticinus, he told them of the capture of the grain store at Clastidium, of Corinna's release, and of the final battle on the Trebia, where Rome's legions were destroyed. Soon, questions were flying thick and fast in broken Greek and faltering Latin, and Sphax heard snatches of similar conversations taking place at the table opposite Idwal and Drust.

Corinna's intimate interview with her mother seemed to have run its course. Smiling, she reached for his hand and squeezed it, a gesture that didn't go unnoticed by the queen, who raised her own hands and began clapping, summoning an army of servants to begin serving the next course.

'I could not help overhearing that our guests have described the momentous events that have taken place in Liguria this winter,' Teuta began, in a voice that transcended the excited whisperings of the Liburnians. 'My own daughter has confirmed the truth of this. But in this house we have no secrets. Malavicus, Volsus, and indeed Aetor, I understand from your line of questioning that you have followed these events closely. Feel free to discuss and question our guests openly, so that we all hear what is being said. Whispers will always be viewed with suspicion.'

It was evident to Sphax that Teuta not only had eyes in the back of her head, but ears as well! It was fitting that Aetor was first to rise to his feet. 'Rumour is sometimes more dangerous than a roomful of whispers, Queen Teuta,' he said in his broken Greek, 'and we have fed on rumour this winter. What is not clear to Illyrians, or Greeks for that matter, are Hannibal's intentions in Italia. Does he intend to occupy Rome and the lands of their allies, such as the Campanians or Samnites? Will Carthage become the new power in Italia? As nephew of Hannibal, surely Sphax must be privy to the highest councils in his army.'

Sphax smiled to himself ... as if Hannibal would allow his impetuous nephew to attend a high council of war! Nevertheless, he could answer Aetor's questions with authority. Rising to his feet, he began, 'Hannibal's intentions are widely known and have been broadcast since the siege of Saguntum: Rome must be destroyed and shorn of her power, otherwise it will remain a threat to us all. As to our intentions in Italia, we have none.' Sphax paused to emphasise the point.

'Carthage has no territorial claims on Italia, in fact quite the contrary, it wishes to see Campania and Samnium removed from the yoke of Rome and their independence restored. After our victories on the Ticinus and Trebia, Hannibal himself issued a decree that all prisoners allied to Rome were to be set free and allowed to return to their homes unmolested. I saw with my own eyes that this decree was upheld.' He was encouraged to see this last statement caused the Liburnians to stare at one another in astonishment.

With a shrug, he repeated, 'Our war is with Rome, not the Lucani.'

'You make it sound as if Carthage is on some mission of mercy, young man, playing the noble liberator,' protested the queen, tartly, 'yet it is Hannibal who has invaded. Rome is simply defending its territory.'

Before Sphax could respond, Idwal had risen to his feet. Judging by the thunderous expression on his friend's face, Teuta was in for a torrid examination. 'So, you consider the homeland of the Boii and Insubres Roman territory? Like Sicily or Sardinia?'

If anything, Teuta rose quicker from her chair, spilling her cup, eyes flashing. 'The Boii and Insubres are fools,' almost spitting the words at Idwal, 'they are as predictable as the seasons! Every few years they rise up against Rome and are slaughtered like cattle. They have not learned to let sleeping dogs lie.'

Sphax was shocked. He could see that Teuta was visibly shaking with rage. He'd never seen such a hothead so quick to anger. She certainly had spirit. Corinna turned to him, shaking her head in disapproval, whilst the Liburnians around the table held their breath.

Unflinchingly, Idwal stood his ground and met the Queen's eyes squarely. 'And now the glove is on the other hand,' he countered icily, fully in control. 'This season the Boii and Insubres have slaughtered Romans like cattle, and are once again masters of their homeland.'

'Hannibal's army is a mongrel rabble,' Teuta sneered, 'drawn from every shithole around the Mediterranean.

Their only allegiance is to Carthaginian silver, and when that runs dry they will melt away like autumn leaves.'

In the face of such venomous provocation, it was remarkable that Idwal's iron control held. But it did. Sphax's cheeks flushed as he felt Corinna's restraining hand on his shoulder.

'Know two things, madam,' Idwal said at last. 'Every man in our army would follow Hannibal to the end of the world. And every man has a bond that unites us far more than silver could ever buy: our sworn hatred of Rome and desire to see her destroyed! Her destruction began on the Trebia and will continue in the spring when we move south.'

'We shall see,' responded Teuta lamely, anger spent and sinking back into her chair. Sphax sensed that Teuta's temper was like a bolt of lightning that would be closely followed by a thunderclap of anger. But both would pass quickly. She had no staying power, or belief in the power of argument. Not so her protagonist.

Idwal had stayed on his feet. Ignoring the queen, he now directed his gaze at the Liburnians. 'Rome's legions are *not* sleeping dogs. They are a pack of ravenous wolves!

'Rome is on the march, driven on by the insatiable ambition of its consuls. Illyria learned this lesson ten years ago, and was reminded of it when legions descended on Pharos two years ago. It all began with Corcyra, but now Pharos, Apollonia and Epidamnos are friends of Rome. As other so-called *friends* have found to their cost, friendship with Rome means tribute and taxes, followed by merchants, colonists, settlements and praetors. Whether Greek or Illyrian, many on this side of the Adriatic have become clients of Rome. Don't be fooled. This is conquest by stealth!'

The Liburnians were once more muttering amongst themselves as Corinna removed her hand from Sphax's shoulder, thinking it safe after the storm had passed. But she was about to unleash a thunderbolt of her own.

'If Rome were to find out that Illyrians are breaking the treaty they signed, a fleet would descend on Rhizon with the next favourable wind. Our shipwrights are constructing keles, mother. A vessel banned by Rome for service with Illyrians! By treaty, a vessel that must not sail south of Lissus.'

Teuta smiled smugly at her daughter. 'But I'm *not* breaking the treaty, Corinna. My shipwrights are constructing them for Philip of Macedon, who is paying me handsomely for the service. Their shipwrights don't possess the skills to build such vessels. I've already sent him a score of master craftsmen to build a fleet of lemboï for Macedon.'

'Philip is constructing a fleet?' asked Sphax, excitedly.

The Queen ignored him, lavishing another self-satisfied smile on her daughter. 'It's of no concern to me what Philip does, as long as he's generous with silver.'

Sphax watched as Corinna sighed deeply and closed her eyes. 'It will be of concern to Rome, mother, believe me. How do you intend to sail five keles down the Adria, past Lissus and into the Aegean sea? Or do Illyrians intend to carry them overland to Macedon?' she added, now incredulous at her mother's naivety.

'Ah!' laughed Teuta. 'That's the beauty of it. Philip is sending crews overland from Macedon to man the ships when they sail south. So Rome can be sure that Illyrian pirates are not aboard, and that Illyria has not broken their cursed treaty.'

Corinna's eyes shot open as she wailed, 'What have you done? By the grace of Hera you're a bigger fool than I thought, mother!'

The banqueting hall suddenly froze as a deafening silence descended, broken only by the sound of Teuta's knife, smashing several plates as it slid down the table as the queen stormed out.

EIGHT

Whenever they had the opportunity, at first light Idwal had been teaching Sphax sword skills so he could use his dragon blade without embarrassment. Both of them eagerly looked forward to these sessions, as much for the cut and thrust of debate about Zeno or Aristotle as the pleasure of physical exercise. After an hour's rigorous exercise in the courtyard of the citadel, Sphax found himself retracing his steps back to the sleeping couch where he intended to wake Corinna in the way she enjoyed, and on that particular morning, he craved.

As he approached the open door of their bedroom he heard voices from within and stopped in his tracks.

'Are you fond of this young man?' It was Teuta's voice, but not the voice of the fire-breathing dragon Sphax had confronted last night.

'I love him, mother.'

'I grant you'll find few prettier! But he is a prince of lands on the other side of the world, and I've just seen him waving a sword around like a little boy.' To Sphax's astonishment he heard them both giggling at this. Teuta's moods seemed to be as baffling and mercurial as his uncle's!

'He has much to learn,' Corinna agreed, 'but give him a jennet to ride and javelins in his hand and he's a different proposition. With my own eyes I've seen him take on ten equites and kill seven of them. In Hannibal's army he's renowned for his courage and intelligence.'

'I see,' said the queen. Sphax hoped she'd been impressed! But without an expression to judge ...

'And how is Idwal regarded?' asked Teuta.

'He's one of Hannibal's most trusted lieutenants.'

'He's a fine man, with a noble bearing. Cavari lands are extensive, Corinna, and Gaul is much nearer our home.' This from the woman who only last night had been hurling insults at Idwal and pouring scorn on his army. Sphax couldn't believe what he was hearing!

'I too admire and respect him, but he is a little stiff for my taste.'

'Not for mine, Corinna ... that's how I would like him!'

'Mother!' But then he heard them both burst into laughter. Sphax could feel his cheeks burning as he hastily turned and fled down the corridor.

* * *

There was so much they had to do that day. Luckily, after last night's storms and tantrums, Teuta had a lot of explaining to do with her Liburnian delegation, who were due to leave that afternoon, so they hoped the queen would hardly notice their absence.

Corinna was eager to get Menda out of Rhizon and on his way to Demetrius. The revelation that Illyria had sent shipwrights to Macedon and was constructing keles for Philip worked to their advantage. If Philip desired a fleet, he would have to pay for it with alliances, not just silver.

As they were about to leave, Corinna gripped his arm and led him off in a different direction. 'There is someone I must greet. He's my childhood sweetheart.'

Sphax was already curious as she led him across the courtyard to a substantial building beneath the citadel's northern wall. As they drew closer he could see that it was a substantial stable block. Entering the semi-darkness, the sounds, sights, and above all the smells were so familiar to him. A stooped, elderly man with greying hair was scolding a young stable boy by enumerating his shortcomings on the fingers of his left hand.

'Good morning, Tatta,' Corinna greeted him jauntily.

'My Lady Corinna?' He exclaimed, beaming at her, 'I was told of your return. What a joy it is to behold you once more.'

Sphax winked at the stable boy, and with a gesture of his chin, suggested he seize his chance. By the time Corinna had introduced him to the stable master, the lad had scarpered.

'You must be here to see Alastor,' said Tatta, turning once more to Corinna.

'How is he?' she asked eagerly.

'Getting older,' Tatta replied as he walked her down an arched corridor lit at intervals by Greek lamps. 'But he's in excellent condition, as you'll see.'

Sphax was impressed. At a guess there was stabling for at least fifty horses in stalls set on both sides of the corridor, each one of a generous size and lavishly appointed. Corinna had never mentioned Illyrian cavalry, so these pampered creatures were for the pleasure of the queen and her court, he realised. Tatta stopped, stooped to remove the double bars from a stall and gestured for them to enter the presence of Alastor.

He could see from Corinna's expression that she was apprehensive, even a little nervous. But her fears, if that's what they were, were misplaced. After sniffing a couple of times to breathe in her scent, the stallion began joyously nickering and stepped towards her. Soon Corinna had her arms around his neck and her cheek nestled against his noble head.

'Isn't he handsome, Sphax?' she cried, overjoyed at their reunion.

'He certainly is!' Suddenly he recalled the name. Alastor was Hades' sleek and fearsome mount upon which he'd carried Persephone back to his underworld lair. Only exceptional horses were given names, and Corinna's stallion was nothing short of exceptional. Powerful yet fine-boned, he stood over fifteen hands tall, and his glossy coat was jet black throughout. There was something about his long neck and upright bearing that gave him a look of haughty disdain.

'He's from the horse-lands of Thessaly,' Corinna explained, 'where they breed fine stallions such as my Alastor.'

At that moment a horse at the far end of the stables began a tremulous, high-pitched neighing, broken only by intervals of agitated snorting. Sphax could hear pawing and the thud of rear hooves against a stall door. In alarm he turned to Tatta, 'That's the sound of an unhappy creature.'

'It's the Egyptian mare,' he groaned, 'the queen paid a fortune in silver for her, but she's wild and willful. Nobody can control her and she won't take bit, reins or saddle. She's the bane of my life!'

Corinna smiled at Sphax, 'With your permission, stable master, would you mind if Sphax took a look at her?'

Surprised, Tatta glanced at Sphax. 'Not at all,' he said, 'if you think it will do any good.'

Sphax hesitated, frowning at Corinna. Reluctant as he was to leave any horse in distress, they were so pressed for time. From past experience he knew that winning over a mare's trust could take up the rest of the morning. He looked for a compromise. 'I would be happy to see what I could do for her tomorrow morning. These things can take time,' he added with a meaningful glance at Corinna.

'Of course,' agreed Tatta, content with this arrangement.

After meeting up with Idwal and Drust they began the steep walk down to the town, the mare's cries still ringing in his ears. To ease Sphax's conscience and take his mind off her distress, he began to allot tasks. Whilst he and Idwal would tackle Menda, Corinna would be completely honest with Scardus, laying bare their plans to form alliances with Illyria and Macedon. They would need his help in acquiring horses and guides for Menda's overland journey to Macedon, so he had to be won over to their cause.

Drust was tasked with taking enough gold and silver to keep the boys in comfort for a few weeks until they returned from Brundisium. Carmo was to be put in charge of the boys' welfare.

Corinna was unhappy about leaving the boys to fend for themselves for what might turn out to be weeks, but there seemed to be no alternative. Then there was the thorny problem of Menda's wife and son, who would remain in Rhizon as a hostage to guarantee his compliance.

'Would your mother take in Elantia and her son, Corinna?' Sphax asked. 'The citadel is secure, at least.'

Corinna frowned. 'You've seen my mother's rage. When we tell her this evening that it was Menda who opened negotiations with Rome and began a whispering campaign that persuaded Demetrius to betray her … I'm not sure how she'll respond to accepting his wife and child as guests. She's quite capable of making their stay … shall we say, uncomfortable.'

'Elantia has such a bold spirit,' said Drust, 'she's quite capable of bribing one of the captains on the quay to take her and the child back to Venetia.'

There was something about the earnestness of Drust's remark that made them all turn and smile. He'd already confessed to Sphax in a whispered exchange that he found Elantia extremely comely. That's when Sphax thought of a perfect solution.

Placing an encouraging arm around Drust's shoulder, he walked with him. 'Corinna is worried about leaving the boys to fend for themselves, and none of us is happy at the prospect of handing Elantia and her son into the custody of the queen.' Sphax took a deep breath. 'How would you feel about staying behind in Rhizon to take care of the boys and become Elantia's guardian until Menda returns from Macedon? Carmo and the other boys have a great deal of respect for you, and you speak their language.'

Corinna and Idwal were beaming at Sphax as he removed his arm from his friend's shoulder, awaiting an answer.

'Won't you need me in the rescue of your son, Corinna?'

'You will be sadly missed, Drust, but I think the fewer of us who turn up in Brundisium the better. It's going to be difficult enough to make four Numidians inconspicuous! I think it's the perfect solution to all our problems.'

'You will be Elantia's guardian,' Sphax empahsised, 'and she and her son will be under your protection.'

'And you'll have to curb that bold spirit of hers,' Idwal teased with a straight face.

'Then if you all feel that's the best way I can be of service, I agree,' Drust said solemnly. 'I will stay behind in Rhizon.'

'If Corinna can spare Zwalia, you will have her help to look after the boys.' Corinna nodded. 'Then all we need to do now is find a villa big enough to keep you all under the same roof,' Sphax added, much relieved at this outcome.

* * *

'Where is your lieutenant, Idwal?' inquired the queen. 'I trust he received my invitation to dine with us this evening?' That evening the four of them reclined on comfortable couches in front of a roaring fire in the audience hall. Sphax and Corinna shared theirs, whilst the queen shared a luxuriously cushioned couch with Idwal.

Even Sphax noticed the queen had taken a great deal of trouble with her appearance that evening. She was wearing her revealing diaphanous red peplos, but gone was the embroidered shawl hiding her bosom, replaced by an amber bauble sunk deep between her breasts. This evening she wore her raven hair long, except for the small braids about her forehead. Somehow the silver-grey had miraculously disappeared.

'Indeed he did, madam, and sends his regrets. But Drust has taken on the responsibility of guardian to our crew of boys, and is attending to their needs this evening.'

'Madam makes me sound like an old maid, Idwal,' she chided with a gracious smile. 'You must call me Caeria, my given name.' Describing herself as an old maid seemed so unlikely Sphax smiled at the thought. But Idwal had been perfectly truthful about Drust.

Drust and his new family were now installed in a grand old villa in need of repairs its current owner couldn't afford. Because of this they'd negotiated a bargain rent on the understanding that the repairs would be undertaken. When they'd packed off Menda with two guides on his mission to Macedon, Sphax had paid particular attention to the parting of husband and wife. It was as he'd suspected. Menda cradled his son lovingly, but gave his pretty young wife a cursory kiss on the cheek and left without so much as a backward glance. It was evident to all that the marriage had not been a love match. But it was equally evident to all— with the exception of Menda—that Drust and Elantia were smitten with each other.

Teuta clapped her hands, summoning servants carrying the gustatio, which they placed on the low tables before them. Sphax's mouth watered at the sight of grilled mackerel, garnished with chopped eggs, leaves and sweet pomegranate seeds.

'Before we eat and drink too much,' Corinna began, 'we need to discuss many things and decide on a course of action.'

'Not tonight, Corinna. My head is spinning with

Liburnian trade routes, Veneti acts of aggression and Hannibal's war in Italia. Tonight we celebrate your return to Illyria. Matters of state can wait upon the morning.'

'You don't understand, mother!' persisted Corinna, exasperated. 'Hannibal himself has given the three of us the power to negotiate alliances and treaties—'

'—Enough! I will not hear another word. May the gods put a curse on all alliances and treaties.' As if to banish such weighty matters, the queen raised her cup and toasted, 'To Bacchus!'

The evening was entertaining enough. Teuta regaled them with stories, embarrassing Corinna with amusing tales of her misadventures as a child. What particularly fascinated the queen was Sphax's descriptions of the desert and the exotic lands of Africa, where gold grew on the ground and elephants roamed the forests.

Pleading fatigue, at midnight Sphax and Corinna excused themselves and rose from their couch. Teuta didn't seem too displeased, and Idwal simply raised his cup in farewell.

As they entered the courtyard they were both struck by the sight of the full moon, sailing high through the star-studded heavens. Sphax was carrying Corinna's shawl which he now placed around her shoulders. Even though the weather had been uncommonly mild for the season, there was a chill in the air that evening.

With a radiant smile, she reached for his hand. 'Come with me, there is something I must show you.'

'Are you not cold, my darling?'

Laughing, she assured him she'd drunk too much wine to feel the cold. Hand in hand they left the citadel by its only gate and began to follow a well-trodden path that led up the mountainside. Though the climb was steep and the path strewn with boulders, everything was so bathed in Selene's silver light it was easy to pick their way. At last they came to a feature in the rock that on first glance looked as if it had been hewn by human hands to resemble a seat, but in fact had been fashioned by nature. Out of breath from the steep climb, they gratefully sat and gazed in wonder at the vista laid out before them. From this height the entire butterfly wings of the lagoon were visible in the radiant moonlight, its waters shimmering in a myriad of silvered ripples. Nestled against his breast, for a while Corinna simply gazed in silence before she spoke at last.

'Don't you wish sometimes that you and I could follow a path such as this and walk into a new life, far away, a life without alliances and treaties, wars and hostages? I've followed this path many times as a girl, it leads over the mountain and into the most beautiful valley I've ever set eyes on. In springtime it's lush with daisies and violets, and in summertime rich in sweet meadow grass. It's a shepherd's paradise, and some days, I yearn for it ...' her voice trailed off.

Sphax didn't answer for a while, gazing thoughtfully into the distance. 'Recollecting my early childhood, as

I did this evening, brings on similar feelings to those you've described; a longing to return to a place of beauty and contentment ... forgotten happiness. But for me it carries with it the leaden weight of sadness and regret.'

He squeezed her shoulder. 'I watched you this afternoon as you smiled at Elantia holding her son in her arms. Despite that smile, there was something almost unbearable in your eyes at that moment ... emptiness, a sense of loss and regret. I've never noticed it before. It felt like a blade twisting in my heart. We must restore Cleon to you, my love. Perhaps only then will you feel whole again.'

Feeling uncomfortable amidst this maelstrom of emotions, Sphax rose to his feet, fashioned a grin and prepared to break the spell. 'So you find my dear friend too stiff for your taste?' he said.

Corinna stared up at him then burst out laughing. 'You eavesdropper!' she scolded as he helped her to her feet.

'Do you think he's managed to escape the charms of your mother this evening?'

He could see by her arched eyebrows she thought not. 'No man could escape the web my mother has spun this evening.'

'I could,' he replied with certainty, as he reached for her hand to guide her down the mountainside in the moonlight.

* * *

'Can you believe it?' ranted Corinna, stomping around their little bedroom in frustration. 'She wants to go riding this morning. Riding! Anything to put off sitting down and listening to our demands!'

Idwal had not turned up for their lesson that morning, so Sphax had gratefully returned to bed to catch up on much-needed sleep. Now he propped himself on an elbow, yawned, and tried to drive the fog of oversleeping from his head. 'That's the problem, Corinna. We have hung Dionysius' sword above her head by a hair, and your mother is stubborn and will not be bullied into a decision. Give her time. Risking open war against a powerful adversary is not to be undertaken lightly.'

'I know ... I know,' she groaned. 'But my mother is not Damocles! She's borne responsibility all her life, and is not shy about making decisions ... some of which have been calamitous—'

'—That's why she's hesitating. Be patient, my darling.'

'A virtue I've never mastered. But you are right,' she sighed. 'Let's go and find breakfast, I'm starving.'

Sphax suddenly remembered. 'There is something I must do first. You go. I'll join you later.'

'What is it?' she asked, puzzled.

'I must take a look at that unhappy mare Tatta was telling us about. My tardiness was preying on my mind last night. I hate to see such creatures suffer.'

Corinna smiled at him indulgently. 'Of course,' she agreed, 'I'd forgotten about the mare. We need to choose you a mount, so I'll come too.'

As if to add to his guilt, what met his ears upon entering the stables were the squeals of a horse in distress. Sphax knew instantly it was the Egyptian mare. Passing a stable master shaking his head, Sphax strode down the arched corridor to the stall where the unfortunate creature was stabled. The moment he caught sight of her his heart leapt, then despaired.

She was the most beautiful mare he'd ever seen. As to her breed; he'd never set eyes on such a creature before, but she was certainly not an Egyptian mare. No wonder the queen had paid so handsomely for her. Sphax had never seen such perfection. Tall and slender, her coat was almost indescribable. The best Sphax could come up with was luminous gold. Bronze didn't come close, and to describe her as the colour of desert sand would have been an insult. Because of her rich luminous coat, something reminded him of the fables of the blazing steed Aethon, one of the immortal horses that pulled the chariot of Helios.

If her grace and beauty were exceptional, her unhappiness was equally manifest. Leaning over the stall's gate, he steadily gazed into her eyes and began his softly spoken repertoire of sing-song sounds and half-words, delivered in a soothing, chant-like tone.

She stopped pawing and snorting the moment he gazed into her eyes, which told him that above all, this mare craved attention. Horses were just as keen to communicate with their human masters as humans were to command them by instruction. But humans had lost the ability to listen and empathise. Sphax had learned to trust his instincts in these situations.

Slowly, ever so slowly, her tail ceased its swishing and her ears pricked forward to listen to him. Without removing his gaze from her or letting up on his sing-song patter, he felt for the bars securing the stall doorway and silently removed them.

Sensing she was now calm enough to approach, Sphax gently swung open the door and stepped into her stall, making each movement slow and deliberate. Still singing, he reached for her mane and neck. For a heartbeat there was fear. He caught it in the flicker of an eye, but it passed. With both hands Sphax gently stroked her mane and neck, singing to her all the while until she was perfectly calm and at ease with him. It was then that he sensed a wave of emotion radiating from her, an overwhelming sense of loneliness, like a prisoner long forgotten and abandoned in her cell.

Still caressing her with his right hand, slowly he turned to stand beside her and face the open door of her stall. With more than a little irritation, for the first time he noticed a small crowd had gathered at the entrance. Corinna and Tatta had been joined by Scardus, two of his guards and several stable boys. This would never do!

Summoning every atom of calm, he whispered, 'I'm going to walk her slowly out of the stables and into the courtyard. I need the passageway cleared of people.' Resuming his singing, he listened for the footsteps to die away before placing his hand on her withers to gently propel her into motion. In this way, side by side, they stepped into the arched corridor and followed its course until they reached the sunlit space of the courtyard where a crowd had gathered.

It was as if the mare had been released from a prison cell. Letting out a funny little snort, she looked as if she was dancing on the spot, and when he stood before her she began to nicker and blow on his face.

'Off you go,' he whispered, giving her a gentle pat on her croup that sent her trotting merrily around the courtyard. Sphax began to whistle in a distinctive way, watching carefully if she moved her ears to follow the sound and locate his position in the courtyard. She did. Next, he stopped whistling, walked to the far end of the courtyard and whistled again, but this time more shrilly. To his delight she trotted over to him and rested her head on his chest, nudging him to be stroked and petted.

It often took days, sometimes weeks, to gain a creature's trust. But this mare had been so desperate for attention and company, it had taken less than an hour. Would she allow him to mount her, though? Sphax was about to find out.

Resuming his sing-song patter, his first problem was her height. On tiptoe he could just about slide onto his own jennet's back, but this mare was almost fourteen hands to her withers, two hands taller than Dido. He would have to spring on to her back, and if he landed clumsily or heavily, Sphax knew she would panic. Tatta had told him she'd refused bit, rein and saddle, which probably meant that nobody had attempted to mount her since. Composing himself, he knew he had to get this right.

He did get it right. For a few moments the mare simply stood still, confused, if not a little surprised by this unexpected development. But when Sphax began caressing her mane, and singing, she soon relaxed and accepted her new burden. Now his only problem was to find a way to ride her.

* * *

'Tatta thinks that all mares bred east of Illyria are Egyptian!' Queen Teuta explained. They were riding side by side, close to the southern shore of the butterfly lagoon, with Corinna and Idwal deep in conversation, following behind. 'I bought the mare you've named Aethon from a Seleucid merchant last autumn. I thought she was the most beautiful horse I'd ever laid eyes on, so I had to have her. I have a weakness for horses, as you've probably guessed.'

'I share your passion, my lady,' Sphax observed, smiling.

'But you are so young! How did you acquire such skills with horses?'

'As soon as we are able to walk, Numidians are taught to ride. Aged six I could pick pebbles from the ground at the gallop, and most of my time in Rome was spent in training chariot horses for the Circus.' He was tempted to add, 'And getting whipped and beaten for my trouble whenever they lost.' But he held his tongue.

'Do all the Numidians in Hannibal's cavalry ride as well as you?'

'Most,' he answered modestly. 'Some better, of course.'

'But I still don't understand,' she asked, genuinely puzzled, 'how men armed only with javelins can defeat Roman legions?'

It had been part of Sphax's training that when riding he was to carry a javelin. By this discipline he'd get used to the feel of it in his hand and could practice threading it with his leather throwing thong. Today he carried his saunion, a slender shaft of Iberian iron a forearm longer than his wooden javelins and twice as deadly.

Now he handed it to the queen. 'Of the five javelins each Numidian carries, one such weapon is an iron javelin such as this. The Iberians call them saunions, and no armour forged by man can withstand them.'

Teuta examined it closely, twirling it between her fingers before testing its balance in her fist. 'Illyrians have no such weapon,' she said, handing it back to Sphax. 'Scardus,' she called to the captain of her guard, riding a few strides ahead. 'Take off your breastplate and hand it to master Sphax.' Obeying his queen, the giant halted in the saddle, fumbled with the straps and buckles behind his back before releasing the breastplate and handing it over to Sphax.

It was a typical muscled cuirass, much favoured by Rome's allies such as the Campanians and Samnites. Crafted from a single sheet of burnished bronze, beaten into shape to resemble an athlete's chest and muscular abdomen, it curved around to protect the wearer's ribcage, but left his back exposed and vulnerable. A fatal flaw Numidians had exploited at the Trebia. For all its enormous size, Scardus' breastplate felt remarkably light in his hands. Wooden javelins would be as much use against it as against an auroch's hide, but a saunion aimed straight and true would stand a good chance of piercing it, as long as the tip didn't strike its many curves …

'Illyrian bronze is much prized for its strength,' commented the queen. 'Would your saunion pierce it?'

'Almost certainly,' he boasted without a second's thought, handing the cuirass back to Scardus.

'You look like a man who relishes a challenge, Prince Sphax. How about a little wager?' she asked, innocently enough.

'That would depend on the nature of the challenge, my lady?'—cursing his boastfulness, and now fully aware of the trap the queen was baiting.

'I'm prepared to wager the golden mare on Scardus' breastplate repelling your iron javelin.'

Sphax froze. But he did see a way out. Forcing a half-smile, 'Alas, Queen Teuta, I'm not a wealthy man, and could never match such a princely wager. I don't possess anything that would come close to the value of your golden—'

'—But you do, master Sphax! There's something I've coveted since I first saw it strapped to your back, and during your morning's exercise with Idwal I was able to examine the craftsmanship of the scabbard and see for myself that remarkable blade in action. It's longer than any Gaulish sword I've ever seen, and the gold and silver inlays on the scabbard alone would match what I paid for the mare.'

There was something mocking about Teuta's arched eyebrows and tight-lipped smile. 'My golden mare for your dragon sword seems a fair wager. And if, as you claim, no armour yet forged can withstand a saunion, it seems I must resign myself to the mare's loss.'

Colour drained from Sphax's face as he considered his dwindling options. He risked losing his most precious possession because of a careless boast. His dragon sword was a treasured gift from Idwal. Made by the smith Aodhán in Nages, Sphax had watched the miraculous process of its forging. The scabbard alone was worth a fortune, its craftsmanship exquisite. Cast in bronze with a gold tip, each side had silver inlays; on one side depicting a dragon, its tongue breathing forth flames, and on the other, a line of elephants approaching a great river.

Be it Agbal, Hannon or Jugurtha, he would have staked his own life on any one of them piercing a breastplate. But they were not here. Through daily exercise his aim was getting better, but he was still rated a novice at the javelin! But refusing the queen's wager meant far more than losing face, it called into question his entire version of events; how Numidian cavalry had decimated Roman legions on the Trebia. Refusing the wager would sow seeds of doubt on the skills of Hannibal's Numidian cavalry!

'I fully understand,' continued the queen, 'if you wish to decline the wager. Your claims about Numidian cavalry and their miraculous saunions do sound rather *fanciful.*' Now he was being called a liar! Teuta's mock-sympathy was worse than her taunting.

Something snapped. 'Then say farewell to your lovely mare, Queen Teuta, for you've just gifted her to me!'

Teuta began directing everyone off the track towards a mossy sward beside the glittering lagoon. His trial by saunion was about to begin. As the riding party began to dismount, handing reins to grooms, an army of servants and slaves leapt into action, unpacking the baggage train of mules. Folding chairs, low tables and even small carpets miraculously began to appear, all placed and ordered under the watchful eye of the queen's chief steward, Pinnes. Soon tables began to groan with the lavish feast of bread, cheeses and a rich variety of cold meats and smoked fish.

Idwal was given a place of honour at the queen's right hand, whilst Corinna sat to her left beside Sphax. Two of the queen's advisors joined their party, whilst Scardus, ominously in deep conversation with his queen, had been given a chair beside Idwal. In front of them, at least forty servants and slaves made themselves comfortable on the grass, staring patiently at the feast laid out on the tables, wondering how much would be left for them.

When Scardus strolled off, Teuta rose to her feet, looking pleased with herself. 'Besides a feast'—she spoke in Greek, largely he guessed, for his benefit— 'I've also provided entertainment for us all,' smiling at Sphax. 'Today we are to witness a demonstration of a weapon unknown to Illyrians. Numidians call them saunions, and claim they can penetrate any metal forged by man. So today we have set Prince Sphax a challenge. Our noble Scardus will place an Illyrian breastplate as a target for the Numidian to aim at with this wondrous missile.

'Our Illyrian bronze is much sought after. To my knowledge no sword or spear has ever penetrated it. So, unless the Numidian's saunion has been forged by the gods, his claim sounds to me like an empty boast.' Sphax heard laughter erupt around the meadow. 'To add spice to this challenge, I have wagered him the golden mare he's tamed this morning, and in return he's wagered the magnificent Gaulish blade you see strapped to his back.'

'What!' Corinna glared. 'You risk Idwal's precious gift on a *boast!*'

NINE

Sphax stared grimly ahead, not daring to risk Idwal's outrage or Corinna's contempt. 'I had no choice,' he said at last, rising to his feet and striding towards Scardus, whose men were binding the breastplate to crossed spears anchored in the ground. He knew that two spears would not be enough for what he intended. Even if he struck the breastplate fair and square, the spears would simply flex, deflecting the saunion. It had to be as solid as a rock to give him a fighting chance. He suggested they use a spare table, turned on its end and resting on its legs, to which they attached the breastplate with knives at the height of a man's chest. Spears were then placed at a steep angle behind it to brace it further. At last Sphax was satisfied the contest was fair.

Besides the saunion, his other weapon awaited him. Being starved of exercise for so long, Aethon knew only two speeds; a gentle trot or a flat-out gallop. A flat-out gallop would do nicely. After he'd dismounted from her earlier, the creature had managed to escape the grooms and had taken off towards the stream to drink, savouring her newfound freedom. But now, hearing his whistle, she trotted back to him, whinnying in his presence and allowing him to mount her again.

Best get this over with, thought Sphax. Delaying would only add to his nerves, and he already felt sick to his stomach. After a silent prayer to Artemis and a touch of her ivory image, he took extra care tying his leather throwing thong. His hands were trembling. Nudging Aethon into a trot, he sensed her impatience but fought to hold her back until she was truly lined up on the target, eighty paces distant.

After her months of confinement, all the creature wanted to do was to run free, unfettered and unhindered by bars, gates and stable masters, so now he gave Aethon her head, pressing her to even greater speed. Within six strides, as the world began to flash by, despite his sickening fear his heart soared in the exhilaration of the moment. And by the time he flung his saunion, ten paces from the target, all his anxiety had evaporated in the thrill of it.

In battle, Numidians rarely see whether their javelins have struck home, for in that desperate moment they're involved in a life or death manoeuvre to turn their mares around and retreat. Today, he could savour his triumph. His spinning saunion had flown straight and true, sinking deep into the breastplate with a satisfying thud.

But Aethon cared nothing for his triumph and had no intention of slowing down! The mare had a mind of her own. Thundering on, the best he could do was guide her in a wide circular arc, relax the pressure of his knees on her flanks and ease himself backwards onto her rump. Eventually she did began to tire, and Sphax was able to bring her back under control, guiding her back to the feasting tables where he dismounted.

Scardus had handed the breastplate to Queen Teuta. As Sphax approached, she sat with it in her lap, carefully examining the hole where the saunion had penetrated more than half its length. Not only that, the table now had a corresponding hole in its polished surface. He was delighted to see her face was set like thunder.

'You are to be congratulated, Queen,' he crowed; 'if this had been Roman bronze my saunion would have gone clean through it. Illyrian bronze is indeed superior.'

'You have met my challenge,' Teuta hissed, less than graciously. 'The mare is yours.'

When he resumed his seat beside Corinna he could see his triumph had done nothing to improve her temper. Finally she turned to him. 'One of these days your recklessness and over-confidence will cost you more than that precious blade of yours.'

* * *

'Let's face it my love, it was a lucky shot,' Corinna teased as she lay naked on their sleeping couch later that afternoon. 'And you might have undone everything that Idwal has accomplished.'

Sphax propped himself on an elbow. 'Luck had nothing to do with it, little mouse!' he returned, grinning. 'Tell me what Idwal's done? I saw you deep in conversation with him all morning. Idwal said nothing as we rode back from the feast together. He seemed more interested in why you were in such high dudgeon, refusing to speak to me!'

Corinna slapped his backside, hard. 'Because I was angry with you! Still am ... at least ... a little. That's why I rode back with my mother.'

'Idwal never doubted I would win the wager. He wasn't angry with me.'

'Well, he should have been!'

'Then tell me what he's done? These accomplishments of his that I may have *undone*?'

He could see that Corinna was savouring the moment. 'He's persuaded my mother to ally the Ardiaei with Hannibal.'

'What!' he cried, astonished. 'When? Why didn't you tell me earlier?' restraining a hand that was about to deliver another slap.

'Because you didn't deserve such good news,' she said between fits of laughter as he grabbed her hands and wrestled her shoulders to the couch.

'What am I to do with you, little mouse.' he joked, grinning down at her. 'When you keep secrets from me?' Releasing her hands and rolling on to his back he asked, 'And how did Idwal get your mother to agree to this?'

'Doing just what we're doing now, my love: pillow talk.'

Sphax laughed. 'From what you've told me of your mother's appetites, I'm surprised he found the time.'

'The Liburnians played their part,' she began. 'Do you remember Aetor, the fellow who was questioning you the night of the banquet?' Sphax nodded. 'Well he advocated an alliance with Hannibal and war with Rome. But the Liburnian position is complicated, Sphax, and they have ulterior motives.'

'Such as their neighbours, the Veneti,' suggested Sphax.

'Exactly.'

'Aetor was trying to explain this,' he added, 'when your mother stormed out.'

'The Veneti's alliance with Rome has emboldened them, leaving them free to attack Liburni lands and shipping. Personally, I doubt if they'll lift a finger in our war against Rome, but they might keep the Veneti quiet.'

'That still doesn't explain why your mother is risking another war with Rome.'

'She admires Idwal and defers to his knowledge of war. He convinced her that Hannibal will defeat any army Rome sends against him. That's why if you'd missed that breastplate it might have undermined his arguments and made him look foolish.'

'And *me* ...' he growled. 'Your mother was goading me about Numidian weapons and tactics all morning. Only a demonstration would have convinced her. That's why

I *had* to pierce that breastplate! Nothing else would have sufficed.'

'I know … I know,' she said softly. 'I understand that now.'

'The wagers were your mother's idea,' protested Sphax, 'not mine. I simply wanted to demonstrate the power of a saunion … but she had other ideas.'

'What you did truly shocked her. Mother told me she'd never seen such a frightening weapon, a weapon that made armour useless. You convinced her of Hannibal's superiority and everything Idwal had been telling her.'

'That just leaves the small matter of Demetrius' return. I fear this will be a far harder nut to crack. We must be at our persuasive best at supper this evening.' Corinna was regarding him with a knowing smile. He knew that look. 'There's something else you're not telling me? Isn't there?'

Feeling the chill in their little bedroom, Corinna sat up on the couch and reached for her chiton, slipping it over her head. 'Your little triumph gave my mother pause for thought. I think for the first time since our arrival it dawned on her that she'd badly misjudged things. I caught her in a reflective mood, so I told her all about Menda.'

'And?' he asked, wide-eyed.

'Demetrius can return to Rhizon, but not to Pharos.'

'Even better!' Sphax declared. 'That's more than we hoped for. You have done so well, little mouse. I'm proud of you!'

'The rupture took place more than ten years ago, Sphax, time enough for anger and bitterness to recede with the years. My mother might be mercurial; burning hot one moment and cold the next, but she doesn't bear grudges. She understands Demetrius was tempted by the high stakes Menda dangled before his eyes.' Reaching for her peplos she added, 'But I wouldn't want to be in Menda's sandals when he returns. I spared no detail of his wickedness.'

Sphax shrugged, dismissively. 'What about the five keles she's constructing for Philip of Macedon?' he asked, shivering, reaching for the folds of the embroidered himation he'd flung to the floor.

Corinna rolled her eyes, 'I can't believe my mother could be so foolish! On their way to the Aegean and Macedon, the vessels would have to put into Greek harbours along our coasts. Within days Rome would have got wind of it. Even if the vessels were crewed by Macedonians, Rome would realise that only Illyrians had the skills to build such ships. Rome would never countenance Rhizon constructing a fleet of fast ships for Philip's growing navy. If it wasn't for the threat of your uncle's army, Rome's retribution would have been swift and terrible.'

'So what's Idwal persuaded her to do?'

'To use them against Roman shipping in the Adria and in defence of Rhizon. He offered her one of Menda's chests to keep the construction of keles flowing. Money well spent, I thought.'

Corinna suddenly burst into helpless fits of laughter. Like a swaddled newborn, her lover had become completely entangled in the folds of his himation. 'You need a handmaid, my love!'

'I do not!' he cursed from inside the cocoon of white linen he was drowning in. 'This garment ... defies me! It has a life of its own.' After much pulling, shoving and cursing, Sphax's head finally emerged from its folds.

* * *

'You forget, daughter, I received news of your husband's murder before you did. With a fair wind, Epidamnos is two days away by ship and only a few days more overland. We heard the rumours and whispers soon enough! Once again Illyrians were blamed and our honour blackened in the eyes of the world. Yet we were innocent of this crime. Arsenios was undoubtedly murdered by his associates ... someone wanted him out of the way. But don't you see? Alkibiades and his wife Alexandra will now be suspicious of you, as they are of all Illyrians. If you ask me, someone wanted it that way.'

The four of them were occupying the same couches they'd lounged upon the night before. But tonight the queen was more than happy to discuss Liburnian trade routes, Veneti aggression or Hannibal's war. That night matters of state could not wait, and not a single toast to Bacchus passed her lips. And Corinna's plan to seek help from Cleon's elderly grandparents in Epidamnos troubled her deeply.

'Cleon is their grandchild, mother. Their flesh and blood!' protested Corinna. 'By all the gods I can't believe they wouldn't want to help us rescue him. And I was an obedient and dutiful wife—'

'— I didn't raise you to be obedient and dutiful! Think for yourself, child. They are the most powerful house in Epidamnos and have everything to lose from offending Rome. As leader of the ruling council, if it became known that Alkibiades was aiding a hostage of Rome he would be finished.'

'How so, mother? Rome has no such grip on Epidamnos—'

'—But it has! Our merchants trade with Epidamnos. The city is a friend of Rome. I've even heard rumours that the ruling council have allowed a Roman garrison in the city. Rome has Epidamnos in its purse.'

'Although you have no proof,' began Idwal, 'I know you suspect Dasius of plotting the murder. Is this correct?' Corinna nodded. 'Everything you've ever told me about Dasius' deranged mind suggests to me that he might have fanned the flames of rumour in Epidamnos, by insinuating that the murder was planned by Illyrians, perhaps even ... by you.'

'But that's preposterous, Idwal!' Corinna exclaimed, outraged. 'Why would I murder my husband, when he alone offered me the only protection I had from the wolves that were gathering around us?'

Sphax followed Idwal's logical reasoning through to its sinister conclusion. 'Because, my darling, Dasius would have closed off your last possible escape route. If your husband's parents thought you had played any part in his death, they would denounce you as a murderess. And once your husband had been eliminated, Dasius would have you exactly where he wanted you. Powerless!'

'You've all lost your reason,' laughed Corinna, 'this is nothing but fantasy.'

'When you look into the eyes of Alkibiades and Alexandra,' Teuta interrupted with an intensity Sphax had never heard before, 'be sure you recognise the gaze of loving grandparents, not a vengeful glare at the murderess of their only son.'

TEN

O n the afternoon of their second day at sea, the headland and hill upon which Epidamnos was built hove into sight. Teuta had insisted they take passage with an old salt named Glavus, who'd told them he'd sailed to the Greek city more times than he cared to remember. His ancient vessel, described as a small corbita by Corinna, had made heavy weather of the light airs the previous day, but that morning the breeze had picked up, driving them swiftly southwards.

They'd all agreed to go below deck before the vessel berthed and tied up against the quay. Waiting for the formalities of taxes, customs and the unloading of cargo before they tried to steal ashore, unnoticed.

At last a hatch opened and Glavus' grizzled bush of a beard appeared above. 'It's quiet up here. Now's your chance.'

Sphax and his men had each selected three wooden javelins to take with them, binding them in sack-cloth and tying strings of onions to them in the hope of fooling the guards at the city's gates. Likewise, Idwal and Sphax's blades had been hidden in a hemp sack. Corinna had taken the precaution of arming each of them with a dagger they'd strapped beneath their chiton tunics. Now all they had to do was to get past the guards. Visitors were never allowed to walk into a Greek city armed.

Agbal picked up his onion strings and Hannon shouldered his sack as they mounted the stairway that led to the aft deck. Entering the twilight that was fast descending on the harbour and the city, Glavus had one piece of advice left. 'Don't stay at the Helios. Behind the temple of Poseidon is a little known hospitium called the Athena. Stay there.'

Except for a handful of fishing vessels readied for tomorrow's catch, as he walked up the wooden companionway, all Sphax could see were vessels tied to iron bollards to sit out the winter.

Corinna pointed to a vessel beached on the far side of the harbour. To Sphax's amazement he saw a Roman quinquereme, around which had been built a makeshift wooden shed to keep the worst of the weather from rotting her timbers. Judging from her fading paintwork, she had seen better days, probably facing his grandfather's Carthaginian quinqueremes off Sicily.

At the harbour gate, recessed into the city's walls, Sphax could make out three guards idly lolling around. They were wearing Boeotian helmets and hefting spears. Corinna had also spotted them and removing her shawl to reveal her face and raven locks, strode forward to throw a casual arm around Idwal's waist.

'What have we here then?' said one of them, feasting his eyes on Corinna.

'Six customers for the Helios,' she laughed, resting her head seductively on Idwal's breast. 'So by the gods let us through and don't make a meal of it,' she added, winking luridly at the three guards. 'This one can't wait to feel my tits and start humping ... and that lot,' waving dismissively at Sphax and his Numidians, 'can only afford a whore between them ... poor girl!'

Amidst the ribald laughter and obscene gesturing, somehow the six of them passed through the gate without arousing the slightest suspicion.

Once out of earshot of the guards Idwal turned to Corinna, 'As the daughter of a queen, you never fail to astound me.'

'A fishwife couldn't have done that better!' observed Sphax, just as amazed.

As they climbed the steep road that led up to the city they could see ahead of them a magnificent agora, lined with arched porticos to keep the good citizens cool in the heat of summer. At the far side of the agora's open rectangle they could also see the colonnaded entrance to a grand temple.

'Is that Poseidon's temple?' whispered Sphax to Corinna.

'No. That's the temple of Hera. Poseidon's is even more magnificent,' she replied, checking her shawl was once again covering her head and hiding her curls. At this hour, with darkness almost upon them, shops were being boarded up and the city looked deserted. They did pass a few men scurrying homewards, Sphax finding it curious that many carried walking sticks they didn't appear to need.

Not since he'd walked through the streets of Massilia and visited the temple of Artemis, six months ago, had Sphax walked through a city that reeked of such power and wealth. The sons of the first colonists from Corinth had grown rich, and showered their city with temples and civic buildings worthy of any in Greece.

It was dark when they reached the temple of Poseidon. Sphax would have to wait until the morning to view its splendour. All he saw of it now were lowering columns towering above him.

But Glavus had been right about one thing: the Athena was so hidden away it was difficult to find. Perfect for their needs. They booked three rooms and closeted themselves in Sphax and Corinna's chamber to discuss how they would approach Alkibiades. And it was only after interminable argument that they finally managed to persuade Corinna to heed her mother's warnings and proceed cautiously.

* * *

Carrying a folding chair and a woven cloth sack, Sphax scrupulously tried to keep two steps behind Corinna.

But she was making it almost impossible for him by her stops and starts, gazing at unshuttered shops or pretending to greet acquaintances on the other side of the street. She was wearing her finest that morning, but had been careful to wrap her shawl so tightly it barely revealed her face. Women were wandering the streets of Epidamnos that morning, followed at a respectful distance by slaves and servants, but they were all similarly swaddled.

Last night, after the endless arguments, Corinna had bought a folding double-leaved wax tablet bound in red leather from mistress Clio, the proprietress of the Athena. Sphax had watched as Corinna had composed her message, rarely having to use the spatula end of the stylus to rub out a word or make a correction. Now the tablet, and its message, lay in the embroidered sack he was carrying.

The morning dawned grey and cloud-laden, threatening rain, and he felt uncomfortable in the role of dutiful slave. He knew that Corinna had only lived in the city as a fourteen-year-old bride for little more than a year. But that was seven years ago. Would she remember the layout of the city? At last she strode out purposefully, heading southwards. Sphax could see they were skirting the eastern edge of the agora, heading for a broad paved avenue, planted with pine trees on its right hand side. This was a residential district, and each successive villa they passed seemed to outshine its neighbour in decoration and splendour.

At last she nodded towards a villa with an arched porticoed entrance which appeared to lead to gardens and an inner courtyard. Walking casually on, she then crossed the street and stopped beneath the greenery of a fragrant cedar.

'Here we wait and observe,' she declared. 'I to sit, whilst my faithful slave stands obediently behind me. Unfold my chair and pass me the tablet.'

'You're enjoying this, little mouse—'

'—Not at all! she retorted. 'I'm simply playing my part in this ridiculous comedy because you, Idwal and my mother begged me to be careful. Left to my own devices I would have stormed into the old man's private rooms and demanded his help ... Cleon is his grandson!'

Sphax sighed, 'We went through all this last night. A message will soften Alexandra's shock. Then she may grant you an interview and you can win her over.' He unfolded the chair and reached into the sack for the wooden, leather-bound writing tablet.

Corinna sat and, dutifully unclipping the stylus, placed the open tablet on her lap. Anyone passing by would see a Greek lady composing an invitation to a birthday or dinner party to be delivered by the slave hovering behind her. And so they waited ...

At least the clouds had lifted and rain looked less likely. Sphax had counted on the fingers of one hand the people who'd passed by on the street opposite. Spotting another, ambling along, he suddenly heard voices from within the arched portico of Alkibiades residence. And there was the man himself, not sixty paces away.

Silver-haired, with a gnarled old face and a beak of a nose, Alkibiades was dressed in a smart saffron-dyed himation, surrounded by chattering attendants. He carried the inevitable stick in his right hand, but Sphax guessed he would have need of it, for the man looked to be at least seventy years old.

Slowly the party made its way towards the city with hardly a glance at the seated lady composing an invitation on the other side of the street. When they were out of sight, Corinna clamped the tablet shut and stood up.

'I'm supposed to deliver that letter, not you!' he warned, exasperated. But by then she was half way across the avenue.

'I'm not playing these games any more,' she called out over her shoulder.

Sphax watched as she slid between the two columns supporting the archway and looked about her. Next he heard the sound of a mellow bell being rung, after which Corinna stepped backwards into the street. Moments later he saw her hand over the folded tablet to an unknown hand inside the portico.

Dragging the chair deeper into the shadows of the pine trees, he slumped into it, heart pounding, and waited. What happened next was extraordinary, and a sign the gods were smiling on them that morning. Swaddled in a woollen shawl, an elderly woman stepped from the archway and flew into Corinna's arms. He watched as they embraced, chattering away to one another with words whose meaning he could only imagine. Instinctively, Sphax reached for his ivory image of Artemis and put it to his lips, as arm in arm, the two women entered the villa of Alkibiades.

It was more than an hour before Corinna re-emerged. Sphax leapt from his chair, folded it and picked up the sack. The street was empty, so he risked walking beside her, anxiously scanning her expression for clues as to how the interview had gone.

'Well?' he asked, impatiently.

'I don't know!' she shrugged. 'She's very kind, and was overjoyed to learn she's a grandmother. But like all Greek wives, she can't even fart without asking her husband's permission. We are to return at noon tomorrow, and you and Idwal have been invited to attend and take refreshment. But she did mention some ugly rumours that had circulated after the death of my husband.'

'Then let's get back to the Athena,' he said, taking up his respectful position a step or two behind her.

She gave him a weary smile. 'Yes. I'm tired and hungry, and desperate to question mistress Clio about those dreadful rumours.'

* * *

'What did she say?' asked Idwal when Corinna returned from Clio.

'Nothing we didn't know already,' she shrugged. 'My husband's vessel was spotted off the coast, south of here, but it was ablaze and must have sunk shortly after. Rumours were rife that Illyrians had sunk to new levels of depravity. Boarding merchantmen, taking what they could after murdering the crew and torching the vessel.'

Sphax asked if there could be any truth in this. Corinna glared. 'Illyrian pirates make their profits not from plundering cargo, but ransoming crews and passengers on board. Merchants pay handsomely for their captains and crews returned ... alive! A rich passenger on board like my husband would have been a lucrative bonus. And why would pirates fire a merchant vessel when they could put a crew aboard, sail her home and auction her to the highest bidder? My husband was not murdered by pirates. Dasius the Pig and his cronies were responsible.'

'But Alkibiades has no way of knowing what you know, Corinna,' objected Idwal. 'For all we know he may still blame his son's death on Illyrians, and you are the daughter of the pirate queen.'

'Did mistress Cleo mention any rumours that you might have been involved in plotting his death?' asked Sphax, almost dreading the answer.

'Yes,' she confessed, lowering her eyes. 'There were more ... shall we say, sinister rumours like that. But I told Alexandra the truth this morning. The whole truth. I'm sure she believed—'

'—Enough!' roared Sphax. 'It seems to me you're deliberately choosing to ignore all the warnings we've been giving you. It's as if you're bent on punishing Alkibiades, not asking for his help. You know perfectly well he won't listen to Alexandra. She's a wife, not an equal!'

Idwal sighed. 'If Alkibiades suspects that you played a part, however small, in his son's murder, by meeting him it strikes me we're deliberately putting ourselves in harm's way.'

'No, Idwal,' she protested sullenly. 'Tomorrow I go alone—'

'—Oh no, Corinna!' demanded Sphax. 'Either we all go, or none of us. Is that clear?'

'So, Corinna,' Idwal continued in his calm, measured tone, 'you must convince us the risk is worth taking.'

For a brief moment, her eyes flickered between the two of them. In the face of such brutal facts, for once in her life Corinna ignored her heart. 'Any Illyrian vessel is bound by Roman treaty from sailing south of Lissus. Therefore, any ship entering the harbour of Brundisium would have to sail from Epidamnos or a Greek colony south of here. As captain of an Illyrian vessel, even Glavus would be denied entry to Brundisium's harbours. Alkibiades controls vast merchant fleets. Only he has the power to compel a captain and crew to risk the crossing in the storm months.'

'Why can't we capture a vessel as we did in Placentia?' Idwal persisted.

'This is not about floating down the Padus, Idwal. To cross the Adria and reach Brundisium we'll need a corbita or a cybaea, a crew of oarsmen and a fair wind.'

'So!' Idwal shrugged. 'We do need Alkibiades after all. That's settled then. The three of us will meet—'

'— No, Idwal!' Corinna pleaded. 'I alone will meet Alkibiades and Alexandra. I'm not prepared to risk you and Sphax.'

Sphax and Idwal laughed. 'Men rule the roost, Corinna,' Sphax protested, grinning at Idwal who was similarly nodding. 'You're overruled!'

* * *

The three of them set off in good time before noon. It wouldn't do to keep Alkibiades and Alexandra waiting. For Sphax, the walk brought a role reversal: this morning he walked beside Idwal and Corinna kept her place a step or two behind. They followed the same route as yesterday, skirting the agora and following the wide avenue past the succession of splendid villas.

Fifty paces before the porticoed entrance to Alkibiades' villa he stopped and turned around to examine Corinna's resolve. 'Are you ready for this?' he asked, concerned. Staring intently into Sphax's sea-green eyes, she pleaded, 'I beg you both. Let me meet Alkibiades and Alexandra alone. Go back to the Athena!'

Ignoring her, the two of them strode on through the archway where they spotted the bell, clanging it several times. But there was no need, a servant seemed to have been placed there to usher them straight through to the courtyard with Corinna some paces behind. Sphax glimpsed peristyle gardens to his right and left before he saw the stooping figures of Alkibiades and Alexandra waiting to greet them. The instant he saw Alexandra's face he knew that something was wrong.

She was shaking her head in distress, her eyes flashing a warning.

'*Flee!*' he heard Corinna scream behind him. But it was too late.

As if from nowhere, Roman legionaries surrounded them. Within a heartbeat he and Idwal had half a score of spears pointed at them.

Behind him he heard muffled sounds as a legionary struggled to grab hold of Corinna. He paid for it with his life. Sphax heard his half-choked scream as her knife tore open his throat. Half-turning, Sphax's last sight was of her bounding for the archway before her second blade flashed, sinking deep into the forehead of the soldier barring her path. He watched as she leaped over his prone body, racing for the avenue to make good her escape. His heart leapt.

'After the bitch!' screamed Alkibiades, his gnarled stump of a face demented with rage. 'She must not escape. She murdered my son!'

Sphax glared with utter contempt at Alkibiades. 'You *stupid* old man! Your friends the Romans murdered Arsenios. Not pirates—'

In that instant Sphax received a forearm smash to his face that sent him sprawling on his back, staring up at three spearpoints.

'The gods will never forgive your betrayal, Alkibiades! May Artemis have mercy on your soul!' was all he managed before a full-blown kick to his head brought down a curtain of darkness.

* * *

As Sphax began to come round he realised he was being half-dragged, half-carried through the streets of Epidamnos by two legionaries. His head and cheek were throbbing fit to burst. He was facing backwards, so all he saw were twenty legionaries bringing up the rear. There was no sign of Idwal.

The legionaries were triarii. He'd killed enough of them on the Trebia to know more than he cared to know about the veteran legionaries that formed the third and last line of a Roman legion. Armed with tall spears and short swords, they carried oval shields and were protected by knee-length mailcoats, rounded Etruscan helmets and greaves on their left shins. The only difference between these men and those he'd faced on the Trebia was their age: the men he was staring at were at least ten years older. Battle-scarred and undoubtedly hardened by service as they were, Rome regarded them as fit only for garrison duty in some flea-bitten backwater of the republic. But judging from the henna-dyed horsehair plumes and trio of black feathers sprouting from every helmet, someone had taught them to take pride in their unit.

Staggering to his feet, despite the pain in his head he shrugged off his escorts, turned around and managed to walk under his own volition. Idwal was directly ahead, flanked by another score of spear-wielding men led by a centurion.

So the rumours were not lies after all. Queen Teuta had been right to warn them of a Roman garrison in Epidamnos, and judging from the numbers he'd so far observed, it consisted of a century of triarii, which meant they were up against eighty men. He didn't care for those odds.

At last they arrived at a ramshackle old villa near the city's northern gate that was being rebuilt and converted into a barracks. The columned entrance to the courtyard was in the process of being dismantled, no doubt to be replaced by guardhouses and a solid gate. As they entered the courtyard, Sphax could see that the extensive peristyle gardens that had once surrounded the courtyard were being grubbed up and cobbled over to provide an exercise yard. It seemed that Rome meant business, and was here to stay.

'Lock these two in a punishment cell,' barked the centurion, 'and bring me the key. I want the rest of you to search the streets for the woman who killed two of my men. Our honour has been defiled. Find the bitch!'

Prodded at spearpoint, they were led to a building that had once been the stables, converted into what the centurion had described as punishment cells. An old stable door was flung open and they were cast into a tiny cell that had once been a horse's stall. Judging from the indecent graffiti referring to numerous cocksuckers, horses hadn't been stabled there for some time, unless they'd mastered Latin.

Two uncomfortable-looking wooden sleeping benches topped by ancient mattresses thinly stuffed with straw were the only furniture the cell seemed to offer. A wooden pail, exuding a malodorous stench had been left between the benches. The stall's wooden doors had been replaced with a single, iron-barred door in a solid frame. As the triarius turned the key in the lock, both of them realised it would have been futile to throw their weight against it.

Once the men had left the stables, Idwal poured out a torrent of instruction in Punic, a language he'd barely mastered but was confident would be incomprehensible to Roman ears. 'We hide Corinna knives. Now!' Both men began frantically unstrapping the belts and sheaths Corinna had armed them with.

Desperately looking around for somewhere to secrete them, Sphax noticed the mattresses were badly torn and threadbare. 'The mattresses, Idwal! Push them deep into the straw.'

Once that was done, Idwal sat back and stared at him, continuing to mangle Punic. 'I Cavari gaesatae … selling sword to Queen Teuta. Have little Greek and no Latin. You much explaining! Think of good story. You speak good Greek … bad Latin.'

Sphax nodded, but all he could think about right now was Corinna. Would she be able to evade the legionaries searching for her? Had she been able to warn the Numidians there was a hue and cry out for her? His men were tough and resilient; with their help she might stand a better chance. Taking ship would be far too risky, the harbour would be the first place they would look. If not by ship, then how could they escape? on foot, by horse? The more he thought about it, the more he thought their chances were slim. But his thoughts were soon cut short by the sound of voices.

A legionary unlocked the door to their cell, and pointing a spear yelled, 'You! Come with me.' Sphax played dumb, but to no avail as the man grabbed the sleeve of his himation and yanked him from the bench.

A moment later he found himself staring at the centurion, who was seated on a wooden stool flanked by two of his men standing stiffly at attention. 'Kneel before Sempronius Falto,' ordered the triarius holding his sleeve. As the man forced him onto one knee, he'd little choice but to obey. Bowing his head at least hid his smile. Falto meant pigeon-toed. Hardly a Roman lineage of distinction, thought Sphax!

Yet centurion Falto possessed the most disconcerting face he'd ever seen. Or rather, it consisted of two faces, divided by a diagonal scar that ran from his left temple across the bridge of his nose, continued down his cheek, ending on the right side of his chin. To the left of the scar, the wound had either failed to heal

properly or become diseased, leaving the skin a permanent blotchy red. To the right of the scar his skin was
the unblemished pale olive he'd been born with.

The instant he'd seen the scar he'd feared for Idwal.
Only a Gaulish slashing blade was capable of inflicting
such a wound, and Falto looked like a man who
nurtured his grudges.

But Sphax noticed something else. Only the right
side of his face seemed alive with feeling and expression.
His left eye could only stare, unblinking, like the corner
of his rigid mouth, twisted into a permanent scowl
and frozen in the moment when the blade had cleaved
open his face. He'd seen such expressions of paralysis
on the faces of old men in Rome, men that limped and
dragged behind them twisted limbs, like shades that
had cheated death. Falto was indeed two-faced, but one
of those faces was already in Hades.

'You are accused of aiding the escape of a hostage
of Rome,' growled the centurion, 'which is an offence
punishable by death. What say you?'

Sphax acted dumb. Still half kneeling, he shook his
head and bleated, 'Non intellego ... quid dicis?'

'The bastard spoke perfect Greek not two hours
ago,' fumed the centurion. 'Fetch Aetius, he speaks
Greek, doesn't he?'

Aetius was eventually found and stood beside his
centurion, looking nervous and flustered. 'Ask him who
he is and what's his business in Epidamnos,' growled
Falto.

Aetius was slow to translate, giving Sphax time to gather his thoughts. 'I am Ramesses,' remembering the name of the only pharaoh he'd been taught, 'an Egyptian from Alexandria now in the service of Queen Teuta of Illyria. My orders were to escort her daughter safely to Epidamnos, nothing more.'

The centurion grunted impatiently when he'd heard Sphax's reply. 'Tell the cocksucker that aiding the escape of a hostage of Rome is punishable by death.'

Sphax glared at the man. 'But this is not Rome, centurion! Epidamnos is a Greek city, subject to Greek laws. Rome has no jurisdiction here and you have no right to detain me and the Gaul.' That earned him a vicious slap to the cheek.

Suddenly beside himself with rage, Falto yelled, 'Tell this piece of excrement that I will do as I please with him. I am the law around here!' Rising to his feet he screamed, 'Strip him and search every fold of that woman's tunic he's wearing, I want to see what the cocksucker's hiding.'

This is what Sphax had dreaded most. He would soon have a lot more explaining to do!

Another man joined the triarius who'd been standing over him, and together they began tugging and tearing at his himation. His ivory image of Artemis was the first thing to be ripped from his neck, followed by a leather purse he carried containing a few silver coins. Both items were tossed to the centurion to examine.

But once stripped to the waist, revealing his bare arms, there was no hiding the fugitivus sign branded on his right forearm. And that's when Tiberius Falto lost all control of himself, descending into a demented madness.

'You're nothing more than a filthy Roman slave!'

ELEVEN

Sphax had never received a beating quite like it. As a slave in Rome he'd received many. Survival had taught him to cover his face with both hands, draw his knees up to protect his belly and clasp his elbows tightly over his ribcage. But this offered little protection from the frenzied monster who was now raining down kicks and blows upon every part of his helpless body.

As the pain became excruciating, his mind slowly sank into a pit of darkness. Just before the numb blackness was beginning to engulf him a voice screamed in his head; 'Fight back! *Fight!*'

His legs and arms were already so badly bruised they felt like molten lead, whilst his chest was on fire, ribs smashed to a pulp. With one last desperate effort he somehow managed to entangle a foot around Falto's ankles, and with the last of his ebbing strength, launched a heel against the centurion's shin. It was one of the last things he remembered, but with satisfaction, for he heard the bastard cry out in pain and sprawl onto his backside.

As Falto rose unsteadily to his feet, Sphax could only look on in horror as the centurion unsheathed his sword, ready to plunge it into his breast.

He owed his life to Aetius and another triarius. By now the centurion was in a state of demonic frenzy. Somehow they managed to restrain him, drag him away and prevent him from committing murder.

* * *

For the next few days Sphax felt barely alive. Unable to speak or move, he lay on the mattress with his eyes closed, but without the relief of sleep. The unremitting pain he felt in every limb of his shattered body denied him this mercy. The worst of his pain was in his chest, which burned with an unbearable fire, causing his every breath to rasp like a death rattle. He doubted whether he had a rib left unbroken.

Before he grew tired of the pastime, Falto enjoyed the satisfaction of slinging the bowl of pigswill they were fed with at Idwal. But once he realised the Cavari was prepared to pick up every last mouthful from the floor, the game lost its charms.

Idwal kept Sphax alive. Swallowing was painful, and chewing impossible, but somehow his friend forced him to drink, and after a day or so, pushed moistened mouthfuls of bread into his mouth and commanded him to eat.

On the third day, when at last he could bear to be touched, with a gentleness that surprised him, Idwal examined every limb of his body, checking carefully for broken bones. On the fourth day he managed to sleep for a few hours and on the fifth, could even whisper a few words in response to a question.

Throughout his ordeal of pain, it was as if Idwal breathed life back into him, renewing and restoring his broken body and soul. Just as he'd kept Sphax's body alive with bread and water, Idwal rekindled his spirit with words of courage, and above all, hope.

Sphax remembered the night Idwal described Plato's cave allegory. He knew the story from one of Elpis' lessons from childhood, but had never really understood it. As a boy, metaphysics had bored him at the best of times, so he'd probably been half asleep the afternoon Elpis tried to explain Plato's insights into the human condition. But something struck a chord with Idwal's telling of the allegory that evening. Something urgent and profound, something that touched upon his present state of mind taught him that only bitter experience could prepare a receptive mind for wisdom.

Idwal described the prisoners as chained in a fixed position, so all they could see on the cave wall in front of them were shadows cast by a fire burning behind them; a fire they could not see or comprehend. In front of the prisoners, Idwal described, was a wall that hid the identity of the people who walked behind it carrying puppets. 'Just as showmen have screens in front of them at which they work their puppets,' he'd quoted from the master.

All the prisoners would ever see were the shadows cast by the puppets. Even the conversations of the puppeteers echoing around the cave the prisoners attributed to shadows on the wall. For the prisoners, these shadows were the only reality they would ever know or understand; much less appreciate that these shadows were only tokens and symbols from the *real* world outside the cave, gifted to them by the puppeteers. The living were condemned to little more than a shadow of a shadow.

'Only the true philosopher, through a lifetime of probing and questioning the meaning of forms, can see through the shadows and reason his way out of the cave and into the radiant light of reality. A monster such as Tiberius Falto will remain chained in the depths of the cave for all eternity, and for that he is deserving of our pity. But we also are deserving of pity, if, even for a moment, we accept Falto's shades and shadows as a measure of our reality.

'It strikes me there is a further analogy to be drawn that speaks to your present condition. Falto has made you a prisoner and chained you to pain and suffering in a cave of his own making. The fire is like your searing pain, casting shadows in the darkness; the only reality you can presently feel and see. But as your strength returns and your body heals, the shadows will surely fade. You, my friend, are blessed with an abundance of courage, fortitude and intelligence, so cast your mind forward to a reality where shadows are banished.

Where your true spirit will never be bound by walls and iron bars!'

There was one shadow, however, that would haunt Sphax in the weeks to come, no matter how hard he tried to banish it from his restless sleep. That shadow came in the form of centurion Tiberius Falto.

* * *

Out of guilt or compassion—Idwal could not decide—it was Aetius who brought them food twice a day and emptied their pail. Giving up the pretence of Punic, Idwal was able to draw him into conversation in Greek and glean much information. Twice a day Idwal gave Sphax a bulletin on the progress, or lack of it, of the patrols searching for Corinna. To their intense relief, on the fourth day after her escape from Alkibiades villa, Idwal learned from Aetius that the search had been called off.

A week after his beating, Sphax felt well enough to sit up on his bench and take part in whispered discussions. His chest still burned, and the slightest movement caused pain, but his body was slowly healing and he was managing to eat the bowls of the filthy slop they were being fed with. Above all, he was beginning to sleep well, and as Idwal constantly reminded him, sleep was his best medicine.

All their night-time conversations centered on conjecture about Corinna's escape. Aetius had never mentioned Numidians, or anyone else in connection with their search for her. Idwal was convinced she'd warned them and they'd planned the escape between them. Increasingly, Sphax came to believe this was the more likely explanation. It also eased his anxiety for her safety on the journey. His Numidians were resourceful and armed to the teeth with javelins, and Corinna would be in possession of the swords they'd left behind at the Athena.

But there probability ended and pure speculation took over. 'They would need horses,' Idwal mused, 'but they would not be difficult to acquire in the farmlands that surround the city.'

'Believe me,' whispered Sphax, regretting his instinctive smile, 'Hannon can *acquire* anything he sets his mind to!'

'Then given horses,' Idwal continued, 'there's only one place they would head for.'

'Rhizon, you mean.'

'Exactly! Where else could they seek help?'

'Help for what, Idwal?' gasped Sphax. 'Even if she can persuade her mother to help, Teuta does not have the resources to storm Epidamnos and rescue us! Its walls are strong and manned by the city's militia and garrisoned by a century of Roman triarii. Queen Teuta will surely counsel caution, and I'm praying Corinna is wise enough to follow her advice.'

'Since when has Corinna ever listened to her mother's advice?'

With grudging irritation Sphax knew he was right. 'I pray she is listening right now, Idwal, for I remember

Corinna telling me that Epidamnos is only a four day ride along the coast. Which means they must have arrived by now.'

Idwal remained silent for a while. After dark it was pitch-black in their cell, so Sphax could only imagine Idwal's expression, but knowing his friend so well it wasn't difficult to picture that

frowning face of his, lost in thought.

At last Idwal spoke. 'In one of our infrequent discussions between bouts of pleasure—'

Sphax had to stop himself laughing. The pain of laughter far outweighed its pleasure. Even so, Idwal heard a strangled chortle from his friend before he continued, 'Caeria told me she possessed ten lemboï and could muster five hundred warriors. More than enough to devastate all Roman shipping in the northern waters of the Adria. That's why she agreed to the alliance with Hannibal. But she was astute enough to realise she would also need Demetrius' help in the long run ... and the support of Macedon, of course.'

Idwal paused for a moment. 'Ten lemboï with five hundred men on board, launched swiftly at that harbour gate would be able to storm it easily. It's just a question of coordination and timing. Dusk or first light would be best. Just think about it, Sphax.'

He did think about it. But what didn't bear thinking about was the certainty that Sempronius Falto would have them both executed before an Illyrian came within sight of the Roman garrison. Sphax raised his fears with Idwal.

'Then we must make ourselves inviolable,' was all Idwal would say.

It always felt comforting to ignore their present incarceration and speculate about a possible rescue, but Sphax was under no illusions. Their spirits might not be bound by walls and iron bars, but their bodies were, and Sphax's wasn't working particularly well at the moment. He changed the subject.

'I'm more interested in your bouts of pleasure with ... Caeria? I must say that Corinna and I were surprised by your ... dalliance.'

Somehow he knew Idwal would not be offended by the enquiry, and indeed, he laughed. 'Surely you've learned by now, my friend, that it's insulting to the gods to refuse beauty and pleasure when it's handed to you on a couch. And believe me, my friend, the queen is still beautiful, neither has age dimmed her appetites ...'

* * *

Sphax was woken by the sound of Idwal scratching another Greek iota on the wall of their squalid cell. He counted them carefully; twenty eight days. Almost another week had passed without sight or sound of centurion Falto, and he and Idwal had gleaned little from Aetius that week.

They were beginning to take on the appearance of street beggars with disheveled hair and beards that were colonising more of their faces each day. But the worst of it was their filthy garments, which were beginning to stink as badly as the slop pail. As endless days dragged into empty weeks, it seemed as if they'd been destined to rot in this stinking hole for all eternity.

But Aetius was talkative that morning. After handing over two bowls of puls and a jug of water, he told them the centurion had a visitor last night.

'And who might that have been?' yawned Idwal. 'A Roman consul?'

'Of course not,' frowned the triarius, sarcasm lost on him, 'it was that old bastard you two were going to meet when we took you ... what's 'is name—'

'—Alkibiades, you mean,' suggested Idwal. Sphax's ears pricked up.

'Yes, that's the bastard, and they were closeted together for half the night.'

'What's going on, Aetius?' Idwal persisted. 'You must have heard something ... there are always rumours?'

Aetius lowered his voice and assumed a comically conspiratorial expression, 'They say that a ship from Brundisium anchored yesterday with an envoy on board with a message from Rome. From Rome, no less!' Aetius' excitement was far from contagious. 'Something's afoot. I know it. I've never seen the centurion in this mood before. He looks ... happy!'

When Aetius and his two jailors left, Idwal turned to him: 'What do you make of it?

Sphax was staring at his bowl of puls, which until now had consisted of stale salted cereals, but this morning contained pieces of chicken and vegetables. He should have been overjoyed. 'Something's wrong ...'

Idwal glanced at his own bowl and smiled. 'We are being fattened up, my friend. But to what end remains a mystery.' They didn't have long to wait for the mystery to be revealed.

Surrounded by triarii, the sinister presence of Sempronius Falto resumed his seat in the stables later that morning, commanding them to bring forth his prisoners.

Sphax's first alarm was that Aetius was not amongst the guards accompanying Falto. Second was the centurion's attempt at high-flown Latin, and third was the sickeningly smug expression on the bastard's hideous face.

'I see that I was right to spare you. Yesterday,' Falto was saying, 'the venerable Alkibiades, elder of Epidamnos, received an envoy and written orders from Praetor Marcus Rufus, high commissioner for harbours in Brundisium. It began with affable felicitations and thanks to the gods for the continued good health of the leader of the Epidamnions.' From the rolling of his eyes, Sphax could see that even the centurion had lost patience with the pace of his own narrative.

'Rufus told us to look out for three bastards who would be working together. One was the daughter of that witch, Teuta. The other two cocksuckers were deserters from Hannibal's army. One of which has a considerable price on his head—a lucrative reward for the fugitivari who brings him in.' Falto couldn't resist a lurid grin of triumph.

'According to this rich bastard in Rome—some cocksucker called Gaius Lucilus—his ex-slave is an eighteen year old Numidian with a fugitivus sign branded on his right forearm. The other we're to look out for is some shit-faced savage from Gaul who answers to the name of Idwal. Praetor Rufus would dearly like to interrogate these two about Hannibal's army. And he says there's a promotion in it for the man who hands them in. Know any cocksuckers who answer to those descriptions?' asked Falto, his men compliantly roaring with laughter.

It was cold in the stable that morning, but the icy chill that was engulfing the pit of Sphax's stomach had nothing to do with the season. The game was up. It was over. Once in Brundisium they would both be tortured before they begged for death to put an end to their suffering.

Defiantly, eyeball to eyeball, Sphax met the centurion's malicious glare, his expression alive with contempt. For the first time he spoke in Latin. 'Allow me to introduce myself, centurion. I am Sphax, son of Navaras, Prince of Numidia.' With an elegant flourish of his hand he gestured towards his friend. 'And you are quite right, this indeed is Idwal, but he is no ordinary Gaul, he's the chief of the Cavari who butchered Rome's legions on river Trebia some months ago.

'What we are certainly *not*, is deserters! If you ever use such foul language in our presence I swear I will kill you. And if you are to receive your reward and promotion, you better see to it that not a hair on our valuable heads is harmed before you hand us over to the praetor.'

Sphax was relieved to see that Idwal was smiling. But the centurion wasn't. 'Alkibiades is finding a captain and crew for our quinquereme,' he growled. 'We sail for Brundisium tomorrow.' Rising from the stool he barked; 'Put these turds in chains and slave collars. And clean them up ... they stink of piss!'

* * *

Aetius, accompanied by two guards handed over their washed garments at dawn the following morning. By stripping to their loincloths to remove the simple tunics they'd borrowed, Sphax hoped the guards would not feel the need to search them again, so there was every chance they might get away with secreting the daggers beneath their himations. The daggers offered the only hope left to them of either fighting back, or a swift way out of this life. Sphax had no intention of being dragged in chains before Gaius Lucilus! But he would wait for him in Hades, if need be.

When Aetius left, they dug the daggers out from the straw mattresses and strapped them over their shoulders so the sheaths rested against their chests, checking each other carefully to make certain that nothing was visible. But the worst was yet to come.

Shortly after congratulating one another on hiding the daggers, four triarii burst into their cell carrying chains and slave collars. Sphax had felt the bite of the iron collar on more than one occasion, but for Idwal this was a new degradation, one he was ill-prepared for. For a while he resisted, until Sphax placed a hand on his shoulder and spoke gently in Greek. 'The puppeteers are sending you a shadow to experience, my friend, and a slave collar can never bind your spirit.'

Sphax was relieved they'd been given collars, and not the full restraint, which included bands around the wrists, restricting movement of hands and arms. Shackled together by an iron chain threaded through a loop in their collars, the two of them were led off and dragged through the streets of Epidamnos to the harbour below the city walls.

To Sphax's eyes the harbour looked exactly as it had done a month ago, except there was a bustle of activity around the re-floated quinquereme tied up against a stone quay as oarsmen, triarii and provisions were being loaded into her cavernous belly. There was no sign of the Roman vessel that had brought Praetor Marcus Rufus' envoy to Epidamnos.

He'd only stepped on board a ship of war once before, and that was after the murder of his parents. Shuddering at the memory, the irony was not lost on him that once again he was sailing to Italia with a slave collar around his neck, but this time his fate would be far worse than slavery.

As they were prodded on to the quay to await their turn to board, Idwal turned to him, 'How are your ribs and legs? We've been confined for a month and you're not fully healed.'

'Holding up,' he replied, grinning at his friend's concern to hide the fact he'd found the walk to the harbour an ordeal. After his Latin speech of defiance in the face of the centurion, they'd spoken only Greek to one another. 'Have you counted the number of triarii Falto is taking with him?'

Idwal nodded. 'Sixty seems rather excessive to me.'

'It leaves the city's garrison rather thin on the ground.'

'If Teuta descends on Epidamnos with ten lemboï, she'll have easy pickings.'

'By the gods, I hope she does!' he said with feeling, absently searching for the goddess's ivory image before he remembered that Falto had ripped it from his neck.

'It looks as if Alkibiades has provided the oarsmen and crew: those men carrying cushions for their arses look like Greeks to me.'

'Only he would have the resources to provide this many men,' agreed Sphax as he felt the prod of a triarius spear on his back ordering them to climb the gangway up to the deck. Made from slender planks of cedar, the deck was little more than a raised platform, eighty paces long above the banks of oarsmen seated in the belly of the vessel's hull. Idwal had told him that a quinquereme had three hundred oarsmen in three tiers either side of the vessel, the hefty oars of the top tiers manned by two rowers, whilst the shortest, by a single oarsman. This meant the belly of the vessel contained thirty banks of ten oarsmen. How was this possible? thought Sphax. From the glimpses he'd caught through open hatches and companionways, it looked impossibly cramped beneath his feet.

Sempronius Falto was beckoning their guards to hurry them forward to the prow of the vessel, above which a great curved neck rose in fading red paint. The centurion looked anxious and impatient, barking orders at all those surrounding him, including a couple of sailors and a grey-haired old salt who looked as if he might be the captain.

'I see we have a welcoming committee,' muttered Idwal.

'Ah … the busy life of a slave of Rome!' To which his friend responded with a hollow laugh.

Looking them up and down, the centurion snapped, 'I want these two kept up here, out in the open where I can keep an eye on them. Tie rope to the ends of their chains and fix them to something solid.' Looking around, their guards seemed confused, as if rope was hard to come by on ship. 'And you, captain, in the name of the gods get us underway. I don't want to spend a night at sea … I'll personally beat those bastard oarsmen of yours if they don't get us to Brundisium today.'

'That may not be possible—'

'—I don't want to hear your excuses ... set the sails or whatever you have to do!' yelled Falto. 'But get us to Brundisium today.'

It was evident the centurion was a reluctant sailor who feared a night at sea. Sphax offered up a quick prayer to Poseidon to send them a tempest rough enough to make Sempronius Falto as sick as a dog. Hearing that their chains were to be fixed to hemp rope had given him a glimmer of hope. Rope could be cut. But chained together as they were, the deck of a quinquereme left few options as to an escape route. Neither of them could swim.

After their guards had done their best with ropes tied to iron cleats on either side of the deck, he and Idwal found they'd been cut enough slack to stand, or on their knees, slide a pace or two sideways. At least they could reach the ropes with their knives. But this offered little more than a vain hope.

At last the moorings were released and the great vessel cast off, drifting on the ebb tide into the deeper waters of the harbour. As if with one voice, three hundred men began chanting as their oars slid into the Adria, pulling on the fulcrum of thole pins to propel them through its waters. With a stiff north-easterly breeze blowing that morning, the crew were already struggling to raise a mast carrying a square-rigged sail, whilst a second, smaller sail on a mast angled forward, was being raised above their heads.

As the headland of Epidamnos slowly receded into the distance, Sphax grew tired of watching the antics of Sempronius Falto. His men had brought a great chair aboard for him, placing it in the stern behind the ship's captain serving the steering oars. There, upon his throne, surrounded by half a score of his men, he watched as the man ranted and berated. Mercifully, Sphax heard not a word, but knew with certainty that sluggish winds, lazy oarsmen and a recalcitrant captain were being cursed for their failures and negligence of his orders.

Sphax slumped to the deck, gathered his garments around him to garner what little warmth they offered, and closed his eyes. He must have fallen asleep, for he felt Idwal's hand gripping his shoulder.

'Wake up, Sphax,' Idwal urged, 'there's something I must see! This cursed chain prevents me from standing without you beside me.'

Getting to his feet, immediately he sensed something was wrong. Falto was ranting at the captain as more of his men appeared on deck. All were staring at something astern of them.

Then Sphax saw them. Still at a great distance, but there was no mistaking the square sails of two vessels. And judging from their steady course, they were fast closing in on the quinquereme.

TWELVE

For the first time since they'd been forced at spearpoint into that squalid cell, Sphax felt a glimmer of hope. But it was a glimmer that could easily be dashed. At this distance it was impossible to tell whether the vessels were Illyrian or not. Most likely they were Greek warships sent by Alkibiades to escort Falto into Brundisium.

But Sphax took some comfort from the fact that the sighting had struck fear and consternation into Sempronius Falto and his men, who might now be called upon to fight as marines; a role they were ill-trained for.

If they were being pursued, any seasoned commander would put his faith in the captain and crew to evade their pursuers and reach safety. But the centurion had lost all reason that morning, and blinded by seething rage, raved against all around him. Sanity was only skin deep with Falto.

Sphax's eyesight being poor—an inherited Barca weakness—Idwal was his eyes. After staring at the vessels for what seemed like an age, he finally turned to him, wide-eyed and excited. 'A black serpent is emblazoned on their sails.'

Instantly he remembered Teuta telling him the serpent god, Illyrios, was sacred to the Ardiaei. A thrill suddenly shot through him. 'Then we are saved! Those vessels are Illyrian. Do you think the queen and Corinna are at the helm?'

'It's possible. But don't count on rescue just yet, my friend,' Idwal cautioned. 'There is the small matter of a Roman quinquereme to be boarded first!'

The vessels were closing so fast that even Sphax could now make out the black serpent on their billowing sails, straining to catch every breath of the stiffening breeze.

'By the gods, Sphax ... they're keles!' Idwal shouted excitedly. 'Remember? The vessels Teuta was constructing for Macedon. They must have worked night and day to get two of them ready for sea.'

'I also remember Corinna telling me they're bigger and more powerful than lemboï. I think Falto's going to have a real fight on his hands,' observed Sphax, gazing once more at the man as he ranted and raved at the captain. 'What in the name of the gods is he playing at?'

Idwal shuffled towards one of the crew hauling on a sheet. 'What's the argument about?' After looking over his shoulder to check no one was watching, the man rolled his eyes in despair. 'That ugly Roman bastard's a shit-faced coward! He thinks we can outrun pirates. Hades will give up its dead before that happens!' The man spat, glaring at Falto. 'Our captain, Lycon, is a Spartan. And if he says we fight ... we fight! Those black-hearted devils don't take prisoners. If they board us they'll feed us to the fish!'

So that was it. Sempronius Falto was raving that if the oarsmen rowed faster, the wind blew harder and Lycon steered a truer course, they could outrun the Illyrians. Denying the evidence of his own eyes, along with reason, Falto had also lost his nerve.

Light and sleek, keles were much smaller and lower in the water, with two tiers of oarsmen either side of the hull and a square sail just as great as the quinquereme's. The pirate queen was closing in for the kill. Flight was not an option.

Sphax stared in disbelief as the captain suddenly thrust the steering oars into a crewman's hands and leaping at Falto, wrestled him to the ground, hands gripping the centurion's throat. Several triarii quickly intervened, roughly hauling the man aside and surrounding him with spears. But he could see the captain pleading with the triarii, gesturing and begging them to listen to him. Slowly the spears were lowered, and he could see they were now listening intently.

Startled by this turn of events, Sphax turned to Idwal. 'What's going on?'

'I think the captain's trying to tell them that if they want to survive this day, they'll have to fight,'

Idwal guessed. 'He's trying to persuade them to take this grand old lady into battle.'

Then the unthinkable happened. A broken Sempronius Falto was led back to his grand chair in the stern at spearpoint! His men had finally deserted him.

Now all around them chaos was unleashed. Orders were barked and crewmen raced to take down sails. More triarii poured on to the deck, this time carrying spare shields and spears. Once the quinquereme was stripped of her sails, her aging timbers began to creak and groan as Lycon slowly brought her about to face her enemies at last. Her massive bronze ram was about to show its teeth.

As helpless spectators, at least Sphax and Idwal now had the best seats in the circus to witness the fight that was about to begin. But it was unnerving to think that beneath them, cutting through the water just below the bow wave was that deadly, triple-bladed ram, cast from solid bronze: it was almost three paces long and weighed more than a stallion. And they would be the first to feel its bite.

Once it became clear the quinquereme was coming about, the keles changed course, widening the gap between them, forcing their enemy to choose a single target. With the advantage of the wind, both vessels were bearing down on them at an alarming speed. But what was worse, the northerly vessel seemed bent on a head-on collision course with a Roman ram.

When disaster seemed inevitable, Sphax screamed, 'Brace yourself!' and they flung themselves to the deck, clinging to the chain for dear life. But to his utter astonishment, the expected sound of bronze ripping through wooden timbers was replaced by cries of wounded men. Swiveling around, he saw that several triarii had been struck by arrows. Some, in their death-throes, had fallen over the latticed railings above the gunnels into the seething waters that narrowly separated the two vessels. Sphax's forehead felt damp from the bow-spray of the keles as she'd surged past.

With nerves of iron, the Illyrian helmsman had left it until the last heart-stopping moment before hauling on a steering oar to clear the ram. Even more impressive was the sight of twenty-four oars being raised as one to avoid them smashing into the quinquereme's heavier oars.

There was no time to ponder near misses. As clear water opened up between the sterns of the two vessels, he caught sight of the southerly keles making her run at them. Judging from the raised oars and angled approach, Sphax could see the intention was to smash her curved prow into the rearmost oars of the quinquereme.

But the quinquereme's diehard Spartan was equal to it. Hauling with all his might on the steerboard oar, Lycon ploughed a southerly course, narrowly saving his oarsmen. Sphax felt a juddering impact on the stern of the quinquereme, but no serious damage was inflicted. Nevertheless, the decks were beginning to be littered with dead and wounded, struck by Illyrian arrows. More triarii appeared to fill their ranks.

Once again Lycon handed his oars to a crewman, but this time he strutted the deck like a true strategos, yelling orders and exhorting his men to fight. Picking up a spare shield he demonstrated the position he wanted them to take up: crouching, right knee on the deck, oval shield covering their body and exposed left shin protected by their bronze greaves. When a score of them took up this position either side of the deck, he begrudged them a grunt of satisfaction and returned to his steering oars.

Poseidon now answered Sphax's former prayer. Within the time it took to turn her aging timbers around to face the Illyrians, the breeze had stiffened and the waves of the Adria broiled, flecked by foaming white crests.

Whilst the lumbering Roman giant was struggling to turn about, the Illyrians had not been idle. Lowering sails, they too had turned about and steering an easterly course, the oarsmen had overtaken them and put half a mile between themselves and their prey. Sphax marveled at the speed and agility of these craft. Lycon had been outsmarted. Once more the keles had the wind and the initiative.

Again the two keles closed rapidly, but this time a quinquereme's breadth apart, intending to use the wind and their skilled oarsmen to smash into their enemy's oars, rendering her dead in the water. At the last moment, two things happened at once.

Lycon hauled on a steering oar to swerve the great ram into the bow of the northerly keles, and anticipating Illyrian tactics, Sphax heard him frantically relaying orders below deck for a hundred and eighty oars to be raised to avert disaster. But it was a bluff.

The Spartan had done exactly as the Illyrians intended. With raised oars, in the teeth of the squalling wind the quinquereme would rapidly lose momentum and come to a standstill. Worse still, she would lose steerage, floundering like a drifting log at the mercy of the boiling waves. This time the keles were closing in for the kill.

At the stately approach of the quinquereme, the keles parted, swerving north and south, the northerly vessel easily avoiding the clumsy lunge of Lycon's ram. Sphax couldn't believe how manoeuvrable these vessels were! In an instant the impediment of sails was removed as the keles circled upwind like hungry wolves to come alongside their helpless victim.

Paralysed by the sight of two keles bearing down on him from the wrong direction, Lycon failed to order the oars to be lowered. It was a mistake that almost proved fatal.

Once again the air was thick with arrows, but now there were new sounds. First came the grating sound of iron grappling hooks biting against the latticed railings of the quinquereme, next came the fearful battle cries of warriors hoisting themselves up the ropes to board the stricken vessel. Soon there was a score of iron hooks binding her fast to the keles flanked either side of her hull.

Lycon was faced with an impossible dilemma. If his crew lowered their oars, the Illyrians would remove or destroy them, even use them to clamber aboard, but leaving them raised meant scores more points of purchase for the grappling irons. So for now they remained aloft.

Helpless and impotent, all Sphax and Idwal could do was lie flat on the deck to avoid the shafts singing through the air and pray the Illyrians didn't mistake them for the vessel's crew. In the heat of battle it was sometimes difficult to distinguish friend from foe.

'Let's cut the ropes, Idwal … whilst we have the chance!' Reaching inside his himation, Sphax drew the dagger from its sheath and began slicing at the rope where it was tied to the chain. Soon they were free, not that it would do them much good.

Already smeared with blood, the deck had become a frenzied battlefield with men slicing, hacking and thrusting amidst the shrieks of the wounded and the screaming oaths of desperate men, locked together in the throes of life or death. Protected only by Phrygian helmets and small round shields, the Illyrians were suffering at the hands of the heavily armed triarii, hefting great oval shields and thigh length mail coats. In a close-quarter fight like this, the Illyrians' long curved swords were no match for the legionaries' short stubby blades, designed for stabbing and thrusting in a tight corner.

Two things saved the triarii. Towering above the keles, the quinquereme's gunnels were exhausting to climb whilst clinging to a swaying rope and gripping a shield. No matter how many grappling hooks stuck fast, it took time and a heroic effort to gain the deck and join the fight, so at no time could the Illyrians build up the decisive numbers they needed to sway the fight.

But it was Lycon who truly saved the day. Wielding shield and spear, somehow he shamed the last of Falto's men cowering amongst the oarsmen to climb the companionways and join the fight. On the deck above, the fight was still finely poised, but the appearance of reinforcements turned the scales. Faced with such overwhelming numbers, the Illyrians reluctantly fell back, sliding back down ropes to the safety of their vessels.

By now the triarii that had fought off the boarding parties were so exhausted they could do little to hamper the Illyrians retreat. Even the courageous Lycon could not persuade his reinforcements to launch a counter attack. They didn't have the stomach for it. So the Illyrians were able to withdraw unmolested, taking some of their wounded with them.

Sphax counted twelve Illyrian and eight triarii dead, spread-eagled along the length of the bloodied deck. 'What now?' he asked, finding it difficult to keep the despair out of his voice.

'We lie low, and fool them into thinking we're still tethered to the ropes.'

At the height of this desperate fight, they'd talked of making a run for it. But chained together and bound by their iron collars, they would have broken their necks climbing down a grappling rope. But now, even that faint hope had been extinguished. To add to their misery, it began to rain. Before long they were shivering and soaked to the skin.

'I can't see the centurion,' muttered Idwal through chattering teeth.

The last Sphax had seen of him he was seated on his throne, a broken man, head in his hands. But Idwal was right. Looking around, he was nowhere to be seen, and the chair was empty. 'He's probably skulking below deck. May he rot there!'

Despite the cold, sodden garments and their hopeless situation, Idwal managed a grin. 'It's not over yet, my friend. This is a setback, not a defeat. I know Caeria. The Illyrians will be back!'

When the last of their warriors and wounded had descended the ropes to safety, the keles had used their oars against the quinquereme's hull to push themselves free and put clear water between themselves and the enemy.

Taking up his place at the helm once more, Lycon ordered the oars to be lowered and the vessel finally lumbered forward under steerage. Idwal remarked that Lycon had not asked his deck crew to raise the sails, which meant he'd given up all hope of using the wind to reach Brundisium. Their easterly course suggested his intention was to limp back to Epidamnos. That city was preferable to the welcome they would receive in

Brundisium, but it only felt like a stay of execution to Sphax.

After throwing the slain Illyrians overboard, the triarii carried their own wounded below deck. Gathered around Lycon, only a few of them remained on deck, the rest having taken the opportunity to shelter from the driving rain on the benches below. All eyes were now riveted on the two keles just ahead of them.

Once they'd drawn clear of the drifting quinquereme, the keles had taken up station a hundred paces off either beam and fifty paces ahead, matching the quinquereme's oars, stroke for stroke. Sphax guessed that keeping pace with a vessel with one hundred and eighty oars would present problems for vessels with fewer than fifty, but Lycon was saving his oarsmen's strength for the next attack, so the quinquereme barely crawled along under steerage. Without sails emblazoned with the sacred black Illyrios, the identity of the keles remained hidden. From what Sphax remembered of his conversations with Corinna, keles were widely in use with Greek cities throughout the Adria and Aegean seas, so all a neutral would see was an aged Roman quinquereme escorted by two smaller scouts.

Through the lashing rain and the murky afternoon gloom, Sphax peered ahead. He thought he saw something on the horizon. 'Is that the coastline ahead?'

Idwal stared. 'It could be,' he said, unsure. 'In this light it's difficult to tell. In any case, we won't reach Epidamnos for—'

He never finished the sentence. In that moment the two keles suddenly raised sails, turned about, and started to bear down on them at great speed. Struggling to their feet, he and Idwal had just enough time to witness this astonishing sight before they were violently flung to the deck as its aging timbers careered sideways, threatening to slide them overboard. It was as if the vessel had struck a reef. Only by clinging on to one another and retying the rope to the end of the chain did they manage to survive.

But it was the sound filling his ears that Sphax would never forget. When they were constructing their camp beside the Padus, he'd watched two woodsmen cut down a giant cedar in a forest where they were harvesting timber. As it fell, it was as if the tree itself cried out in its death throes as it crashed to the ground, bringing down lesser trees in its path. Now he heard the same sickening sound of splintering wood, smashed and ripped asunder.

All along there had been a third keles beyond the horizon, out of sight, awaiting her moment to pounce. Now she had raced to catch them unawares, smashing into the larboard oars of the quinquereme, rendering the vessel useless and dead in the water.

This time the boarders had the advantage over the triarii. The third keles had ground to a halt amidst the splintered wreckage of oars, directly below the quinquereme's hull. With lightning speed, scores of grappling irons had been cast, and now Illyrian warriors were climbing aboard in twos and threes. The tables had been turned.

Now the Illyrians had the numbers to charge forward, quickly overcoming the startled triarii that had stayed on deck. Any triarii attempting to join their comrades above deck were quickly dispatched. To their bravery, many tried, but all were wounded or slain in the attempt, and the companionways soon became choked with Roman dead.

Sphax watched as the valiant Lycon sank to his knees, surrendering his vessel. He was relieved to see him left unharmed at the helm. Behind him, scores more grappling hooks were biting on the stern rails where the other two keles had come alongside.

There were now perhaps fifty Illyrians striding the deck, bolting hatches and guarding the companionways. There could be no escape for the men trapped below, and Sphax could only imagine the carnage and panic splintering oars had wreaked on the hapless oarsmen, packed together on the benches below.

Sphax and Idwal had not moved since they'd been thrown to the deck and narrowly escaped being thrown overboard. Everything had happened so quickly all they could do was watch and wonder. Lying flat on the deck they were virtually invisible, and believing the prow to be deserted, none of the Illyrians had thought to check it or the companionway leading to it. It was time to make their presence known to their rescuers.

Hastily untying the rope that had saved them from drowning, and wary of standing on unsteady feet, they began crawling down the deck on their hands and knees. They hadn't gone far before Sphax stopped, his heart leaping in sheer joy. Corinna had climbed aboard and was standing beside Drust. Scampering up the ropes behind them his three loyal Numidians quickly formed a guard around her.

Corinna was holding his dragon sword aloft to attract everyone's attention. He felt sure she was about to order a thorough search of the decks below, the obvious place to detain prisoners. With a profound sense of relief, Sphax begun to smile at the irony. Here they were, not seventy paces from their saviours, yet no one was aware they were safe and unharmed.

But someone was only too aware of their presence. At that moment he was staring up at them from an unguarded companionway.

In fact, in his fevered mind, his prisoners had never left his brooding thoughts since he'd gone below after the enemy first boarded. He'd known all along they couldn't rely on the Spartan to save them. Especially after he'd turned his own men against him. But now he was standing beside his faithful lieutenants, Marcus and Antonio Sabinus. He could always rely on them.

Sempronius Falto would save the day. Only he had a plan! Only he would be the hero of the hour. Falto drew his sword and marched up the unguarded companionway.

Sphax gasped in terror at the sight of the centurion and his guards emerging from the darkness below. What new horror was this?

THIRTEEN

'Get to your feet,' snarled Falto, yanking the chain that bound them so viciously it left them choking as they struggled unsteadily to their feet. Standing behind the two of them, swordpoint pricking Sphax's side below his aching ribs, Falto ordered Marcus and Antonio Sabinus to take up station either side of them.

Yet nobody noticed them. In the general mayhem, boarders were still assembling at the stern of the vessel sixty paces distant, where Corinna was busily organising parties to begin searching below deck.

It would never do to ignore Sempronius Falto, especially in his present deranged state of mind.

'Look to me!' he screamed in exasperation. 'Look to me! ... you shit-faced bastards who dare ignore me! I, Sempronius Falto have seen through your games. If the daughter of the pirate witch wants to see her lover alive, she'll do exactly as I say.'

Falto now had the attention he craved. Striding up the deck, Corinna, Drust and the Numidians stared aghast at this unexpected threat.

'That's close enough,' Falto commanded, switching the blade to Sphax's throat to ensure compliance.

'We will do you the courtesy of listening,' said Corinna, brazenly grinning at Sphax before adding; 'after which I will kill you and feed your filthy carcass to the fish! Our intention was to capture this vessel and use it to sack Epidamnos. It is *you* that has played our little games. As for your prisoners ... they are of no consequence.'

'You lie, bitch!' yelled Falto. 'You lie!'

Corinna laughed, defiantly. 'Have it your way, centurion,' she bluffed with a shrug, appearing to turn her back and gesturing the men to walk away.

Ever since his beating, a shadow of fear had entered Sphax's soul, weighing on his spirit like some leaden anchor. Somehow, hearing Corinna's laughter and rejoicing in her courageous defiance made his soul sing once more. The spell was broken. Suddenly he felt free ... to choose between the light of reality or eternal shadow. Falto was a monster. He must die.

'*Wait!*' Falto screamed. 'You will not come between me and my greatest triumph,' he raved. 'I will deliver my prisoners to Praetor Marcus Rufus and receive my reward. Sempronius Falto will not be denied ...'

Sphax stopped listening, every faculty stirring into life with a clarity he hadn't experienced for weeks. He considered his options. Should they use the daggers? They might have time to deal Falto a mortal blow, but the two guards? Chained together as they were, fighting off two spear-wielding triarii with knives was madness. They would be dead before anyone could intervene. It was then he noticed his Numidians had already threaded their javelins.

Catching Agbal's eye, he slowly turned his head sideways to gesture at the triarius standing beside him. After repeating the gesture, the young Numidian nodded faintly, muttering something under his breath to Hannon standing beside him. He now had Hannon's attention. Tilting his head to indicate the triarius beside Idwal, Sphax waited for the Numidian to signal he'd understood. Agbal and Hannon were amongst the finest shots in his eshrin. From fifteen paces they couldn't miss.

Falto was still listing his demands and boasting about how he'd outsmarted them all. Noticing the darting eyes and subtle nods, Corinna guessed something was afoot. Having bluffed indifference, she now hung on to Falto's every word, nodding solemnly to encourage him to continue.

During his speech, Falto had shifted his sword-point to Sphax's lower ribs, barely a forearm's width from Idwal's right hand. Taking a risk, Sphax turned slightly towards Idwal, raised his eyebrows and stared fixedly at his friend before switching his gaze to Falto's sword pricking his ribs. In Sphax's heightened state of awareness, he could have sworn he saw a half-smile play across his friend's lips before he too nodded.

Holding up a hand to stop the tirade, Corinna suddenly exclaimed, 'We accede to all your demands,

Sempronius Falto,' thereby guaranteeing the man's undivided attention. Her timing was perfect.

'Now!' screamed Sphax, twisting around to coil his length of chain around Falto's neck like a noose. A moment later, a dying body spewing blood from the javelin lodged in his throat careered into him, sending them both sprawling to the deck and forcing Idwal to his knees. But Sphax gripped the chain as if his life depended on it, so as he fell he dragged the centurion with him. They landed facing one another, Sphax's hands already tightening on the iron noose.

Sphax looked up to see Idwal on his knees, about to plunge the centurion's sword into Falto's breast. 'No!' he commanded, 'He's mine!'

With the last of his strength he pulled Falto towards him so they faced one another, eye to eye. And so it was that Sphax stared into the bulging eyes of Sempronius Falto as he took the last breath of his miserable life. With each deliberate twist of an iron link, he delivered the monster deeper into the depths of Hades. When he could no longer feel his foul breath on his cheek, Sphax let go and rolled aside.

That's when Idwal finally plunged the blade between Sempronius Falto's shoulders to make certain their ordeal was over, and Falto was returned to the shadows where he'd always belonged.

* * *

When at last Corinna held him in her arms, her joy was soon tempered by concern. Sphax winced as they clung to one another. Idwal quickly described the beating he'd received from Sempronius Falto and the fragile state of his health. Corinna immediately demanded food, fresh clothing, and above all, ointment and a physician. If they were honest, he and Idwal enjoyed the fuss and attention they received that afternoon. After the loneliness of their cell, it felt reassuring to hear the good-natured banter of Drust and the Numidians, and the bread and cheese tasted as if they were savouring it for the first time. The physician pronounced Sphax's ribs were healing well and the knitbone oil dulled his aches.

When they'd stripped and searched the bodies of Sempronius Falto and his lieutenants for the keys to their slave collars, a leather pouch had been discovered out of which Sphax's precious ivory image of Artemis fell to the deck. As he watched the sight of the centurion's naked body being tossed over the side, he re-threaded it, returning it to its rightful place on his breast. Moments later, the rain miraculously ceased and the wind died, returning the roiling seas to a tranquil calm. Sphax wasn't sure whether to attribute this sign from the gods to Poseidon welcoming the monster, or a reward from Artemis for the recovery of her image.

Well within the hour thirty-six legionaries had surrendered and been stripped of their uniforms, and an entire crew of Epidamnion oarsmen had agreed to row for Illyrian silver. Lycon was once more back at the helm.

* * *

That evening the deck of the captured quinquereme was made to glow with the mellow light of Greek lamps. Benches had been found and placed in a broad semi-circle for the score of honoured guests, along with cloaks and shawls to keep out the evening chill. Wine flowed freely, and what little food was left aboard the four vessels was handed out generously.

For reasons they couldn't fathom, Sphax and Idwal had been placed opposite Teuta, Corinna and a distinguished looking Greek, not on either side of them as precedent demanded. To compound the irony, they found themselves sharing Sempronius Falto's commodious throne, the one the centurion had occupied on his brief journey to Hades.

Sphax and Idwal had both questioned Corinna and Drust as to how Alkibiades came to receive a letter and envoy that described them in such perfect detail? How could this be? they'd pestered. By way of response, all they'd received were enigmatic smiles and reassurances that all would be revealed in the evening's entertainment.

'It's time we spared you the misery of ignorance,' declared the Greek sitting beside Teuta, rising to his feet and grinning at them both. 'For your entertainment— and let's face it, you're both in need of amusement—

Corinna has devised a storytelling of your rescue. As I'm to deliver what she describes as the prologue, I must first introduce myself. I am Demetrius of Pharos.'

Sphax gasped. So this was the man who'd betrayed Teuta and taken the infant king Pinnes under his wing. Menda's mission to bring about a reconciliation between the two of them had obviously been a spectacular success!

Since the moment Sphax caught sight of him in the company of Teuta, he'd been drawn to him. Dressed in his finest war gear of muscled cuirass and hoplite helmet topped by a mane of madder-dyed horsehair, Demetrius had the commanding presence and noble bearing of a man soldiers would willingly follow into battle. That evening he'd discarded armour in favour of an embroidered cloak dyed in the deepest azurite, above a simple woolen chiton. His thick raven curls, without the slightest hint of grey, framed a handsome face set with piercing dark eyes and generous lips that seemed in continual search of amusement. But there was something about his thrusting chin and bearing that reminded Sphax of Corinna.

'From what my queen has told me,' he began, 'her daughter arrived some four weeks ago after escaping from Epidamnos in the company of her faithful Numidians. Corinna insisted work completing and fitting out three of the keles begin the following morning. I myself arrived at Rhizon a week later to a joyous reconciliation with my queen and positive news from Philip of Macedon regarding the proposed alliance with Hannibal.'

At this welcome news Sphax and Idwal exchanged significant looks. At least that part of their mission had been a resounding success.

'At Corinna's insistence,' Demetrius continued, 'in haste we set course for Epidamnos the following morning in three keles. It may come as something of a surprise to you, but our vessels have been on station, yet out of sight of Epidamnos for the last three weeks, guarding every approach to the harbour. At night we beached our vessels in a secluded bay south of here to take on food and fresh water before returning at first light.

'To our surprise, on the second day of our vigil, a Roman merchantman sallied forth from the harbour. Her captain hadn't the stomach for a fight, surrendering upon our approach. Once aboard her, we discovered a sallow, disagreeable creature named Sarius, who turned out to be nothing less than the chief steward of Alkibiades.

'What's more, he was carrying a letter!' Demetrius suddenly grinned at Corinna. 'I think the tale would be better continued by you, my dear ... I can barely write my name in Greek! Letters and scholarly academy are beyond a simple soldier like me. Besides,' he added sourly, 'I seem to recall you interviewing the man for hours ... when all the queen and I wanted to do was throw the wretch overboard!'

Corinna was laughing as she got to her feet. 'What we hadn't realised when you two were taken prisoner, was that Alkibiades would be equally intrigued as to why his daughter-in-law was accompanied by a Gaul and a Numidian.

'He might be ancient, but Alkibiades is not senile. Gauls and Numidians could mean only one thing for a hostage of Rome: I'd escaped to Hannibal's army and was now under his protection. So what were a hostage of Rome, a Numidian and a Gaul doing on the other side of the Adria attempting to rescue Cleon from Brundisium? Alkibiades would surely reason that Falto's prisoners were men of status, and he'd already learned from Alexandra that we'd come from Rhizon. The steward told me Alkibiades suspected my mother was behind this.

'This I'd gleaned from my interviews with Sarius. The letter made things doubly clear. It was addressed to Praetor Marcus Rufus in Brundisium and Sarius had been ordered to deliver it in person. I'll spare you the ingratiating prose! In short, it asked the praetor to make urgent enquiries of Rome as to who Sempronius Falto's prisoners might be. And it warned Rufus that Queen Teuta might attempt to rescue her grandson Cleon, advising him to remove the child to the safety of Rome.' Corinna's face twisted into a scowl. 'The safety of Rome!' she cried, staring at Sphax. 'Cleon's removal to Rome has always been my darkest fear ... it would put him beyond my reach!'

Demetrius placed a comforting arm around her shoulder. Sphax found this intimacy disconcerting.

Corinna had told him she'd known Demetrius since early childhood, but that was a long time ago, before the small matter of his betrayal.

'To continue the tale,' began Demetrius, returning to his chair beside the queen, 'that's when Corinna came up with the most ridiculous, far-fetched, hair-brained scheme I've ever had the misfortune to countenance,' he teased, hoping to lighten her mood.

Ignoring Demetrius, Corinna quickly regained her composure and the thread. 'It seemed obvious to me that if we could convince Alkibiades you two were of great importance to Rome, and must be handed over to the praetor immediately, Alkibiades would order Falto to deliver you to Brundisium by the swiftest means possible. In other words, by that quinquereme languishing in her shed in the harbour.

'With a fair wind, that vessel was the only ship in the harbour capable of reaching Brundisium in a single day, and Alkibiades could easily supply a captain and three hundred oarsmen.

'All we had to do was convince Alkibiades of your importance and the urgency of the situation. I must say there was a certain irony and amusement in the fact that all I had to do was tell him the truth!

'After all, my darling, you are an ex-slave and a wanted man. Gaius Lucilus would pay an emperor's ransom to see your head on a spike. And Idwal is a trusted lieutenant of Hannibal, privy to his plans and intentions. We had Alkibiades' ship, all we needed now was someone to act as envoy and deliver my letter.'

Suddenly, a curly-haired man dressed in an ancient toga leapt to his feet and began bowing and gesturing, full of his own importance. 'I am Sextus,' he spoke in fluent Latin, winking and capering before their throne, 'envoy of Praetor Marcus Rufus, commissioner of harbours in Brundisium, deliverer of the most perfect forgery Alkibiades would ever hold in his hands. Written by the fair hand of Corinna in the noblest of Latin, it told Alkibiades that he held two prisoners that were of great importance to Rome.'

Sphax looked to Corinna for enlightenment, but her only response was an enigmatic smile, before raising a finger to her lips.

'This missive,' continued Sextus, 'described the exploits of Idwal, lieutenant in Hannibal's army, not to mention a Numidian, Sphax, slave and branded fugitivus, wanted for the murder of Marcellus, son of Gaius Lucilus. But there was more … This Numidian, the letter informed, was none other than the nephew of Hannibal himself. And at the Trebia had slain the tribune Manius Quintus in mortal combat.'

Paused, a mischievous glint in his eyes before clapping his hands in triumph. 'Such detail! Such exquisite, intimate detail this letter provided, even down to the exact position of the fugitivus sign on the Numidian's right forearm.

'Whosoever read such an authorative letter would marvel at the author's knowledge of the prisoners described therein. But the letter was not so much a missive as a command.

'Rome wanted those prisoners! The centurion Sempronius Falto was to deliver them immediately into the hands of Praetor Marcus Rufus in Brundisium.

'At my suggestion,' Sextus crowed, 'Corinna consented to add a sweetener that would appeal to Falto, offering the man who handed over the prisoners a generous reward and certain promotion.' With a final capering flourish, Sextus added, 'As envoy, I myself was questioned at length by the aged Alkibiades and was able to elaborate and embroider the detail contained in the letter. My part in this deception is now history.'

Corinna continued the storytelling. 'I calculated it would have taken two days for the steward's vessel to reach Brundisium. So allowing ten days for Rufus to enquire of Rome, and a further two for the return journey, all we had to do was wait two weeks, then send the vessel back to Epidamnos. We'd already bribed the captain and crew to keep their mouths shut.

'That's where Sextus came in, impersonating Rufus' envoy. And before you ask, he really was a Roman citizen and an actor by profession. But after finding himself shipwrecked, he decided piracy was far more lucrative. I've known him since childhood, and learning he was aboard my keles, I asked him to take on the role of envoy.' On cue, Sextus stood and performed another elaborate bow, milking the laughter before resuming his seat.

'So, we put Sextus aboard and a guard on Sarius. When our impostor had completed his mission successfully, we packed Sarius and the vessel off to Rhizon. The rest you know.'

'But what you don't know,' exclaimed Demetrius, rising once again to his feet, 'is that we thought Corinna's plan was madness! The Queen and I urged we storm the city under the cloak of darkness and come to your rescue. But Corinna wouldn't hear of it. She convinced us it was far too risky. From what she'd gleaned from Sarius, Falto was a monster, and would execute you both before we got within sight of the garrison, or that he would use you as hostages to save his miserable skin.'

Demetrius paused and gazed at Corinna. Again, there was something disconcerting about that look, something in his eyes and indulgent expression. 'From what we've witnessed this afternoon, Corinna has judged the man's character perfectly. She was right to stay our hand ... in truth, she has been right all along.'

Corinna then did something that surprised him. Folding Demetrius' hands in her own, she raised them to her lips. Whether it was this touching moment, or the solemnity in the Greek's voice, something moved Sphax.

Rising to his feet he stood before Teuta and Demetrius before kneeling and bowing his head. Sphax recalled the sight of the Illyrian dead sprawled on the deck, sacrificed to save them. 'We are eternally in your debt. In repayment, we will move heaven and earth to come to your aid should you need it. This I swear before you.'

'Noble sentiments!' laughed Demetrius. 'But I wouldn't do too much swearing of allegiances, young man, it might land you in big trouble later.' Sphax knew exactly what he was referring to.

To everyone's relief, the queen was laughing louder than Demetrius. 'You silly boy! You didn't think we would leave you both to rot in a Roman cell, did you?'

Demetrius was serious for a moment. 'You have our clever daughter to thank for your rescue. We just executed her plan. Perfectly, I must confess.'

Sphax blinked. Had he heard correctly? Sphax got to his feet and turned speechlessly towards Corinna, standing beside him. She was smiling and nodding. He had heard correctly. He was standing before Corinna's father.

* * *

Later, they spent a cold sleepless night huddled together on an uncomfortable mattress below deck. It should have been a night of bliss. But Sphax was in considerable pain from the day's exertions, and both of them were preoccupied, locked away in their separate thoughts.

Tomorrow it seemed, they would storm Epidamnos and ransom the city.

Sphax had never stormed a city, but from everything he'd been told by the veterans who'd sacked Saguntum, it inevitably descended into meaningless slaughter. A frenzied bloodbath, followed by unallayed rape and pillage, did not sit well with his conscience that night. At the same time, he knew that Corinna had only one thing on her mind: how to take vengeance on that snake, Alkibiades, who would have conspired with Rome to condemn Cleon to a lifetime of separation and exile from his mother.

Giving up on his battle with sleep, Sphax gently untangled his arms from Corinna, grabbed his bearskin and wrapped in his himation, climbed the nearest companionway up to the deck. He was cheered by the sight of a fulling moon, casting its golden glow from the starlit heavens. Tomorrow at least would dawn bright and clear.

Even at this hour most of the lamps were still blazing as servants stowed away the last of the benches and wine, but even so, the night watch were alert. Sphax was challenged twice before he'd slumped into Falto's chair.

He must have fallen into an uneasy sleep, for the next thing he remembered was Corinna standing above him, running her fingers through his hair. 'What a delightful way to be woken,' he yawned.

'Move up, little dove, there's enough room on that thing for the two of us.'

'Especially for a little mouse,' he grinned, obliging her. 'You can't sleep either.'

'Not without you beside me ... at least not on this special night,' she said, draping his bearskin cloak around them both.

They sat in silence for a while before Sphax's thoughts turned to Demetrius. Reaching for her hands beneath the bearskin he said, 'It's not every day you discover a long-lost father. It must have come as quite a shock.'

'In some ways ... when they first told me, three weeks ago,' she agreed, 'but I've often suspected it because of the love and kindness he's always shown me. In any case, I never believed *her* stories about my father. A good liar needs to be a consummate actor and possess a good memory. My mother has neither quality.'

Corinna slowly shook her head. 'We don't choose our parents, the gods do, but now that I've had a few weeks to get used to the idea, I can think of worse fathers. Even after he'd betrayed us, I could never find it in my heart to hate him, and after I found out about Menda's foul part in it, I began to pity him. After all, he lost everything.'

'I must say I admired him from the moment I set eyes on him.'

'He does have a noble bearing, doesn't he?' she smiled. 'His courage and bravery have never been questioned.'

'At least Menda redeemed himself.'

'In my eyes, Menda will always remain irredeemable,' she declared, shaking her head. But then she suddenly grinned. 'Drust was the only person in Rhizon who couldn't wait for Menda's return.'

'Drust!' Sphax exclaimed, surprised. 'What about Elantia?'

'She turned out to have the tongue of a common fishwife and a temper sharper than a serpent's fangs. When I asked for men to crew my keles, he was the first to volunteer,' she laughed. 'Poor Drust ... it seems he's not lucky in love.'

'Indeed.' Drust's love life was not uppermost in his mind at that moment. Abruptly changing the subject he asked, 'Will the plan to capture the harbour gate in Epidamnos succeed?'

'It had better! Otherwise we'll have to kiss goodbye to Epidamnos and I'll never get my hands on Alkibiades' scrawny neck.' She shot him an anxious look. 'You tell me. You're the soldier ... what do you think?'

When Demetrius explained the plan earlier that evening he felt reasonably confident it would succeed. But after they'd gathered the volunteers together on deck and drilled them for an hour, Sphax began to have reservations. They just looked *too* Illyrian!

'What worries me is that it *will* succeed.'

Corinna looked confused. 'What do you mean?'

'My men have told me stories of the sack of Saguntum. They're the stuff of nightmares, Corinna, nothing short of debauchery and senseless slaughter. I wouldn't wish such a fate on my worst enemy—'

'—Where's profit in senseless slaughter?' she laughed, shocked. 'We're Illyrians, not Hannibal's mercenaries. In the name of the gods, why would pirates undertake an eight month siege? Illyrians have never seen profit in such labour. Let's face it, a half-starved chicken is hardly worth fighting over. Yes, there will be drunkenness. But if this interferes with ransoming the place, it will be stamped out.

'Believe me,' she scowled, 'left to my own devices I would have steered a course for Brundisium and my son. But I owe them so much, Sphax! My mother's mind is set on ransoming Epidamnos, and the city may indeed prove to be a crucial piece in our negotiations with Philip of Macedon. He's desperate to occupy the place and gain a foothold on the Adria.'

'And what of Alkibiades?' asked Sphax. 'Is he to become yet another victim of Illyrian pirates?'

'No!' Corinna smiled. 'Hera has gifted me the perfect solution to Alkibiades.'

FOURTEEN

In the greying half-light before dawn, the ageing Roman quinquereme glided into the harbour of Epidamnos under a hundred oars. Lycon was on the steering platform, his oarsmen and crew spared by their solemn oaths, sworn under pain of death. Beside crew with ropes ready to make the vessel fast, on deck stood thirty hand-picked volunteers, stiff and immaculately dressed in borrowed uniforms, hefting shields and spears. Amidst them all, seated on the great oaken chair, sat their centurion, wearing a muscled cuirass and rounded Etruscan helmet sprouting a trio of black feathers. With both cheek guards lowered, little could be seen of his handsome face.

Half a mile away, standing bleary-eyed above the battlements of the harbour gate, twenty militiamen looked on, yearning for the comfort of their sleeping couches. Every man of them loathed a night watch, but their relief would be here soon. At least the sight of the quinquereme, limping back to harbour like a dog with its tail between its legs had provided some laughter and entertainment. Everyone in Epidamnos knew the old girl was rotten and riddled with worm! What did arrogant Roman arseholes know about maintaining a warship? Now here she was, back for repairs after no more than a day at sea. That evil-tempered bastard, Falto, would demand the gates be opened so his men didn't have to break step on their march back to barracks. It would never do to cross Sempronius Falto. 'Down to the gates,' someone was already yelling. 'Prepare to release the bars and welcome the cocksuckers back to Epidamnos.'

Below the quinquereme's deck it was a different story. In the near darkness and expectant hush, packed as tightly as a flock in a sheep pen, there was hardly room to scratch an itch. Sphax, Corinna and the Numidians had slowly felt their way along the rowing benches to the bow, where, through the narrow gap between the top rowing benches and the upper deck, they had a clear view of the harbour gate recessed into the city's walls. This was where Demetrius planned to march his men brazenly through the gate and into the city.

It was risky, and Sphax had his doubts. If Demetrius' impersonation of Falto aroused the slightest suspicion, or his men lost their nerve, those gates would be barred and they would receive a shower of spears for their trouble. Then there would be nothing for it but to sail straight back to Rhizon. Without battering rams or scaling ladders, there wasn't a hope in Hades of taking any of the city's three gates, and no one had come up with a better plan.

It seemed to take an age to tie the vessel to the iron bollards and make her fast. Anxiously, they listened as the wooden boarding ramps were fixed in place to the deck and the first of the triarii gingerly descended to the quayside, the noise of hobnails on the wooden boards deafening. Outside the darkness of their wooden walls, the sun had risen, suffusing everything in a blood-red light.

The previous night, Sphax had warned Demetrius' chosen thirty not to stand idly around, but to form themselves into a column of five ranks, six men abreast—a legion's standard marching formation—and they were to do this in perfect silence. But that was practice! This was the real thing, and anything could go wrong.

When three ranks had taken up the formation on the quay, Demetrius himself strode out stiffly to take his place behind the third rank as the last two ranks formed up behind him. So far so good, thought Sphax, heart pounding. They looked disciplined, yet unhurried.

As he heard Demetrius yell, 'Forward,' Sphax's heart was in his mouth. This was the bit that worried him. Could they keep in step with each other? The deck of a rolling vessel was hardly the place to practise this, so they'd settled on Sphax demonstrating the pace by marching up and down.

'You taught them well,' whispered Corinna, 'they look good to me.'

'Don't tempt the fates,' he murmured, fingering his ivory image nervously. The column was now eighty paces from the gate and still in reasonable order. When they got within sixty, something quite unexpected happened. Without a single challenge or cry of halt, the gates began to creak open, as if by magic.

In that instant Sphax realised there must have been an overwhelming temptation for Demetrius to yell, "Charge!" and rush the gate. Instead, he kept his cool, and his men their nerve. 'I shall simply march into Epidamnos with my men, Sphax,' he'd told him last night with a great grin on his face. Now he was about to do exactly that ... in some style!

When the first cries of battle from the gate were heard there was a sudden stampede for the companionways. Two hundred Illyrians were now eager to join the fight.

It might have offered the best view of the city's gate, but the bow was far from any companionway, which meant they would be amongst the last to leave the vessel. Corinna seemed unconcerned. Peering due west she announced that three keles were about to enter the harbour with three hundred reinforcements, adding 'Illyria has taken her first city from Rome.'

'It's not over yet.'

'Oh yes it is!' she snorted. 'The only men capable of resistance are under guard in my mother's keles, and Idwal will make sure the handful that are left in the garrison surrender.'

'What about the city's militia? Surely they will—'

'Shopkeepers! Bakers! Moneylenders!' Corinna was laughing now. 'They're not warriors! They don't even make good watchmen. As we've just witnessed.' The gangway between the rowing benches was almost clear by now. 'Come on, before we miss the entertainment.'

Sphax had never thought he would hear the bloody business of storming a city described as entertainment.

As they walked down the quayside the next thing to surprise him was his Numidians. Except they no longer seemed to be *his* Numidians. With Agbal a pace in front and Hannon and Jugurtha either side of her, Corinna seemed to have acquired a personal bodyguard. He found himself trailing behind, superfluous. The worst thing was the silence. What had got into them?

Yesterday he'd noticed how proudly they were wearing knives in fancy sheaths strapped to belts around their waists. No doubt gifts from Corinna. They could hardly keep their hands from fingering the ivory hilts this morning.

'Stop!' he shouted in his mother tongue. The three Numidians obliged, turning around to stare at him. 'What's going on, Hannon?'

'What do you mean, Sir?'

'Have you three decided to join an Illyrian eshrin?'

'Of course not,' said Jugurtha, thrown by the question.

'Then why are you surrounding Corinna like bodyguards?'

The three of them looked sheepish, bemused.

'Spit it out!' Silence.

'It's like this, Sir,' began Jugurtha, his pale blue eyes avoiding Sphax's, 'when you were taken, well ... as you weren't able to ... I mean ... we all swore to protect the Lady Corinna. She doesn't mind, Sir.'

'She says she likes being bodyguarded,' Agbal chipped in.

Sphax was finding it a struggle not to burst out laughing. 'I can see that, you slackheads.'

'We've just got into the habit of it ...' added Agbal, lamely.

'Well, would the three of you mind if I walk beside my lady. I'm perfectly capable of defending her myself ... and in the name of Ba 'al Hamūn, talk to one another! It's unnerving *not* to hear you three babbling on about something or other.'

By now Corinna had worked out what this little discussion might be about. Beaming at him she recited, 'Sastanàqqàm Indek tifut n- imidiwàn Tiled tasnit.'

Sphax groaned, switching to Greek. 'Your grammar is atrocious! Anyway, why are you learning Numidian?'

'They were lost without you, Sphax,' she explained, suddenly serious. 'They began following me around like children, so I gave them a job. And how else am I meant to talk to them? They have no Latin or Greek.'

She did have a point, and he knew he was being childishly possessive about her, and *his* Numidians. 'I'm grateful for the protection you've given Corinna, men,' he said in Tassynt, the purest form of Numidian, 'I shall not forget it.' By the time they reached the harbour gate, Sphax could hear idle banter from the three of them striding along behind him.

After speaking to the Illyrians left in charge of prisoners and the gate, Corinna re-joined them as they began to climb the steep paved road that led to the agora. 'He's going to be insufferable after this!' she laughed.

'Who is?'

'My father! He's going to bore us to death with the story of how he marched into Epidamnos with just thirty men and disarmed the guards before they could cry, "All hail to Demetrius of Pharos!"'

'And his men,' asked Sphax, 'any wounded?'

'Not a scratch,' she reported, still chuckling. 'As I predicted, our shopkeepers and bakers simply laid down their arms and now they're in the guardhouse, laughing with their captors and grumbling about their empty bellies.'

'The militia or their captors?' he enquired, mightily relieved.

'Both,' she replied dryly. 'I've instructed a party to forage breakfast for them all.'

By the time they reached the grand open space of the agora, the sun had fully risen in a cloudless blue sky, promising a mild spring-like day. The place was crowded, but not with Epidamnions. Jubilant Illyrians were wandering around in small groups, drifting in and out of the colonnaded walkways, where the shops were located.

'There's my mother,' said Corinna, pointing to a great throng standing outside the temple of Hera on the far side of the square. It was easier to pick out the giant figure of Scardus, captain of the queen's guard, his bronze Phrygian helmet head and shoulders above the rest.

As mother and daughter greeted one another, Sphax stepped back and gazed up in wonder at the sculptures on the temple's pediment. Painted in dazzling gold, ochres and crimson against a background of the deepest azurite blue, they depicted Hera, holding her lotus sceptre, seated beside Zeus on the throne of Heaven, flanked by lesser gods. They seemed so real and life-like; a cast of godlike actors about to step onto a dazzling sunlit stage.

Below this was an exquisitely painted frieze illustrating images and symbols associated with the goddess. Sphax understood the peacocks drawing Hera's chariot, but was puzzled by the images of cuckoo birds.

He was so enraptured by the beauty of it all he hadn't noticed Corinna linking an arm through his and following his gaze. 'Does it not fill you with awe and wonder?' she said.

Feeling the warmth of her breath on his cheek only deepened his reverie. 'It does, my darling.'

'This is where I brought my first offerings for the goddess and learned something of the mysteries of worship and devotion.'

'And in Brundisium?' he asked.

'I made my offerings at a small shrine, in the Greek quarter.'

'Isn't there a magnificent temple to Juno in the city?'

'Juno is *not* Hera, Sphax,' she corrected, with a scowl.

'I've forgotten the significance of the cuckoo, can you remind me?'

'Then shame on you,' she gently chided. 'By transforming himself into a cold bedraggled cuckoo, Zeus tricked her into holding him against her breast. It was then that he raped her, and it was only to hide her shame that she agreed to marry him. For me the bird represents the eternal power men hold over women. Take note, and contemplate the imagery, for I intend to have the bird engraved on my tomb.'

Before he'd time to contemplate anything, Teuta joined them. Looking up, she took in the entire pediment, cornice, frieze and capitals with a cursory sweep. 'Magnificent. They tell me it cost over two hundred talents of silver to build. This is such a rich city, we will do well here.'

'I'm sure you will, mother,' agreed Corinna absently, eyes still fixed on the frieze.

'Once we've lightened this place of its gold and silver and the men have drunk their fill, we'll sail for Brundisium. It will only be a day or so.'

'That will not be necessary,' Corinna replied tartly. 'I intend to go alone.'

'We've been through this a thousand times, Corinna! Why don't you listen?' Teuta was glaring at her daughter. Through gritted teeth she continued, 'It's a Roman city, crawling with legionaries and a fleet at anchor in the harbour. You can't do this alone. You'll need all the help you can get! And need I remind you, Cleon is *my* grandson.'

This was all news to Sphax. He'd not been a party to those thousand arguments. But there was something about the queen's conviction and certainty that set alarm bells ringing. Cheering suddenly broke out on the north side of the agora, bringing the spat between mother and daughter to a close.

'Ah! Demetrius returns with my handsome Gaul,' the queen reported, her eyesight sharper than Sphax's. 'Judging from his reception, it seems the city is ours.'

By now men were teeming into the square from every direction, suggesting that the reinforcements aboard the three keles had also arrived. Demetrius strode over to them and stood before the queen, removing his borrowed helmet; his look of triumphant satisfaction was there for all to see.

'The north and south gates have been taken,' he proclaimed, raising his voice so all would hear, 'and what remained of the Roman garrison has surrendered to Idwal. Every soldier of Epidamnos has laid down his arms and is now our prisoner, and every citizen has locked and barred their doors in fear and trembling. The city is yours, my queen!'

Cheers and shield thumping broke out amongst those within earshot of Illyria's new hero, but quickly Teuta raised her arms to stifle it. She wasn't about to be upstaged by her ex-lover! Instead she would steal his thunder ... and the applause.

When silence was restored and all eyes were on her, she began. 'By your courage and bravery, today Illyrios has arisen from the wilderness of obscurity and struck a great blow against our enemies. A mighty Roman garrison has been defeated and surrendered'—hardly, thought Sphax—'and the Greeks who for so long have stolen our trade and commerce will at last be made to pay. So, as you walk peacefully through its streets, tell the good citizens of Epidamnos that they have nothing to fear from us: we Illyrians are here only to lighten their burdens and relieve them ... of their gold and silver.'

When the laughter died down she continued. 'Find the city's elders, their magistrates and oligarchs. Bring them to the courthouse beside this temple of Hera, so they may grovel, haggle, and wail when I tell them my price for the ransom of their city. I have settled on four hundred talents. Just think of it, men ... four hundred talents of silver! Wealth even beyond the dreams of Midas.

'And as I stand before you this day, I swear by Illyrios that every man will receive his fair share of this great wealth. So be jubilant! Silver will soon be showering on your heads like rain from heaven.'

There was indeed jubilation, as the crowd erupted into a frenzy of cheering, foot stomping and slapping of shoulders. Teuta certainly knew how to rouse her audience.

'We should go,' said Corinna. 'We need to get to Alkibiades before my mother's men. That would ruin everything.'

Before Sphax could ask how or why, she'd turned on her heels to round up Idwal and Drust, gathered in earnest conversation around Demetrius and her mother.

Soon the seven of them were striding purposefully along the broad avenue they'd taken on that fateful morning a month ago. But now there could be no Sempronius Falto lying in wait for them, and Idwal had assured them the Roman garrison had surrendered without a fight. Apparently, news of the death of their centurion had not been met with universal lamentation.

But Corinna was most anxious to learn that Clio, proprietress of the Athena hospitium, was safe and unharmed. Drust assured her she was, and as ordered, he'd placed three men to guard the door to her establishment.

The only one amongst them to feel *un*-assured was Sphax. 'What are you going to do, Corinna, when we confront Alkibiades? As the gods are my witness, I know he is lower than a serpent's belly, but even so, he is old and frail … I would have qualms about doing him harm.'

'Who said anything about doing him harm? At least not in the way you're thinking of. I've found the perfect solution to avenge ourselves on Alkibiades, one that will not harm a single hair on his serpentine head!'

'Which is?' asked Idwal, skeptical.

'You'll just have to wait and see,' she replied, gesturing for them to cross the avenue and continue under the cover of the pine trees. 'This is where I hid from the legionaries after you two were taken.'

Sphax could see that the land fell away in a series of terraces, eventually reaching the sea shore, he guessed. Scattered amongst the pines he could see villas and tiled rooftops, but there were also places where the trees were dense and overgrown, offering places to hide. After a few hundred paces they arrived at the place where he'd planted the folding chair for Corinna to write her letter to Alexandra. But unlike that morning, today the villa was a hive of activity.

In the courtyard beyond the porticoed entrance, they could see servants carrying great wooden chests, and horses and carts being saddled and made ready for departure.

'It looks as if our snake is about to crawl from his hole and make a run for it,' observed Drust.

'He won't get far,' laughed Sphax, 'Demetrius has taken all the gates and posted guards.'

'And guards can be bribed,' snapped Corinna.

'How far is the southern gate from here, Corinna?' asked Idwal.

Corinna seemed lost in thought. 'Not far,' she said, absently.

'Then I suggest we make our move,' said Idwal, reaching for his sword.

'Wait!' cried Corinna. 'He might be doing our work for us. This might yet serve our purpose—'

'But you still haven't told us what that purpose is, Corinna,' fretted Sphax, exasperated.

'I say we rush the place now,' said Drust, 'whilst we still have the chance.'

As everyone considered what to do next, the decision was taken out of their hands. Two laden wagons, followed by a stately carriage and a string of riders on horseback began to rumble out of the courtyard onto the paved avenue.

'Quick,' yelled Corinna. 'Into the trees before we're spotted. The gate's only half a mile down the hill.'

Taking to their heels they charged deeper into the trees then headed south, staying parallel with the avenue. But their quarry had the advantage. Whilst they were dodging trees through thick undergrowth, Alkibiades and his entourage were on horseback and in wheeled wagons, and judging from the grinding racket Sphax could hear, the horses were being driven hard.

By the time the trees abruptly gave way to a paved road beneath the city's walls they were all panting and gasping for breath. And one glance at the gate told them they were almost too late.

Sphax recognised the gaunt, stooping figure of Alkibiades opening a chest a servant had placed on the ground before the dozen or so guards posted at the gate.

Corinna had been right: silver could open any door. Two of the guards were already beginning to remove the bars from the gate.

'They're Demetrius' men,' observed Drust, 'from Macedon.'

'Then they might not answer to us,' Idwal observed.

'They will answer to me!' snarled Corinna, marching boldly towards them shrieking, '*Seize them! Seize them!*' Leaving Sphax and the others no alternative but to follow in her wake.

When Alkibiades turned to stare at the harpy bearing swiftly down on him he uttered but a single word. '*You!*' he spat.

But on recognising Sphax and Idwal his anger instantly evaporated, replaced first by utter confusion, then abject fear. 'This is not possible,' he moaned, paling visibly. 'Falto delivered you to Brundisium—'

'—Wrong, serpent!' Corinna raged. 'The letter you received was written by me, and delivered Falto straight into our hands. You were so easily deceived, old man!'

'Thread your javelins,' Sphax muttered under his breath to the Numidians. He had that sinking feeling that at any moment this could turn ugly.

'I have come to take my son's inheritance. Which means I'm going to relieve you of all your wealth … down to the last as! Do you understand, Alkibiades … your last as!'

'Thieves! Robbers! Brigands!' quavered Alkibiades, backing away from her to the relative safety of his carriage.

'Starting with this,' she said, bending down to pick up the chest brimming with silver coin.

A laced boot suddenly flicked the lid shut and rested itself firmly on top of the chest. Its owner leered down at her. 'Not that, lady. That's ours. We've just negotiated a deal with that toothless old fart. They get free passage through the gate ... we get the chest. That's the deal, so hands off.'

Corinna slowly straightened up and stared at the man. With his lantern-jaw, beak of a nose and thatch of matted red hair, Sphax guessed he was Macedonian. He certainly wasn't Illyrian. Other than a sheathed sword on a chain belt around his waist, he had no weapons. But this didn't seem to bother him, and the ten men gathered around him more than made up for his deficiency in weaponry.

'Do you know who I am?' She asked, stepping backwards whilst adjusting the folds of her woollen himation.

'You're the daughter of that she-wolf, Teuta,' he glowered, before shrugging dismissively. 'So what!'

'And your illustrious name, soldier?' she enquired, overly polite, fumbling with her dress as she took her place beside Sphax.

'Orestes, bitch! What of it?'

'I need a name to place over the cross you'll be crucified on when my mother catches up with—'

'—We'll be long gone by then,' he sneered, 'Macedon has no interest in your squabbles with Rome.

We're here to fill our purses and women's slits. Nothing more. This chest of silver will repay us handsomely for our trouble.' To add further insult, Orestes' remarks provoked great guffaws of laughter amongst his men.

Corinna's right hand now disappeared under the folds of her himation. Six pairs of eyes were watching her every movement, and waiting, for a signal ... a cue. They knew only too well what was hidden there. As Sphax had predicted, it was about to turn ugly.

It happened in a heartbeat. A desperate heartbeat.

First came the glint of an ivory knife handle as it carved its way through the air. Next, the whirr of three spinning javelins, flung at point blank range with deadly accuracy.

Orestes' hands reached instinctively for the object that had lodged itself deep within his throat, but by then his eyes were glazing as he sunk to his knees spewing blood. His companions either side of him met the same fate as the iron barbs of javelins tore into their flesh. Death had come so swiftly that none had time to register a departing cry of agony. Charon would greet them all in silence.

Before Sphax had reached over his shoulder to draw his dragon sword it was all over. Three more javelins and Corinna's last knife had already flown.

That's when the yelling and pleading began, as the surviving Macedonians flung down their weapons and took to their heels in terror. Four of them were trapped on the wall above the great arch of the gate—

the only way down for them was a stone staircase already strewn with four of their dead.

'Mercy, gracious queen! Spare us! Take pity on us ...' they were caterwauling, pleading to surrender.

'Throw away your weapons and come down,' Sphax commanded, 'and you'll be spared. The killing is over.' Shields, spears and swords suddenly rained down on the paved road and the dead beneath the walls. The four of them came down and fell on their knees before Corinna.

'You are unworthy allies of Illyria,' she said coldly, hardly bearing to look at them. 'Macedon is far, I suggest you begin your journey home at once,' and turning her back on them she joined the Numidians recovering their javelins and knives from the dead.

That's when Alkibiades rolled his last throw of the dice. In the vicious struggle that had just taken place beneath the gateway, they'd almost forgotten about him and his fleet of wagons and riders. The southern gate was still barred shut, but the paved road at the foot of the walls was clear. Seizing his opportunity he began yelling at the wagoners and carriage to whip their horses forward, along its path.

Before Sphax had gathered his wits the two wagons and carriage had thundered past him, but the four riders in their wake had been slow to urge their mounts forward. As a chestnut stallion came abreast of him at the trot, he leapt for the saddle. Straddling a leg over its back, he grabbed a rein in his left hand

and a fistful of the startled rider's tunic in his right hand. Terror-stricken, the chestnut suddenly reared, depositing its former rider painfully on the roadway. By a near miracle, Sphax managed to stay on the stallion's back. Urging and soothing the beast to calm down, at last he regained control, dropped the reins and gently nudged his knees into the stallion's shoulders.

Soon he'd overtaken three horsemen and Alkibiades' carriage and was rapidly gaining on the leading wagon. When he came alongside, he felt the waspish sting of leather bite into his shoulder. As a last resort the desperate driver was using his whip on Sphax, rather than his horses. As the lashes continued to rain down on him he had no alternative but to draw his sword, the sight of which brought the man to his senses. Frantically reining in the yoked mares, he brought the wagon to a juddering halt, leapt from his seat and ran for his life.

Sphax breathed a sigh of relief. It had been a foolish thing to try. If any of Alkibiades' servants had been armed, the outcome might have been very different. Still holding his dragon sword in his right hand he pointed it menacingly at the last of the wagoners and then at the riders surrounding the carriage. 'Try anything like that again and I swear I'll kill you. Get down from your horses and the wagon.' Glaring at the driver still holding the reins of the carriage horses he yelled, 'You too! Drop the reins and climb down.'

Knowing the game was up, Alkibiades had remained in his carriage. When Corinna, Idwal and Drust finally joined him on foot, the Greek was stubbornly refusing to get out and face them, even though Sphax had asked him politely to do so several times. It was Alexandra who eventually opened a carriage door and stepped gingerly out to stand before them.

Her skin had taken on the unhealthy colour of yellowed old parchment, and her deep-set grey eyes looked utterly dejected and exhausted. Even in the bright sunshine she had a thick woollen shawl about her head and stooping shoulders. 'I'm truly sorry, Corinna, he wouldn't listen to me. He's never listened to me ...' her voice trailing away.

Sphax could see a mixture of anger, pity and compassion playing about Corinna's face as she smiled sorrowfully at her mother-in-law. 'I never thought he would listen,' she sighed. 'It was *you* I wanted to tell. Not him! You deserved to know the truth about Arsenios' murder. I mourned a husband and the father of my child, but you grieved for an only son.'

Whilst this conversation was taking place, Idwal and Drust untied the hemp covers from the two wagons and examined their contents carefully. Shaking his head in disbelief, Idwal turned to Corinna. 'There's more gold and silver in this wagon than the four hundred talents your mother is demanding as ransom for the entire city.'

'I would wager that my wagon contains more gold than yours,' jibed Drust.

'Then my grandson will not be cheated of his rightful inheritance,' pronounced Alexandra, reaching for Corinna's hands. 'I beg you, daughter, it is my fervent wish that I look upon the face of my darling grandson before I die. Let us pray to our goddess Hera that you will be successful in rescuing Cleon, and that I may yet hold him in my arms.'

'I too pray to our goddess for his safety and the strength to accomplish this task.'

'You are brave and resourceful, my dear,' and turning to smile at Sphax, she added, 'and blessed with steadfast friends. You will succeed.'

'Look, Alexandra, there isn't much time. Are your servants loyal and trustworthy?'

'Those that have stayed are.' Looking closely at them for the first time, Sphax noticed that two of the riders travelling on horseback were women, not that much younger than Alexandra herself. He prayed the one he'd pushed off the chestnut stallion wasn't badly hurt.

Leading Alexandra by the hand, Corinna opened the carriage door, and after they'd embraced, helped her to take her seat beside her husband, slumped with his head in his hands, broken and defeated. Corinna couldn't bear to look at the man.

Raising her voice so all the servants could hear, 'You must not return to Epidamnos. The city is not safe,' she warned. 'You must all leave by the southern gate and follow the road to Apollonia. It is two days' journey, but Apollonia will give you refuge. Take the chest of silver we left by the gate.'

Corinna then turned to the servants gathered around the carriage. 'Will you swear to serve your mistress Alexandra, and see to it that she arrives safely in Apollonia?' Sphax saw that they were all nodding solemnly. 'Good. Then may Hera grant you a safe journey.'

'Would you escort Alexandra and her servants back to the gate and see that all this is done, my darling?'

'If you say so,' Sphax said, returning her smile with a questioning frown. 'But what about Alkibiades? Is he to go free? He's cost so many lives ...'

'The gods will be his judge, not I.'

'Then what?' asked Idwal.

'To the harbour, to load a keles with my son's inheritance.'

Idwal laughed. 'Your mother will be furious when she finds out.'

'To quote a Macedonian brigand's last words,' she explained with a mischievous grin, "we'll be long gone by then."

'Where?'

'Brundisium, Idwal. Where else!'

'Your mother asked you to wait for her and Demetrius before you sailed for Brundisium, Corinna.' Alarm bells were once more ringing in Sphax's ears. 'We may need their help.'

'I will rescue my son. Not them!'

Sphax got the sinking feeling that their real trials were just about to begin.

PART THREE

THE
HOSTAGE
OF ROME

FIFTEEN

'It feels like old times,' Sphax said wistfully, keeping half an eye on Phoenice, star of the north. They'd been wondering how long it had been since they'd last stood gazing up at the star-strewn heavens, Sphax's bearskin cloak draped around their shoulders. Six weeks or eight meant little more than a blink of an eye in the vast eternity of stars above their heads, all that mattered was the joy they felt at that moment.

Corinna had named her own keles the *Hera* and chosen her crew carefully. Coming aboard he'd been greeted by some old friends. The elderly Illyrian salt, Glavus, had been made captain, and amongst the oarsmen were Carmo and Elpis, the slave boys they'd freed on the Padus. Besides oarsmen, a keles could carry up to a hundred warriors, but Corinna had settled on fewer than eighty, chosen for their skills with a bow rather than the sword: a superior weapon in a fight at sea, she claimed.

Once Alkibiades' chests had been loaded into the belly of the vessel—much needed ballast according to Glavus—the gods of the wind had been generous, gifting them an auspicious easterly that had filled the great sail adorned with the serpent Illyrios. Now they were not far from the coast of Italia, with Glavus and the oarsmen catching up on much needed sleep whilst Corinna took the steering oars.

Glancing behind her at the fingertips of grey light gathering in the east, she asked Sphax, 'Waken our captain, my darling. Dawn is approaching and the coves and shoreline north of Brundisium can be treacherous. I don't want to run her aground. Glavus knows this shore better than his own face in a mirror.'

It never ceased to amaze Sphax how quickly an old salt like Glavus woke from deep sleep. One moment he was snoring his head off, next he was wide awake enough to tie a sheet or take the helm. By the time he arrived back on the steering platform with Sphax, the greyness was transforming itself into shafts of gold and pink, and ahead of him lay the coast of Italia.

'Look to the south-west, Sphax.' Glavus pointed to a broad bay on the distant horizon. 'That's the stag's head, the outer harbour of Brundisium, open to the Adria, yet offering some shelter. Beyond that lies a narrow passage that leads to two inner harbours resembling a stag's antlers. The northern antler is the greater, almost a mile of perfect anchorage. The finest in Italia.'

'The two harbours are rather like the butterfly lagoons at Rhizon,' Corinna added, 'but narrower and less extensive.'

'Take a last look, my friends, for I dare not bring the *Hera* any closer. The sight of our serpent sail would stir up a hornet's nest and we'd soon have Roman triremes for company! Time to waken our oarsmen and take down our sail.'

* * *

'I'd rather enter by the Appian gate,' suggested Corinna, 'it will be busier than the northern gate, with less likelihood that we'll be stopped or searched.'

It was late in the afternoon when Sphax caught his first sight of the walled Roman city of Brundisium. Shortly after dawn they'd beached the *Hera* in a rocky cove four miles north of the stag's head and dragged her ashore. The land thereabouts looked flat and featureless, reminding him of the plains beside the Padus: empty of tracks, farms and settlements, a perfect hiding place for their vessel. But they would have to return within four days. Water would not be a problem, but their supplies of food were meagre, and by then the crew would be running low.

The *regina viarum* was indeed busy that afternoon, choked with everything from bullock carts to grand carriages filing along its polished stone causeway. They found progress faster following the course of the stone wall beside its ditch than trudging behind some snail-paced wagoner, already late with his shipment of barley from Tarentum. The Via Appia was the longest and most trodden Roman road in the whole of Italia.

Corinna had been right about the gate. The guards were so overwhelmed with crowds that afternoon the seven of them were ushered through without so much as a glance.

Once inside the walls Sphax felt he was back in Rome. Not the Rome of the Capitoline or Palatine, but the Rome of the teeming, squalid Subura, with its canyon-like, shit-strewn streets overlooked by four-story insulae and cheap tabernae and brothels. Drains seemed to have been overlooked when the architects laid out this district of Brundisium. At times the stench was unbearable.

Leading them through a maze of alleyways, Corinna finally halted them outside the arched gateway of a crumbling old stabulum. 'This is as far from the Greek quarter as it gets. I shouldn't be recognised in this district. Neither is it the sort of hostelry where customers are asked awkward questions.'

'What's the food like?' asked Agbal, eyeing the place suspiciously. Sphax translated for the amusement of the rest of them as he and Idwal found the counter and booked three rooms.

Swaddled in a shawl that hid most of her face, Corinna gave them a guided tour of the city before nightfall. Not all the city was as unsavoury as the district around their stabulum. But to Sphax's eyes the streets looked mean and narrow, too much brick, stone and mortar crammed into too little space. As dusk began to fall he was yearning for a broad avenue or the open agora they'd marveled at in Epidamnos. Brundisium's forum did possess a porticoed walkway and a fine basilica, but by comparison looked pinched and cramped, no bigger than the fish market down the road.

What *was* impressive were the two interlinked harbours. The northern naval harbour stretched for almost a mile, flanked by the city's wall and lined with stone quays, sheds and warehouses, whilst the anchorage pointing in a southerly direction seemed to be given over to commerce and trade. Set on its gigantic blocks of stone and great fluted columns, the temple of Juno towered above the quayside where the Appian way met the Adria. This was the true heart of the city, its soul. Brundisium was born of the sea and lived from its bounty.

Corinna counted thirty triremes, several fives and even a seven tied up alongside the northern quays. And that was not to mention scores more beached and covered with makeshift wooden shelters on the shore opposite.

It was getting dark as they made their way back through an archway in the walls to the steps of the temple of Juno. Four hundred paces to the east, in a vast square, stood two impressive buildings Corinna was keen to point out. The first was obviously a legionary barracks with turreted gatehouse and walls enclosing an exercise yard. But it was the grand palace beside it that attracted their attention.

After Corinna's cunning forgery, it seemed strange to be staring at the residence of Praetor Marcus Rufus,

Roman commissioner for harbours in Brundisium. Ridiculous as it sounded, Sphax felt as if he knew the man! Yet the only place they were ever likely to meet was on a battlefield.

As the place was crawling with sentries and guards, Corinna was eager to move on. By then Sphax had exchanged meaningful looks with Idwal. The legionaries were all triarii. As in Epidamnos, these elderly veterans had been posted to one of Rome's distant outposts to raise the eagle and keep the peace.

* * *

'What next, Corinna?' Idwal, along with the rest of them were sitting uncomfortably on the hard wooden floor of the Numidians' room, that being the biggest of the three they'd been allotted.

'In the morning I'll ask the slave boy who served us this evening to take you and Sphax to an address in the Greek quarter by the southern quays. There you must deliver a message to Nikolaos to meet us in the Golden Cockerel tomorrow evening—it's a popina off the forum. You two speak Latin as well as the natives. I dare not visit or show my face around the southern quays. Since Dasius I have enemies, and may be recognised.'

'Who is this Nikolaos?' asked Sphax. 'Can he be trusted?'

'Yes. I would trust him with my life!' Corinna was adamant. 'He was my servant, a simple, hardworking soul.'

'So why don't we pay Nikolaos a visit, ask him where the steward whose holding your son lives, and rescue Cleon,' shrugged Drust.

Corinna sighed. 'His name's Titus Voltina. But it might not be as simple as that, Drust. After my blunders in Epidamnos getting two of you arrested, I'm determined to exercise more caution this time.'

'Think about it, Drust,' explained Idwal. 'By now everyone in this city must know of our victory on the Trebia. And because of its Greek connections, they may know something of how the Greek garrison of Clastidium surrendered to Sphax and his Numidians. We don't even know whether Hannibal released the scores of Brundisians Sphax captured. If he has, they may be here, in this city! Then there's the small matter of a hostage of Rome going missing. Rumour breeds rumour ...' Idwal sighed, smiling at his fellow Cavari. 'These are deep, perhaps even dangerous waters, my friend. I agree with Corinna, we walk as thieves in the night ... stealthily.'

'Tell us about this Titus Voltina. We know he worked for Dasius and that snake, Lucanus Flavius, but we know little more,' Sphax pointed out. 'Why did Dasius choose him to be Cleon's guardian?'

'He didn't. Flavius chose him. And he's not spine-less ... in fact, he's very good at what he does, and his services were much sought after. It's just that he's not exactly a man of action ...'

'What does he do?' asked Idwal.

'He's a treasurer and secretary. He worked for Flavius to begin with, then for Dasius. He kept records and tallies, ledgers and accounts, made sure their warehouses were piled high and silver flowed into their coffers. He's middle aged, talks of nothing but numbers, weights and measures, and I was never able to get more than a few words from his wife. They don't have children. What more can I say of him? ... he's steady, reliable and insufferably dull.'

'Not exactly the father figure you were hoping for then?' grinned Sphax.

Corinna laughed. 'No! At least he may have taught Cleon his numbers.'

'And you've no idea where this ... secretary lives,' pondered Idwal.

'No. Flavius took the precaution of finding a new residence for him and his wife *before* we sailed for Ariminum. It's even possible that he's no longer in the city.'

So far, Sphax had rapidly translated their conversations into Numidian.

'Dog's twat, captain!' Hannon exclaimed, 'we're as much use here as a eunuch in a brothel. None of us has any Latin and we don't know this place. We may as well go back and join the rest of the crew.'

Understanding some of what Hannon had said, Corinna raised her hands in protest. 'I need you!' but that was the extent of her Tassynt. Switching to Greek: 'Tell them, Sphax! I need spies and lookouts. I might even need their javelins before we get out of this place.'

So it was decided. Agbal, Jugurtha and Hannon would stay.

* * *

Down an alleyway behind the basilica lay the Golden Cockerel. Few customers were seated on the rough benches of the bar downstairs, but the rooms above were doing a brisk trade, judging from the steady stream of men ascending the stairway, and given their satisfied expressions upon descent. Like many such low establishments, profits were made between women's legs, not from the sour wine or indifferent food they served.

Sphax was surprised Corinna had suggested it as a meeting place. But on the other hand, the bar was badly lit, a long way from the Greek quarter, and like its customers, anonymous.

Before they'd set foot in the place, Sphax had positioned Agbal and Jugurtha at either end of the alleyway. No one was going to spring any nasty surprises on them that evening.

'He's late,' mumbled Idwal into his cup.

'Don't worry, he'll come,' Corinna replied confidently.

They'd been sitting in silence for almost an hour when Sphax noticed Hannon eyeing the customers climbing the stairs a little too enviously. 'Go and check up on our lookouts, Hannon,' he ordered.

At the threshold Hannon passed a man dressed in a grubby brown chiton, eagerly searching the faces in the bar. Catching sight of Corinna, his face suddenly beamed with delight. For a moment the two of them simply held each other's hands and grinned at one another.

'My lady, I cannot tell you what a joy it is to see you again … and you look so well.'

'You too, Nikolaos! Sit down,' gesturing to the bench beside her. 'Sphax, bring the man a fresh cup and pour him wine. We have much to talk about.'

For a while, Sphax, Idwal and Drust listened to the anecdotes and polite enquiries about friends and acquaintances. At least it gave Sphax the opportunity to study the face of the man they were trusting with their lives. Any moment a score of legionaries might descend on the bar, and their lookouts would only give them a fighting chance of escape.

Clean shaven, with a shock of black curly hair that swept on to his shoulders, he guessed Nikolaos to be about ten years older than himself. But there was something about the man's soft brown eyes and bluff, open expression that spoke of honesty and innocence. All his instincts told him this was a simple, straightforward man, incapable of guile or deception.

For all her good-natured banter and expressions of concern, Sphax couldn't help noticing Corinna wasn't giving anything away about her own life over the past year. It was she that was asking the questions, gently probing. At least one nugget of information proved to be useful and made Corinna's position in Brundisium a little safer: to Nikolaos' knowledge, none of the Greeks who'd set out to garrison Clastidium with Dasius had so far returned.

Their ears pricked up when she casually dropped into the conversation, 'And tell me something of that dry, humourless man, Titus Voltina. Is he still wedded to columns of figures and that plain wife of his?'

'Haven't you heard?' Nikolaos exclaimed. 'Since he's come up in the world he's put on airs and graces. These days he won't give the likes of me the time of day!'

'How so?' Corinna asked, now curious.

'Ever since he was appointed quaestor,' Nikolaos lowered his voice to a whisper, 'to that Roman bastard, Praetor Marcus Rufus, the man's become an insufferable, pompous ass, full of his own importance. That's what happens when ordinary folk live in that grand mansion.'

The lighting was dim in the bar where they sat, but what colour Corinna retained, drained away by the time Nikolaos' had finished his tirade. She looked as white as a winding sheet. Sphax reached out for her hand. It was shaking.

Idwal broke into the black cloud of silence that had descended on them. 'I didn't realise the man was from the equestrian class—'

'Equestrian!' Nikolaos snorted. 'He's a bag of shit, lower than a snake's belly ... he has no class!'

'When was Titus appointed to this grand position?' Idwal continued.

Nikolaos scratched the stubble on his chin. 'The day lady Corinna sailed with Dasius. I seem to recall he moved into the praetor's residence that very same day.'

So that was it. Lucanus Flavius had set this up before they sailed for Ariminum with Corinna. Dasius, for all his evils, was incapable of such vindictive malice. But from everything Corinna had told him of Flavius, the man was indeed capable of snatching Cleon from his mother's breast, hours before they sailed, and depositing him with Titus and his wife in the praetor's mansion. By this means he would have a power over Corinna like no other!

It also occurred to Sphax that Nikolaos had no knowledge of these terrible events, otherwise he would have asked Corinna about Cleon. 'Have you seen Titus Voltina's wife since she moved into the praetor's residence?' he asked.

Nikolaos scoffed. 'Mother and I hardly move in the same circles as a quaestor! Besides, the place has over a hundred rooms and a huge garden in the courtyard. I've never seen her on the street, but these days she's got slaves to do her fetching and carrying.'

Sphax recalled the imposing columned entrance to the mansion, its great walls and tiled roofs, along with the sentries, guards and patrols milling around outside. It would be easier to storm the Servian Gate in Rome.

With a great effort, Corinna managed to compose herself. 'They took my son from me, Nikolaos, just before we sailed. They tore him from my arms. I tried to fight them off, but it was hopeless ... then I begged and pleaded ... yet they still took him.'

'Who did this, Lady Corinna?'

'Lucanus Flavius' ruffians,' she sighed. 'Flavius must have done a deal with Titus. He would get him quaestor, if Titus and his wife took my son.'

It was Nikolaos' turn to be shocked into silence. Then he blurted, 'But he was just a babe in arms!' continuing through gritted teeth, 'Those bastards ... those evil, scheming bastards! May they rot in Hades.'

'Then you'll be pleased to know that Dasius and Flavius are already there,' Idwal interjected. 'But would you be prepared to help us?'

'That's why we're here, Nikolaos,' Corinna added fervently, 'to rescue my son from Titus and his wife.'

'Of course, my lady! But what can a poor Greek do when up against Rome?'

'Can you tell us something of Titus Voltina's habits?' asked Sphax. 'When does he leave the residence? What time of day does he return? Who does he meet or speak with?'

Nikolaos was more than happy to oblige, and went on to describe the meticulous habits of a man so set in his ways he was as predictable as tomorrow's sunrise. Come winter, spring or summer, every day was exactly the same as the next for Voltina. Piecing together what the Greek had described, Sphax began to think aloud.

'So Titus works on his tallies and accounts or as the praetor's secretary in the mornings, and at noon precisely, sets out on his regular tour of the wharves and warehouses.' He would order Agbal to dog the man's every step tomorrow to confirm this.

Corinna was staring at him. 'So what, Sphax!' she snapped. 'Weren't you listening? Titus Voltina is a man of habit ... how will this get us past the sentries and into the praetor's residence? There are hundreds of rooms in that mansion. We need to find out which rooms he and his wife use. That's where we'll find my son.'

Sphax wasn't going to argue with her in her present desperate state. But if he'd learned anything from his uncle, it was that the first part of solving a problem was collecting as much information as possible, however inconsequential or trivial it might seem.

Idwal tried to calm the choppy waters by making a sensible suggestion. 'Do you know anyone who visits or makes deliveries to the praetor's residence, Nikolaos? A baker or butcher? A tradesman, perhaps?'

The man was scratching his chin again. 'The praetor's slaves and servants visit the markets and forum most days,' he said at last. 'But I'll give it some thought ... I must know someone who visits the residence.'

And that's how they left it, agreeing to meet Nikolaos in the Cockerel in two days' time. The walk back to the stabulum was conducted in gloomy silence. When they were alone together in their room, Sphax took hold of her hands. 'We will find a way, Corinna, I swear we will find a way.'

'I know ... I know,' she sounded broken, defeated, fighting back tears. The desperate, shuddering gasps of sobbing came later that night, as she clung to him in the darkness.

SIXTEEN

'You can't send poor Agbal out like that,' Corinna objected, 'he'll be arrested!'

'Why?' asked Sphax, alarmed. 'He came with us yesterday without being arrested.'

'Only because I insisted the three of them hid their hair in their hoods.'

'By the gods, Corinna, what has their hair got to do with it?'

'This city has all races and peoples, from Egyptians to Libyans and Nubians. Most Brundisians would not be able to tell the difference. But they would recognise a Numidian if they saw one. Those gold rings in their hair give them away. They'll have to go.'

'Dog's twat, do you know what you're asking? Numidians are not a vain people, but their hair is … sacrosanct. The braids and rings represent status and dignity … who they are. Asking them to unbraid their hair would be an insult.'

'It's not the braids—some Libyans and Nubians wear braids—just the rings. If they don't remove them, they may as well carry javelins and ride around the city on saddleless mares yelling "Ahboojiah!"

Sphax burst out laughing. 'That means 'jump'. I think you meant 'ahbiejiah,' which does indeed mean 'charge!' I suppose it would be alarming if Agbal rode around the city asking everyone he met to "jump!" '

For the first time that morning Corinna smiled. 'I think this needs to come from you,' he said as an afterthought. 'They might just listen to you. I'll go and fetch Agbal.'

Agbal was fetched. In her crude Tassynt and with Sphax's translations from the Greek, Corinna patiently explained why he had to remove every single gold ring from his braids. During the explanation, Agbal visibly turned a paler version of himself, and at the end of it was rendered so speechless he had to send for Hannon and Jugurtha to confirm his ears had not deceived him. Now the three of them listened patiently, as once more she explained her reasons for removing their rings. There was a brief discussion when she'd finished, after which they began unthreading the rings from each other's braids.

When the Numidians left, Sphax stared at her. 'From now on, I think you should command my eshrin. You have them eating out of your hands. At least you're smiling again—'

'I have little to smile about, believe me,' she sighed. 'If only Titus Voltina had not been made a quaestor. He and his wife would still be living in some house in the city or the country hereabouts. The seven of us could have descended on them, forced them to hand over Cleon, and be safely aboard the *Hera* by now. Now we have to contend with what amounts to a citadel ... armed guards and sentries.'

'Blame the malevolent mind of Lucanus Flavius for that. He intended to put Cleon beyond your reach.'

'It's more devious than that, Sphax.' Corinna closed her eyes. 'I'm such a slackhead! I should have seen it straight away. Reading that letter we intercepted, I was so outraged by Alkibiades asking Praetor Marcus Rufus to remove my child to the safety of Rome, it blinded me to a truth staring me in the face.'

'It's not blindingly obvious to me, Corinna. Explain?'

'Rufus arrived at his post in Brundisium months after that lecherous vermin, Lucilus Manlius, left for Liguria. Manlius, if you remember, was the previous commissioner of harbours in Brundisium. The day Rufus arrived in the city, Dasius, Flavius and I were already aboard ship, ready to sail. Dasius and Flavius never met Rufus, I'm sure of it.' Corinna suddenly opened her eyes and narrowed them. 'Rufus does not know that Titus' child is not his own, but the son of a hostage of Rome.'

'Surely not. Flavius must have told the praetor—'

'How could he? I'm telling you. They never met!'

'Then it must have been Titus.'

'Why?' she objected. 'If he'd told the new praetor he'd lose control of Cleon. It's a praetor's responsibility to hold a hostage of Rome, not the job of some minor official, and if Titus lost control of Cleon, so would Flavius. Flavius' power over me would have been broken. That's what Alkibiades was trying to warn Rufus about in that letter. Right under his nose he was harbouring the son of a hostage of Rome, who might be rescued at any moment. I'm convinced Rufus has no idea who Cleon is.'

'Then that's to our advantage, is it not?'

'Perhaps.'

'But it means we're only up against Titus, not Marcus Rufus, Praetor of Rome.' Sphax smiled. 'I refuse to believe we can't get the better of such a dull and tedious creature.'

* * *

Except for a pair of old men playing knucklebones beneath the only lamp that had been lit that evening, the downstairs bar of the Golden Cockerel seemed gloomier and quieter than usual. But as before, business was brisk in the rooms above. Nikolaos was already waiting for them, and looked pleased with himself.

After Sphax poured him a cup of wine which he downed in a gulp, he turned to grin at Corinna. 'The gods are smiling on us, my lady. This afternoon I spoke to a neighbour of mine, a tax collector for the Greek wharves, a man called Damon. He answers to Titus Voltina alone, and visits him every week to hand over his tally of revenues.'

'In Rome,' sneered Sphax, 'publicani are seen as little more than thieves and extortionists. What makes you think your tax collector is any better? Or can be trusted?'

Taken aback, Nikolaos flushed. 'But I've known him for years. He lives with his mother and unmarried sister.'

Corinna was smiling benignly. 'You have to admit, Nikolaos, you are a trusting soul, unlike Numidians, who are less generous. My late husband's dues were paid on the Roman wharves, and the publicani who collected them had no such scruples. Though I've never met the man, I know Damon by reputation, and from what I recollect, he is to be trusted.'

'He's Greek, my Lady, not a Roman thief! Every merchant and captain in the city trusts him ... has done for years ... that's why he always wins the contract. I tell you he's as straight as a groma. And by the gods, don't ever try to bribe him! He'll throw it back in your face.'

'My ... a publicanus who can't be bribed,' sniffed Sphax. 'That's a turn up!' Corinna glared at him, raising her eyebrows to the heavens, but the sarcasm was lost on Nikolaos.

'Well done and thank you, Nikolaos,' Idwal intervened, ever the diplomat. 'All we need is someone who can get us into the praetor's residence: the rest we can manage ourselves. Your friend sounds like the perfect candidate.'

Until now, Drust had been listening thoughtfully. 'When you spoke to Damon, did you mention Corinna, or her late husband?'

Nikolaos's expression betrayed his uncertainty. Reaching for the comfort of the stubble on his chin he recollected, 'I might have mentioned in passing that I was servant to Lady Corinna and shifted cargoes for Arsenios. Did I do wrong?'

'I don't know,' considered Drust. 'You tell me. Other than yourself, it would be dangerous for us to trust anyone in this city.'

'How did you persuade him to meet with strangers?' asked Corinna.

For a moment Nikolaos looked sheepish before beginning hesitantly, 'I ... I told him some friends of mine suspected a merchant of ... cheating. I told him they would pass on ... information, and it was in his interests to meet with you.'

'Perfect!' laughed Corinna, incredulous that this trusting soul was capable of such a deception.

Sphax's eyes were suddenly drawn to a scuffle that had broken out on the stairway. Two men were cursing one another. He watched in frozen horror as a knife blade flashed, followed by a chilling scream. Flinging his victim violently from the stairs, the assailant bounded down the remaining steps, through the door and out into the night. After hitting the tiled floor hard, his victim rolled a couple of times before coming to rest at Nikolaos's feet, spewing blood from a great rent in his belly. He was still alive. But his eyes were glazing over and he was not long for this world.

Idwal sprang to his feet. 'We must all leave. Now!'

Sphax put his arm around Corinna's shoulders, and stepping over the blood-soaked body, steered her towards the door. Drust noticed Nikolaos had not moved, sitting rigid and horror-stricken, staring at the pool of blood gathering at his feet. Dashing back into the bar, Drust yanked him by the arm and manhandled him out into the alleyway. A dog barked in a nearby street and Nikolaos almost jumped out of his skin. There was neither sight nor sound of the murderer.

'Join Agbal at the entrance to the alleyway,' Sphax said urgently. 'I'll go and collect Hannon and Jugurtha.'

They met up half a mile away in a similar alleyway, listening carefully for footsteps or the signs of a hue and cry. Nothing, just deadly silence.

'That place is getting too rowdy for my liking,' observed Drust drily. But only Idwal raised a smile.

When Sphax explained to the Numidians what had happened, Dubal growled, 'I hope she was worth it.'

'What makes you think it was an argument over a woman?' asked Sphax.

Jugurtha sighed wearily, 'Isn't it always?'

For the first time since they'd fled the Golden Cockerel, the moon emerged from behind clouds, bathing their anxious faces in shadow and silvered light. The shocking viciousness of the murder had left a foul taste in their mouths. The warriors amongst them understood killing all too well. But not murder.

Corinna collected her thoughts. 'Where and when did you arrange this meeting with Damon, Nikolaos?'

'Tomorrow night ... back there. I mean ... where we've just left,' he shuddered.

'Then we must think of somewhere more respectable. Could you ask Damon to choose, and we'll fit in with whatever arrangements he cares to make?'

'Of course, my lady. I'll speak to him first thing tomorrow and let you know in person. Where are you staying?'

Corinna told him, adding 'After what's happened tonight, are you happy to walk home alone, Nikolaos?'

'Of course,' he said, putting on a brave face.

* * *

There was much to do before their meeting with Damon that evening. Hera's crew had to be re-supplied, so a wagon and horses had to be hired, and everything from lentils to olive oil bought at the city's markets and loaded on the wagon. Neither had it helped that they were four hands light for these tasks. Someone had to stay behind at the stabulum to await Nikolaos's visit, and Sphax had insisted it was Jugurtha's turn to dog Titus' movements that afternoon. Corinna had been furious, but Sphax was adamant: until they had a clear picture of the quaestor's movements, a Numidian would tail him every day.

It had taken until the early hours of the morning for the four of them to hammer out a convincing story to put to Damon. Sphax's scepticism at the prospect of dealing with an *honest* publicanus hadn't helped, and Idwal's labyrinthine questioning for every conceivable contingency had stretched Corinna's patience to near breaking point. Then there was the small matter of Idwal and Drust's magnificently drooping mustachios. Like the Numidian's gold rings, Corinna insisted they would have to go. Greeks had no such fashion. Except for the Numidians, none of them had slept much and tempers were frayed that morning.

When Sphax returned to the stabulum after watching Idwal and Drust clatter through the Appian gate on the wagon, he found Corinna soundly asleep and Jugurtha already on his way to the praetor's residence. Agbal had seen no sign of Nikolaos, and Hannon was perched on his favourite stool in the bar downstairs, fingers in a bowl of pickled sardines.

Asking Hannon to waylay Nikolaos in case he missed him, Sphax decided to meet the Greek in the city to save him a journey and ensure Corinna slept on, undisturbed. There was only one direct route from the Greek quarter, so he was confident he would see him sooner or later.

So, on a glorious spring-like day, he found himself strolling along the streets of Brundisium, enjoying the midday sunshine as much as time to himself. After less than a mile he caught sight of Nikolaos on the other side of the street, hooded, head bowed, scurrying along like a mouse trying to avoid a cook's cleaver.

After waiting for a bullock cart to pass, Sphax skipped across the street and stood in his path. Head still bowed, Nikolaos tried to dance around him before looking up to see who was blocking his path. 'Oh … it's you, Sphax! Sorry … I wasn't looking.'

Sphax had to stop himself laughing. 'Are you alright, Nikolaos? You look worried.'

'It's nothing. It's just that … last night unnerved me, somewhat.'

'It unnerved us all, Nikolaos. But don't worry, I can't see you getting into a knife fight over a whore.' Gazing up and down the quiet street for somewhere to sit, he suggested, 'There's a bench outside that taberna, let's sit for a moment. Corinna's sleeping, so I decided to come and meet you and save you a journey. Can I buy you wine … or some food perhaps? It is midday, after all.'

'Thank you, but no. I ate prandium with mother at home before setting out, but I wouldn't say no to resting my feet a while.'

They sat in the sunshine, Sphax listening carefully to his directions to find the taberna Damon had chosen as a meeting place. It was only after Nikolaos had finished his lengthy description that Sphax noticed the man. And only because for an instant their eyes had locked, before the other had jerked his head away.

He was standing across the street from them, intently studying the expensive saddles and fancy horse gear on display in a shop selling leather goods. Barefoot, and dressed in a tattered grey chiton, Sphax guessed he was a year or so younger than himself, and judging from his appearance, was not a citizen looking for a new saddle. There was something furtive and deliberate about his loitering. Sphax smiled to himself. Jugurtha was probably employing the same tricks and subterfuge at that very moment to avoid Titus Voltina. More successfully, he hoped.

Nikolaos had been followed. He was certain of it. Sphax made up his mind.

Without any warning he shouted, 'Quis es?' bounding across the street. Sphax had never seen anyone move so fast in his life. Turning on his heels he sprinted down the street like an athlete, dodging everyone in his path with a skill Sphax couldn't hope to match. He gave chase, but after fifty strides the youth ducked out of sight into an alleyway. Sphax arrived in the alley breathless and gasping, and saw immediately it was hopeless. He'd entered a labyrinthine maze of alleys and passageways, and the youth had vanished. Sphax walked slowly back to the bench where he'd left a startled Nikolaos.

'Do you think that was the murderer?' he asked, wide-eyed, in some alarm.

Sphax had to stifle a laugh. 'Silencing the witnesses you mean. One by one!' He grinned cheerily at him. 'No, Nikolaos. That young man was following you. For what reason is unclear, but he's not our murderer.'

* * *

For the second time since leaving the stabulum, Corinna asked. 'You understand why I can't risk Jason's bar, don't you?' The seven of them were striding down the street where he'd chased the youth, earlier that day.

'Perfectly, my darling. I don't want you anywhere near the place. Point us in the right direction when we reach the market. At least by setting out early, you won't have to return by yourself in the dark,' Sphax assured her, side-stepping the real reason he'd insisted on them arriving at Jason's taberna an hour earlier than the time set for their meeting with Damon.

He'd kept it to himself that someone had been following Nikolaos. They were all jittery enough after last night's incident at the Golden Cockerel; there seemed little reason to add to Corinna's anxieties. An extra hour would give them plenty of time to look around the Greek quarter and post his Numidians at all the likely approaches to the taberna. He didn't want any surprises that evening.

'Don't you think it strange, though?' Corinna mused.

'What?'

'That Damon chose a taberna on the same street where I lived with my husband and son. Jason's is a popular and respectable bar, but it's only a few hundred yards from our villa.'

'As you say, it's a popular bar. He may live close by ... even on the street where you lived.'

When they reached the forum where the fish market was held, Corinna reached for his hand. 'This is as far as I dare go. Beyond the market anyone may recognise me.' Idwal and Drust gathered round them as she carefully instructed them how to proceed.

'You must go, my love, it's dangerous for you to linger here,' said Sphax, anxiously scanning the faces of people crossing the empty square.

Following Corinna's directions, in less than half a mile they found themselves standing outside Jason's taberna. One glance told them this was not a low dive like the Golden Cockerel. In the spacious bar downstairs, customers were already eating at tables spaced around a glowing brazier, whilst upstairs, guests would be arriving or preparing for cena. Corinna had told him the establishment also functioned as a hospitium.

'I have an idea,' Sphax suggested to Idwal and Drust. 'I think we should all separate and wander round the neighbourhood until we're familiar with the layout of the streets and alleys. If we meet up here in an hour, we can compare notes before we post my men on watch.'

'You're getting mightily suspicious, my friend,' said Idwal, shaking his head.

'There's something I haven't told you. I don't want you to say anything about this to Corinna, but someone was following Nikolaos this afternoon.'

'How do you know?' asked Drust, alarmed.

'Because I spotted him watching us, idly loitering around on the other side of the street. When I challenged him he turned and fled. I gave chase of course, but couldn't catch him.'

'So your suspicions are far from groundless, Sphax,' observed Idwal. 'You're right to be cautious. But who would gain anything by following Nikolaos? What did the man look like?'

'Just a scruffy urchin of sixteen or so. What I mostly saw was his back, but for an instant I did get a good look at him, and might recognise him if I saw him again. I'm sure he was hired to follow Nikolaos.'

'By the man we're meeting tonight, perhaps?' Idwal said with a twisted smile.

'At least you intercepted him in the city, far from our stabulum,' pointed out Drust.

'I think that's what the lad had been hired to find out. So at least I foiled that part of his employer's devious plan, whatever it might be. And only by the luck of the gods,' Sphax admitted.

As Idwal and Drust went their separate ways, Sphax explained carefully to his Numidians that they were now on a scouting mission to spy out the lie of the land and would meet up in an hour. He refrained from mentioning Nikolaos' mysterious shadow.

* * *

The elderly Greek tending the counter pointed out Damon, sitting alone at a table closest to the brazier. It turned out to be unnecessary. Other than the tax collector, the bar was now empty. But what caught Sphax's eye was the display of dishes sunk into the counter. They looked more than appetising, and he was famished. After ordering food, they stepped into the low-ceilinged room lit by soft Greek lamps, and hovered by Damon's table.

'I am Elpis, friend of Nikolaos,' Idwal began, 'and these are my friends and partners, Attikos and Telamon.' Sphax and Drust bowed in turn. 'May we join you?'

Damon gestured to three empty chairs without a hint of a welcoming smile. Sphax guessed he was a man of some forty years, but it was difficult to judge because his clean-shaven complexion, bald head and bulging brown eyes gave him the appearance of an infant child grown suddenly old. 'You're not from these parts, I take it?'

'No,' replied Idwal, who'd agreed to do most of the talking, 'we are merchants and traders from Tarentum. We own three cybaeae and trade mostly with Syracuse and Catana in Sicily.'

'Bit young to be merchants,' sniffed the tax collector, 'don't you think?'

'Two of our fathers established the business many years ago,' parried Idwal, 'and Telamon's father is still our senior partner. My father is retired.' It was already clear they would have need of Idwal's agile mind before the night was out.

'Nikolaos said you had information for me. He mentioned something about cheating ... a merchant ... it all sounded a bit vague to me.'

Idwal fell silent whilst a servant busied himself around the table placing knives, wine and bowls of food before them. When the boy had left he said, 'Believe me, Damon, there's nothing vague about it. We could only tell Nikolaos the half of it, of course.'

Damon placed his knife in his empty bowl, and pushing it aside, poured himself a cup of wine then carefully diluted it from the jug of water. 'I suppose you're going to tell me the other half, eh?' he said at last, staring pointedly at Idwal.

'Either you or Praetor Marcus Rufus.' That made Damon sit up! Sphax smiled to himself. Idwal now seemed to have the measure of the man. Mentioning the praetor had not figured in the playscript they'd concocted, but it seemed to have worked.

'That serious then. Go on, I'm listening.' And now he was, thought Sphax.

And so Idwal launched into the narrative the four of them had spent an entire evening inventing and then picking holes in until they'd got it right, or so they hoped. Somehow they had to convince Damon that Titus Voltina was cheating by creaming off tax and custom revenues to set up a shipping merchant in Tarentum they'd named Publius. All of them had enjoyed painting a colourful portrait of this Roman rogue, to the extent that they almost saw him as flesh and blood. Publius had risen to become their chief rival in Tarentum. However, the rise had been suspiciously rapid and fortuitous. Too good to be true.

How could a lowly merchant, owner of a battered old trading craft, rise so swiftly through the ranks to a position where he was commissioning cybaeae and building new warehouses every few months? Had he come into an inheritance? A windfall? Married a rich widow? Telamon's father, their senior partner, began to make enquiries.

Sphax was studying Damon's reactions intently. Like any good actor, Idwal had mastered and rehearsed his lines well, and judging from Damon's expressions so far, he was holding the stage and had his audience in the palm of his hand.

'Publius had not come into an inheritance or married a rich widow,' Idwal continued his tale. 'His newfound wealth was a complete mystery. But in the course of our enquiries, we discovered a significant connection with Brundisium. One of Publius' employees, a shifty character called Marcus, once worked with Titus Voltina in a trading company set up by the Greek, Dasius, and a Roman called Lucanus Flavius.'

Sphax was pleased to register that Damon's eyebrows rose significantly at this revelation. Corinna had been convinced that Damon would remember the trading company her late husband ran with Dasius and Flavius. Good lies were far more convincing when spiced with truths.

Idwal was rapidly approaching what they'd decided would be the dramatic climax of their fiction. 'We began following Marcus months ago. We discovered that he visited Titus Voltina every month at his residence in the praetor's mansion. Last week we apprehended and searched him after he left the Appian gate. This is what we found.'

With theatrical aplomb, Idwal reached inside his himation for the leather purse which he dropped beside Damon's empty cup. 'Open it. See for yourself.'

Loosening the leather drawstring, Damon let several silver didrachm spill onto the table before deftly scooping them up and tossing them back in the purse. As if judging its weight and value, he bounced it a couple of times in the palm of his hand before handing it back to Idwal.

'Not enough for a new vessel … but a warehouse, perhaps? And this is just one month's *investment*,' noted Idwal, summing up his case.

Damon sat back, breathing heavily and lost in thought, his brown eyes sunken, staring at some point on the ceiling.

They had now reached the crux of their little drama. It would never be enough to cast suspicions on Titus Voltina's probity and honesty: somehow they had to gain access to his private quarters in the mansion. This next step had been hotly debated in their discussions last night. Sphax had argued that their arguments so far were little more than circumstantial, and at worst, hearsay. And why should Damon trust three strangers as witnesses? Tossing a purse of silver onto a table might be a dramatic gesture, but it was hardly evidence! It was Idwal who realised their *lack* of evidence was the key to opening the doors of the praetor's mansion.

'This proves nothing, of course,' Idwal continued, appearing to founder his own case on the rocks of reason. 'Though the three of us sitting here can testify that Marcus entered the praetor's mansion a poor man and left it wealthier to the tune of this purse, we cannot prove it was given to him by Titus Voltina. Though we have witnessed the two of them together on numerous occasions on the quaestor's tours of the naval wharves, it still proves nothing.

'So, if we took our case to a magistrate, it would falter. It would be our word against his. The wretch would protest his innocence and squirm his way out of it.' Idwal paused significantly and shaped a smile. 'But there is a way.'

Damon's eyes descended from the ceiling and locked onto Idwal's. Sitting up in his chair, his pale eyebrows invited Idwal to continue.

Idwal wiped his smile. 'If we could gain access to Titus Voltina's quarters in the mansion, the evidence would be staring us in the face, written in the fair hand of the man himself. On his scrolls and tablets, the monthly tally of revenues collected will be there for all to see, and could easily be compared with the monthly tallies collected by honest publicani such as yourself. We know Voltina's tally will fall short, that the scales will not balance to the tune of this purse.' Idwal held it once more in his hand. 'But until we examine those scrolls and tablets, we will never be able to prove it. It will be his word against ours.

'Numbers do not lie. Voltina would be condemned by his own hand, and we would have a case for the magistrates.' Eyeing Damon steadily, Idwal picked up the sharp end of his spoon and began extricating clams from their shells.

'I'm not due to make my weekly visit to the quaestor for another three days,' said Damon at last. 'This is such a delicate matter I hesitate to pursue it further until I've made discreet enquiries of my fellow publicani. You must understand these are very serious accusations, and as far as I'm aware, Titus has the complete confidence of Praetor Marcus Rufus.'

Last night they'd agreed that it was vital to force Damon's hand, to drive him to urgent action. The more time he had to ruminate on their story, ask questions or make awkward enquiries, the less likely they were to get away with it.

Tarentum was less than two days away by horseback, and although arch rivals, the two cities had close trading ties. Sooner, rather than later, Damon would find out that Elpis, Attikos and Telamon along with their shipping company were little more than fictions, a chimera invented by the three of them to ensnare him in a conspiracy that would be his undoing.

'I'm afraid time is not on our side, Damon,' Idwal explained firmly. 'We have to return to Tarentum in two days' time, and however discreet, I fear any enquiries you made of your fellow tax collectors would find their way back to Voltina. Rumour spreads faster than the plague when silver is it at stake. After we waylaid Marcus and found that purse, we ordered a slave of ours to escort him back to Tarentum, without letting him out of sight, but Marcus is wily and cunning, I wouldn't put it past him to find a way to warn Voltina. No, Damon,' reaffirmed Idwal, shaking his head, 'we have to act fast and we have to act now.'

'When were you thinking of searching the quaestor's rooms?'

'Tomorrow afternoon, when Voltina is on his rounds of the wharves—'

'—Impossible!' cried Damon, aghast. 'Three days is not long to wait … let me make some enquiries … ask questions.'

'With every delay, our rival Publius steals a march on us, Damon. With Voltina's silver, Publius is out to ruin us!' Idwal appealed to his fellow conspirators for support. Sphax and Drust duly began nodding their heads with theatrical solemnity, playing to their undecided audience.

'I say again, Damon, we must either search the quaestor's quarters tomorrow, or go straight to Marcus Rufus and explain our suspicions to him. In which case the praetor will order the search. Either way, Voltina's scrolls and tablets will be scrutinised for malpractice tomorrow afternoon.' Sphax got the sinking feeling this was Idwal's last throw of the dice.

There was a long and uneasy pause, followed by a deep sigh of resignation before Damon murmured, 'Tomorrow it is then.'

There was not a trace of the triumph Idwal must have been feeling as he asked, 'Where? What hour shall we meet?'

'I will decide and send a boy with a message. Where are you staying?' Doubt still lingering at the fringes of his every question.

It was asked innocently enough, but Idwal was not falling for that. 'At the hospitium hard by the Appian Gate,' he lied, 'but surely there is no need. Can we not decide now, to save you the trouble?'

There was another awkward pause. 'Very well then. We could meet in the Arcadia at the eastern end of the porticoed walkway in the forum. It's less than half a mile from the praetor's residence. Would an hour after midday suit?' asked the tax collector, examining their faces in turn.

'Until then,' agreed Idwal, draining his cup and preparing to leave.

Too late, Sphax realised there was a calamity waiting to happen outside. Hovering opposite the entrance loomed Agbal, looking as if he was about to greet them with his habitual toothy grin. Sphax hung back, frantically shaking his head.

It was only by a slender thread that the publicanus had agreed to help them. Finding out that more men were involved, some of whom had been posted outside to keep an eye on him, might have pushed the man's suspicions over the abyss.

With a presence of mind that belied his years, Agbal had the good sense to ignore them and barge past Damon on his way into the taberna.

SEVENTEEN

D amon was late. Judging from the monumental sundial in the forum—a crowd-pleasing gift to the city from its praetor—by almost half an hour. Leaving Corinna, Idwal and Drust at a table near the Arcadia's entrance, Sphax had posted himself some distance away so he could watch out for Damon's arrival, the cue for him to join his Numidians outside the praetor's mansion, half a mile away.

In case things went disastrously wrong when they entered the mansion, last night they'd decided that Sphax and his men should post themselves outside, and stay alert to any sudden alarms from within. At least the four of them could take care of the sentries posted at the entrance. But Sphax prayed this desperate measure would not be necessary.

And now *he* was late. He quickened his pace. Ahead of him the gaunt, four-square walls of the legionary barracks came into sight, and as the Appian curved gently eastward he would soon see the praetor's mansion and the magnificent columns of the temple of Juno.

But instead, with his next step what caught his eye were three Numidians sprinting towards him, beads of sweat gathering on their brows as they jostled through the crowds. In the pit of his stomach he knew the sky had fallen in. Something was wrong. Something was *very* wrong.

Being the youngest and fittest, Agbal arrived first. Between rasping gasps for air he spluttered, 'They've already set out ... we must warn them!'

'Who, Agbal? Who's set out?'

'That fellow you met last night ... the tax collector,' Agbal gasped, 'he's with Titus Voltina and legionaries. We must warn Corinna!'

So that was it. They'd been betrayed. Why in the name of Artemis had they trusted the bastard? A wretched tax collector! Titus would recognise Corinna the instant he caught sight of her. Hannon and Jugurtha arrived, panting, hands gripping their javelins rolled in sackcloth, panting for breath.

'Why did I not pass them, Agbal?'

'They set off up the street by the temple, the one that runs parallel to the Appian,' he explained, breathing more steadily.

Sphax's thoughts were racing. 'Were the triarii carrying shields?' They all nodded. That should slow them down at least. 'How many?'

'Ten,' gasped Jugurtha.

'We can deal with ten,' he said, thinking aloud. 'An ambush?' Staring in turn at Hannon and Jugurtha he pleaded, 'We must go! Corinna is in great danger. Keep up as best you can.' Nodding at Agbal to join him, Sphax began to sprint back along the Appian.

It was a market day in the forum, crowded with shoppers and traders stalls. Forcing their way through the crowds they halted at a fruit seller's stall where he'd stood earlier. From here they had a good view of the colonnaded entrance to the Arcadia. One glance told Sphax they were too late.

Flanked by several triarii, Damon was about to enter the taberna whilst a tall man, dressed in a spotless toga, organised sentries to guard the entrance.

'Is that Titus Voltina?' he asked Agbal, who'd followed the man for an entire afternoon.

'Yes. What do we do now?'

'Pretend to buy apples and wait for Hannon and Jugurtha.' They didn't have long to wait.

Voltina had disappeared inside the taberna, leaving four triarii idly standing around under the porticoed walkway, two either side of the open door. If Jugurtha was correct about the numbers, and usually he was unerringly accurate in this respect, only six legionaries were inside. Sphax noticed the entrance to the Arcadia would only allow two men to walk through it abreast. All he had to do now was decide on a favourable moment to strike, and with javelins flying, find some way of warning Corinna, Idwal and Drust to make a run for it.

Deciding the triarii would be at their most vulnerable as they escorted their prisoners out of the door, Sphax gathered the three of them together. In hushed tones he quickly explained what he had in mind. When he was satisfied they'd understood, the four casually sauntered off to take up their positions.

Beginning a one-sided conversation in Greek with Agbal, they casually strolled over to a position some five paces to the right of the sentries. Fumbling for his knife, Sphax stole occasional glances at the backs of the legionaries to check they hadn't moved. By now he knew Hannon would be in place, idly gazing at the wares in a jeweller's on the opposite side of the entrance. Jugurtha had already taken up his position, twenty paces directly opposite the doorway of the taberna.

Out of the corner of his eye, Sphax detected movement at the entrance to the taberna as Jugurtha yelled, 'Ahbiejiah!' A word Corinna would surely recognise.

Leaping at the nearest triarius, Sphax sank his blade deep into the man's neck above his mailcoat as Agbal wrenched the other sentry's head back, slicing his knife across his bare throat. On Hannon's side of the entrance a triarius already lay twitching on the ground, whilst the second backed away, levelling his spear. That's when Jugurtha's knife found his unguarded back.

Amidst more screams of inflicted pain, Corinna bounded from the entrance, closely followed by Idwal and Drust, bloodied knives in their hands.

They were all gathering around Jugurtha when two triarii leapt through the doorway screaming curses, shields raised and spears levelled. Idwal's knife deflected one spearpoint, but the other stuck Drust a glancing blow on his hip before Sphax and Agbal's knives sliced into the man's neck. Idwal, Hannon and Jugurtha were slashing away as the surviving triarius backed away, thrusting his shield before him, but he was soon cornered and dealt with.

Now more triarii appeared at the doorway. Corinna screamed for knives. As blades spun and flashed through the air with lethal accuracy, the entrance to the Arcadia became choked with three more Roman dead. Then all went deathly silent.

By his calculations, they'd accounted for all the legionaries. Damon and Voltina were probably cowering at the far end of the bar, praying for a back entrance. Sphax wanted to storm in and wring their filthy necks! But they had to get out of there. By now they'd attracted a crowd of horrified onlookers, staring in shocked silence at the carnage the seven of them had wreaked.

His blood up, Sphax bellowed, 'We will cut the throats of any who stand in our way! Disperse and go about your own business.'

Sphax offered his arm for support, but Drust waved him away. 'I'm fine, Sphax. It's only a flesh wound.'

As they set out for the stabulum, the crowds miraculously melted away, leaving them to casually weave their way through the stalls. By the time they left the forum and sought the shadows of an alleyway, once again they'd become anonymous and unnoticed.

Sphax had only one thought in his head. On all counts they had failed. Right now they needed all the help they could get. By the gods, why hadn't Corinna listened to her mother?

* * *

Drust had made light of his wound. When Corinna examined it shortly after they'd arrived back at their rooms she saw it was serious, and would need to be cleaned up and stitched. So for the next hour she busied herself tending to Drust, keeping her from dwelling on far darker thoughts, more distressing and painful than the Cavari's wound. That at least would heal. Whereas Corinna's situation now seemed irretrievable.

Their plan to rescue Cleon had failed, even before it had begun. Now it appeared her son was lost to her forever, a captive of a scheming quaestor, locked away in some unassailable mansion guarded by two centuries of legionaries. Later, when they were alone, she poured out her heart.

'What have I done to offend her?' Corinna railed. 'Hera has abandoned me. Deserted me! She's left me to the fate of cruel Clotho, the coldest of the Moirai. What am I to do, Sphax? What am I to do?'

He could offer few words of consolation. 'We all swore to rescue your son, Corinna, and that's what we're going to do, by whatever means, no matter how long it takes. I for one will not leave Brundisium without Cleon.'

'Drust has already suffered on my account,' she fretted, fighting back tears, 'I fear the price for my son's return might be too high.'

'Drust came here willingly, out of choice, Corinna,' he pointed out. 'Today we have failed. But we are not giving up. Tomorrow we put our heads together and come up with a fresh plan.'

That night sleep evaded him. Corinna was either tossing and turning or restlessly rising from their bed to sit on a couch by the shutters, lost to dark thoughts and misery. At some point he must have fallen into a light sleep, for he suddenly woke to the acrid smell of smoke. Something was burning.

Leaping out of bed he saw that Corinna was asleep on the couch, but at some point she'd kicked over a Greek lamp on the floor. Oil had spilt out onto a bundle of clothes, now ablaze. Quickly putting out the flames, he reached over and opened the shutters to clear the room of smoke. Dawn was breaking somewhere in the east.

Corinna slept on, oblivious. He was about to wake her so she could return to bed, but thought better of it. Once awake, she might not be able to fall asleep again. Finding his bearskin cloak he draped it around her and left her to sleep on.

It was then he remembered. Sphax had once deliberately set fire to a stabulum as a desperate diversion to draw a thief from a stable. Only, it had worked *too* well. He'd ended up burning the place to the ground. Sphax recalled their names: Marcus and mistress Clodia. Thieves and cheats who'd maltreated his beloved Fionn for years. Recalling their names brought back the rage he'd felt that evening. His war with Rome had begun that night.

That's what was missing from these furtive days in Brundisium. Righteous anger and hatred had been replaced by subterfuge and fear. Every day they walked amongst their enemies praying they would not be recognised for what they were: Rome's nemesis.

This was not a Greek city. It was a Roman cesspit, full of tax collectors, quaestors and magistrates, including a praetor elected by the senate of Rome. Everything about the place made his skin crawl. Sphax had forgotten he was at war with Rome. He was not born a soldier, but fate and necessity had ensured he'd become one. Brundisium must burn. With that thought he knew exactly what they must do.

* * *

'My men and I will set fire to every warehouse and trireme in the Roman harbour. Once Glavus has enough firelight to see by, he will guide the *Hera* into the northern harbour and burn every trireme and quinquereme tied up or beached on its foreshore. By starting such a conflagration, we not only threaten the city, but Rome's naval power in the Adria. The ensuing mayhem will create a stampede, as every legionary stationed in Brundisium will gather to douse the fires and save what they can. In other words, we create the most devastating diversion imaginable.'

'And how will this help us rescue Cleon?' demanded Corinna, for some reason shocked by the plan. They were gathered in the Numidians' room to hear Sphax's latest ideas.

'On his way back to the mansion, you, Idwal and Drust will seize Titus Voltina, take him prisoner and hold him at knifepoint until we begin our great conflagration. Once the flames are at their height, amidst the panic and confusion, you march him into the mansion with a blade at his throat. If our diversion has done its work, every single legionary will be fighting fires in the harbour, not standing guard outside the mansion. We use Voltina himself to lead you to his apartment in the mansion. He's already witnessed what our knives can do, so he's hardly likely to refuse, is he?'

'Then what?' argued Corinna. 'We walk calmly through the Appian Gate, I suppose?'

'No! Of course not,' Sphax snapped back angrily, irritated that she could not see his plan would work. 'We board the *Hera*—which by that time will be alongside a Greek wharf—and sail happily away with Cleon cooing gently in your lap!'

'It's brilliant, Sphax,' exclaimed Drust. 'Not only do we strike a blow against Rome, we rescue Cleon into the bargain.'

'But it won't work, Drust!' cried Corinna.

'Why not, Corinna?' Idwal asked, astonished by her response. 'Why are you so set against Sphax's plan?'

'How will we find Voltina?' she asked sullenly. 'The warehouses by the Roman yards are a labyrinth. Where will we hold him before you start these fires? Then there's the small matter of Glavus navigating the northern harbour in the dark.'

'Because I ordered Jugurtha and Agbal to follow Voltina, I know precisely where he will be at any given hour. And what's wrong with holding Voltina here, in this stabulum, for a few hours? Only his wife will notice his absence,' Sphax shrugged. 'As to Glavus navigating the northern harbour, he's told me himself he knows it like the back of his hand. The Ides is in three days' time, when the moon will be at her fullest. I suggest we plan for that date so the *Hera* can find her way along the coast and into the stag's head. Believe me, once she's inside the northern harbour, the flames will have turned night into day. There will be firelight enough to thread a needle!'

Sphax stared at Corinna, but she remained silent, eyes downcast. He was just as puzzled as Idwal by her objections. 'Is there something you haven't told us, Corinna? Some other reason why you're not happy with my plan?'

'Four years ago there was a terrible fire that started in a warehouse on the Greek wharves.' Sphax caught the sorrow in her eyes. 'Many people perished, including women and children. It was terrible, a calamity. Many friends of ours lost everything ... everything, Sphax,' her voice trailed.

'Did it spread to the Roman quays and naval yards?' asked Sphax, beginning to understand her fears.

'No,' Corinna admitted.

'Then I believe the fires we start will not spread to the Greek wharves,' he assured her. 'Besides, my intention is to fire warships and trading vessels, but a few warehouses going up in flames wouldn't hurt!'

'In view of what you endured four years ago, Corinna,' Idwal began reasonably, 'I quite understand why you have a horror of fire. But we are at war with Rome, and Brundisium is a Roman city. The Greek quarter is small and insignificant compared with the power that sits anchored in that northern harbour. For my part I would happily set a torch in the Roman barracks and the praetor's mansion. Given that we have the chance to reduce Rome's Adriatic fleet to ashes, we would be neglecting our duty if we didn't grasp this golden opportunity!'

'You're right,' she sighed, 'I'm being irrational. Especially when you consider that I almost set fire to this place last night! I'm sorry, Sphax. It is a good plan.'

'Sphax once burned a stabulum to the ground,' Idwal informed a shocked Corinna. 'He's never told you that tale, has he?'

* * *

Three days had seemed like plenty of time to prepare. But there was so much to do, and in any case, the *Hera* would need to be re-supplied before the Ides were upon them. There was much discussion whether torch staves bound in hemp or hessian burned longer. Then there were the endless arguments about the merits of oil, pine resin, sulphur or lime. Because they could burn in water, Corinna insisted the *Hera's* torches should be coated with sulphur and lime, the traditional Roman method of torch making. From his experience of burning down stabula, Sphax favoured the combustive qualities of pine resin, whilst Drust swore by hessian torches soaked in olive oil, remembering the annual processions to the temple of Artemis in Massilia. It would appear that the races of Gauls, Illyrians and Numidians would never reach accord on the subject of torches.

It was only when Idwal calculated the likely number of torches they would need to fire the entire Roman fleet that they realised they were in trouble. It ran into hundreds, not to mention the quantities of pine resin and beeswax it would take to encourage the flames to spread quickly.

Then Corinna remembered a workshop in the city which manufactured torches for weddings and funerals. Idwal was sent out to investigate, and if possible, buy up their entire stock. That's when they received their next shock.

Within the hour he returned, flushed and agitated. 'It's not safe out there. The city's crawling with legionary patrols. They're stopping people in the street, questioning them. We'll have to lie low for the rest of the day I'm afraid.'

'We did kill ten of the bastards yesterday,' grinned Drust. 'And being Roman, they will make someone pay.'

'Probably the good citizens of Tarentum,' laughed Sphax, 'if they believed any of our story. But seriously, Idwal, my men and I will have to risk it this evening. We must scout out the area around the harbour and naval quays in the dark. I don't want to leave it to chance in three days' time.'

Corinna shot him an anxious look. 'You will be careful, my darling, won't you?'

They were indeed the very model of caution, but it didn't stop them from almost blundering into a patrol on a street behind the barracks. By sheer good fortune they found an alleyway to dive into. But the patrols were new and worrying. They'd never encountered them before at night. Sphax prayed it was simply Roman jitteriness after the events at the taberna, and would ease in a day or so. But the knowledge of the quays and warehouses they'd gained that evening far outweighed the risks.

* * *

'I've come with some information that might concern you,' explained Nikolaos as he joined Sphax and his men at a bench in the bar of the stabulum.

It was late afternoon. They'd spent a laborious day heaving supplies on to three wagons Idwal had hired that morning. Amongst the jars of pickled sardines and barley were far more exotic items such as sulphur, lime and rolls of flax, items so incongruously juxtaposed any customs official would be scratching his head at the sight of them all together. But at least they'd solved the torch-making problem. Glavus had a crew of over fifty. They would have to make them. With the city once more free of legionary patrols, Idwal had at last tracked down the torch-making workshop. To the astonishment of the Greek proprietress, he'd paid in silver to purchase her entire stock. Now they would have more than enough torches to fire every warehouse on the quays.

By the time Nikolaos entered the bar and sidled towards their bench, Sphax guessed that Corinna, Idwal and Drust would be approaching the cove where they'd dragged the *Hera* ashore. They were expected back in the city at midday tomorrow, in time for the final act of their mission.

'Do you know if you were followed here, Nikolaos?' demanded Sphax, anxiously. It had been his first concern when he caught sight of the Greek.

'I doubled back on myself twice, to check, so I'm sure no one followed me.'

Sphax was relieved. 'I have much to tell you, Nikolaos. But first, what is this information that might concern us?'

As Nikolaos launched into a long-winded account of the rumours that were flying around the Greek wharves, it soon became clear to Sphax that it was indeed of concern to them. And if the rumours were true, they might be forced to change their plans.

A small fleet of warships had been sighted off the headland, south of the city. They were too far out to sea to identify with any certainty, but rumour had it they were Carthaginian. It had put the wind up Rome, which had long feared Carthage might blockade Brundisium or Tarentum. But Rome had always felt secure in the winter months, outside the sailing season. The sighting had changed this view.

It would take a week to find crews and make the warships in the naval harbour seaworthy, Nikolaos told him. Which meant that Brundisium was particularly vulnerable. Tarentum always had seaworthy vessels ready to meet a threat to Sicily, but not so Brundisium. 'Therein lies the problem,' he'd said, 'there's a rumour the praetor's summoned three triremes from Tarentum. Just in case …'

'How soon could they get here?' Sphax had asked in some alarm.

Nikolaos had considered this for a moment. 'Tomorrow at the earliest … certainly by the next day.' Sphax had found himself fingering his ivory image and praying to the goddess that it was the latter.

EIGHTEEN

Sphax and Agbal were checking the selection of fire strikers they would use that evening when Jugurtha came to tell him there was an old woman in the bar downstairs, begging to speak to him. Intrigued, he followed Jugurtha down to the bar.

Swathed in a hooded brown himation framing a mournful face resembling a wrinkled, sun-dried grape, she must have been at least fifty years old. Staring at him she asked, 'Are you Sphax?'

'Yes, mother. What do you want of me?'

'Nikolaos is my son. Last night ...' her voice suddenly faltered and silent tears began to flow down her cheeks. Recovering a little, she started again. 'Last night legionaries came to our apartment and took my son away.' Jugurtha found a chair for her.

For a moment Sphax was speechless, shocked by the news. 'Sit down for a while and tell me exactly what happened.' Yesterday he'd advised Nikolaos to avoid Damon after the tax collector's betrayal of them. But he'd never expected anything like this. All Nikolaos had done was arrange a meeting. He was perfectly innocent of their devious plotting, and they'd always been careful to spare him the details.

'I was preparing our evening meal when five of them burst in like bulls at a cattle market, saying he was arrested. They grabbed hold of him and started dragging him out of the door before I'd a chance to ask their business.'

'Are you certain they were legionaries, and not vigiles?' The difference was crucial. Vigiles were civilian thief-takers, in charge of law and order. Only a praetor had the authority to order legionaries to arrest a citizen.

'Vigiles don't carry spears and shields, Sir, or wear fancy helmets. They were legionaries all right. My Nikolaos hasn't a bad bone in his body. Why have they done this, Sir?' Once more the tears silently rolled down her cheeks.

'I can assure you your son is innocent of any crime. But think carefully, mother, did the soldiers say anything else to you?'

After a couple of bouts of snuffling she was able to reply. 'They said they'd come on the orders of the quaestor, Titus Voltina.'

So he was behind this, not Damon! What Voltina had done was illegal in Roman law. Sphax guessed this was very much *unofficial* business; the quaestor had persuaded a few triarii to snatch poor Nikolaos, scare him witless and bring him back to the mansion so he could be questioned. Nikolaos was such a trusting and simple soul he would not know his rights, and would believe he'd been truly arrested. 'How did you know to come here and ask for me?'

'The soldiers had no Greek. Before they took him away, my son told me to come here and ask for the Lady Corinna or you. He said you would know what to do. I beg you, Sir, please help us.'

He did know what to do. But even if they freed Nikolaos, there would be consequences, and a price to pay, for both of them. Sphax wondered if mother or son had considered this. 'If we are able to free your son—and this is not certain—you will never again be safe in this city. Titus Voltina will seek revenge, and find a way to destroy Nikolaos.' Smiling softly into her eyes, he added. 'You will have to leave your home, mother. Are you prepared for this?'

She held his eyes. 'My son is all I have in this life, I will go where he goes.'

'Then go home and gather together any possessions that are precious to you and can be carried by hand. It will be tonight.' He said a few words in Tassynt. 'Jugurtha will escort you home.'

* * *

It felt good to hold Corinna in his arms once more, but his news distressed her.

'Voltina is turning out to be a vindictive viper,' she said angrily, after digesting what he'd told her. 'We can't allow poor Nikolaos to suffer on our account.'

'Agreed. Tonight Voltina will be forced to release him. I promised his mother.'

'It might not be that simple, my darling. He might have been removed from the mansion.'

'Then let's pray he hasn't, and you can rescue him. Nikolaos' mother is a remarkable lady, willing to sacrifice everything for her beloved son, just as you are for Cleon. We must do all we can.'

'And we will!' Corinna assured him. 'But three triremes will be more than a match for my poor *Hera*. Should we find out if they've arrived?'

'Our plans are now as fixed as the stars,' Sphax shrugged. 'Knowing or not knowing will not change the outcome the Moirai have chosen for us. We are truly in the hands of the gods now.'

'Is there any good news?'

'Yes. Rome has stopped patrolling the streets and questioning its citizens.' She would have to settle for this.

* * *

Late in the afternoon Agbal set out with Idwal and Drust to apprehend Titus Voltina. Underneath their cloaks they were armed for battle, having smuggled swords, knives and even javelins in the wagons they'd brought back from re-supplying the *Hera*. Returning within the hour with an outraged quaestor, they deposited him in the Numidians' room after binding his hands and feet.

Dressed in an expensive, saffron-dyed toga, Voltina had the pretensions of an eques but the manners and speech of a plebeius. Tall, clean shaven and thin as a stick, his receding black hair was cut short in tight curls, imitating the Roman style. He sat stiffly upright on the couch, glaring contemptuously. Though there was something gangling, almost comic about the man, there was no mistaking the calculation in those darting grey eyes. They missed nothing, like a profit and loss tally, evaluating the world on what could be gained.

'Why did you take Nikolaos? What have you done with him?' Sphax demanded in Latin.

'Shouldn't you be asking why you have taken *me*, a citizen of Rome?' he retorted, his voice piercing and high pitched.

'You are a minor provincial official, not entitled to citizenship. Answer my question!'

'The Greek is of no importance. Whereas you have taken prisoner a quaestor of Rome. When Marcus Rufus hears of this he'll have you tied in a sack and thrown in the harbour.'

For some reason, Sphax thought the image amusing and burst into laughter. 'I think you're referring to the Roman punishment for parricide. Joining me in the sack would be a snake, a monkey and—'

'You deserve nothing less!' Voltina hissed.

Sphax wiped his smile. This was going nowhere. Reaching for the dragon sword he'd placed provocatively between them, Sphax slowly unsheathed it, resting the point of the blade against Voltina's cheek. He watched as the last of the quaestor's defiance drained from his face. 'We need you alive, Voltina. But that doesn't mean I can't inflict a little pain on you … or perhaps a lot of pain, if you don't answer my questions. Which is it to be?'

Voltina nodded, now compliant and obligingly terrified. 'Tell me why you took Nikolaos,' Sphax repeated.

'To find out where you were hiding. Damon and I never believed that drivel about men from Tarentum! But the moment I clapped eyes on that Illyrian bitch in the taberna, I knew her game. She's trying to get back that brat of hers, isn't she? She'll never get away with it.'

'Oh, I think she will, Voltina,' Sphax answered steadily, switching the point of his sword to the man's throat. 'The question is, will you?'

'What do you mean?'

'Once your former employer—an unsavoury character called Dasius, I believe—told her that you were holding her son, she ripped out his miserable throat. And when she confronted another of your employers, one Lucanus Flavius, she sank her knife into his back. Your ex-employers are dropping like flies.' Sphax paused to let this sink in. 'I'm afraid to tell you this, Titus, but your own life hangs by a thread. Corinna is a vengeful creature. If you want to see tomorrow's sunrise, my friend, I would do *exactly* as she says.'

Voltina was staring, eyes glazed, the fight knocked out of him. Withdrawing his blade, Sphax sheathed it. 'Where are you holding Nikolaos?'

'In the child's nursery.'

'Did three triremes arrive from Tarentum this afternoon?'

'Yes,' the quaestor replied in a lifeless monotone, 'the crews have gone ashore. I'm supposed to pay them tomorrow.'

'Then I hope you're still alive to do it, Quaestor.' He left the room, ordering his men to resume guard of their prisoner.

* * *

Midnight had been agreed as the hour of the great conflagration. As Glavus navigated the *Hera* into the northern harbour, he was to light a lamp to signal his position to the Numidians waiting on the northern quays. This would be the cue to set a torch in Brundisium and put her to the flame. But to gauge midnight accurately, he and Corinna had to measure the full moon's arc through the heavens and mark its zenith, which meant periodically standing in the courtyard of the stabulum to make the necessary observations. On their sixth visit, Corinna judged the time had come. After embracing and wishing her luck, he and his men stole into the night.

It felt good to be holding javelins in their fists once more. In truth, he'd known that none of his men had felt comfortable skulking in the shadows of this Roman city, teeming with their enemies. Now the pretence was over, the mask removed. Once more they were proud

Numidian warriors, at war with these people and their legions, praetors, and tax collectors. They were about to go into battle.

Sphax made sure this new bold spirit he'd sensed in his men didn't lead to carelessness. They still needed the shadows. Over the last two nights they'd taken it in turns to scout the streets in the darkness to check on legionary patrols. The fact that they'd encountered none was no guarantee they wouldn't blunder into one tonight. Laden as they were with javelins, axes to break down doors and sacks containing torches and pine resin, movement was in any case slow and awkward.

With Jugurtha scouting sixty paces ahead, they progressed in short bounds, waiting for him to signal the all-clear before joining him and repeating the process. In this way they worked their way through the alleyways behind the legionary barracks and approached an archway in the city's wall that gave access to the stone quay. Once through, they would get their first glimpse of the moon reflected on the glittering waters of the northern harbour.

Standing beyond the archway, Jugurtha looked cautiously about him then waved them forward. They had made it. In the vivid moonlight, Sphax found himself staring down the mile-long length of the quay, with its wooden warehouses backing onto the city wall and vessels of every description tied up alongside.

Corinna had impressed on him that it was imperative to find the triremes from Tarentum and fire them the moment they spotted the *Hera's* signal. Those three vessels offered the only threat to the *Hera*, but that threat was considerable. She'd also warned him that even through the crews had gone ashore, guards would have been left aboard that would have to be dealt with.

Anxiously the four of them scanned the harbour. Sphax's heart sank when Agbal's keen eyes spotted the triremes, beached half a mile away across the water on the northern bank.

Gathering the others in the shadow of the wall he whispered, 'There is nothing we can do. Unless we could swim like otters we can't reach those triremes. So now we go back to our original plan and fire the four buildings and warehouses we selected the other night. Agreed?' They all nodded. 'Agbal's on watch for the signal. Once he's seen it he will run to each of you in turn. Only light your torches on his command. We have much work to do, so be off with you, Agbal, and may Ba 'al Hamūn guide you this night.'

Fifty paces away lay a building Jugurtha had selected because of its size. None of them had managed to gain access to it, but its two storeys and tiled roof spoke of its significance, and by some margin it was the grandest building on the quay. Its solid chain and rusted iron lock should have prevented entry, but Jugurtha pointed out that the wood securing the chains was rotten. One deft blow of Hannon's axe and they were in.

The moment torches were lit they realised they were in an incendiary's paradise. This was the harbour's chandlery. Surrounding them were coils of hemp rope, sails, oars, masts and spars, everything that a vessel required to stay afloat. Better still, in a corner lay orderly jars of tar for waterproofing, and wood preserving oils. The entire building was nothing less than a tinder box awaiting a spark. They left Jugurtha piling sailcloth around the jars of tar and oil.

He and Hannon soon had torches, kindling and pine resin set up in their respective targets; a covered timber yard stacked high with planks, and a warehouse full of jars of oil. Agbal had selected his own target: a huge shed piled with woollen fleeces and rolls of cotton cloth. Sphax found the door stubborn and resistant. When Hannon joined him they switched their attentions to a shuttered window, which did finally give way, Sphax worrying about the noise they were making.

Climbing inside, Hannon lit a torch, looked around and began whistling to himself. After he'd doused the torch and climbed out he whispered, 'There's so much wool in there he'll have to get out fast, before he's roasted mutton!' Now there was nothing left to do but return to their stations and await Agbal.

'Go ahead, Sir, the *Hera's* arrived!' Sphax had his torches already lit, all he had to do was toss them into the piles of wood shavings and wait for Hephaestus to work his magic. Once he was sure it had taken he joined Jugurtha, already waiting on the quay outside Hannon's warehouse.

When Hannon joined them Sphax smiled jauntily: 'Who's going to win the wager, do you think?'

They looked sheepishly at their captain. 'You know about that?'

He didn't, but had guessed they would place wagers on whose building burned down first. They were Numidians, after all! And Numidians would wager on who had the longest toenails. Refusing a wager was worse than spurning a cup of wine. 'Count me in,' he grinned, looking up to see Agbal charging towards them.

Encumbered as he was by sacks and javelins, Agbal arrived panting yet with a great grin on his face. 'Watch this!' he declared proudly, with the excitement of a boy telling his father of his latest triumph.

The four of them turned to stare at the fleece shed, two hundred paces down the quayside. As they watched, a blood red glow began to spill out from the shutters they'd smashed, intensifying in colour through orange to pale yellow with every passing moment. With a deafening whooshing roar, the entire roof of the shed became engulfed in flame before crashing to the ground. Great flame-clouds of sparks and choking smoke filled the air. The violence and suddenness of the conflagration caused them all to take an involuntary step backwards. Agbal had won the wager.

If the fleece shed was the first to burn, Jugurtha's chandlery was by far the most spectacular. As a slave in Rome, Sphax had seen entire blocks of three-storied insulae go up in smoke. For the city's tough street urchins, a fire was an entertainment, just as popular a public event as chariot racing, and young boys gave as much thought to families trapped on upper stories as they gave to the deaths of charioteers.

In a series of violent eruptions, great gouts of flame shot skywards as the various materials stored in the chandlery ignited and burst into flames, refueling the fiery furnace. But by that time they'd torched a score of vessels tied up at the quayside, including a quinquereme they'd managed to scramble aboard. The heat on the quayside became intense. A strong easterly breeze fanned the flames, which soon engulfed neighbouring buildings and vessels. Selene's soft silent light had been transformed by Hephaestus into a roaring inferno.

Above the crackling roar he could now hear human cries and shouts of terror as people ran through the archway onto the quay, their shadows making dizzying patterns in the firelight. At first he could only make out citizens, but these were quickly joined by men in helmets, flames reflecting on burnished bronze. The heat was becoming unbearable, and they were beginning to cough and choke amidst the clouds of smoke. It was time to return to the shadows.

'Follow me. We'll watch from the steps of the temple,' Sphax yelled between bouts of coughing. 'Light your spare torches and sling them at that cybaea,' pointing to the last vessel in the line, four hundred paces down the quayside. When the last of their torches, along with sacks of pine resin and sulphur had been tossed onto its deck, they took to their heels.

Brundisium's temple of Juno Curitis, wielder of the sacred spear, sat on a lofty plinth that could only be reached by a single flight of steps. Its towering columns supported a terracotta pediment adorned with a statue of the goddess about to hurl her spear. From its columned portico the vista was unsurpassed, and the sight that met Sphax eyes would make the goddess weep.

The entire northern harbour was encircled by a flaming ring of fire. Glavus and the *Hera* had done their work. Rome's Adriatic fleet was burning.

Unlike Hera's temple in Epidamnos, Juno Curitis' temple turned its back on the citizens of Brundisium; it had been planned to face the narrow entrance to the harbour and the stag's head beyond. Rome's protectoress in time of war was hurling her spear at the Adria.

Sphax suddenly realised the temple was both a warning and a symbol of intent for all the peoples who lived on the shores of the Adria. Gods should not be there to serve man, or the insatiable ambitions of a state! Juno Curitis sanctified Roman power and conquest. Hers was an *unholy* alliance. Sentiments so far removed from Corinna's understanding of the suffering and compassion of Hera, he found them abhorrent. What had Corinna said? "Juno is *not* Hera."

In a state of unthinking madness, Sphax dropped his javelins and bounded back down the steps. Sprinting through the arch he raced towards the burning cybaea. He neither noticed nor cared about the hordes of people gathered on the quay beside her. Without a moment's thought or hesitation, he leapt on to the vessel's burning deck and snatched up three blazing torches.

Astounded by this extraordinary demonstration of bravery, the crowds decided he was a hero. As he jumped from the deck they began cheering. He disappeared down the quayside, laughing to himself. They had nothing to cheer about! If they'd only known what he was going to do with those torches they would have torn him limb from limb, or nailed him to a crucifix. Sphax was about to commit the most heinous crime in the Roman canon of Twelve Tables.

His first thought was to place the torches against the huge twin panelled doors of the temple, but on closer inspection, he saw they were lined in copper. But his luck was in. They were not locked. Throwing the weight of his shoulder against one of them, it began to creak open.

He didn't need his torches to see the place was empty. Around him burned scores of lamps, suffusing the interior with a soft yellow light. Before him stood a fearsome statue of the goddess, three times his height. Alarmingly, the spear she was about to hurl seemed to be aimed directly at him. Sphax studiously avoided those accusing eyes.

Then he saw exactly what he'd been looking for—a long wooden table that almost stretched the width of the temple. It was a libations table for offerings, and it was groaning with fruit and jugs of wine. Affixed to it at both ends were ornate wooden screens that almost reached to the ceiling. Some of the gifts had been placed inside large bronze jars emblazoned with a peacock design. Pouring out their contents, he picked up two of them.

'Is this wise, Sir?' It was Jugurtha's voice. Startled, Sphax swung around to see his men staring at him.

'It doesn't do to insult other folk's gods, captain,' echoed Hannon. 'And burning down their temples … well, that's just asking for trouble.'

Sphax struggled to explain the unexplainable. How could he *explain* a gut feeling, some instinct deep within his being? Pointing to the stern face of the goddess he said, 'Juno is not a goddess, she's just a symbol of Rome's power and authority. Every time you face Roman legionaries in battle, you can wager your life on it they've sacrificed to this woman and prayed for victory. Think of it this way: I'm just getting rid of their best general.'

With that he placed one of the bronze jars beside a leg of the libations table below the wooden screen, plunging two torches into it so the flames licked up the wood.

'I don't like this, captain,' groaned Agbal, 'I don't like it one little bit.' But he was wasting his breath. He'd seen that look on his captain's face before. It was an expression that brooked no discussion or argument.

And by then his captain had placed the last blazing torch in a jar on the opposite side of the temple.

'My work's done,' declared Sphax. 'Time to get out of here.' They followed him reluctantly, shaking their heads.

* * *

The wharves of the southern harbour were different in design from the Roman quays. Set on piles driven into the mud, some of them jutted into the harbour at right angles from the shore. They had selected the first and longest of these jetties as the place where the *Hera* would briefly tie up to let them aboard. Sphax paced the wooden planking impatiently. There was no sign of either the *Hera*, or Corinna, Idwal and Drust. All they could do now was wait and pray.

Nervously fingering his ivory image, Sphax continued to pace, anxiously staring at the fiery glow to the north west, his thoughts in turmoil. Had the *Hera* run into difficulties? Was she already battling for her life against three triremes? If so, the odds were impossible. But the question that repeatedly stabbed away at his thoughts was: where was Corinna?

'It's the *Hera*,' cried Agbal, pointing. 'She's entering the harbour.'

Sphax followed the direction of Agbal's finger, and could just make out a shape like a sleek shadow, heading towards them. Soon he could hear the regular oar-beats as the craft scythed through the moon-rippled waters.

Ropes were tossed onto the jetty which he and his men secured to the wooden piles as best they could. Soon the craft was made fast and they climbed aboard.

Glavus made his way over to him from the stern, his face set like thunder. 'Why did you not tell us about those three triremes?' he shouted accusingly. 'Their crews are gathering and they'll soon be afloat.'

'We only heard the rumours yesterday. They arrived today, so there was no way we could have warned you,' Sphax explained. 'How long have we got?'

Glavus was shaking his head, 'Not long, lad.' He turned to make his way back to the steering platform. 'Not long at all,' he said over his shoulder.

Sphax rested his forearms on the gunnels and stared down the jetty. Beginning a silent prayer, he addressed it to Artemis, Hera, any god, goddess or deity that would listen. Time passed. He stared, prayed and waited. Time passed, then stood still. Something must have gone wrong.

Then, as if in answer to his prayers, they appeared. Corinna, Idwal and Drust were running as best they could down the jetty. Behind them he recognised Nikolaos, carrying his mother like a babe in arms. Crewmen from the *Hera* leapt onto the jetty and began tearing at ropes whilst Glavus barked orders to his oarsmen.

Idwal thrust a woollen bundle into Sphax's outstretched arms as Jugurtha and Hannon reached out for Nikolaos' mother. Within a few heartbeats everyone was aboard. Sphax found himself staring into the face of a doe-eyed infant, half asleep, innocently oblivious to the predicament he was in.

'Row!' yelled Glavus. 'Row as if your lives depend on it. Row like Argonauts, like men possessed. It's our only hope!' All around him grim-faced archers began stringing bows and reaching for their quivers.

Gently, Sphax handed a sleeping Cleon to his mother and joined Idwal and Drust on the prow, peering anxiously into the darkness. 'You two will be late for your own funerals,' he jibed. 'What happened?'

Idwal grimaced, his lips twisted in a joyless smile. 'Voltina's wife wouldn't give up the child. She clutched him to her breast and backed away. Then she picked up a knife from a table and threatened to slit Cleon's throat rather than give him back to Corinna.'

'Would she have done it?' he asked, horrified.

'Oh yes! By this time she was raving as if she'd been possessed by Morrigú. I'm convinced that after killing the child, she would have sunk the knife into her own breast.'

'What did you do?'

'I picked up a silver candle holder from the table and hid it behind my back. When I got close enough, I leapt at her and landed a blow to her head.' Idwal turned away and stared down into the rippling waters. 'I'm sure I killed her, Sphax … I've killed an innocent woman.'

That wasn't quite true, thought Sphax, but this wasn't the time or place to discuss Idwal's misplaced sense of guilt.

They were about to join the northern harbour, and one glance in that direction confirmed his worst fears. Silhouetted against the blazing shoreline like a fiery sunset were the dark shapes of three vessels. And they were bearing down on them fast.

'Triremes off the port bow,' he yelled.

'Row!' came a desperate command from the stern.

They were now in a life or death race for the narrow entrance to the stag's head. If the *Hera* reached it first, she would escape into the darkness and vast expanse of the Adria, disappearing like a thief in the night. But if the triremes reached it first and blocked the entrance, they would be forced to stand and fight impossible odds.

Like two javelins aimed at the same target, he could see that their courses were beginning to converge. As they drew closer, he could make out the nearest vessel's oars as they rose and fell. Beneath his feet he felt the *Hera's* timbers strain and tense with the effort.

They were close enough now for Sphax to see legionaries mustering on the trireme's deck. She was the swiftest of the three, and with every stroke, was beginning to draw ahead of them.

When all he could see was her stern, she subtly changed course, veering south to force them on to the rocky shoreline directly ahead. Rome had gained the entrance to the harbours.

They had lost the race.

NINETEEN

They had lost the race. But not the battle. Not yet. He'd seen for himself how fast and manoeuverable keles were when faced with Rome's lumbering giants. Triremes had one hundred and seventy oarsmen whilst they had barely fifty, but the *Hera* was light and sleek, her crew skilful and experienced, and sixty Illyrian bowmen would inflict fearful execution on any vessel attempting to close with them.

Sphax, Idwal and Drust joined Corinna, squeezed awkwardly on the lower bank of rowing benches, her sleeping son on her lap. Glavus, already changing the *Hera's* course, was shouting for his crew to haul on a spar and raise the sail.

'Glavus is about to use this stiff breeze to give our oarsmen a respite,' she said by way of explanation. 'We have to fight in the northern harbour where we'll have room to manoeuver. We'll have the tide to contend with, but the southern harbour is smaller and such a tangle of wharves we could easily find ourselves trapped. Don't worry, if anyone can get us out of this rat-trap, it's Glavus.'

'I'm afraid Drust and I are as much use as a two-legged horse,' Idwal sighed.

'Not so!' Corinna objected. 'Take over the oars from Carmo and Elpis, they're strong boys, but they will be tiring. And you, Sphax, gather your Numidians. Glavus will surely bring us close enough for you to loose off javelins.' Her words were such a hopeful rallying cry they felt ashamed of themselves and rushed off to do her bidding.

Without spilling a breath of the wind, the *Hera's* outsized sail enabled them to outpace oars and give oarsmen some respite. But it was all too brief. Already they were abreast of the smoking ruins of the chandlery at the western edge of the harbour; soon they would have to come about and face their enemies.

But with grim satisfaction, now Sphax could see for himself the extent of the mayhem four Numidians and an Illyrian keles had wreaked on Brundisium. They had indeed dealt Rome a blow. The waters of the northern harbour were surrounded by a raging ring of fire, many of its vessels and warehouses were still ablaze, whilst the burned-out hulks of warships littered the northern shore. Even the great temple of Juno was glowing a vivid orange, attesting to its fierce internal fires. Sphax prayed it had become a beacon of despair.

Glavus was once more bellowing orders as sheets were untied and the spar lowered. *Hera* was coming about to confront two triremes fast bearing down on them. As the oarsmen gained their steady rhythm, the dancing reflections on the rippling surface of the water created the illusion they were floating on a sea of fire.

Whilst the *Hera* held her steady course down the middle of the harbour, the northerly of the two triremes matched theirs. They were now on a collision course, the tactic plain; the trireme intended to smash its lethal bronze ram into their bow. If this happened, the *Hera* would disintegrate instantly: all that would remain of her would be a collection of splintered timbers, flotsam bobbing on the waves of the northern harbour.

Sphax watched horrified, a knot gathering in his stomach as the southerly trireme now altered her course to run close in and parallel with the stone quay. Passage through the southern half of the harbour had now been effectively blocked. They now had no choice but to pass the northerly trireme on her starboard bow.

Immediately, Glavus began hauling on the oar to swing them north, at the same time yelling a constant stream of orders to his oarsmen. The trireme's captain responded similarly, veering his vessel to starboard. They were so close now, Sphax couldn't bear to watch.

When collision seemed certain, Glavus screamed, 'Raise!' and the *Hera* swerved violently to starboard as the larboard oars were raised as one. Sphax felt the hull judder and quiver beneath him as the *Hera's* bows smashed into the trireme's leading oars. Rising up,

Illyrian bowmen were now pouring deadly volleys of arrows at legionaries gathered on deck. The distance was too great for Sphax to risk a javelin, but Agbal hurled, and the three of them cheered when they saw it had not been wasted.

By feinting a course to the north, they'd fooled the trireme's captain. Veering north himself, he'd opened a widening gap between the two Roman vessels which they'd somehow managed to squeeze into. It had been touch and go! But once more they had open water ahead.

Thinking aloud, Sphax said to his men, 'We need Corinna up here.' Leaping down to the lower rowing platform he followed its course until he found her, seated on a chest under the steering platform, cradling Cleon in her arms. Knowing nothing of their recent near brush with disaster, she was smiling lovingly at her son.

'Look, Sphax! Carmo and Elpis have made a little cot for my baby out of an old rope chest.' Sphax watched as the boys began stuffing sailcloth into the makeshift cot, supervised by Nikolaos' mother.

He hated what he had to say next. 'My love, we desperately need you on the gunnels. We are still in grave danger. Glavus will need your advice, and Idwal and I have never fought at sea ... we *need* you!'

For an instant there was a look of resentment etched on Corinna's face. But only for an instant. With a sigh she rose to her feet and handed her precious bundle to Nikolaos' mother.

'I swear, my lady,' began Nikolaos solemnly, 'we will defend your son with our lives.'

Corinna seemed satisfied. Following Sphax along the rowing benches they clambered up to the gunnels on the bow, where the Numidians were staring at the harbour entrance.

'What's Glavus planning next?' asked Sphax, peering at the trireme that had been left straddling the entrance to the harbour. 'I feel like a mouse cornered by three cats.'

'Mice can squeeze into the smallest of holes, Sphax. That one's anchored herself bow and stern across the channel, but there are gaps we might be able to steal through. No harm in taking a look. That's what I would be thinking, and it appears that Glavus has had the same thought.'

They were now no more than a hundred paces from the vessel. It looked as if the *Hera* was being deliberately aimed at the gap between the trireme's fishtail stern and the rocks marking the northern shore. As the distance closed, it looked to Sphax that even a rowing boat would struggle to clear the gap. A judgement Glavus must have similarly made, for at the last moment the *Hera* veered to starboard, smashing itself into the trireme's stern below a steering oar, causing the entire hull to swing violently back on its anchor. But a keles didn't have the bulk or momentum to break such bonds, and the anchor held. They had smashed a steering oar and created momentary confusion, but that was all, and now the vessel was drifting back to her original position.

Anyone not clinging for dear life to her gunnels when the *Hera* struck had been thrown to the rowing benches by the impact. As his Numidians gingerly got to their feet, Sphax watched as the Illyrians rushed to the larboard bow and began picking off any legionaries still on their feet. Already the *Hera* was drifting away from her stern on the tide. He could hear Glavus shouting orders to raise the sail and come about.

Only now were the unwieldy triremes coming about at the western edge of the harbour, more than a mile away. At least it would give Glavus plenty of time to think about his next move, and heavy work for the Roman crews, rowing against wind and tide.

'Don't you think your Illyrians should be more sparing with their arrows?' Sphax suggested, 'We will have a real fight on our hands before the night is out.'

Corinna seemed lost in thought and didn't reply. 'I have an idea I want to put to Glavus,' she said distractedly, quickly making her way to the steering platform. Sphax watched as they began an animated conversation interspersed with elaborate hand gestures. Even if they hadn't been speaking Illyrian, they were too far away for him to have heard a word. But what she did next was even more puzzling.

Standing in the belly of the hull, she addressed her Illyrians in what sounded to Sphax like a rousing battle speech. Indeed, it ended with cheering and back slapping before Corinna raised an arm to stop it, ordering them to get on with some unknown task she'd set.

With growing alarm, he watched as the Illyrians began opening chests containing everything from rope ladders and grappling irons to additional weapons and armour. Bowmen were strapping swords to their sides and hefting round buckler shields. Surely Corinna was not considering boarding one of the triremes! It would be madness. They simply didn't possess the numbers for that. It would end in failure and needless bloodshed.

'What are you doing?' Sphax yelled at her. 'You're risking your son's life on some hair-brained plan that will end in disaster! We don't have the numbers to board a trireme.'

'That's where you're wrong!' she screamed back. 'If we can ground one of them, all we need to do is disable her, not capture her.'

'What's the point of disabling her?'

'Because this flood tide will eventually refloat it, you slackhead! We must put it out of the fight.'

Shouting at one another was getting them nowhere, and Corinna was adamant, her mind made up. The situation was now so desperate it was time to put forward his own plan. In his view it was the only possible course of action once they'd lost the race for the harbour entrance and their last hope of escape. She wouldn't like it! But he had to convince her. It was their best chance.

'There is an alternative,' he pleaded gently, walking over to where she stood, glaring at him. 'We could set you and Cleon down on the north shore. This is your only chance of escape. You two would simply disappear into the night.' A thought suddenly occurred, 'My men will escort you, and those two boys, Carmo and Elpis can go with you. You escaped before from Epidamnos, remember. You can do it again. This way you will survive to find your way home.' Sphax paused and stared into those lovely hazel eyes. 'You and I both know we are in a fight we cannot hope to win. We are lost. It's over. So please, Corinna. I beg you! Do as I suggest.'

She gazed at him for a moment, anger forgotten. 'One woman has already met her death clinging to my son. I can hardly blame her for the fierce love she showed, and her courage was undeniable. I would feel ashamed if I didn't have the same courage to fight for my son, to cling to him and defend him with my last breath.'

'But it's—'

'—I will not hear of it, Sphax. Glavus agrees my plan offers our best hope. Help me make it succeed. As a last resort, if it fails, we'll beach the *Hera* and *all* of us will make a run for it.'

He doubted whether there would be time for a last resort, but it seemed it was the best he could hope for. 'What do you want me to do?'

'Defend the *Hera* whilst I and my Illyrians disable the grounded trireme.'

Is that all? thought Sphax. With a handful of javelins!

With a fulling sail and the benefit of the tide, the *Hera* was now surging towards the northern harbour and her enemies. Glavus was already easing her towards the northern shore, and the triremes were likewise adjusting their course to intercept them.

Sphax knew they would not make the same mistake twice. He was right. The vessels had closed the gap between them; not even a mouse could squeeze into that hole.

'I'm praying these captains from Tarentum don't know this harbour as well as Glavus,' Corinna mused, as much to herself as Sphax. 'There's so little water on the northern shore it's easy to run aground. A keles might get away with it, but not a lumbering trireme. If we can only tempt them towards the shoreline, Roman pride won't allow them to let us slip through their fingers once more.'

On this northerly shore they were sailing in semi-darkness. There were no warehouses here, and by now most of the ship-sheds had burned down, the vessels they housed little more than charred hulks. Some were still alight, but not enough of them to cast much light. Sphax sensed, rather than felt the *Hera* being nudged slowly towards the shore, as if Glavus was feeling for the mud on the harbour bottom, listening for its tell-tale grinding and restraining pull. Grounding the *Hera* would be fatal.

Idwal and Drust joined them on the larboard gunnels. Relieved of their duties at the oars, they had dressed in their finest war gear. Idwal was wearing his priceless mail coat and cape, helmet glinting with silver inlays and cheek guards, a long Gallic blade strapped to his waist. Drust was dressed in similar magnificence, but without the additional protection of a mailed cape.

Sphax laughed at the sight of them. 'I feel as if I'm back at the Trebia.'

'Let's hope the outcome will be the same,' grinned Drust.

Unbuckling his dragon sword, Sphax asked, 'Where's Cleon, Corinna?'

'Still sound asleep in his cot beneath the steering platform with Nikolaos, his mother and the boys watching over him.'

'You will have more need of this,' he said, handing his sword to Corinna. 'Cleon is now my son, and I swear I will defend him.'

'Let's pray you don't have to,' she replied, anxiously staring at the two triremes, now little more than three hundred paces distant and closing rapidly. They all felt a sudden juddering sensation beneath their feet. Seeing their looks of alarm, Corinna reassured them, 'This is as close to the shore as Glavus dare take us.'

The grinding and juddering continued intermittently, but it didn't seem to affect the *Hera's* speed much. All eyes were now fixed on the triremes, two hundred paces away. If the trireme closest the shore didn't alter course, the *Hera* would smash into her portside oars, which would be just as disastrous as a grounding, leaving her dead in the water. Glavus was giving the Roman captain little choice: either he shipped his oars and lost steerage, or risked the shallow waters of the shoreline. As the *Hera* continued to grind and judder, Sphax counted down the distance.

It all happened so fast. Veering towards the shore, the northerly trireme ground to a sudden halt amidst the sickening sound of splintering timbers.

Above the cacophony, Corinna and Glavus began yelling orders. As the *Hera* veered away from the shore, oars were shipped and sail lowered as sixty Illyrians rushed to the starboard gunnels carrying everything from grappling hooks to rope ladders.

Desperately, the second trireme veered towards them hoping to intercept. But it was too late. Open water between the triremes now beckoned, and the *Hera* glided into it.

Giving the bow and its ram a wide birth, Glavus steered onto her starboard bow and aimed the *Hera's* prow at the trireme's double row of oars, dangling uselessly over the side.

Again Sphax recoiled from the sound of splintering wood. Glavus was using the *Hera* as a mighty axe to splinter the trireme's oars. At last the *Hera* came to a juddering stop at the ninth row.

By then the iron claws from a score of rope ladders had bitten into latticed railings and Illyrians were swarming on to the deck of the stricken vessel like a pack of ravenous wolves.

Corinna had been right. They did have the numbers. Sphax hadn't counted the oarsmen; as skilled with sword and buckler as they were at oars.

Sphax watched anxiously with Idwal, Drust and his Numidians as the fight on the deck degenerated into a series of isolated skirmishes between outnumbered legionaries and swarms of marauding Illyrians, whose bowmen were picking them off at close range.

'Take a look at this!' It was Glavus, who'd arrived panting on the portside gunnels after traversing the length of the vessel from the steering platform. Half a mile away, the other trireme was laboriously coming about, but would soon have the advantage of the wind and tide. 'Our oars have been shipped, so they can come hard alongside. We may as well invite the bastards aboard!'

'Could we push the vessel away with our oars, once it came alongside?' suggested Idwal.

'Maybe, if we had half a crew. But they're over there,' he grunted, nodding towards the deck of the grounded trireme.

'Agbal,' Sphax yelled, 'hand me your javelins. Climb on to the deck of the trireme. Find Corinna and tell her that the *Hera* will be taken unless she sends me oarsmen immediately. Go, lad. *Now!*'

As Agbal leapt down to the lower rowing benches, Sphax shared out the javelins between Jugurtha and Hannon. All eyes were now riveted on the trireme, coming slowly about.

'She'll ship oars to cut her speed,' Glavus explained without taking his eyes off the vessel. 'As she does so she'll throw out grappling irons to hold us fast and bring her to a stop. Cut those ropes if you can. Our greatest threat lies amidships, where the hulls will touch. Bearing in mind the trireme's deck is taller by a man's height, all the bastards have to do is leap on us.'

'None of them have faced Numidian javelins or tasted Gaulish iron, Glavus. Let them come,' growled Sphax, climbing down to the lower rowing platform in search of swords for himself and his men. He found three swords with long curved blades, much favoured by Illyrians. Designed purely for slashing, they required little skill to be effective. Grabbing three small buckler shields for good measure, he began climbing back up.

It worried him that Idwal and Drust lacked their great oval shields. Sphax turned to Idwal, offering up the bucklers. 'Would these be of any use?'

'It's a selfless thought, my friend. But you will have need of them more than us.' Under the circumstances, he was amazed to see Idwal smile. 'I'm sure I can persuade a triarius to *lend* me his.'

Idwal's confidence was infectious. Sphax found himself grinning. 'This is not a cavalry action, Idwal. We follow your command. Place us where we'll be most effective.'

Sphax found himself standing amidships beside Glavus, who'd armed himself with spear and shield. Idwal and Drust stood either side of them and Idwal had posted Jugurtha and Hannon on either flank.

With a knot of fear gathering in his stomach and quickening heartbeat, Sphax stared at the trireme fast bearing down on them and carefully threaded his saunion. A final thought occurred. Between them they had only thirteen javelins. Every barb had to count. 'Numidians,' he yelled, 'don't waist javelins on legionaries perched on the deck of the trireme. Slay only those who leap down to assail us.'

With oars raised, the towering hull of the trireme came abreast of them amidst the sound of iron grappling hooks biting into gunnels and the steering platform. As the ropes holding them fast began to strain and tighten, the tide and sheer momentum of the trireme threatened to tear the *Hera* away from the grounded trireme off its starboard bow. With every timber groaning and creaking, somehow she held fast. But now three vessels were gripped by iron claws, with the hapless *Hera* trapped in the middle.

First came the spears. Backing away, they found themselves dancing and dodging or taking shelter on the lower platform. Before the fight had even started Sphax's buckler was rendered useless by a pilum buried too deep to remove.

The first to leap aboard was a centurion in search of glory. It proved a short-lived quest. Idwal's blade cleaved the man's head from his shoulders. With its plumed helmet still attached, it bounced from bench to bench on its descent into Hades. Idwal had his shield.

Next to die was a triarius, lunging at Drust with levelled spear. Nimbly stepping aside, Drust swept his sword in a scything arc that opened the man's throat in a bloody shower. Then everything happened at once. Faster than thought or deliberation could ever command, now pure instinct and the desperate will to survive took hold of Sphax.

His saunion ripped into a throat before his next javelin found a veles' chest. Down to his last javelin, he reached for his Illyrian blade in time to slash wildly at faces lunging at him. His last javelin found the neck of a hastatius.

But there were so many of them, and they kept coming. Sphax was reduced to frenzied slashing just to keep them at bay and stay alive.

Someone suddenly leapt onto his back, sending him sprawling to the ground with such force that his sword slipped from his grasp. Unknown hands gripped his throat in a choking grip, fingernails clawing his flesh as thumbs pressed ever deeper into his neck.

With a supreme effort he managed to shake him off, his assailant rolling over before coming to rest against a rowing bench. Sphax cursed the gods. In single combat, why were his adversaries always a head taller and twice his weight?

Struggling to his feet he backed away, but the triarius had grabbed his sword and was about to finish him off. Too late he remembered his knife. But before he could reach it another knife flashed over his right shoulder, burying itself deep into the man's left eye, sending him screaming backwards onto a rowing bench where Idwal found him and finished him off.

Sphax turned to see Corinna standing behind him, arm still poised with the effort of the throw. Smiling to himself, he realised now why the gods had chosen a taller opponent.

By now the air was thick with arrows and Rome was in retreat, their men desperately trying to scramble back aboard their trireme. 'What kept you?' he asked, failing miserably to make light of the fact that she'd just saved him from certain death.

'It seems I arrived just in time,' smiled Corinna, visibly relieved. Gathering her thoughts she added, 'We need to cast these triremes adrift.' Switching to Illyrian she began bellowing a string of orders. Soon a score of men were hacking away at the grappling ropes binding the *Hera* to the trireme, whilst a dozen more were retrieving rope ladders and grappling irons that bound them to the grounded vessel.

Casting around for his men, he saw them bent on their knees beside Idwal and Drust, leaning over a fallen comrade. It was Glavus. Skewered by a triarius' spear.

Sphax felt a stab of guilt. He was standing at Glavus' right hand when the legionaries leapt down to begin the fight. Idwal had placed him there. He should have remained steadfast at the old man's side, defending him, protecting him. Instead, in the frenzy of that moment his only thought had been to slay his enemies, to grind them into dust, to toss them overboard with a javelin in their throat.

Maharbal, his general and great mentor had once told him, "When faced with a choice between glory and duty, always choose duty. Duty sometimes brings glory, but there is no glory to be had in neglecting one's duty."

Once again he'd failed.

Sphax watched as the four of them solemnly raised Glavus' body to their shoulders and made their way slowly down the rowing benches to the steering platform. Once they recognised the burden being carried, every Illyrian stepped swiftly aside, and with bowed heads, placed hands over hearts as a mark of respect and farewell. When Glavus had been positioned in a place of honour behind his vacant steering platform, Sphax sought out Corinna to break the ill tidings and confess his neglect of duty.

'You are a Numidian warrior, Sphax, trained to assail your enemies, not hold back to defend those weaker than yourself,' Corinna reflected. 'You are absolved of all blame for his death,' she added, solemnly shaking her head. 'Glavus was no warrior, but he embraced his fate willingly, as should we all. Let us honour his passing, not mourn his fate.'

Idwal had joined them and listened in silence as Sphax had confessed his neglect. Now he spoke up. 'Of the twenty bodies I counted strewn over the rowing benches, thirteen were slain by javelins. If you, Hannon and Jugurtha had not made every javelin count, we would all be sharing the ferry with Glavus, as Charon rowed us across the Styx.'

* * *

Cut loose from each other, the *Hera* and the larboard trireme began drifting eastwards on the vagaries of wind and tide, but the *Hera's* crew were well drilled and the first to man oars. This and her inherent manoeuverability ensured she was first to come about and face westwards. Corinna had taken over the steering oars. Sphax and Idwal standing resolutely beside her.

Instead of turning about to pursue them, the three of them watched with sinking hearts as the enemy trireme returned to the stone quay to take on board scores more legionaries, fresh for the fight that was surely to come.

Little had changed. An enemy trireme had been grounded and disabled, but another lay anchored, barring the harbour entrance and with it their only means of escape. Meanwhile, their immediate enemy was now teeming with fresh men, spoiling for a fight.

Corinna was staring grimly at the vessel blocking the harbour entrance. 'I'm going to try and ram the anchored trireme one last time. If we can strike her amidships, at her weakest point, we may do enough damage to ...'

'And if we can't?' questioned Idwal, bleakly.

'I'll beach the *Hera* on the northern shore,' she sighed. 'Even if the gods favour us, I fear that few of us will escape. After what we have inflicted on their city, Rome will hunt us down like dogs!'

His Numidians, along with any Illyrians with arrows left in their quivers had positioned themselves at the bow. Even at this desperate hour they were still determined to inflict pain and death on their enemies. At whatever cost.

Corinna pointed the *Hera's* bow at their foe and began chanting rhythmically to coordinate her oarsmen. Creaking under the strain, the vessel began to gain speed.

Fingering his ivory image, Sphax turned around to stare at the smouldering stone quays for the last time. The trireme had cast off and was now in pursuit of them. They had thrown the last dice. Tumbling through the air the die would fall and come to rest as the gods decided their fate.

With his eyes locked on the anchored trireme, now only four hundred paces distant, Sphax found the shouting and cheering that had broken out amongst the men gathered at the bow puzzling. What were they thinking? Didn't they realise they were about to strike a trireme with all the force and power their oarsmen could muster? Some were even dancing around! Surely they would be thrown overboard when the *Hera* struck?

Then he lifted his eyes and gazed beyond, into the waters of the stag's head, lit by the first fingers of dawn's golden light. At first he thought his eyes were deceiving him. Turning to Corinna he cried, 'How can this be?' But there could be no mistake.

Driven by wind, tide and three hundred oarsmen, the vast hull of a quinquereme loomed into sight, heading for the harbour entrance at great speed and flanked by two keles. Painted on her great square sail, fulling and billowing in the breeze was the black serpent of Illyrios, come like some ancient demon from the underworld to destroy all who dared stand in her path.

It was not a Carthaginian fleet that had been sighted off the headland south of Brundisium. It was Illyrian! And the raging ring of fire and flame around the harbour of Brundisium had acted as a beacon, a call to arms, to war! Queen Teuta and Demetrius of Faro had answered that call and were leading the charge.

All the oars aboard the *Hera* ceased their work as men scrambled to the gunnels to stare with bated breath. As the great bronze ram of the quinquereme neared its target, Sphax too held his breath.

In the space between heartbeats the anchored trireme ceased to exist. Amidst the thunderous roar of splintering timbers the vessel was torn asunder, split in two as easily as a woodsman's axe cleaves a log. One moment she was there, bobbing idly at anchor, and in the next, all that was left of her was a tangle of wreckage, slowly sinking below the waves. But *Illyrios* sailed majestically on, as if she'd brushed aside nothing more than a twig caught in her path.

Open-mouthed, and without a word to one another, the three of them turned around to stare astern at the trireme that had been relentlessly pursuing them. Her helmsman, suddenly realising the dire peril she was in, began to swing the vessel's bow southwards.

'The captain's realised he hasn't time to come about, so he's making for the Greek quays,' Corinna observed with a tension that was evident. 'But I'm sure he's misjudged our quinquereme's speed.'

He had. But he almost got away with it. Sphax could only imagine the sheer terror of the crew as they rowed for their lives with the great hulk of the quinquereme bearing down on them at speed.

She was about to enter the Greek harbour when *Illyrios* caught her a glancing blow forward of her steering platform. One of the trio of spikes on the quinquereme's ram must have bitten home, deep below the trireme's waterline. *Illyrios'* momentum and great bulk did the rest, slicing along the length of the vessel's hull as a knife fillets the flesh of a fish.

Swinging hard to larboard, *Illyrios* shook herself free from the stricken trireme and began to come about, lowering her starboard oars.

Already listing heavily from the fatal rent gouged below her waterline, Sphax stared aghast as the trireme suddenly keeled over on her side, her tall mast, spar and flapping sail striking the water with a whip-like splash. Within moments she'd disappeared beneath the waves amidst a seething cauldron of bubbles.

It was over.

As the quinquereme swept past the *Hera's* starboard bow she received rousing cheers from all the crew gathered on the gunnels. Corinna already had her son in her arms. Now she raised him high above her head so all aboard the quinquereme could see that Illyria's future king had been rescued. All Sphax could recollect later was the fleeting image of Teuta herself, dressed in her finest war gear, waving a spear like some triumphant sea-nymph.

The soft light of dawn now stretched over the vast horizon of the Adria, bringing to an end this night of fire and flame, death and destruction. Gathering Corinna and her child tenderly in his arms, he sniffed the salt-laden breeze from the east; it smelled sweet with the promise of safe passage and journey's end.

HISTORICAL
NOTES

I t is often understated how geographically wide-ranging the Hannibalic Wars (Second Punic War) became. By the time of Hannibal's defeat at the Battle of Zama in 202 BC., war had raged over the Iberian peninsula, transalpine Gaul, the Italian peninsula stretching to its heel at Tarentum, the Greek and Illyrian Adriatic, Greek states such as Macedon, and finally to Africa itself. Hannibal's army contained contingents from all races and peoples bordering the shores of the Mediterranean, including Lusitanians (modern Portugal), Numidians, Libyans, and of course Gauls from transalpine Gaul. There is even evidence for a contingent of Cretan archers.

After the death of Hiero II of Syracuse (one of Rome's staunchest allies) in 215 BC, unrest spread to Sicily. A Carthaginian whispering campaign weaned his successor, Hiero's grandson Hieronymus, away from an alliance with Rome. Hieronymous' murder only intensified the factional fighting, and for a time Sicily was drawn into the war. Even far flung Ptolemaic Egypt and Syria's Seleucid empire were almost drawn into the conflict through the ongoing rivalries between Ptolemy IV, Antiochus III, and Philip of Macedon.

So, this titanic struggle for hegemony between Carthage and Rome can be seen as a truly Mediterranean-wide conflict.

Nowhere are the Hannibalic Wars more complex, and indeed confusing, than in the Greek sphere of influence. Ever since Pyrrhus' invasion of Italy in 280 BC and his costly victories—that's where we get the term *pyrrhic victory*—Republican Rome kept a watchful eye on events across the Adriatic and Aegean seas. In the patchwork of states and autonomous cities run by anything from elected democratic councils to outright despots, the Greek world was plagued by endemic warfare.

Leagues and counter-leagues, such as the Aetolian and Achaean, were perhaps the first attempts at Greek federalism, but Rome played them off against each other, usually to curb the great power in the land, Macedon, and its young king, Philip V. When Philip negotiated an alliance with Hannibal in 215 BC (the negotiations cover a period of two years, so my conjectures in *The Hostage of Rome* that initial contacts were begun in 217 BC might not be far from the mark), and Rome learned of its detailed clauses (yet another thrilling story of espionage, subterfuge and adventure), she promptly declared war on Macedon.

Rather than setting the cat amongst the pigeons, this precipitous action by the senate could well have backfired, leading to Rome's destruction. Macedon at this time was allied to the powerful Achaean league. If the two of them had launched an assault on Italy's Adriatic seaboard at the same time as Hannibal was rampaging through southern Italia, Rome's very survival would have been in doubt, and the entire history of western Europe would have been re-written.

If I were to write a counterfactual history of the Hannibalic War, Rome's ill-advised declaration of war on Macedon would be my starting point!

Which brings me to Illyria (modern day Albania, Montenegro and Croatia), a kingdom on the margins of the Hellenistic world, yet dotted with isolated Greek coastal colonies such as Pharos, Epidamnos and Apollonia. Cities that had come under Rome's *protection* and sphere of influence. At times, the relations between Illyrians and Greeks was far from neighbourly. For their part, Greeks saw Illyrians as not much better than barbarians. By the time *The Hostage of Rome* begins, Rome had already launched two expeditions against Illyria: the first, to curb Teuta in 229 BC, and the second, to put an end to Demetrius' raiding and piracy by occupying Pharos in 219 BC. After his defeat, Demetrius fled to Macedon.

There can be little doubt that queen Teuta and Demetrius of Pharos were colourful characters. In this period it's almost unheard of for a woman to ascend a throne and rule in her own right, so we must assume she was a powerful and charismatic individual. However, the portrait the Greek historian Polybius paints of her is most unflattering:

> listened with an insolent and disdainful air ... answered with womanish passion and unreasoning anger.

But there again, Polybius is a notorious misogynist! The passage in his *Histories* that most intrigues me is where he obliquely hints that Teuta and Demetrius might have been more than just friends. If this is to be inferred, Demetrius' switching sides echoes the ancient Greek dramatic trope of love and betrayal.

Speculation aside, history offers us no help (or a golden opportunity for the historical novelist!). After Rome banishes Teuta to Rhizon, she vanishes without trace from the historical record. I simply refuse to believe that this queen of womanish passion and unreasoning anger would be content to live out the rest of her days in a quiet backwater of northern Illyria. For instance, we do know that the great fleet Philip amasses was built by Illyrian shipwrights. Who supplied them?

Similarly, after Demetrius' eviction from Pharos, he is barely mentioned by later historians. It is known that he became a trusted lieutenant of Philip and fought in Macedon's many wars, but beyond this, he remains a blank.

As a great deal of the action of *The Hostage of Rome* takes place at sea, I think it might be helpful for readers if I say a little about piracy and warfare at sea. In the Greek world piracy was as endemic as warfare, but rather than ship-on-ship actions, it was far more profitable for states to sponsor mercenaries, who would gather a hundred lemboï together, descend on a coastal city, capture it, then ransom it, the state taking its cut.

Illyrians were notorious for this form of piracy. This is how Teuta's late husband, Agron, and Demetrius of Pharos acquired their great wealth, and why Rome was prepared to launch consular armies to quash such anarchic lawlessness. Nothing incensed the Roman senate more than threats to its merchants and seaboard trade.

Other than raiding and piracy, historians have little to say about the war at sea in the Hannibalic Wars, for the simple reason that Rome overwhelmingly dominated the seaways, possessing vast fleets that patrolled the central Mediterranean. Carthage still maintained a large fleet, but underplayed her hand, and offered Hannibal little aid when he most needed it.

For Rome, the magnificent harbours of Tarentum and Brundisium were key to the war at sea. Tarentum was tasked with providing warships that could counter any sudden Carthaginian threat to Sicily, whilst Brundisium, as gateway to the Adriatic, beached her vessels in the storm months but was expected to resume patrols in late spring.

Warfare at sea was brutally simple: vessels could either be rammed and sunk, or boarded and captured. In the First Punic War, being new to naval warfare, Rome preferred to rely on her seasoned legionaries to board Carthaginian vessels and take them. She even invented a spiked boarding bridge called a 'raven,' which could be lowered quickly onto an enemy deck to enable legionary marines to cross in overwhelming numbers.

During the Hannibalic Wars the workhorse of the Roman navy was the trireme, a decked vessel of thirty-seven meters with its oarsmen arranged in banks of three, one above the other. Additional propulsion came from a large square-rigged sail amidships, and a much smaller, forward-pointing bow sail. Typically, it was armed with a triple-spiked bronze ram, and flat out, could reach speeds of 10 knots (11.5 mph). Speed enough to slice through an enemy hull as easily as a can-opener! A favourite tactic was to attack from the rear, shredding banks of oars before swerving the ram into the exposed hull.

Relics such as quinqueremes from the First Punic War had been mothballed and maintained in weatherproof sheds in most Roman harbours during this period. Eight metres longer than triremes, with two rowers assigned to each upper tiers of oars, quinqueremes were heavier and faster, but far less manoeuverable than triremes.

With the rapid advances in naval technology during this period, one is reminded of the naval arms race in the early twentieth century, and the scramble to build bigger and more powerful dreadnoughts. Besides quinqueremes (fives), there is evidence of sevens, eights, and even nines, constructed using twin-hulled, catamaran style technology, but these were built for prestige and status, not for their dubious fighting qualities.

Illyrian shipwrights were never interested in these lumbering giants, instead putting their ingenuity into designing and building much lighter and sleeker craft, with good speed and above all, superior manoeuvrability. The ubiquitous lemboï was the pirates' vessel of choice. Undecked, up to eighteen metres long, four wide and without sails, it relied on a single row of oarsmen either side of the hull, yet it could reach remarkable speeds in short bursts.

Keles proved to be a natural development of the lemboï's tried and trusted design, without sacrificing its manoeuvrability. Considerably longer and broader in the beam than lemboï (but still a lightweight by trireme standards), they carried a double bank of oarsmen (up to forty-eight warrior/rowers) in addition to a great square sail. Within the undecked hull, a keles had the capacity to carry up to a hundred warriors. Seventy years after the events I describe in *The Hostage of Rome*, celes (in the Latin) would become the scouts of the Roman navy, the eyes and ears of its fleets.

To our modern sensibilities the practice of hostage taking seems shocking, invoking images of highjack or terrorism. In the classical world such images had yet to be implanted. Hostages were a common occurrence, guaranteeing compliance of treaties, alliances and agreements. On the whole, hostages were treated well, especially if they were highborn. The historian Polybius was himself a hostage, spending seventeen years in Italy as teacher, client and advisor to the Scipio family.

Finally, I must say a few words about Brundisium. I have already described it as Rome's gateway to the Adriatic. But its importance can be gauged by the fact that one of the earliest and most trodden roads in Italy led from Rome to Brundisium. The Appian way, queen of roads, reached its end overlooking the harbour, marked by two giant columns seventeen metres high. One of these columns still stands today, an ancient sentinel, guarding the harbour entrance. In *The Hostage of Rome* I take liberties with these columns, imagining they supported a great frieze and pediment above the entrance to a temple dedicated to the Roman goddess Juno, protectoress and defender of Rome. It makes perfect sense to me, but unfortunately, I can offer no archaeological evidence to back up my claim that a temple ever existed on this site.

Originally, Brundisium was a Greek trading post, but by the time Sphax and Corinna arrive within its walls, it had become a major colonial outpost of the Roman Republic. Its outer harbour—the stag's head— led to two vast inner harbours—the stag's antlers— via a narrow channel. These sheltered inner harbours, providing space for entire fleets to lie at anchor, was why Rome regarded Brundisium as crucial in her war efforts against Hannibal, and why each year the senate elected a praetor to be Commissioner of the Harbours of Brundisium.

Dear Reader

Thank you so much for reading *The Hostage of Rome*. If you have enjoyed the story, I would really appreciate it if you took the trouble to write a review on the site where you purchased the novel. Just a simple sentence is always helpful! If, like me, your favourite place to buy books is from a bookshop on the High Street, you can still write a review on Goodreads or any site where you enjoy sharing your passion for books. Please contact me on my website if you have any questions about Sphax and his adventures. I'd love to hear from you!

www.robertmkidd.com

I'm also on

Facebook & Twitter

If you would like to read more about Sphax's adventures, why not try the first book in The Histories of Sphax Series—*The Walls of Rome*.

The Walls of Rome

THE HISTORIES OF SPHAX SERIES

⟿ BOOK 1 ⟿

218 BC. Sphax is seventeen and haunted by the brutal murder of his parents at the hands of Rome. After ten years of miserable slavery he will make his last bid for freedom and go in search of Hannibal's army and his birthright. He will have his revenge on the stinking cesspit that is Rome!

Destiny will see him taken under the wing of Maharbal, Hannibal's brilliant general, and groomed to lead the finest horsemen in the world – the feared Numidian cavalry that would become the scourge of Rome.

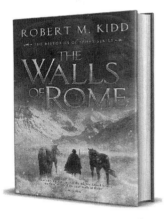

From the crossing of the great Rhodanus River, Sphax's epic journey takes him through the lands of the Gaul to the highest pass in the Alps. This is the story of the most famous march in history. A march against impossible odds, against savage mountain Gauls, a brutal winter and Sphax's own demons.

Reviews from book bloggers

Robert's writing is so impressive that it's hard to believe it was his debut novel. Wonderfully rich in historic detail, the plot is grounded around actual historical settings and characters. The fast pacing narration, great action-packed scenes, and the description of the locations, weaponry, tribes of Gaul, and the different battle techniques of the Numidian cavalry immersed me in the story. I was drawn in and didn't want to put this down.

Sumit

The writing is wonderful. The descriptive nature of this book just let me get lost in the story. Not only is this story descriptive, it's also fast-paced and riveting. I didn't want to put this down.

Jessica Belmont

The Winter of Winters

THE HISTORIES OF SPHAX SERIES

❧ BOOK 2 ❧

218 BC. Hannibal's exhausted army staggers down from the last Alpine pass like a rabble of half-starved savages, the remnants of a once magnificent army that had set out from the Rhodanus with such hope. Now there is no way back. With the legions of Consul Publius Scipio closing fast, Carthage needs its Gaulish allies like never before. But where are the Insubres? Where are the Boii? Where are the thousands of warriors pledged by solemn oath?

In the maelstrom of battle, Sphax, nephew of Hannibal, forges a reputation as the scourge of Rome. But will his ingrained recklessness and quest for honour set him at odds with the forbidding genius of his uncle? Only one thing is certain in this winter of winters, a great battle is coming that will decide the fates of Rome and Carthage.

Reviews from book bloggers

If you are someone who enjoys historical fiction I would definitely recommend this book, everything about it is amazing!

Sophie – bookreviewaholic.blog

I love this book. I typically enjoy historical fiction like this, but this one really stood out to me.

The pacing is phenomenal, and really kept me glued to the pages from start to finish. The suspense and action picks up and slows down nicely in a way which kept me interested, but not overwhelmed.

This is one of my favourite reads so far this year, and I can't wait to read more of the series.

Veronica – babybackbooks

The first book was so good I was hoping Robert M Kidd had continued on his A-game for this one, well, for me he had. The story is as immersive and compelling as the first.

Everything about this book had me glued to it. The battle is an epic one and had me speeding through the pages faster than I was before that.

Will be waiting for Robert's next one and hoping it is soon. He has a love for this historical period and it shines through every word in the book.

Sharon Rimmelzwaan – sharonbeyondthebooks

Hostage of Rome

THE HISTORIES OF SPHAX SERIES

⤛ BOOK 3 ⤜

217 BC. Rome has been savaged, beaten and is in retreat. Yet, in that winter of winters, her garrisons cling on behind the walls of Placentia and Cremona, thanks to her sea-born supplies. If he could be freed, a hostage of Rome may yet hold the key to launching a fleet of pirates that could sweep Rome from the seas. For that hostage is none other than Corinna's son Cleon, rival heir to the throne of Illyria, held in Brundisium, four hundred miles south of the Rubicon.

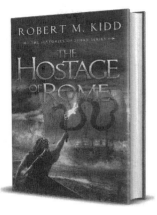

But Hannibal is set on a greater prize! Macedon is the great power in Greece, feared even by Rome. Its young king, Philip, is being compared with his illustrious ancestor, Alexander the Great. An alliance with Macedon would surely sound the death knell for Rome.

Given Hannibal's blessing, Sphax, Idwal and Corinna face an epic journey against impossible odds. Navigating the length of the Padus, past legionary garrisons and hostile Gauls, they must then risk the perils of the storm-torn Adria in the depths of the winter. If the gods favour them and they reach the lands of the pirate queen, only then will their real trials begin.

Printed in Great Britain
by Amazon

85922126R00217